D0104998

Just Princesses

Silver dragon books

written by
Crystal Velasquez

pictures by
Manuel Preitano

colors by
Beezz Studio

words by
Matt Krotzer

edited by
Jessica Rossana
Dave Franchini

production & design by
Christopher Cote
Ashley Vanacore

managing editor
Jennifer Bermel

publisher
Joe Brusha

Joe Brusha President & Chief Creative Officer
Christopher Cote Art Director
Pat Shand Writer & Editor
Dave Franchini Assistant Editor
Jessica Rossana Assistant Editor
Joi Dariel Production Manager

John Lyons Director of Sales & Marketing
Jennifer Bermel Director of Business Development
Jason Condeelis Direct Market Sales & Customer Serv
Stu Kropnick Operations Manager
Ralph Tedesco VP Film & Television

silver dragon

Just Princesses, July, 2016. First Printing. Published by Silver Dragon Books Inc. an imprint of Zenescope Entertainment Inc., 433 Care
Drive, Ste. C, Horsham, Pennsylvania 19044. Silver Dragon Books and its logos are ® and © 2016 Silver Dragon Books. All rights reserved.
Princesses, its logo and all characters and their likeness are © and ™ 2016 Silver Dragon Books, Inc. Any similarities to persons (livin
dead), events, institutions, or locales are purely coincidental. No portion of this publication may be reproduced or transmitted, in any
or by any means, without the expressed written permission of Silver Dragon Books except for artwork used for review purposes. Printed in
ISBN: 978-1942275343

Just Princesses

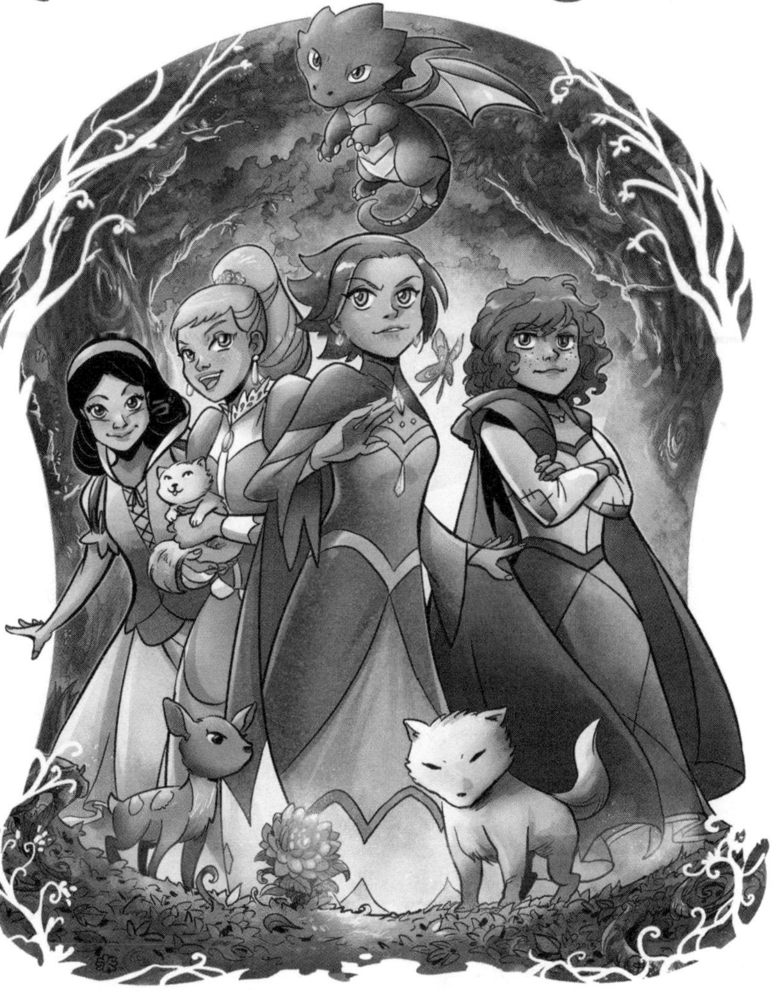

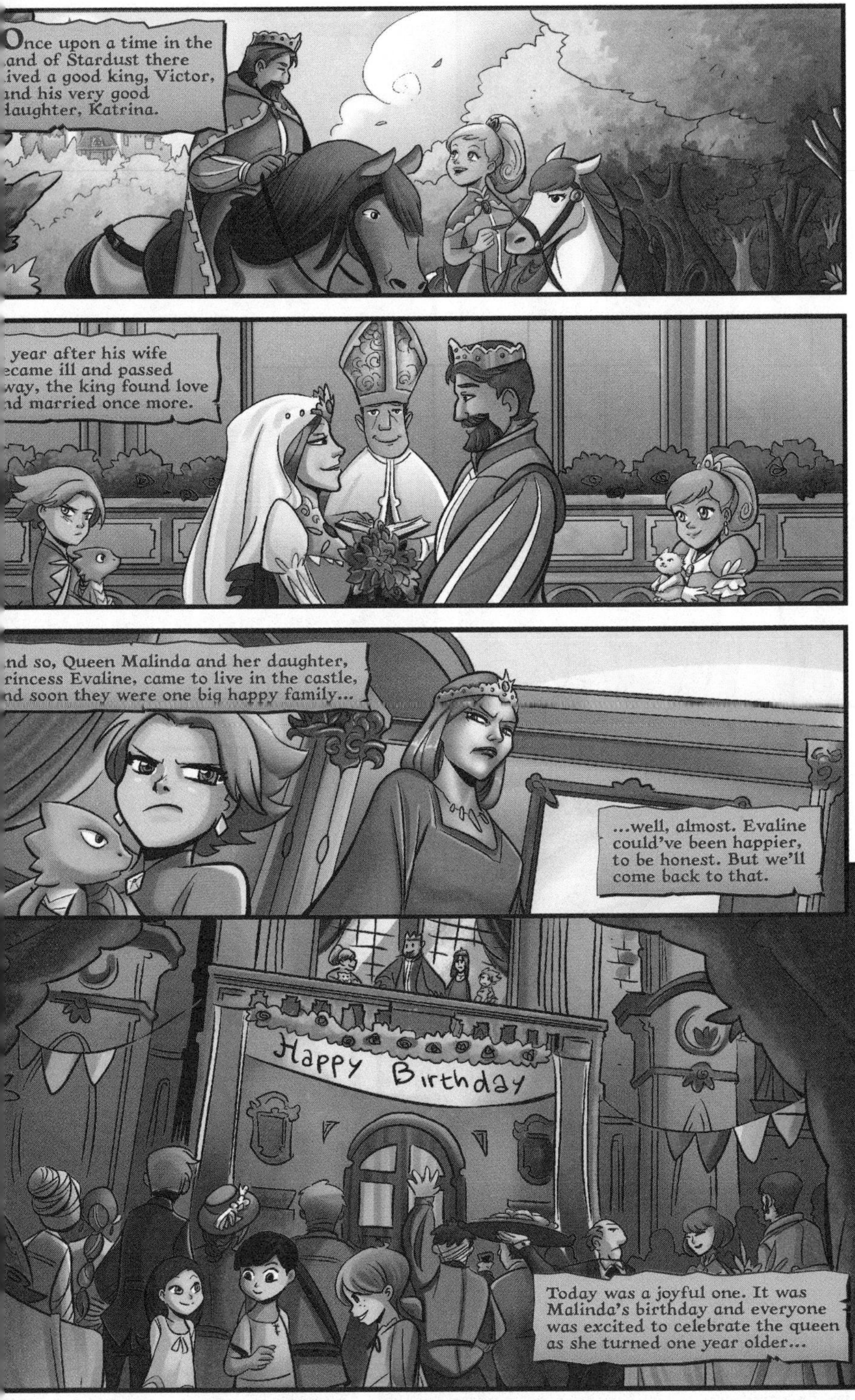
Once upon a time in the
and of Stardust there
ived a good king, Victor,
nd his very good
daughter, Katrina.
year after his wife
ecame ill and passed
way, the king found love
nd married once more.
nd so, Queen Malinda and her daughter,
rincess Evaline, came to live in the castle,
nd soon they were one big happy family...
...well, almost. Evaline
could've been happier,
to be honest. But we'll
come back to that.
Happy Birthday
Today was a joyful one. It was
Malinda's birthday and everyone
was excited to celebrate the queen
as she turned one year older...

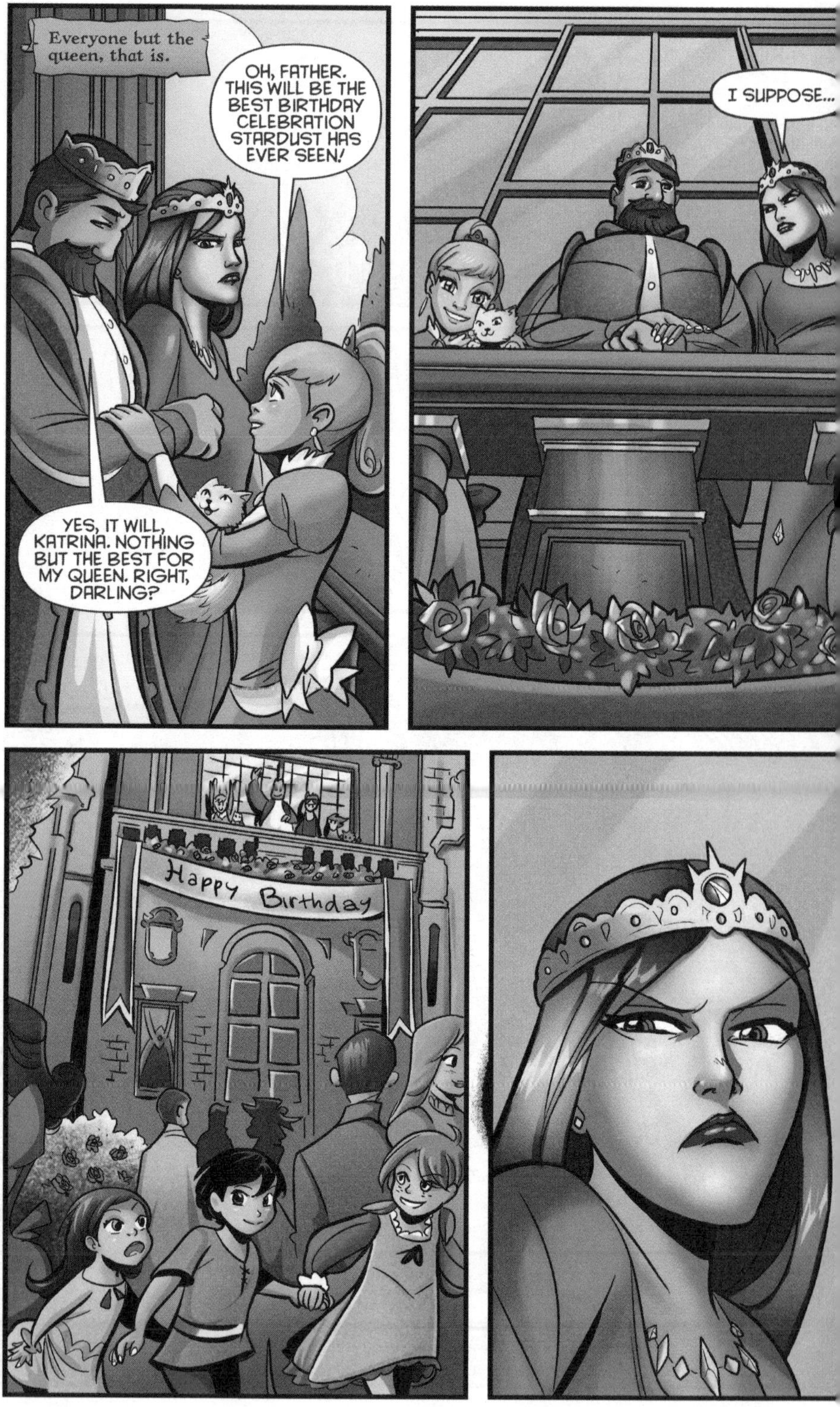
Everyone but the queen, that is.
OH, FATHER. THIS WILL BE THE BEST BIRTHDAY CELEBRATION STARDUST HAS EVER SEEN!
YES, IT WILL, KATRINA. NOTHING BUT THE BEST FOR MY QUEEN. RIGHT, DARLING?
I SUPPOSE...
Happy Birthday

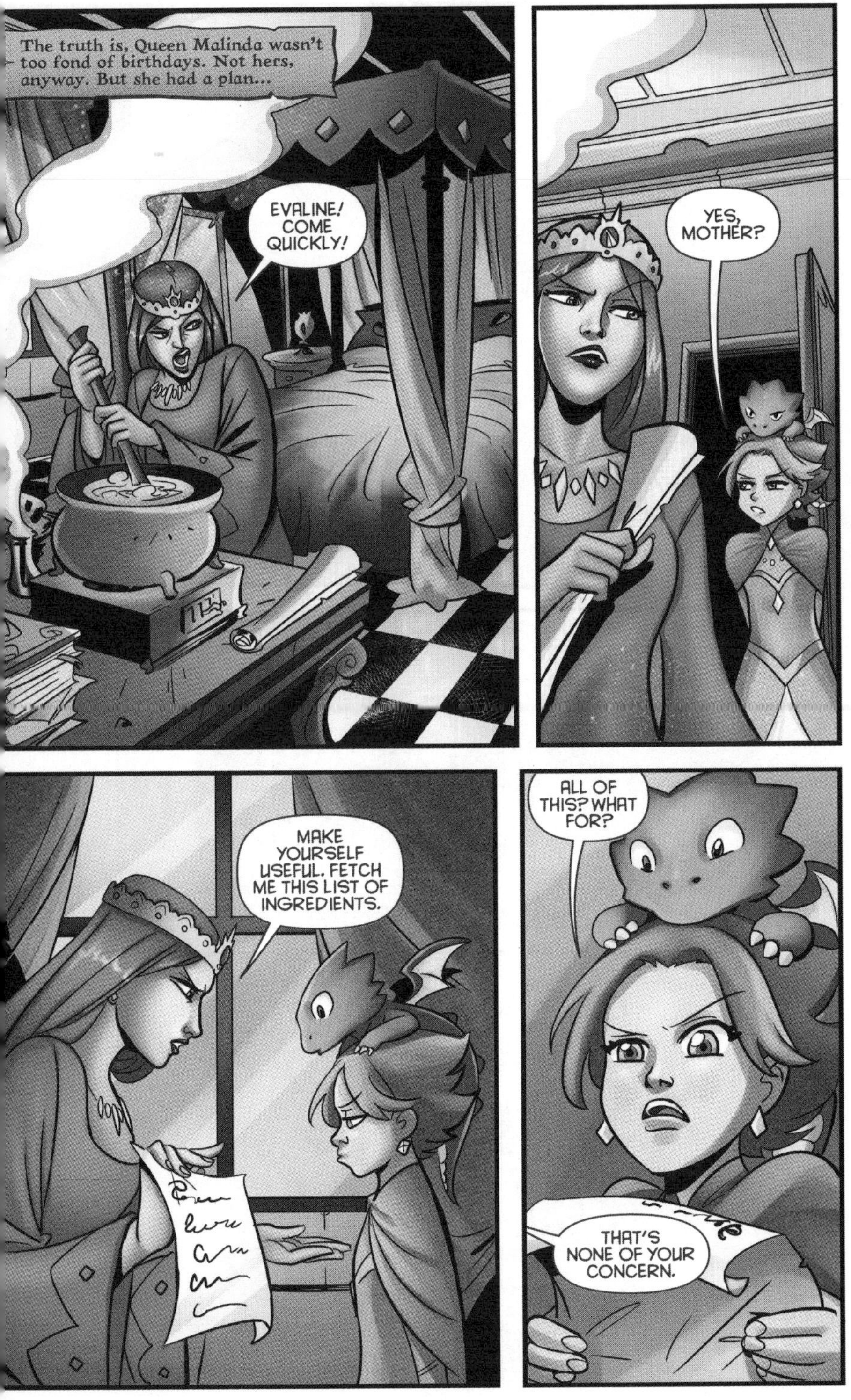
The truth is, Queen Malinda wasn't too fond of birthdays. Not hers, anyway. But she had a plan...
EVALINE! COME QUICKLY!
YES, MOTHER?
MAKE YOURSELF USEFUL. FETCH ME THIS LIST OF INGREDIENTS.
ALL OF THIS? WHAT FOR?
THAT'S NONE OF YOUR CONCERN.

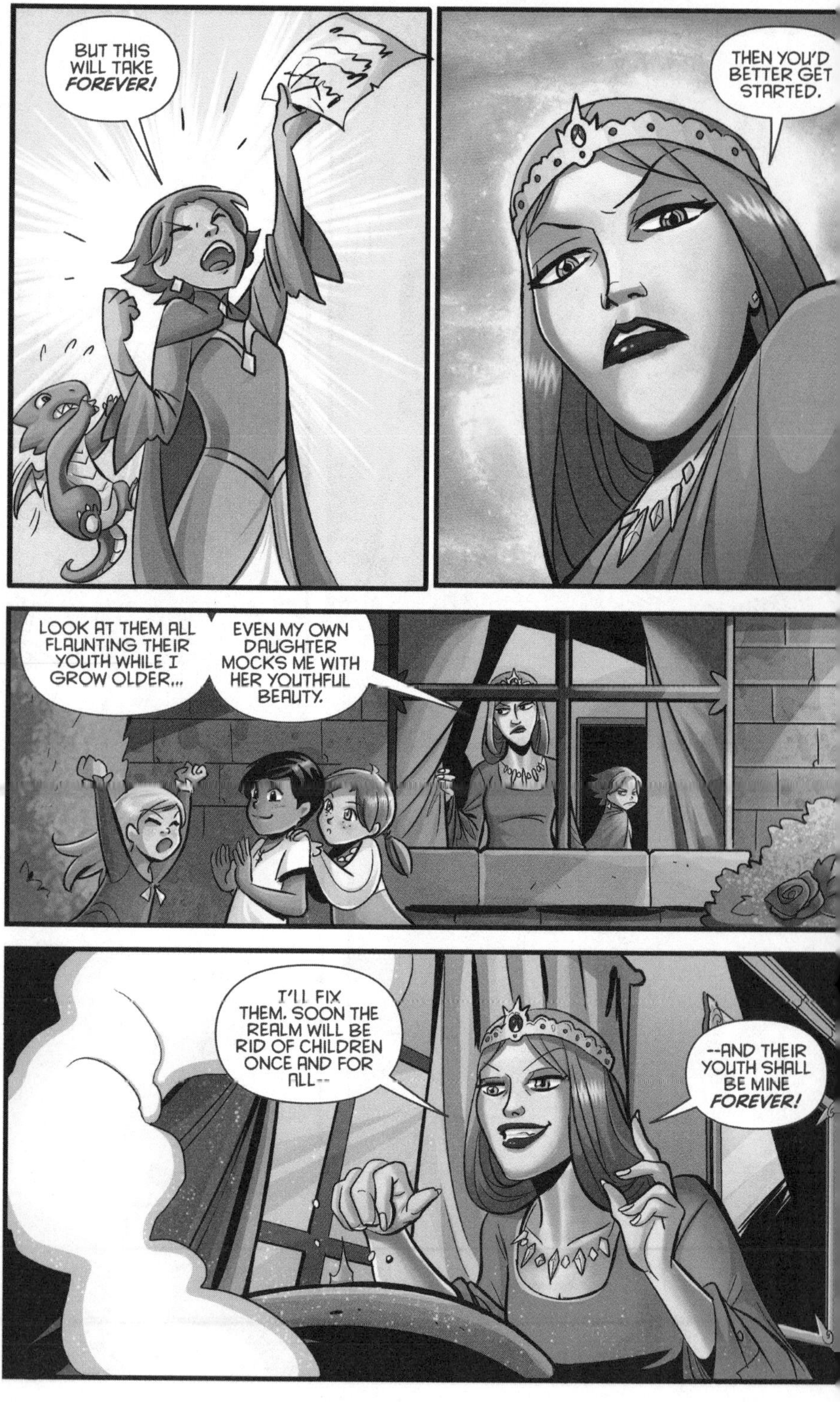
BUT THIS WILL TAKE *FOREVER!*
THEN YOU'D BETTER GET STARTED.
LOOK AT THEM ALL FLAUNTING THEIR YOUTH WHILE I GROW OLDER...
EVEN MY OWN DAUGHTER MOCKS ME WITH HER YOUTHFUL BEAUTY.
I'LL FIX THEM. SOON THE REALM WILL BE RID OF CHILDREN ONCE AND FOR ALL--
--AND THEIR YOUTH SHALL BE MINE *FOREVER!*

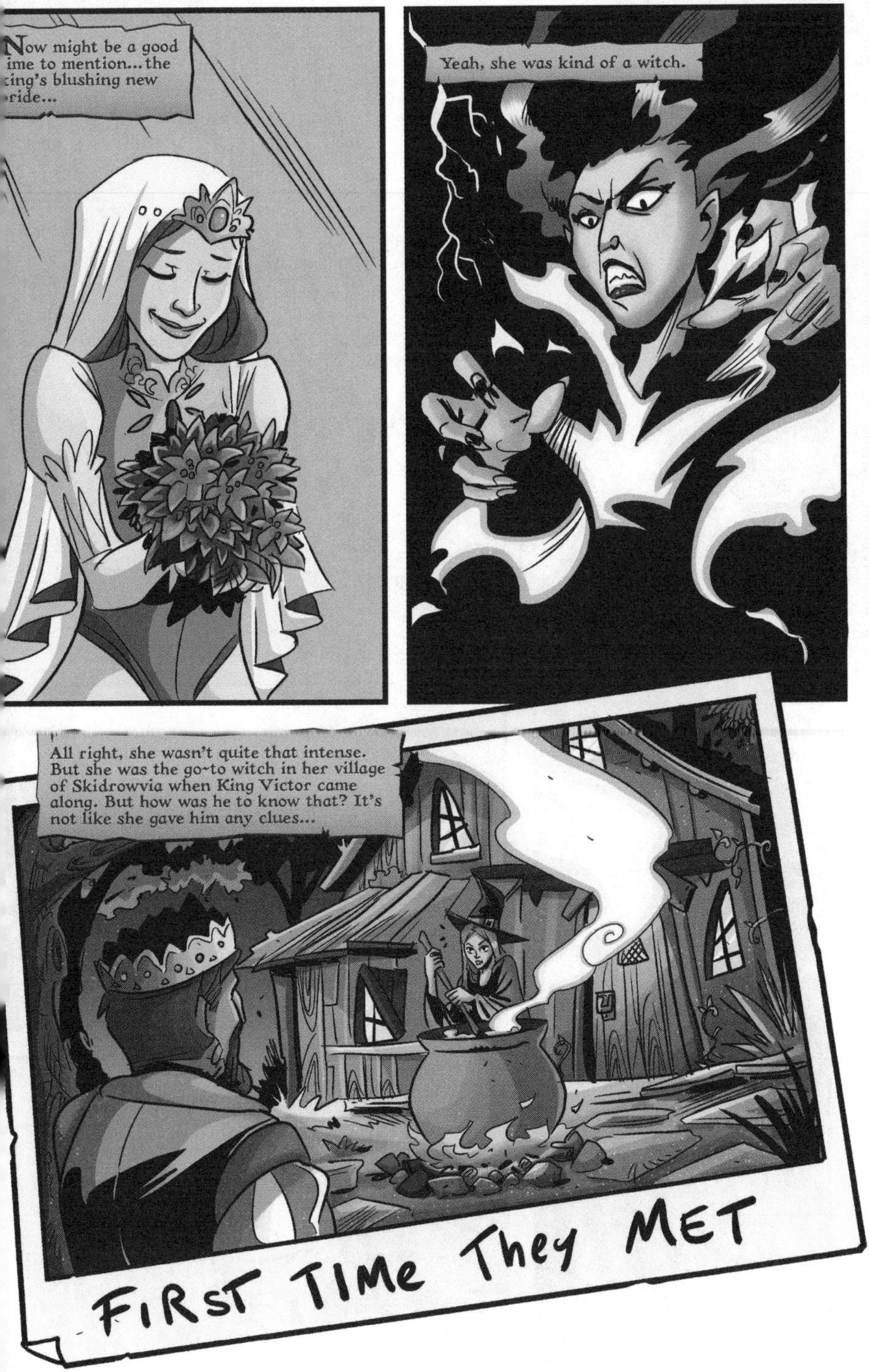
Now might be a good ime to mention...the ing's blushing new ride...
Yeah, she was kind of a witch.
All right, she wasn't quite that intense. But she was the go-to witch in her village of Skidrowvia when King Victor came along. But how was he to know that? It's not like she gave him any clues...
FIRST TIME They MET

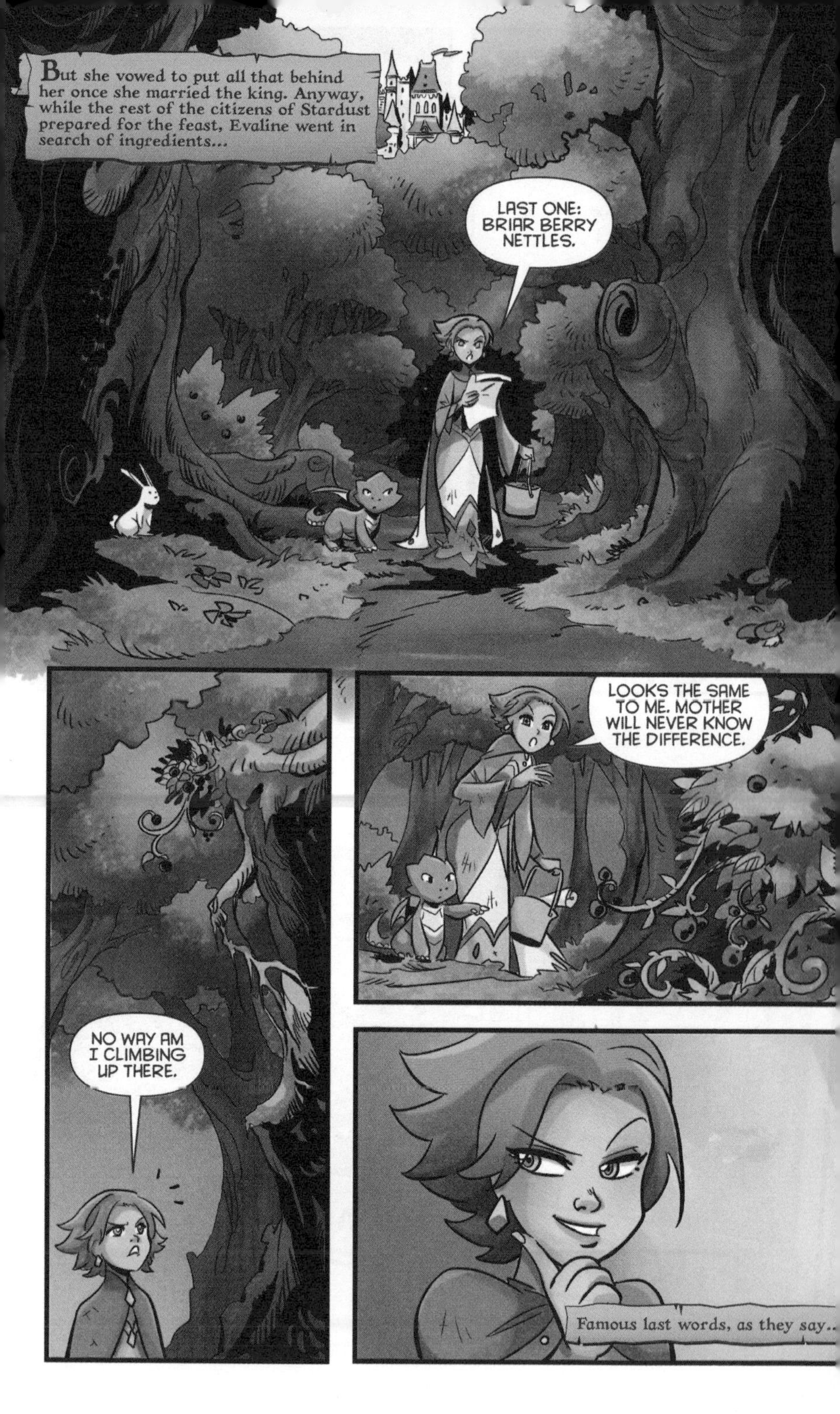
But she vowed to put all that behind her once she married the king. Anyway, while the rest of the citizens of Stardust prepared for the feast, Evaline went in search of ingredients...
LAST ONE: BRIAR BERRY NETTLES.
NO WAY AM I CLIMBING UP THERE.
LOOKS THE SAME TO ME. MOTHER WILL NEVER KNOW THE DIFFERENCE.
Famous last words, as they say...

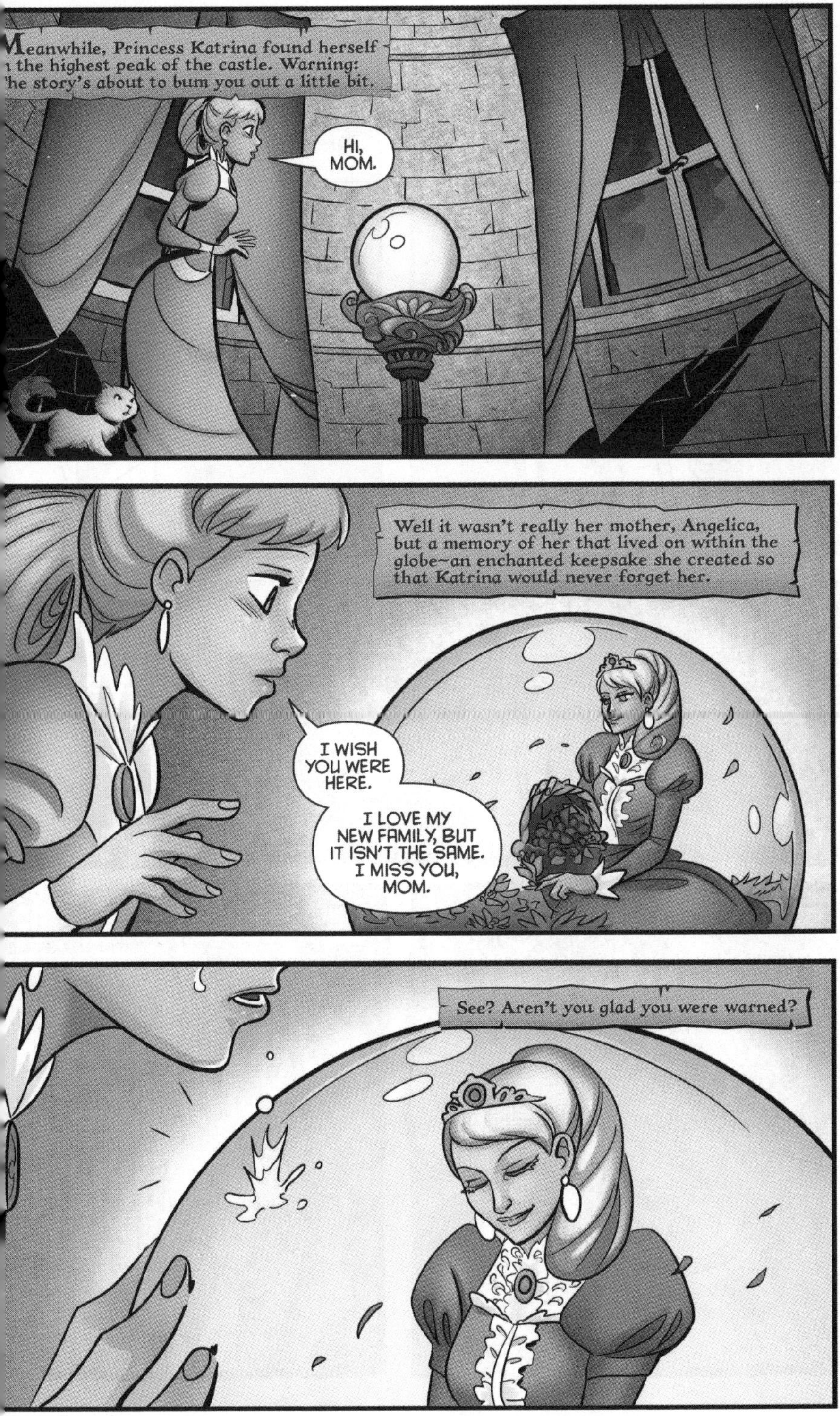
Meanwhile, Princess Katrina found herself in the highest peak of the castle. Warning: the story's about to bum you out a little bit.
HI, MOM.
Well it wasn't really her mother, Angelica, but a memory of her that lived on within the globe~an enchanted keepsake she created so that Katrina would never forget her.
I WISH YOU WERE HERE.
I LOVE MY NEW FAMILY, BUT IT ISN'T THE SAME. I MISS YOU, MOM.
See? Aren't you glad you were warned?

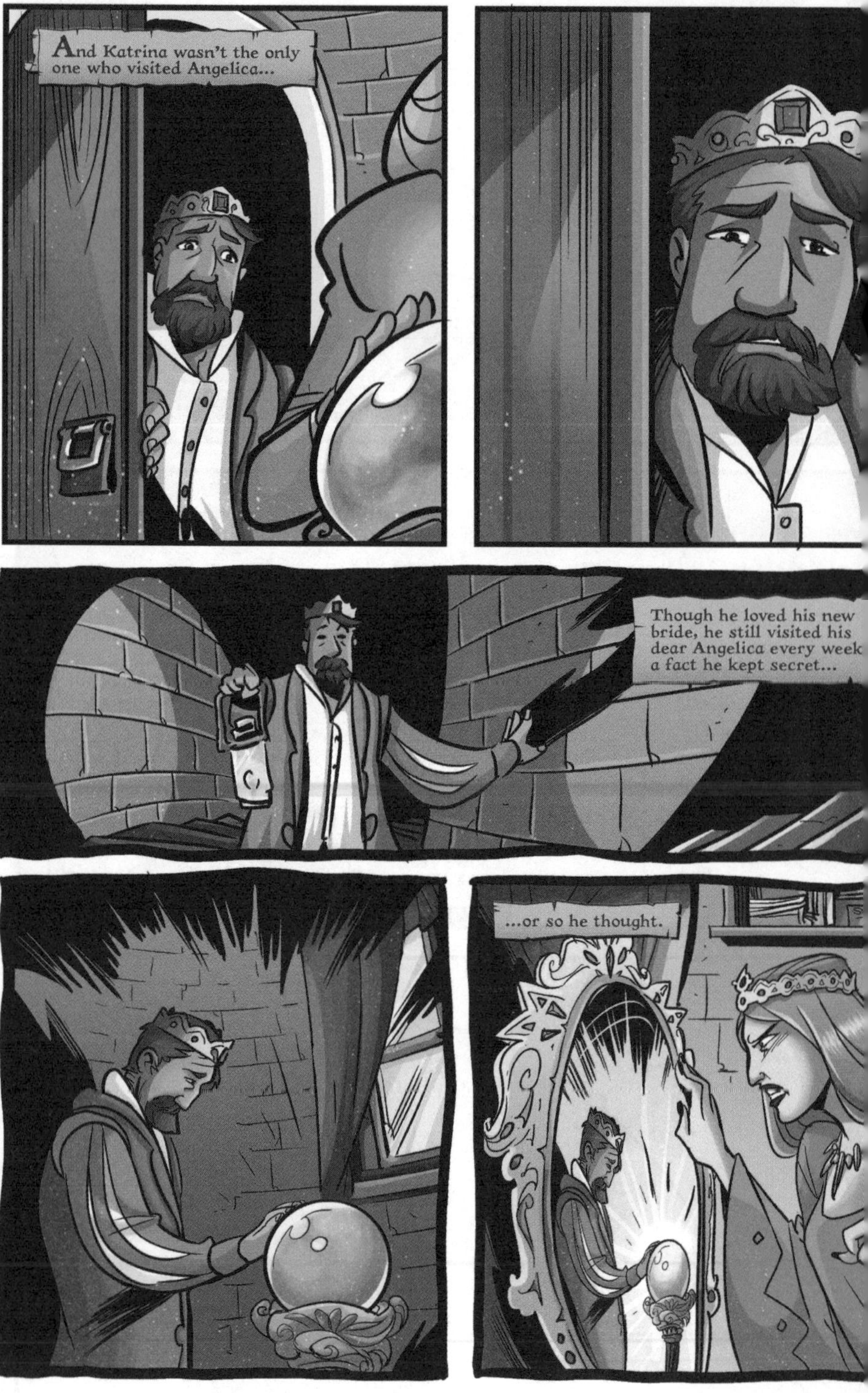
And Katrina wasn't the only one who visited Angelica...
Though he loved his new bride, he still visited his dear Angelica every week a fact he kept secret...
...or so he thought.

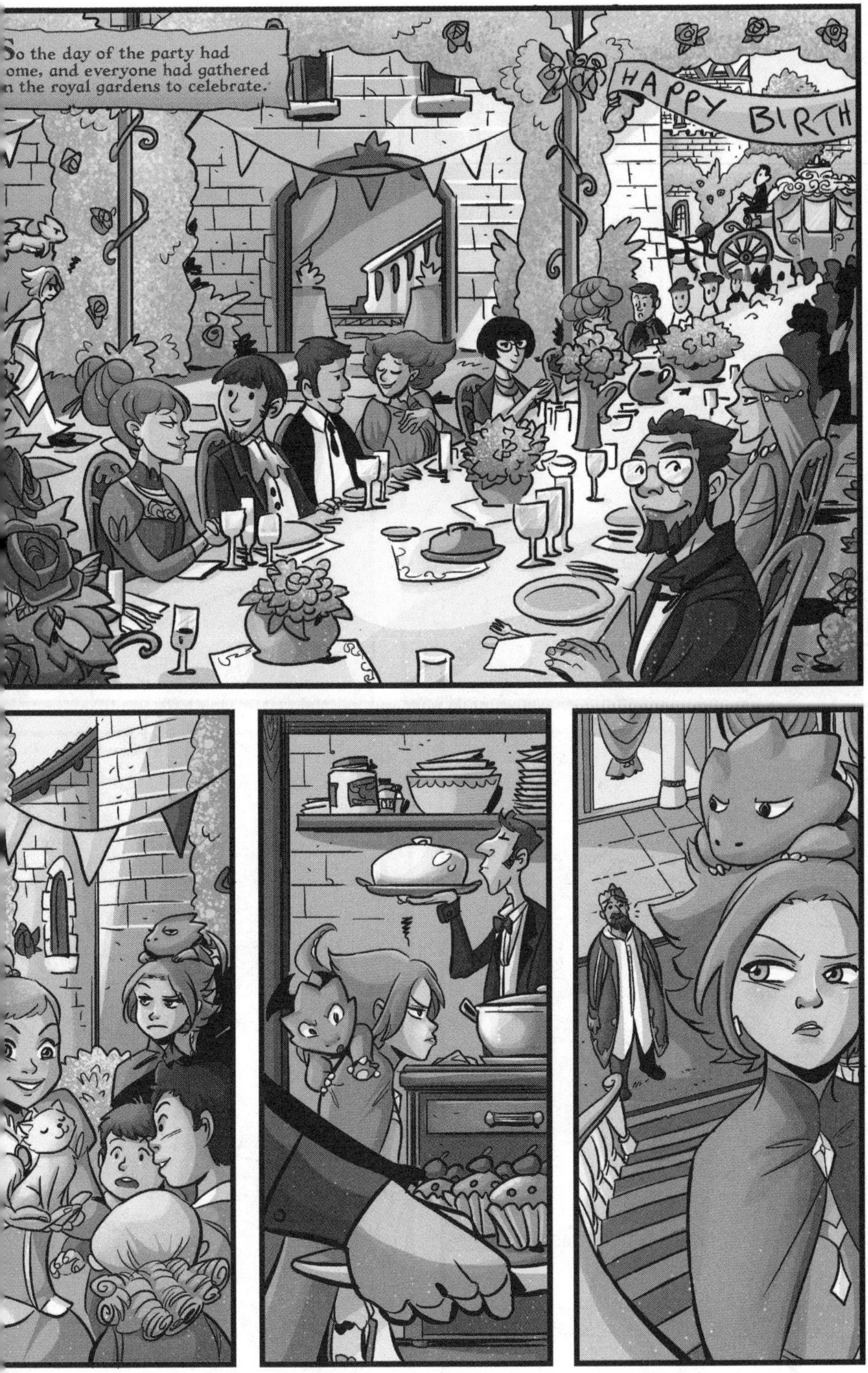
So the day of the party had
come, and everyone had gathered
in the royal gardens to celebrate.
HAPPY BIRTH

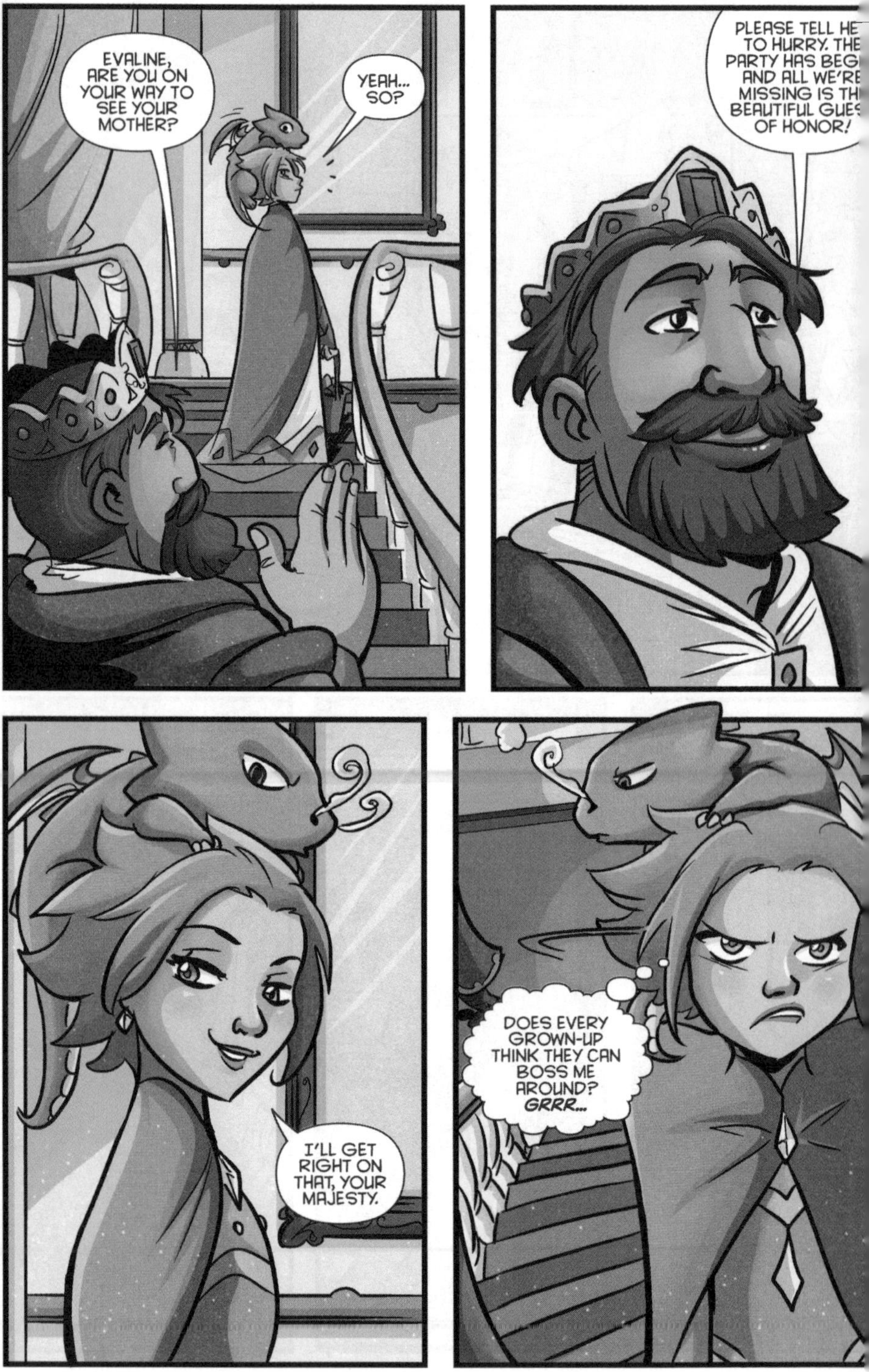
EVALINE, ARE YOU ON YOUR WAY TO SEE YOUR MOTHER?
YEAH... SO?
PLEASE TELL HE TO HURRY. THE PARTY HAS BEG AND ALL WE'RE MISSING IS TH BEAUTIFUL GUES OF HONOR!
I'LL GET RIGHT ON THAT, YOUR MAJESTY.
DOES EVERY GROWN-UP THINK THEY CAN BOSS ME AROUND? *GRRR...*

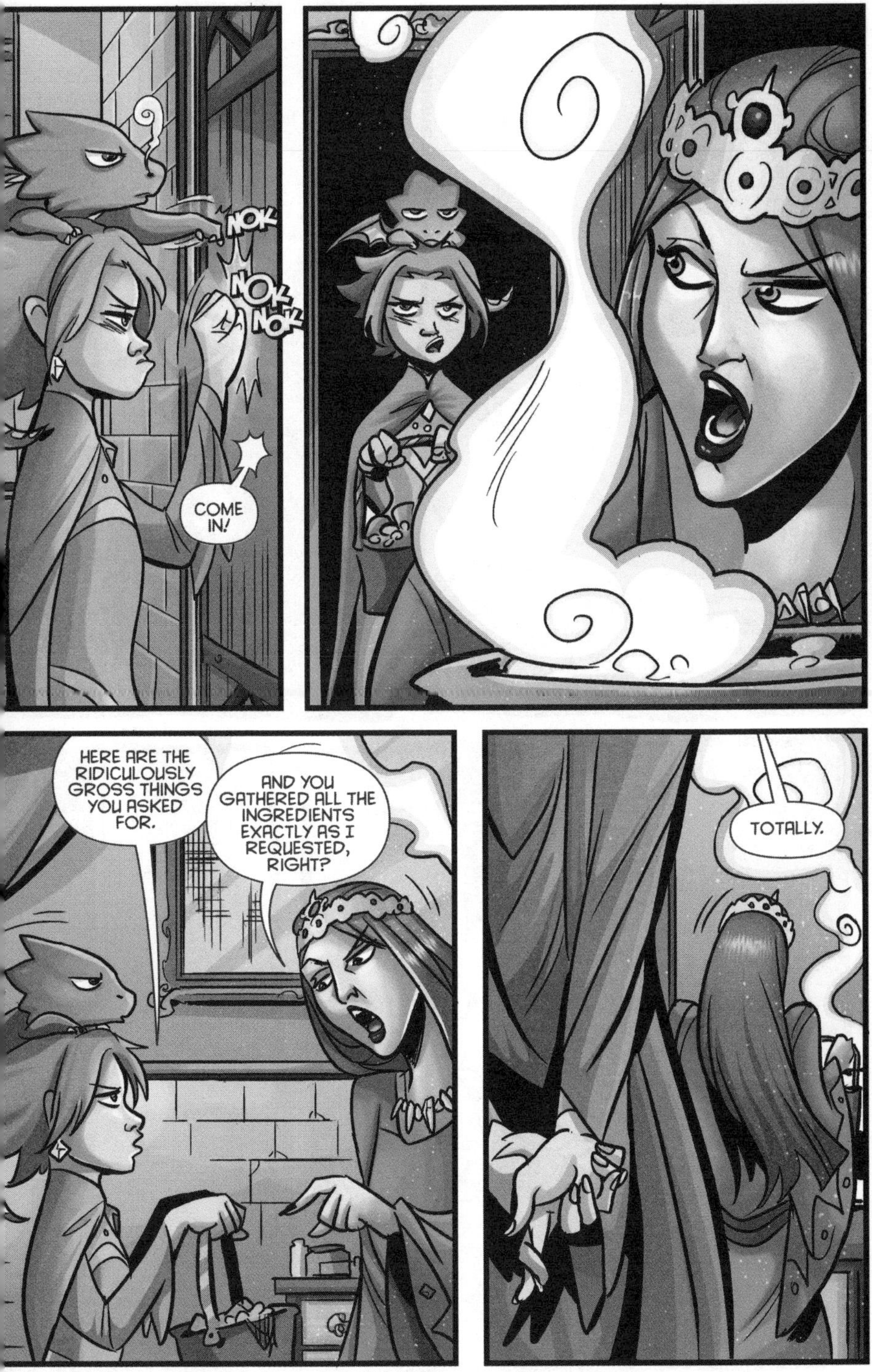
NOK
NOK NOK NOK
COME IN!
HERE ARE THE RIDICULOUSLY GROSS THINGS YOU ASKED FOR.
AND YOU GATHERED ALL THE INGREDIENTS EXACTLY AS I REQUESTED, RIGHT?
TOTALLY.

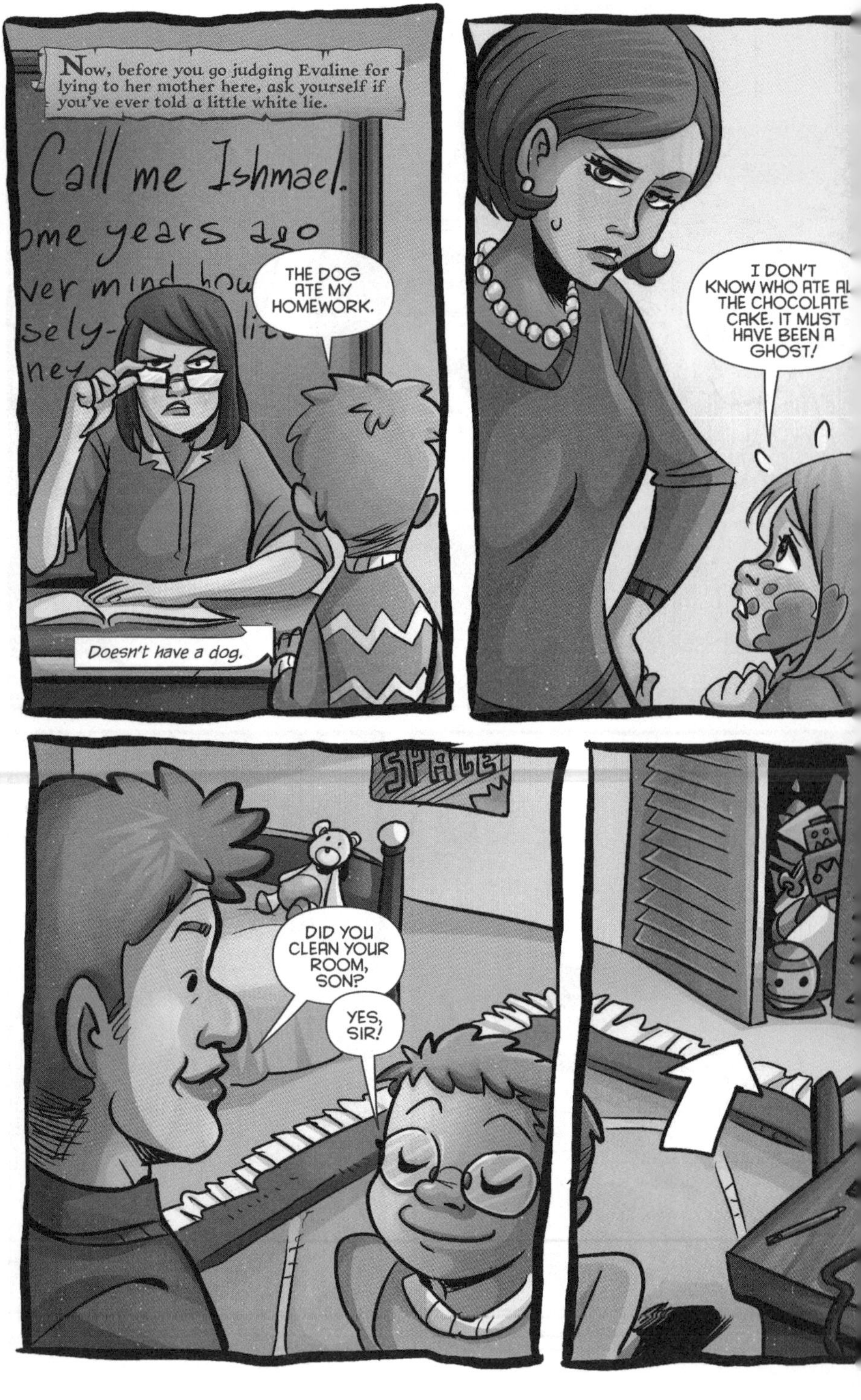
Now, before you go judging Evaline for lying to her mother here, ask yourself if you've ever told a little white lie.
Call me Ishmael.
ome years ago
ver mind how
sely-
ney
THE DOG ATE MY HOMEWORK.
Doesn't have a dog.
I DON'T KNOW WHO ATE AL THE CHOCOLATE CAKE. IT MUST HAVE BEEN A GHOST!
SPACE
DID YOU CLEAN YOUR ROOM, SON?
YES, SIR!

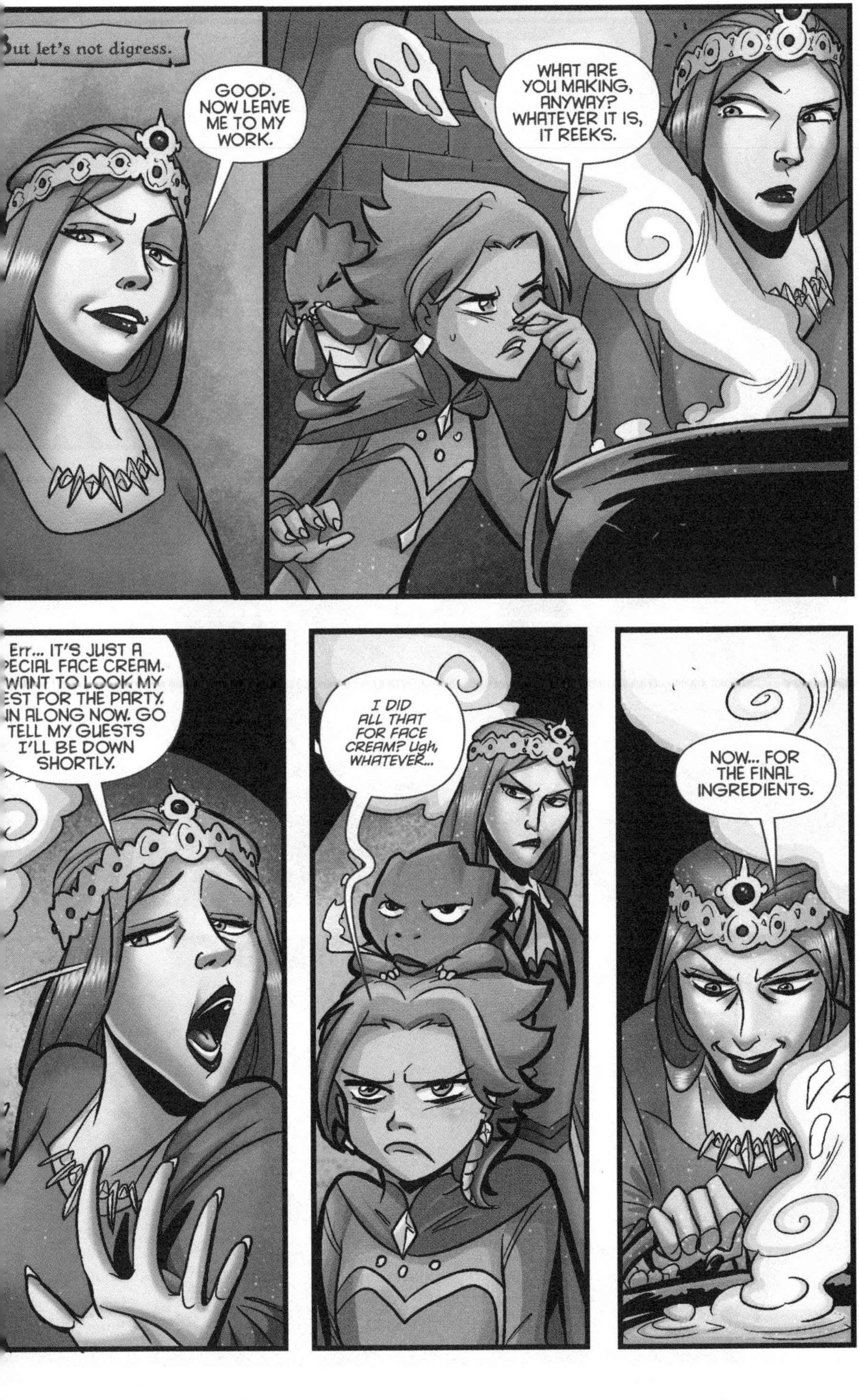
But let's not digress.
GOOD. NOW LEAVE ME TO MY WORK.
WHAT ARE YOU MAKING, ANYWAY? WHATEVER IT IS, IT REEKS.
Err... IT'S JUST A PECIAL FACE CREAM. WANT TO LOOK MY EST FOR THE PARTY. IN ALONG NOW. GO TELL MY GUESTS I'LL BE DOWN SHORTLY.
I DID ALL THAT FOR FACE CREAM? Ugh, WHATEVER...
NOW... FOR THE FINAL INGREDIENTS.

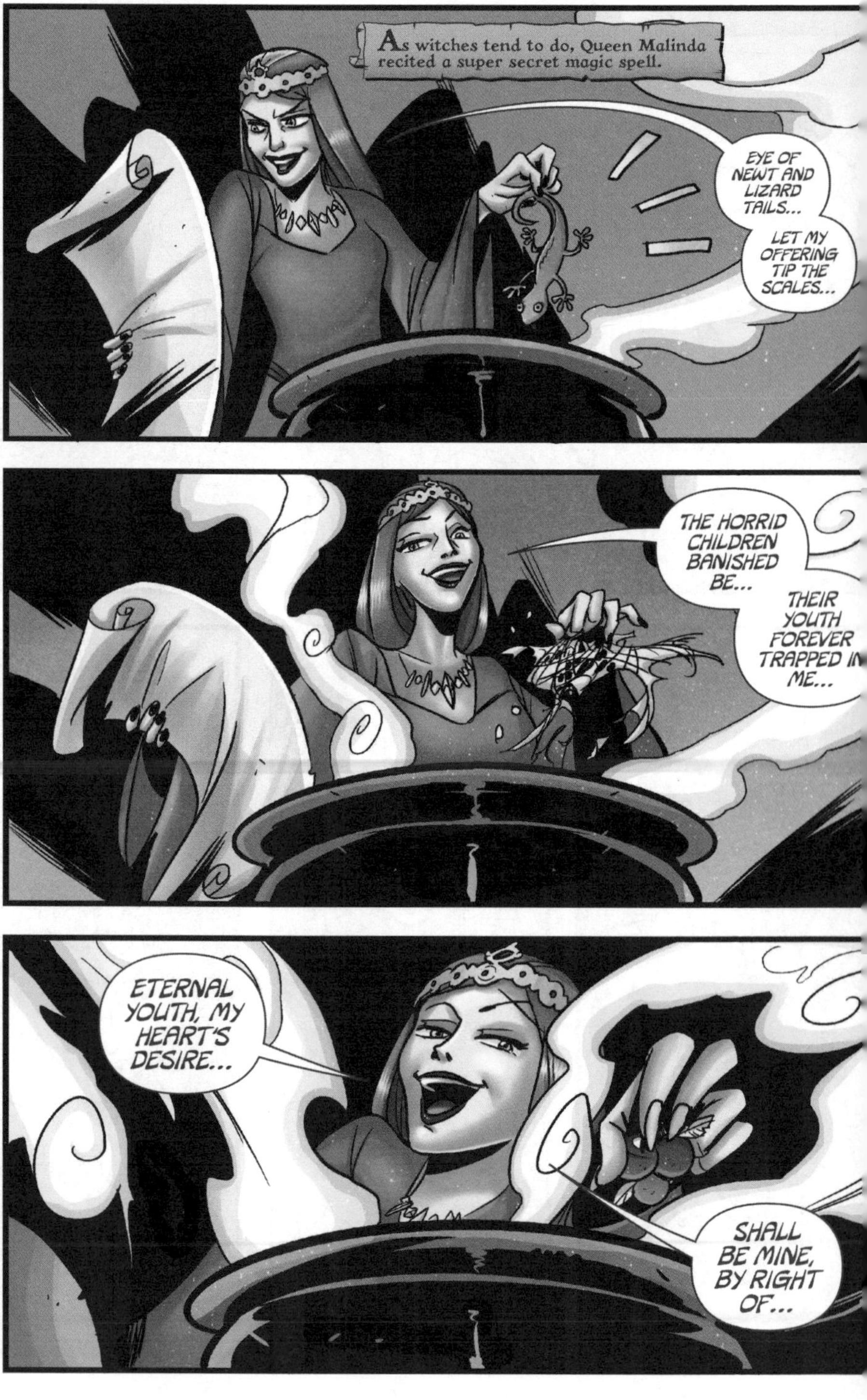
As witches tend to do, Queen Malinda recited a super secret magic spell.
EYE OF NEWT AND LIZARD TAILS...
LET MY OFFERING TIP THE SCALES...
THE HORRID CHILDREN BANISHED BE...
THEIR YOUTH FOREVER TRAPPED I
ME...
ETERNAL YOUTH, MY HEART'S DESIRE...
SHALL BE MINE, BY RIGHT OF...

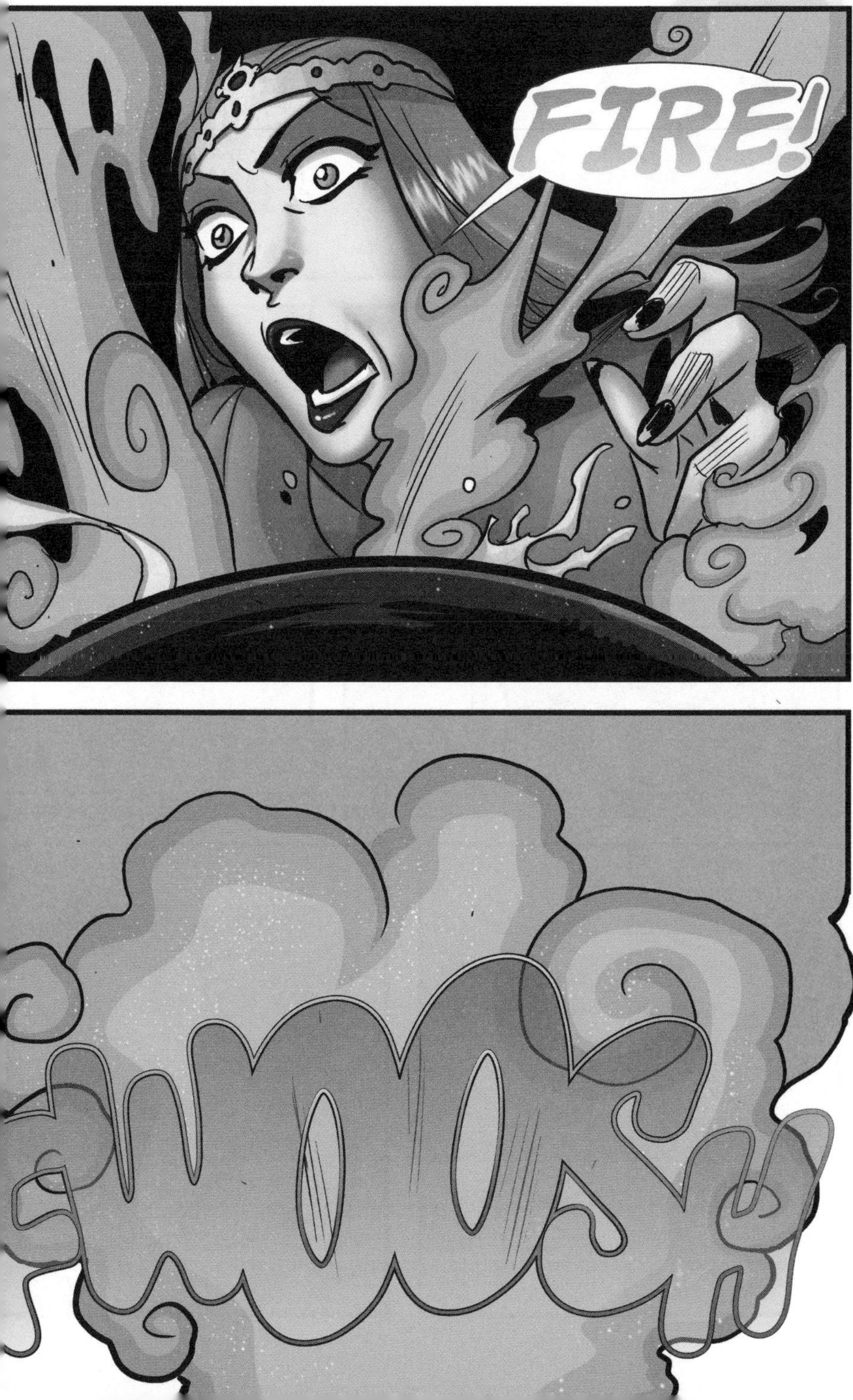
FIRE!
WHOOSH!

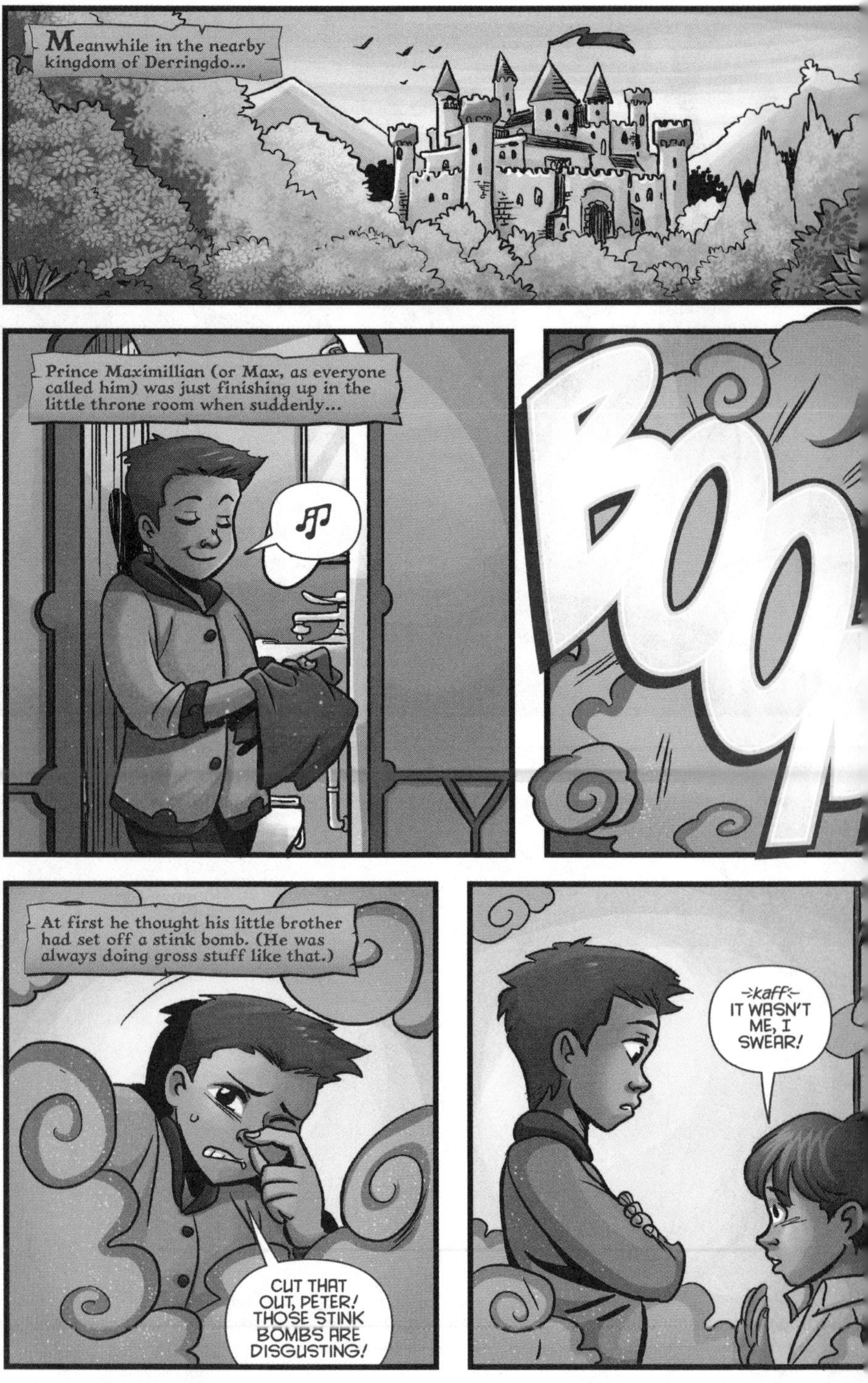
Meanwhile in the nearby kingdom of Derringdo...
Prince Maximillian (or Max, as everyone called him) was just finishing up in the little throne room when suddenly...
At first he thought his little brother had set off a stink bomb. (He was always doing gross stuff like that.)
CUT THAT OUT, PETER! THOSE STINK BOMBS ARE DISGUSTING!
kaff
IT WASN'T ME, I SWEAR!

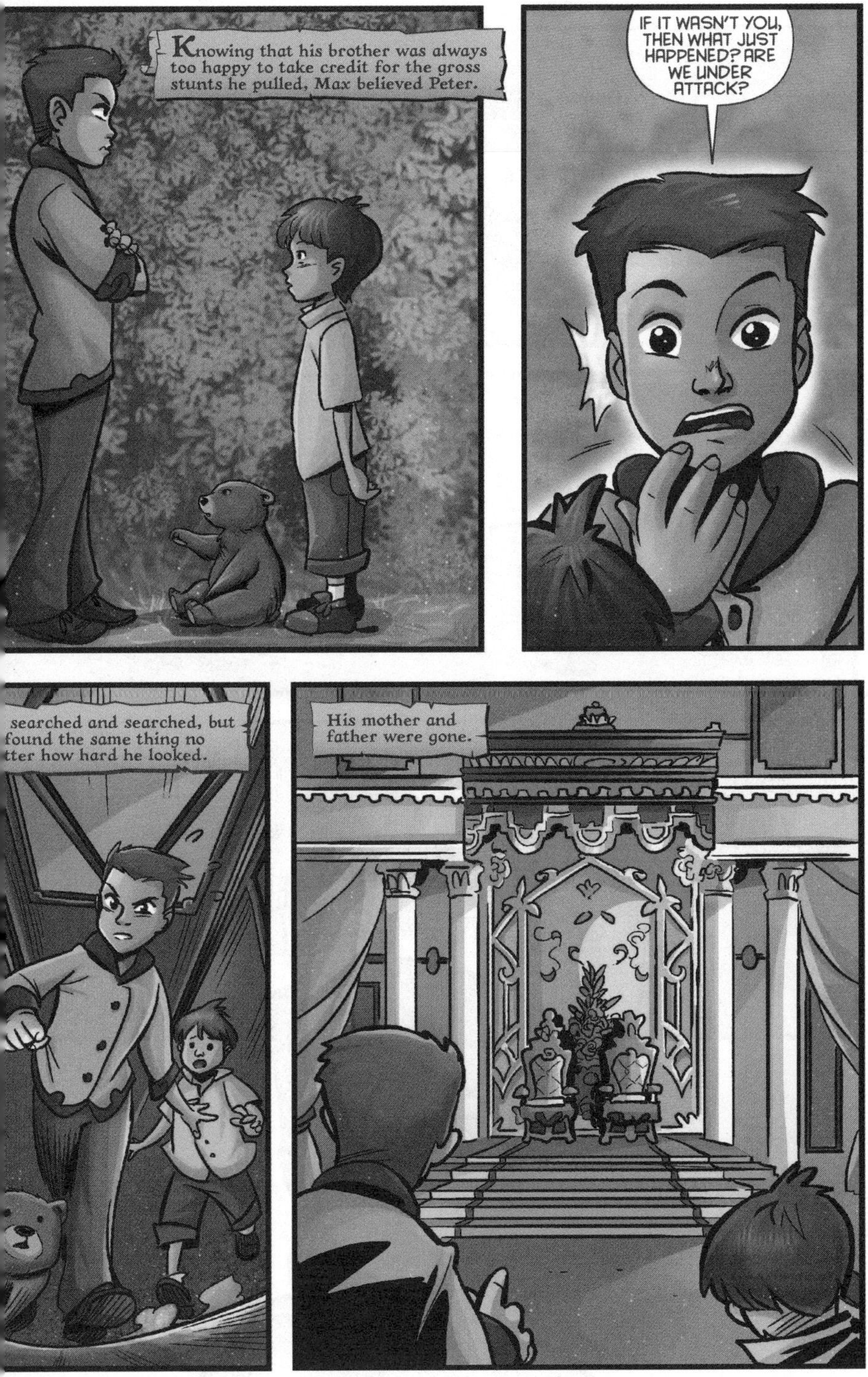
Knowing that his brother was always too happy to take credit for the gross stunts he pulled, Max believed Peter.
IF IT WASN'T YOU, THEN WHAT JUST HAPPENED? ARE WE UNDER ATTACK?
searched and searched, but found the same thing no tter how hard he looked.
His mother and father were gone.

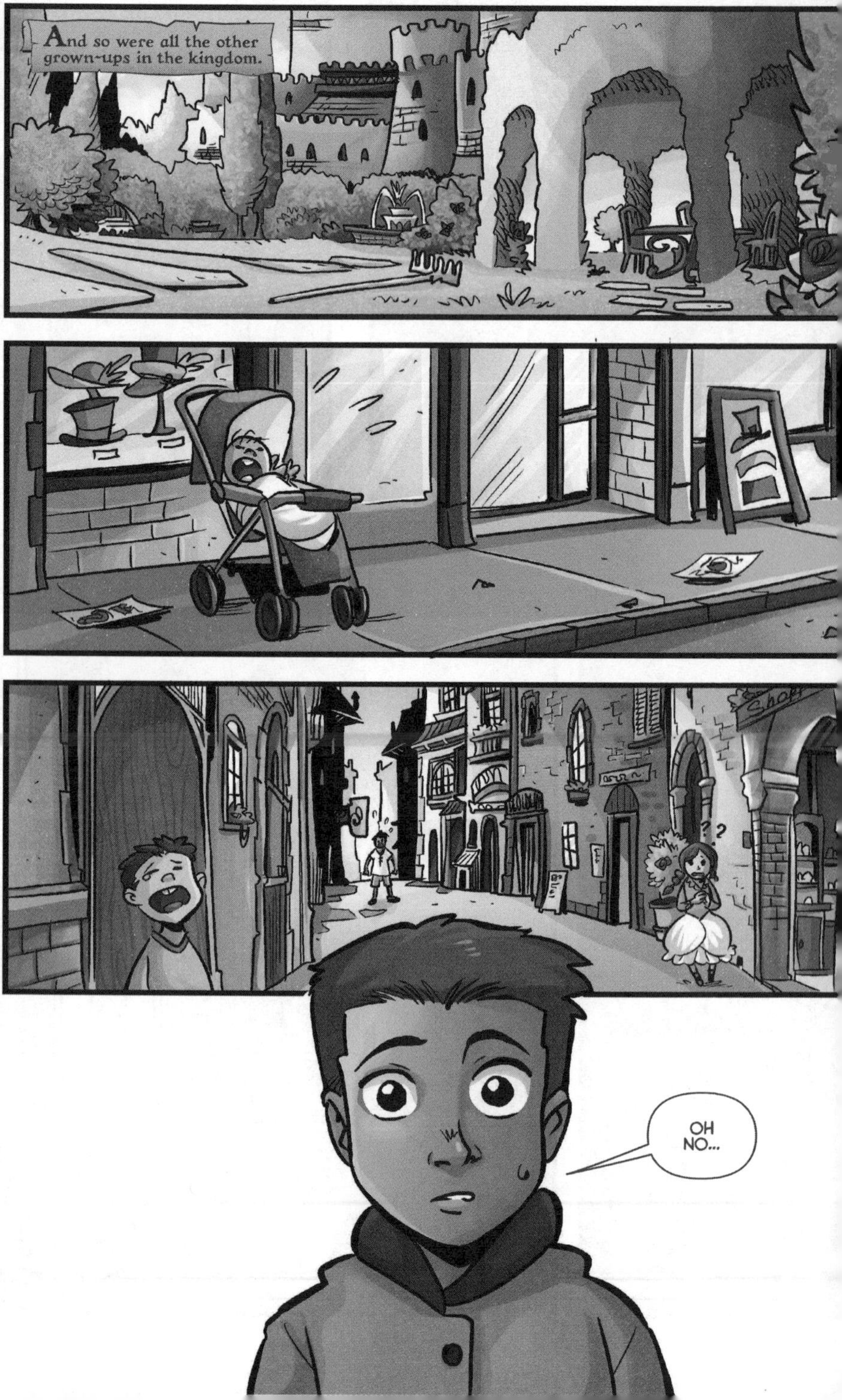
And so were all the other grown-ups in the kingdom.
Shop
OH NO...

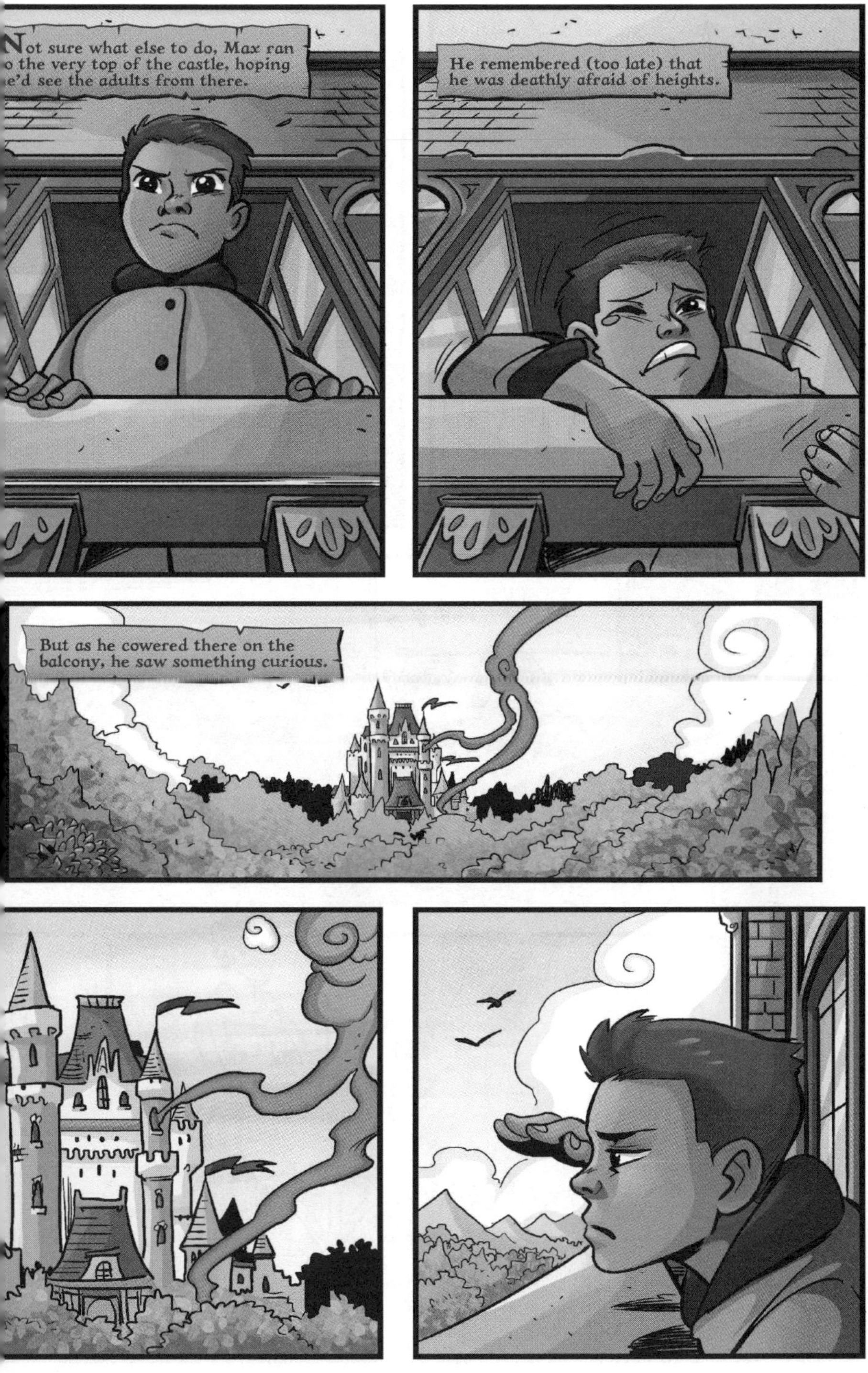
Not sure what else to do, Max ran
o the very top of the castle, hoping
e'd see the adults from there.
He remembered (too late) that
he was deathly afraid of heights.
But as he cowered there on the
balcony, he saw something curious.

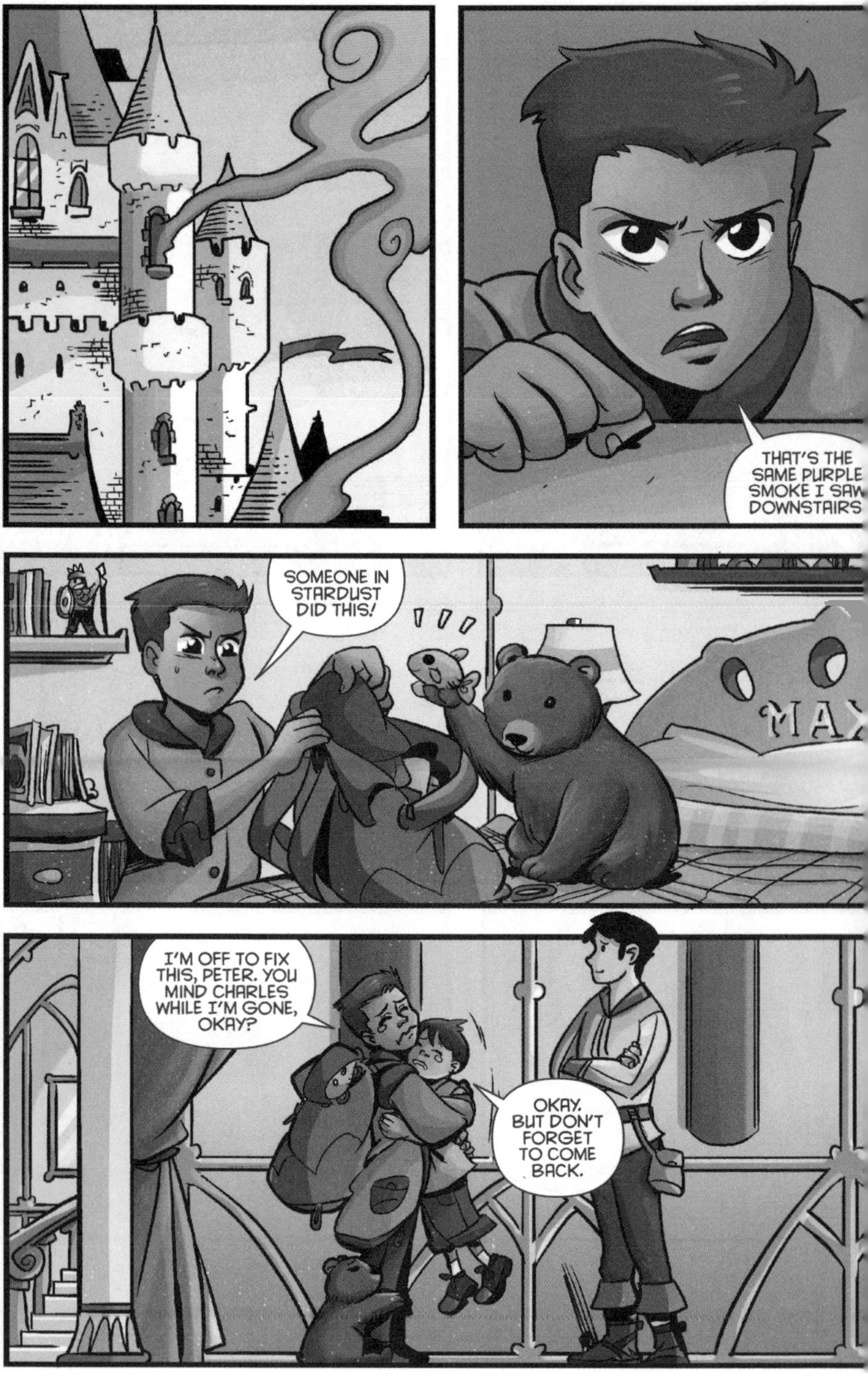
THAT'S THE SAME PURPLE SMOKE I SAW DOWNSTAIRS
SOMEONE IN STARDUST DID THIS!
I'M OFF TO FIX THIS, PETER. YOU MIND CHARLES WHILE I'M GONE, OKAY?
OKAY. BUT DON'T FORGET TO COME BACK.

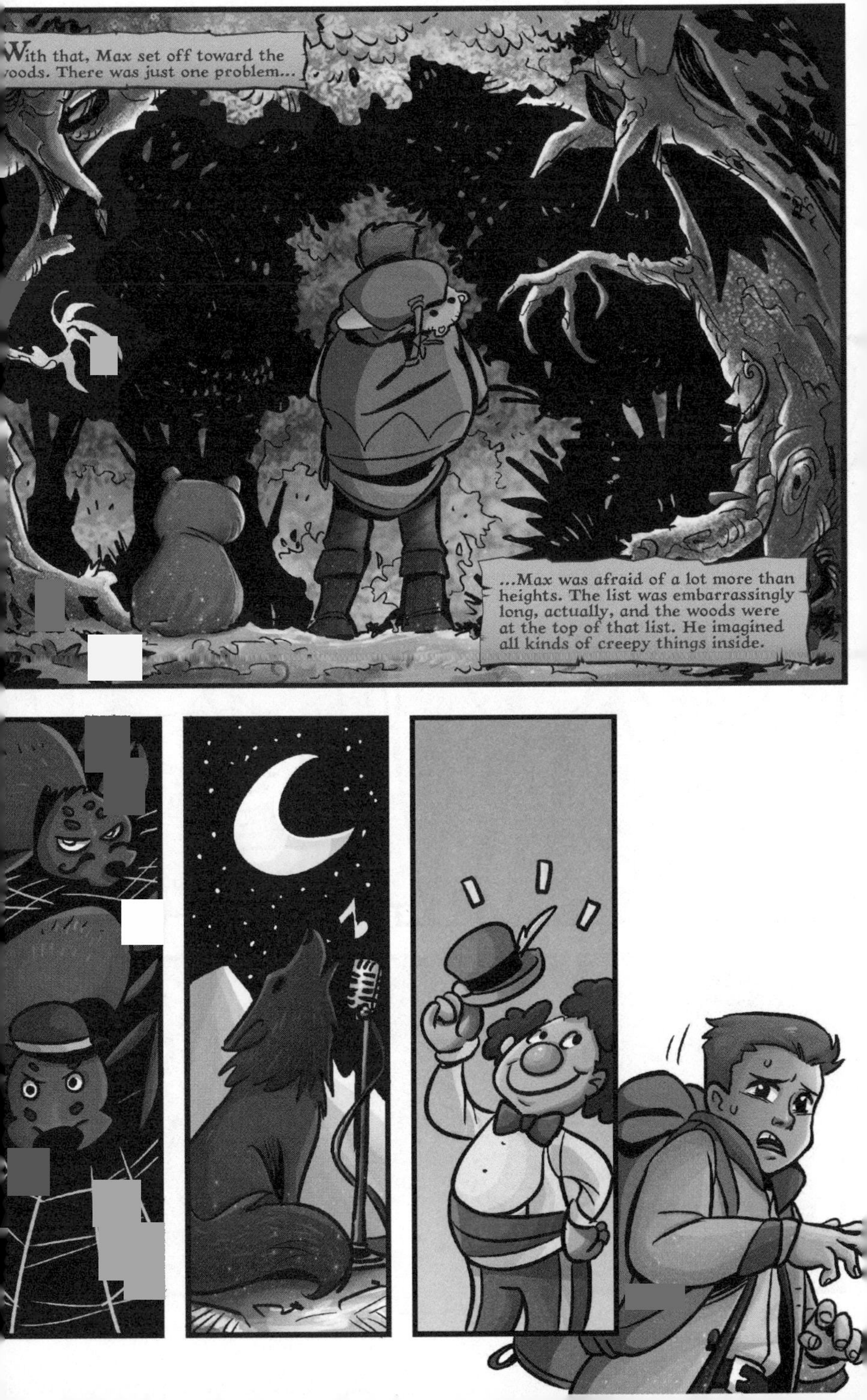
With that, Max set off toward the woods. There was just one problem...
...Max was afraid of a lot more than heights. The list was embarrassingly long, actually, and the woods were at the top of that list. He imagined all kinds of creepy things inside.

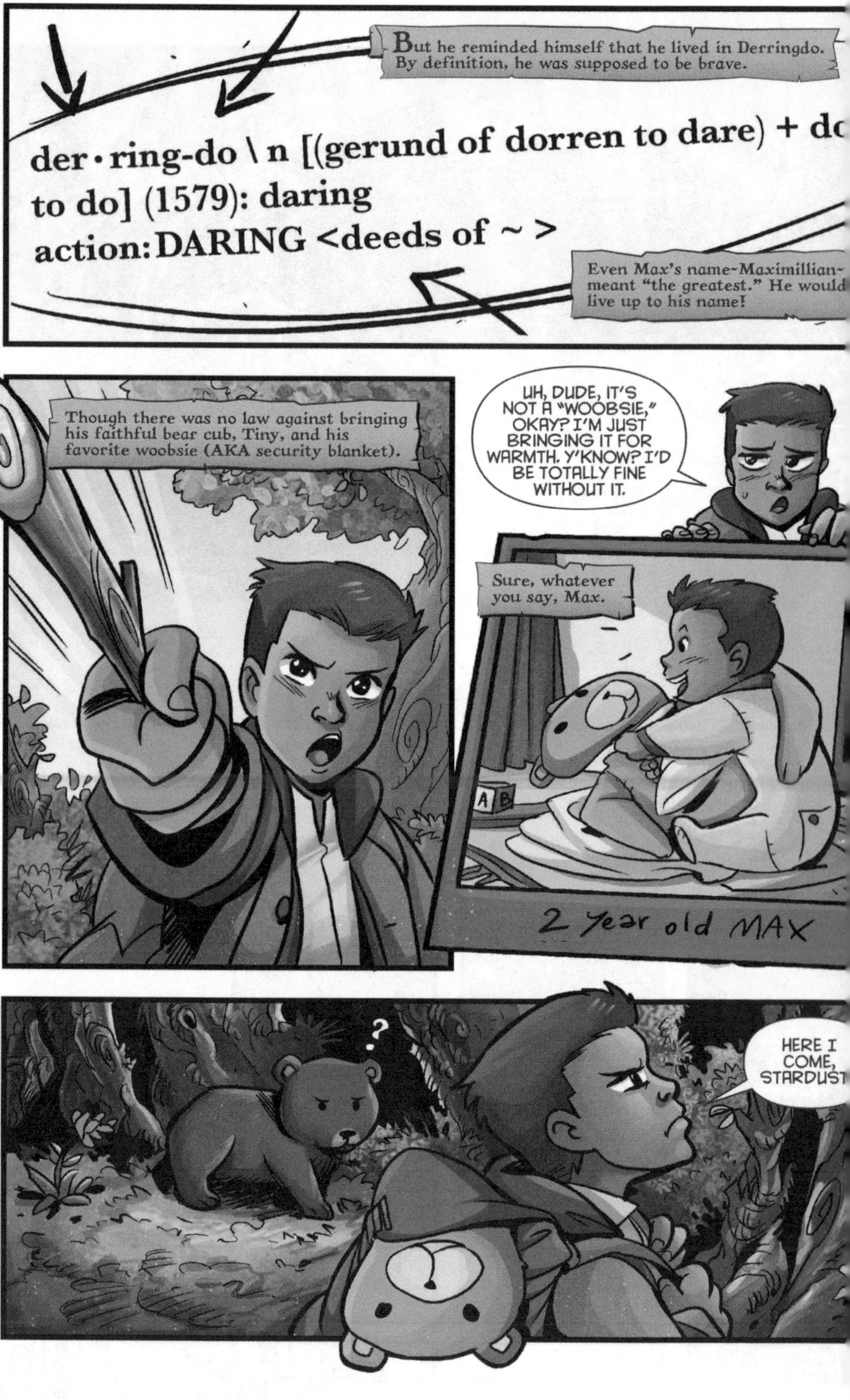
But he reminded himself that he lived in Derringdo. By definition, he was supposed to be brave.
der • ring-do \ n [(gerund of dorren to dare) + do
to do] (1579): daring
action: DARING <deeds of ~ >
Even Max's name~Maximillian~ meant "the greatest." He would live up to his name!
Though there was no law against bringing his faithful bear cub, Tiny, and his favorite woobsie (AKA security blanket).
UH, DUDE, IT'S NOT A "WOOBSIE," OKAY? I'M JUST BRINGING IT FOR WARMTH. Y'KNOW? I'D BE TOTALLY FINE WITHOUT IT.
Sure, whatever you say, Max.
2 year old MAX
HERE I COME, STARDUST

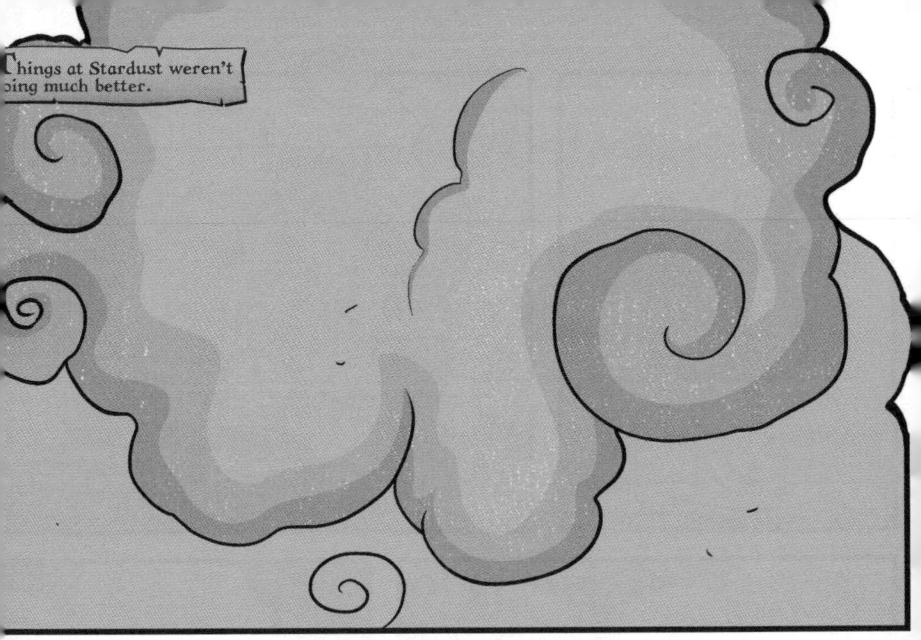
Things at Stardust weren't
oing much better.

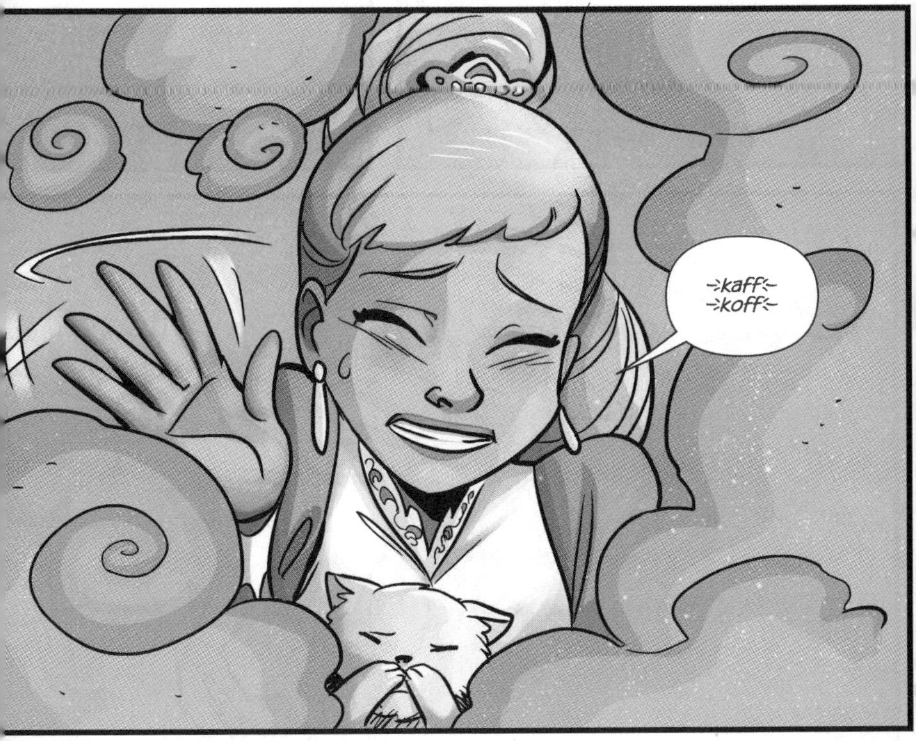
kaff
koff

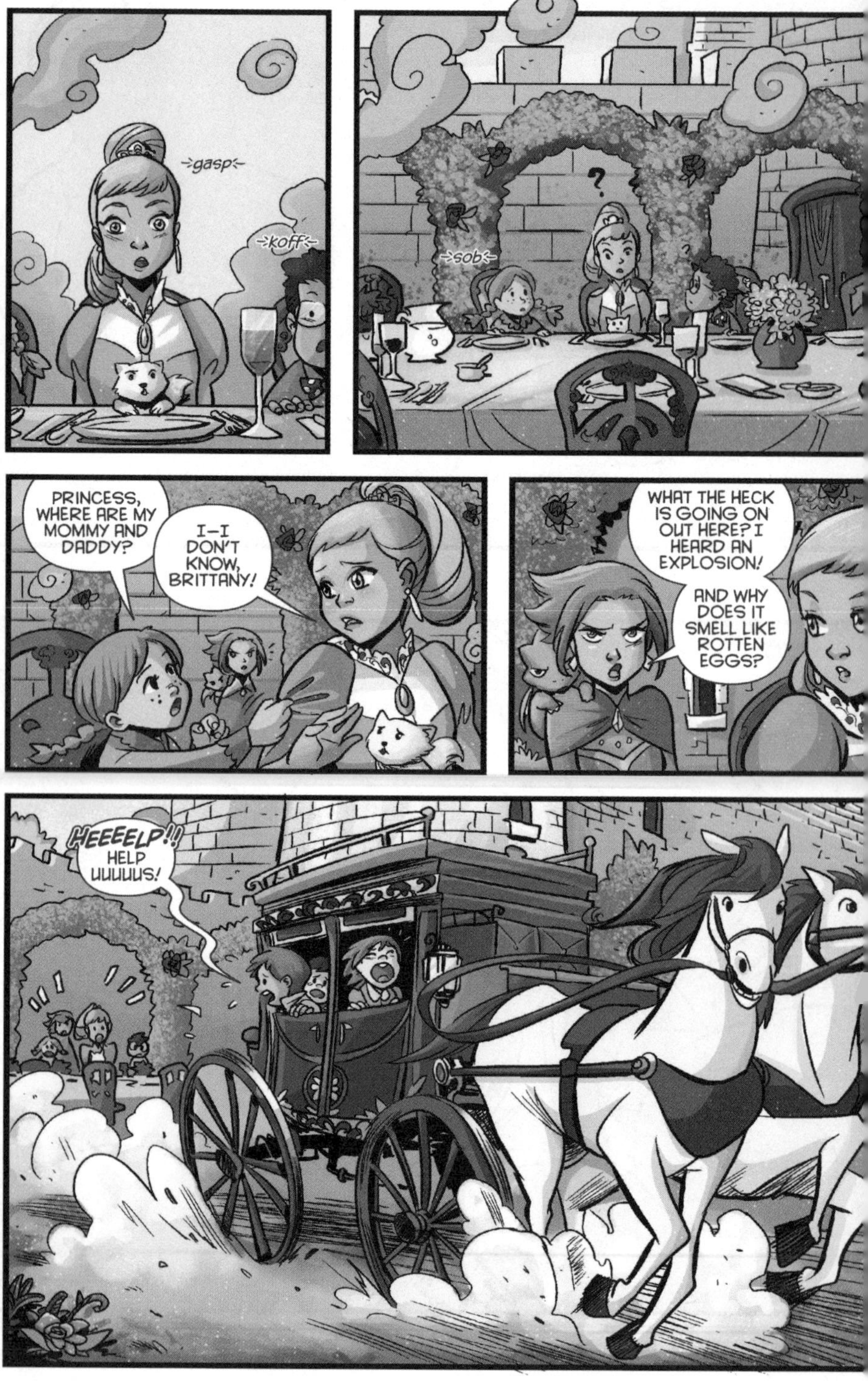

gasp
koff
?
sob
?
PRINCESS, WHERE ARE MY MOMMY AND DADDY?
I—I DON'T KNOW, BRITTANY!
WHAT THE HECK IS GOING ON OUT HERE? I HEARD AN EXPLOSION!
AND WHY DOES IT SMELL LIKE ROTTEN EGGS?
HEEEEELP!!
HELP UUUUUS!

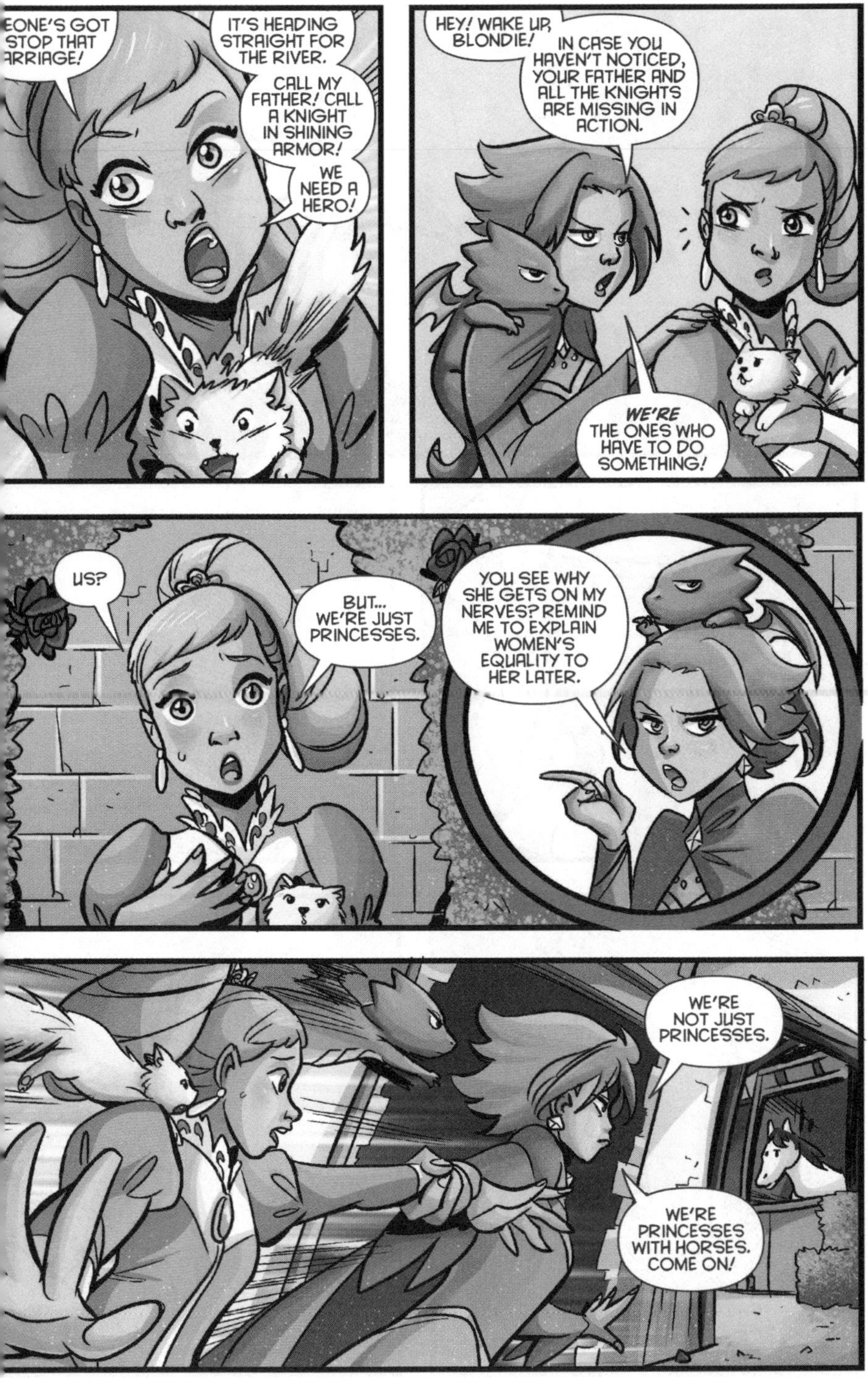
EONE'S GOT
STOP THAT
ARRIAGE!
IT'S HEADING STRAIGHT FOR THE RIVER.
CALL MY FATHER! CALL A KNIGHT IN SHINING ARMOR!
WE NEED A HERO!
HEY! WAKE UP, BLONDIE!
IN CASE YOU HAVEN'T NOTICED, YOUR FATHER AND ALL THE KNIGHTS ARE MISSING IN ACTION.
WE'RE THE ONES WHO HAVE TO DO SOMETHING!
US?
BUT... WE'RE JUST PRINCESSES.
YOU SEE WHY SHE GETS ON MY NERVES? REMIND ME TO EXPLAIN WOMEN'S EQUALITY TO HER LATER.
WE'RE NOT JUST PRINCESSES.
WE'RE PRINCESSES WITH HORSES. COME ON!

JUMP ONTO EVALINE'S HORSE! I'LL TRY TO STOP THE HORSES.

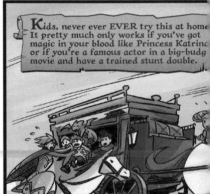

Kids, never ever EVER try this at home. It pretty much only works if you've got magic in your blood like Princess Katrina or if you're a famous actor in a big-budget movie and have a trained stunt double.

WHOA, GIRLS. *WHOAAA!*

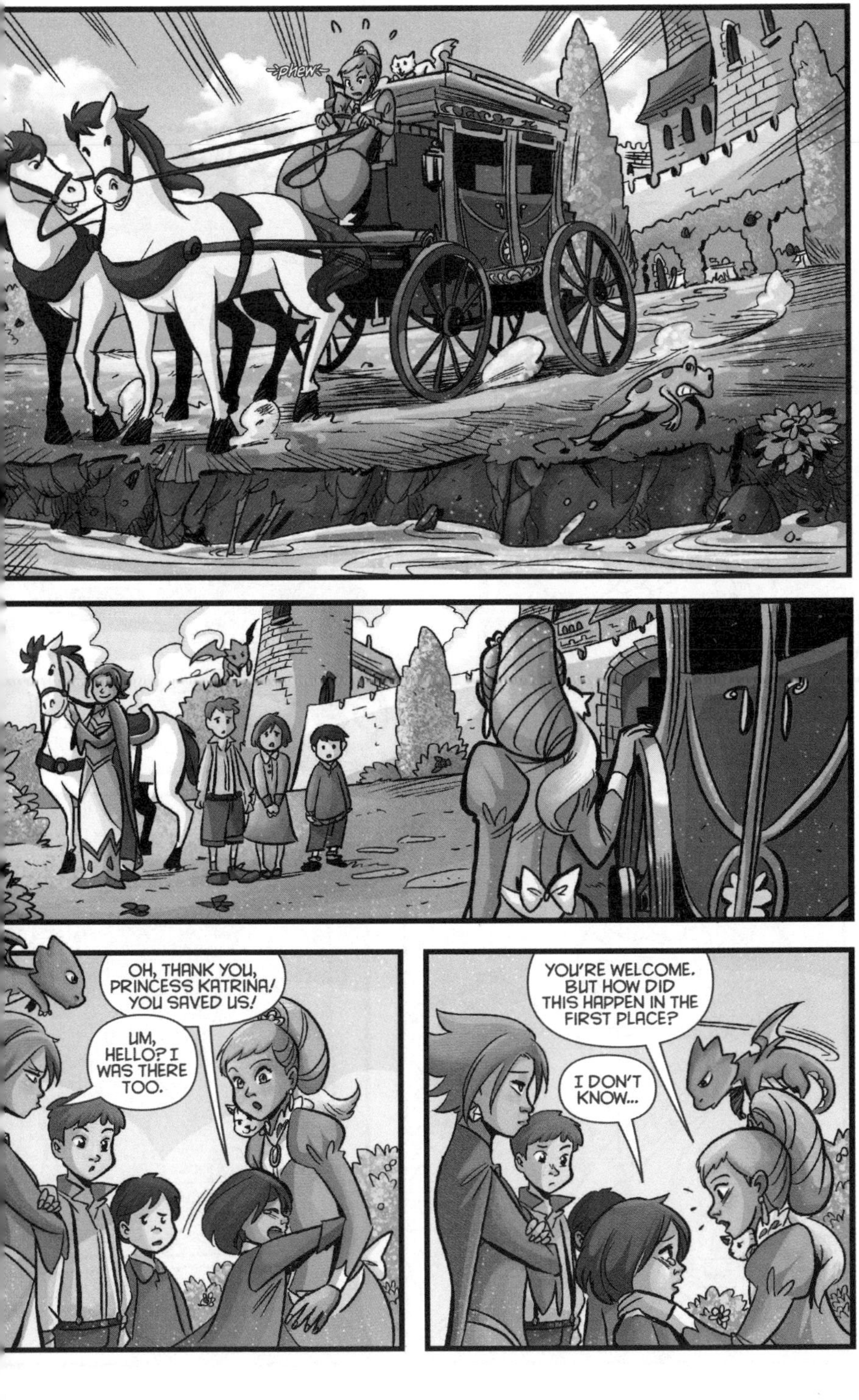

phew
OH, THANK YOU, PRINCESS KATRINA! YOU SAVED US!
UM, HELLO? I WAS THERE TOO.
YOU'RE WELCOME. BUT HOW DID THIS HAPPEN IN THE FIRST PLACE?
I DON'T KNOW...

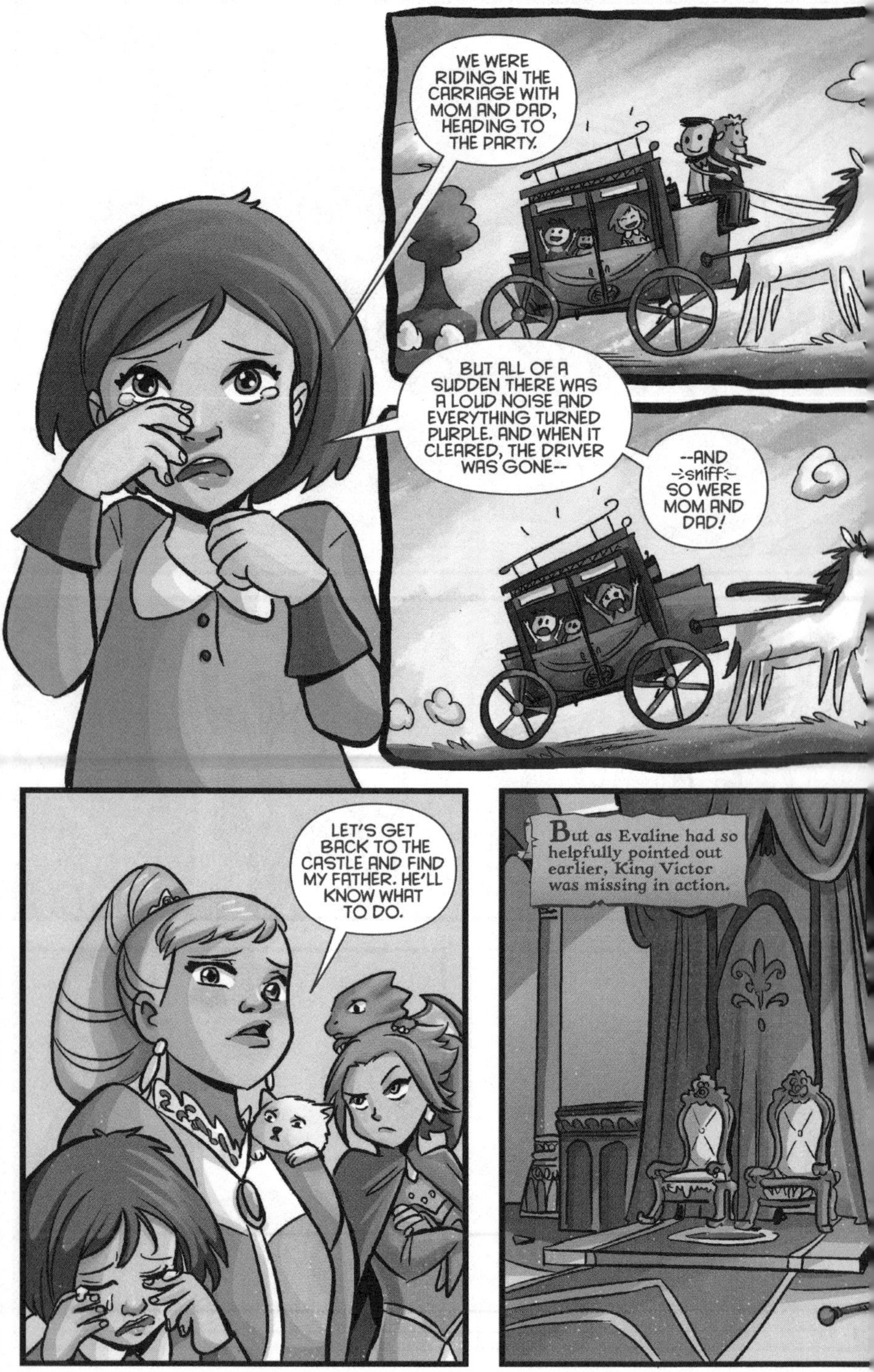
WE WERE RIDING IN THE CARRIAGE WITH MOM AND DAD, HEADING TO THE PARTY.
BUT ALL OF A SUDDEN THERE WAS A LOUD NOISE AND EVERYTHING TURNED PURPLE. AND WHEN IT CLEARED, THE DRIVER WAS GONE--
--AND *sniff* SO WERE MOM AND DAD!
LET'S GET BACK TO THE CASTLE AND FIND MY FATHER. HE'LL KNOW WHAT TO DO.
But as Evaline had so helpfully pointed out earlier, King Victor was missing in action.

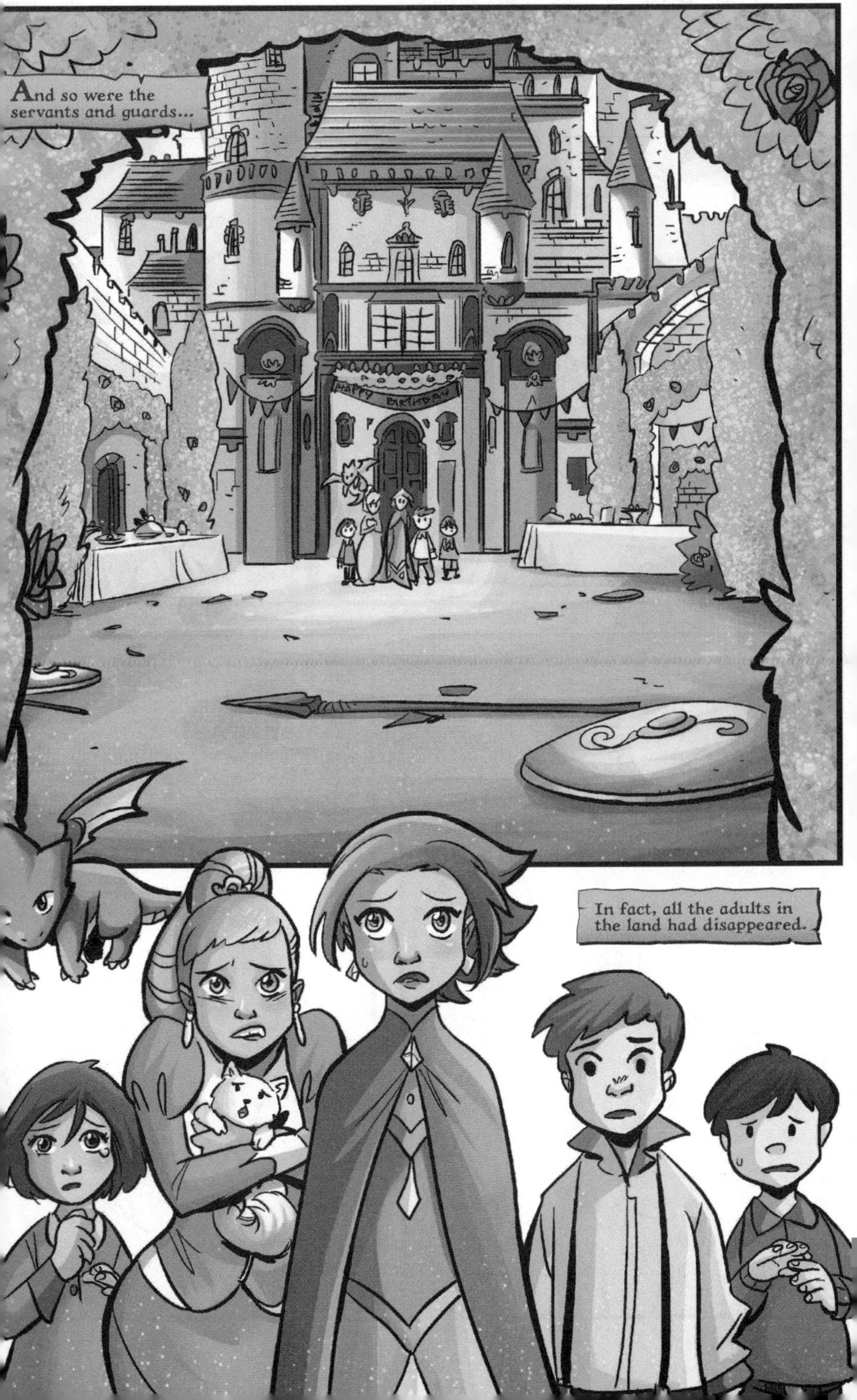
And so were the servants and guards...
HAPPY BIRTHDAY
In fact, all the adults in the land had disappeared.

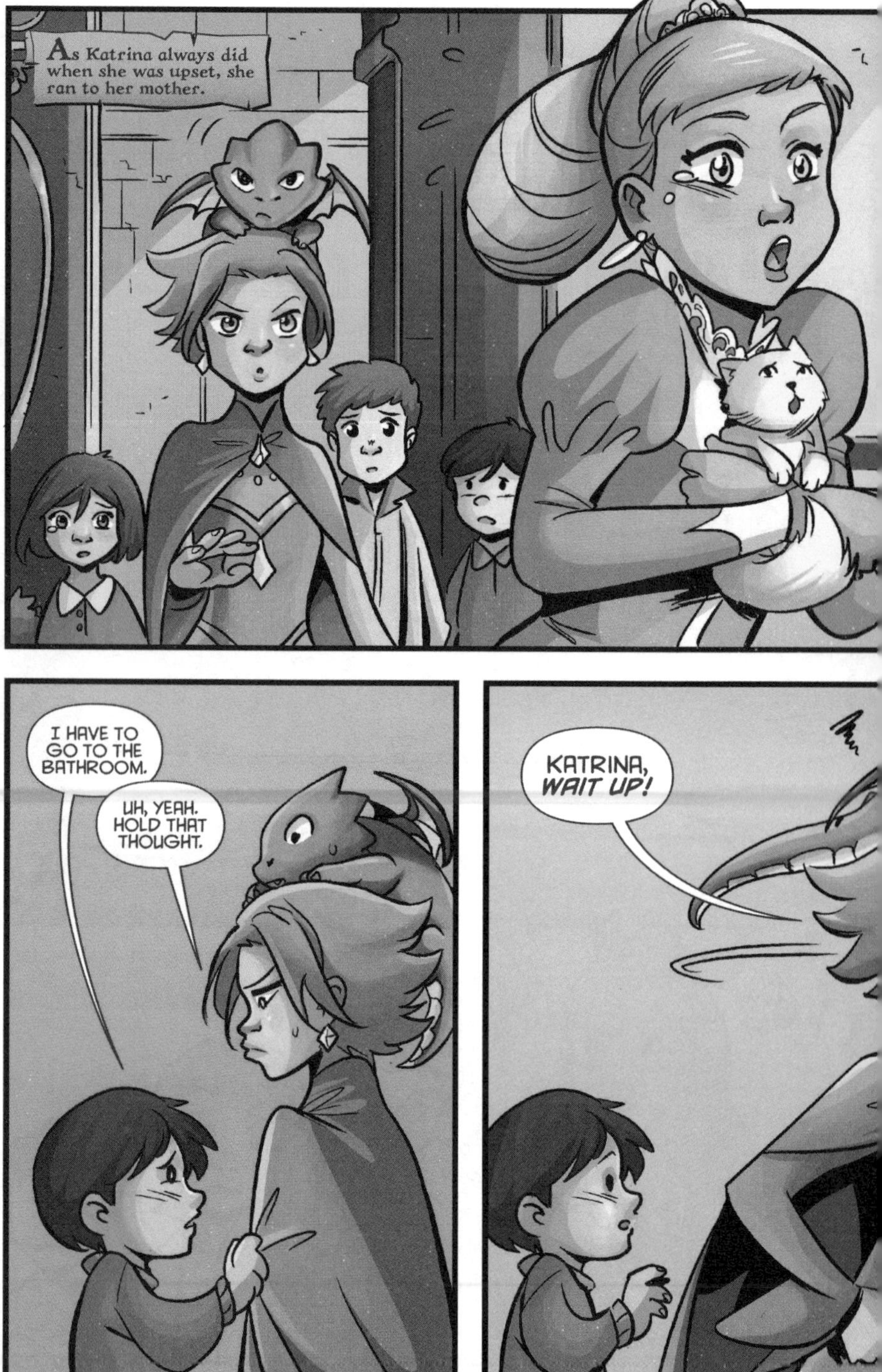
As Katrina always did when she was upset, she ran to her mother.
I HAVE TO GO TO THE BATHROOM.
UH, YEAH. HOLD THAT THOUGHT.
KATRINA, WAIT UP!

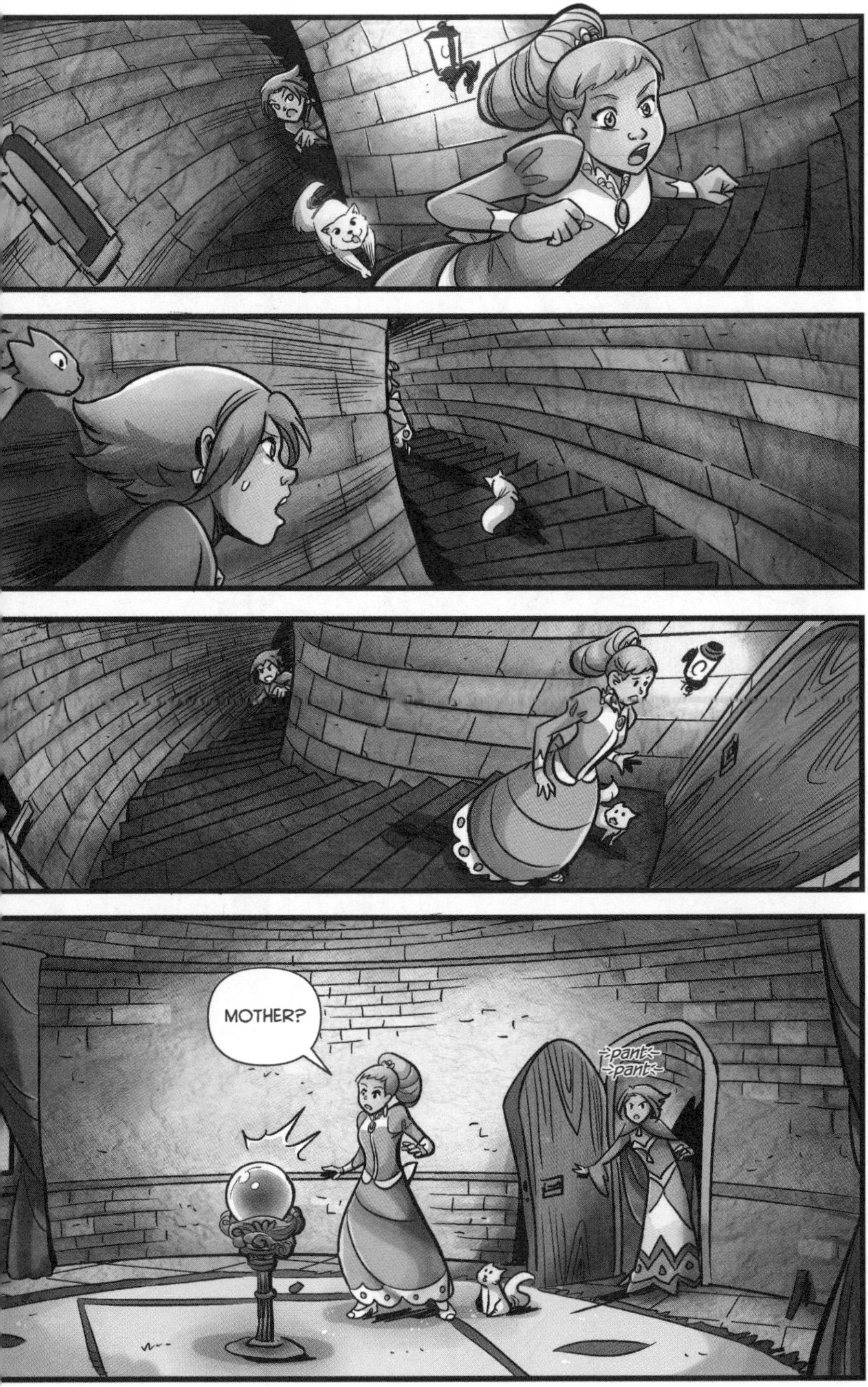
MOTHER?
pant
pant

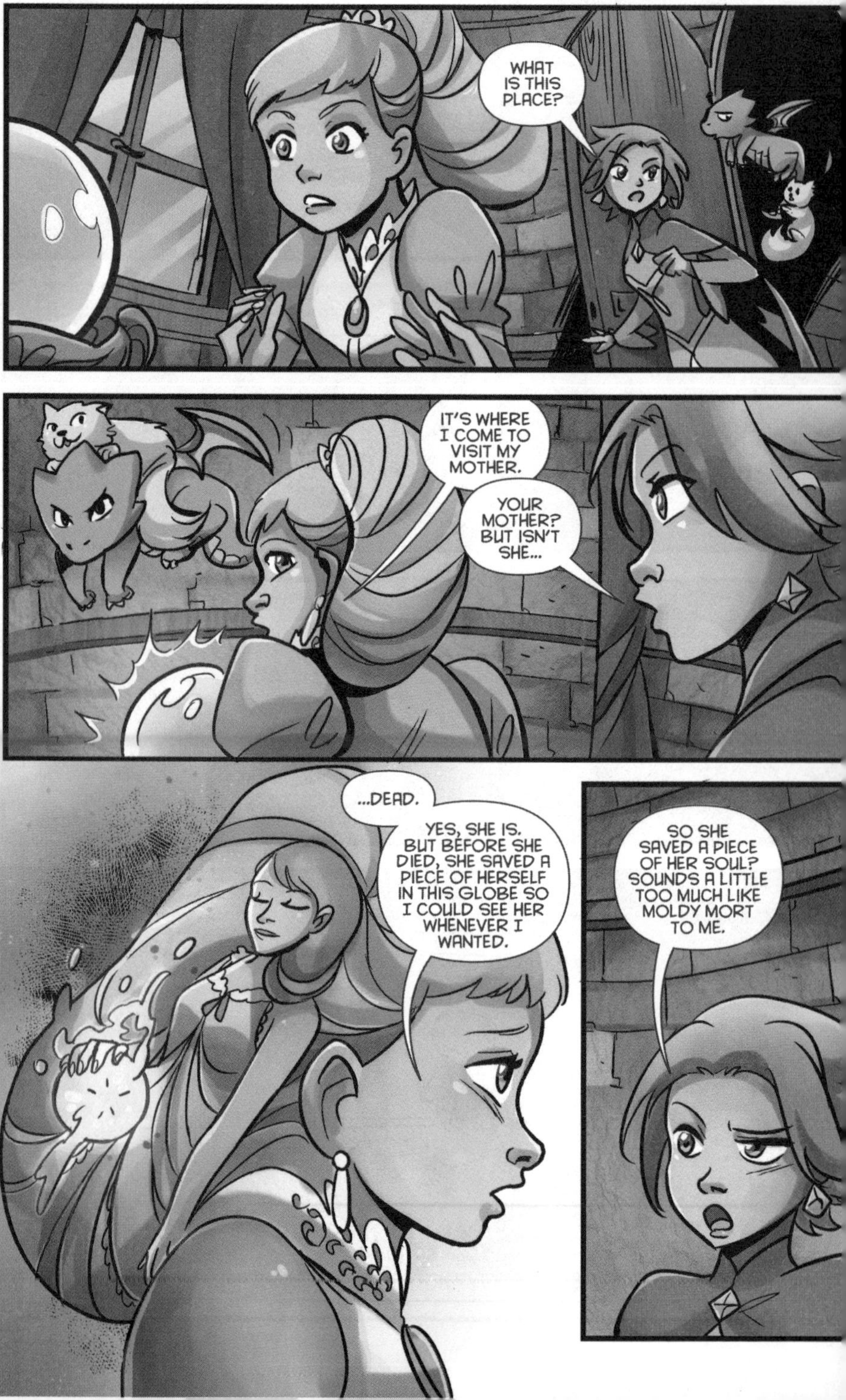
WHAT IS THIS PLACE?
IT'S WHERE I COME TO VISIT MY MOTHER.
YOUR MOTHER? BUT ISN'T SHE...
...DEAD.
YES, SHE IS. BUT BEFORE SHE DIED, SHE SAVED A PIECE OF HERSELF IN THIS GLOBE SO I COULD SEE HER WHENEVER I WANTED.
SO SHE SAVED A PIECE OF HER SOUL? SOUNDS A LITTLE TOO MUCH LIKE MOLDY MORT TO ME.

Surely you've heard of the infamous evil wizard Moldy Mort, who sought to live on forever by hiding part of his soul in a piece of moldy cheese.

NO ONE WILL EVER THINK TO LOOK HERE!

Yeah, he really didn't think that one through.

IF YOU DON'T MIND, WE HAVE A BIT OF A CRISIS GOING ON OVER HERE?

SO HARD TO FIND GOOD NARRATORS THESE DAYS...

Right! Sorry. Back to the princesses...

IT ISN'T LIKE THAT. IT ISN'T HER IN THE GLOBE, EXACTLY. IT'S REALLY JUST A LIVING MEMORY OF HER. SHE DOESN'T EVEN KNOW I'M HERE.

COME CLOSER. I'LL SHOW YOU.

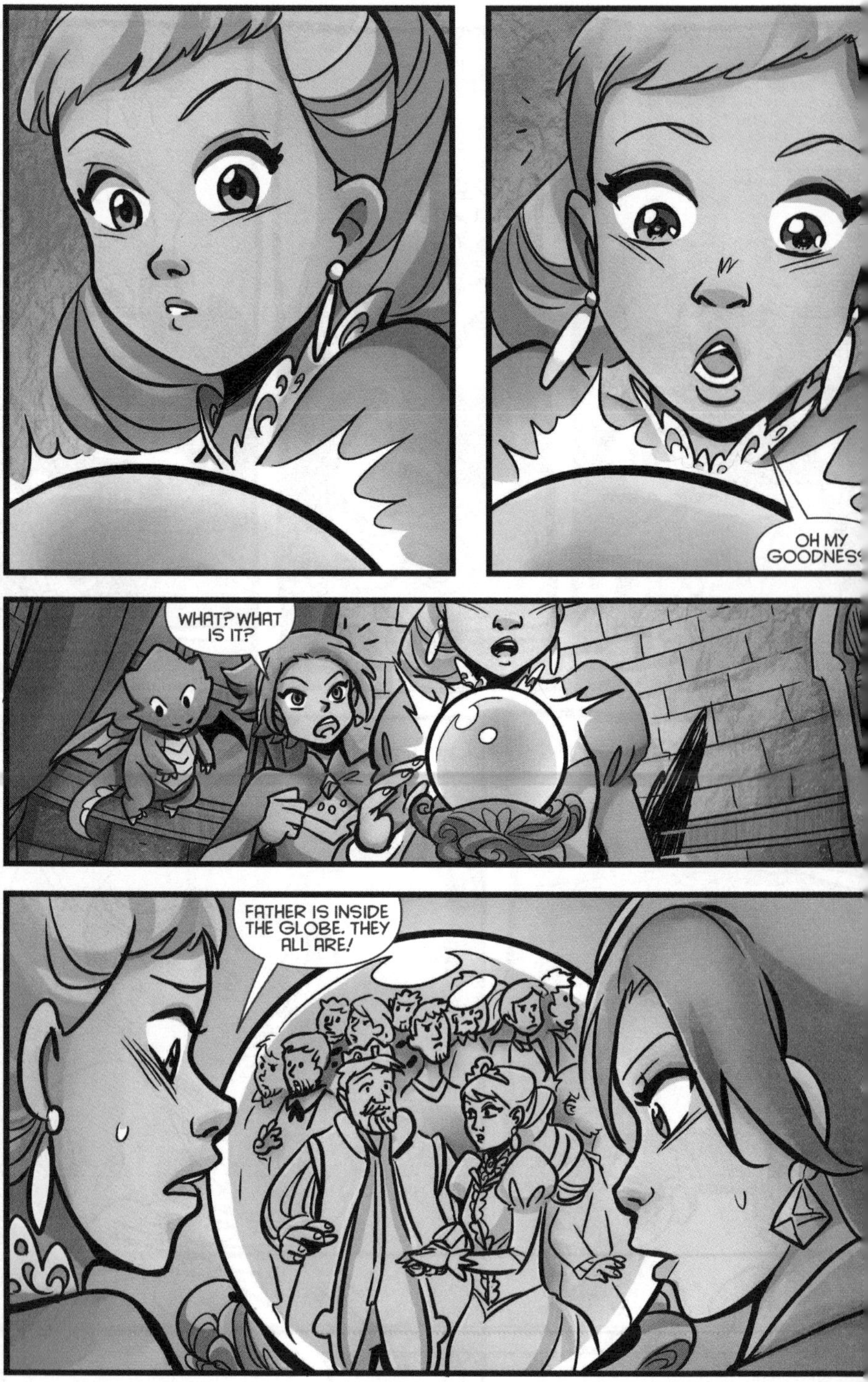
OH MY
GOODNESS
WHAT? WHAT
IS IT?
FATHER IS INSIDE
THE GLOBE. THEY
ALL ARE!

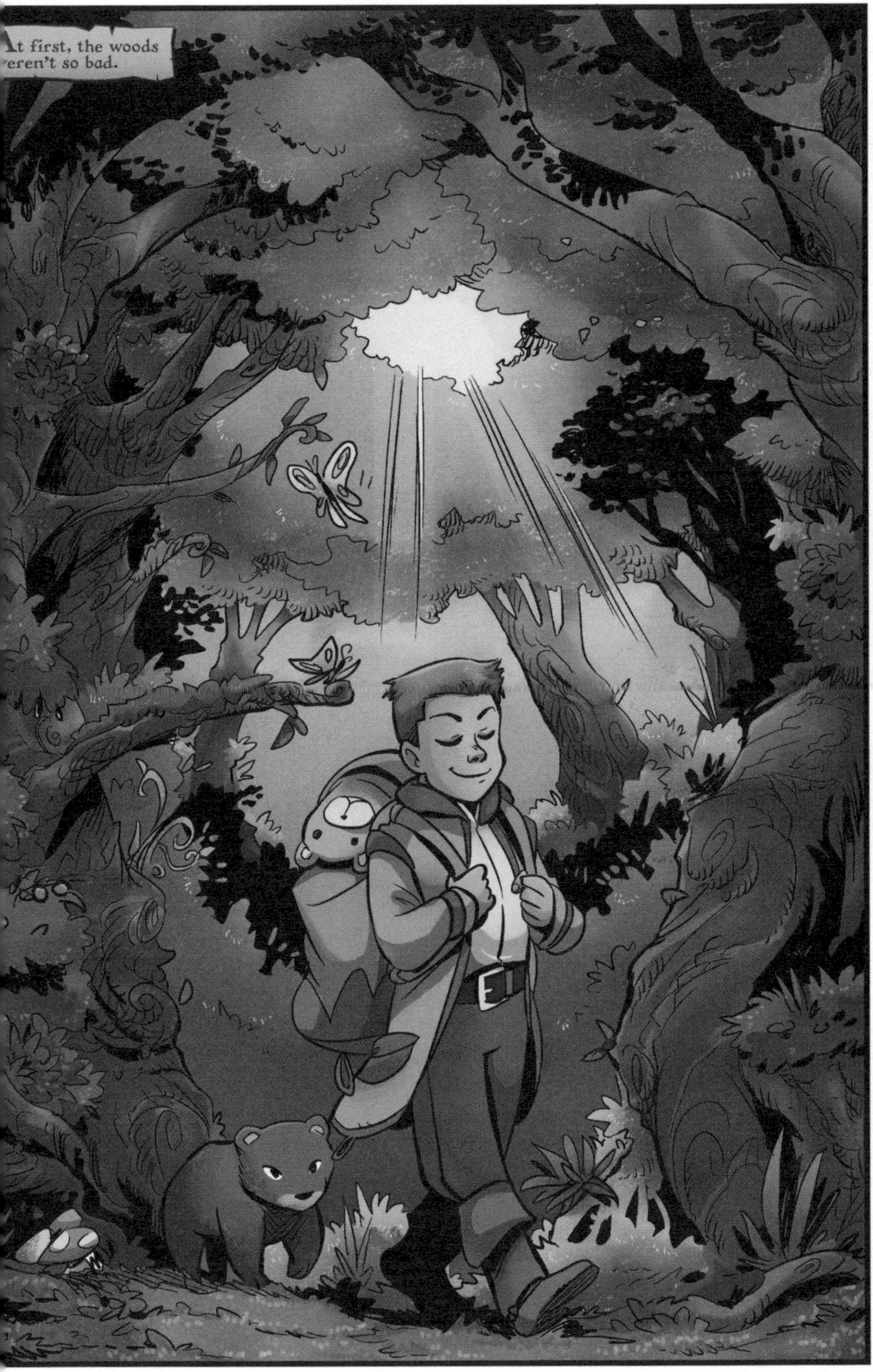
At first, the woods
weren't so bad.

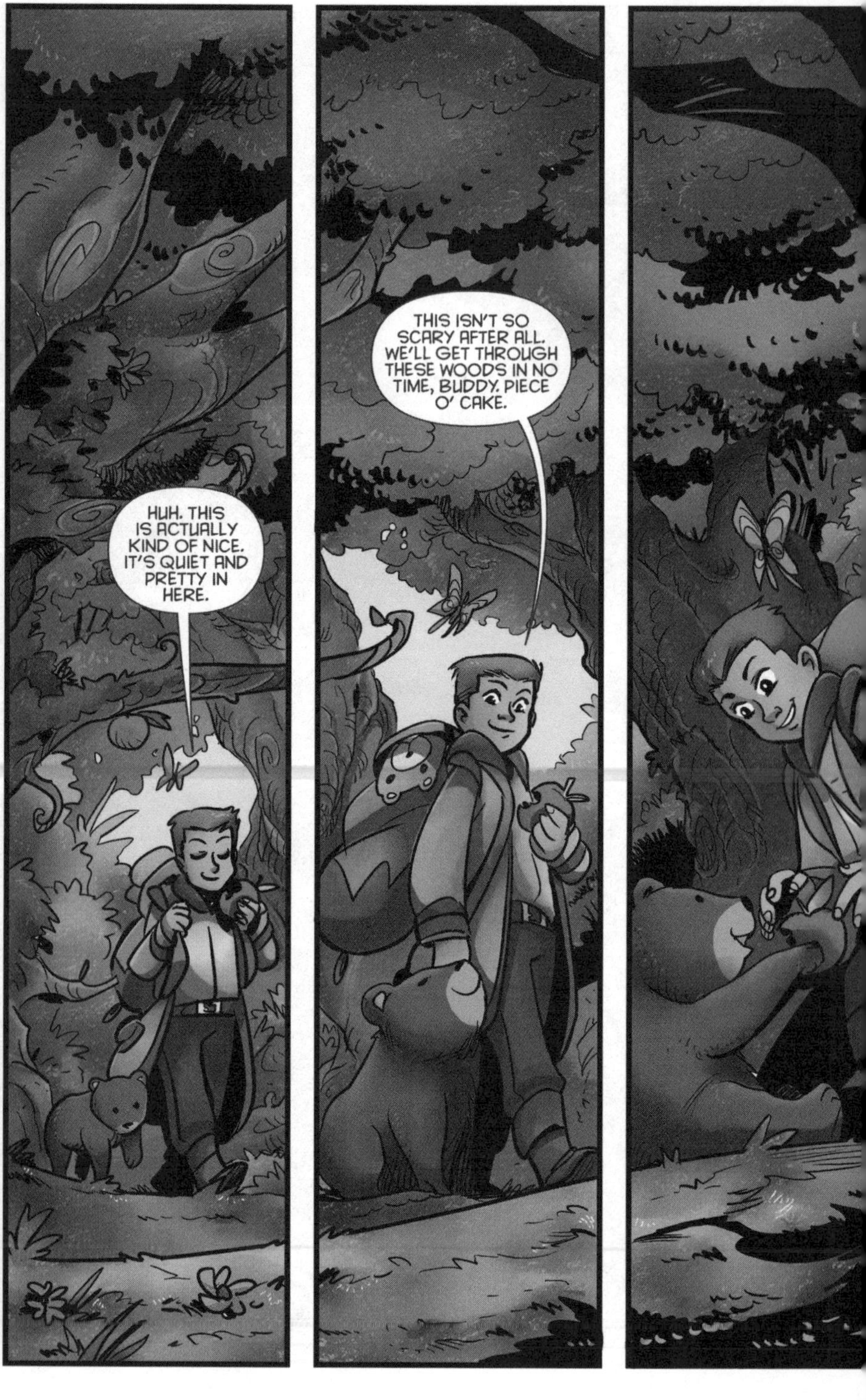
HUH. THIS IS ACTUALLY KIND OF NICE. IT'S QUIET AND PRETTY IN HERE.
THIS ISN'T SO SCARY AFTER ALL. WE'LL GET THROUGH THESE WOODS IN NO TIME, BUDDY. PIECE O' CAKE.

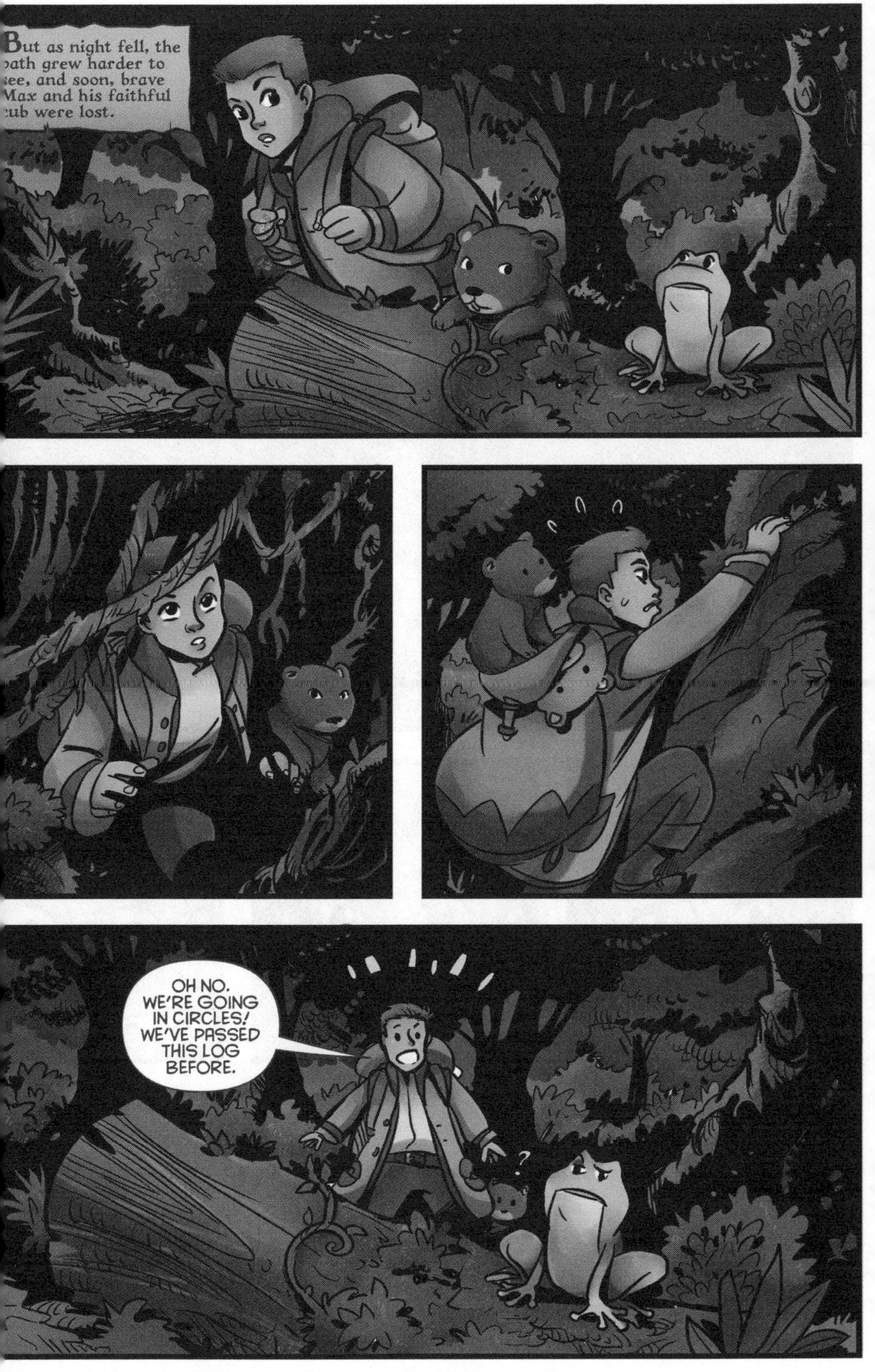
But as night fell, the path grew harder to see, and soon, brave Max and his faithful cub were lost.
OH NO. WE'RE GOING IN CIRCLES! WE'VE PASSED THIS LOG BEFORE.
?

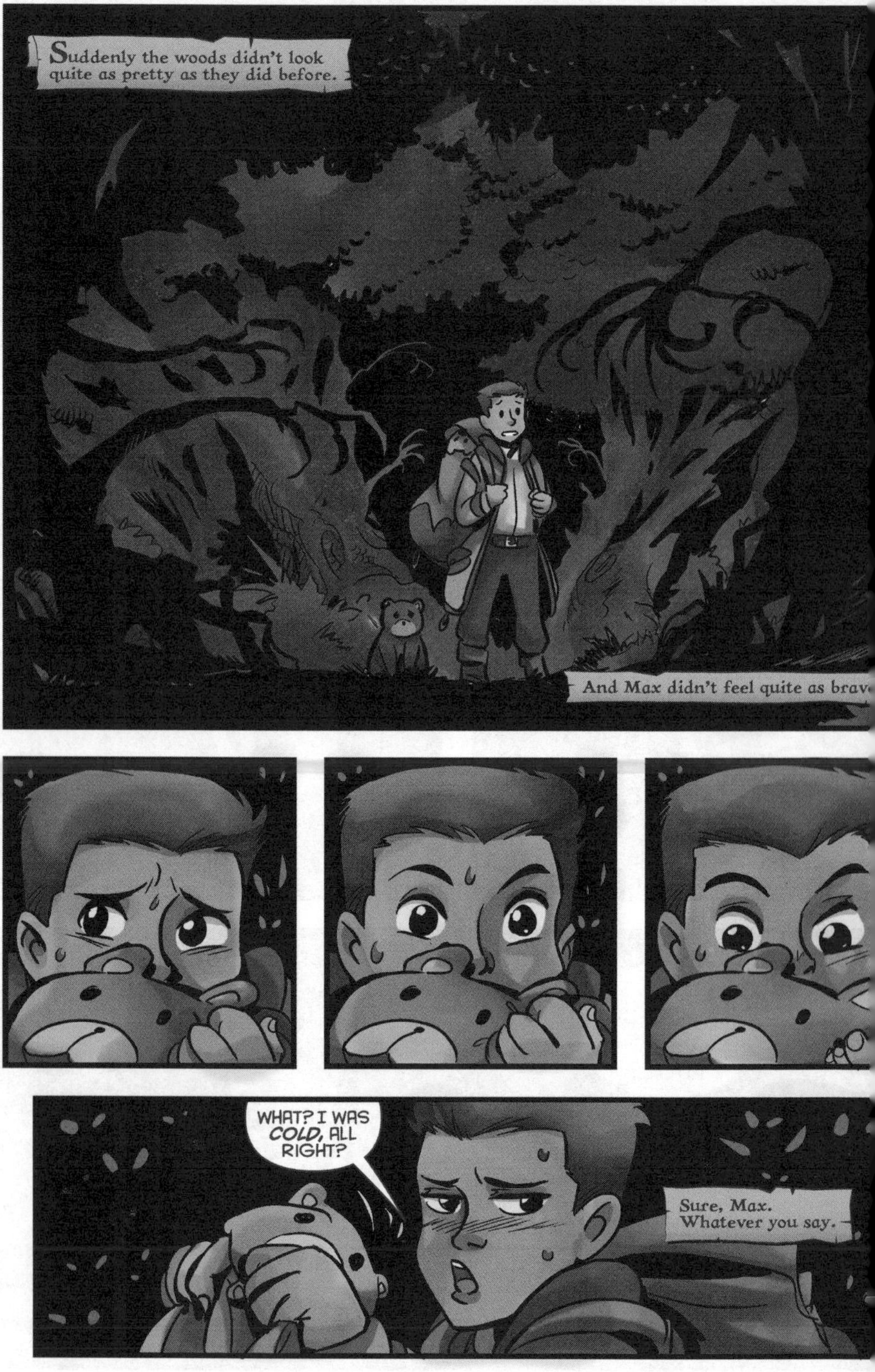
Suddenly the woods didn't look quite as pretty as they did before.
And Max didn't feel quite as brav
WHAT? I WAS COLD, ALL RIGHT?
Sure, Max. Whatever you say.

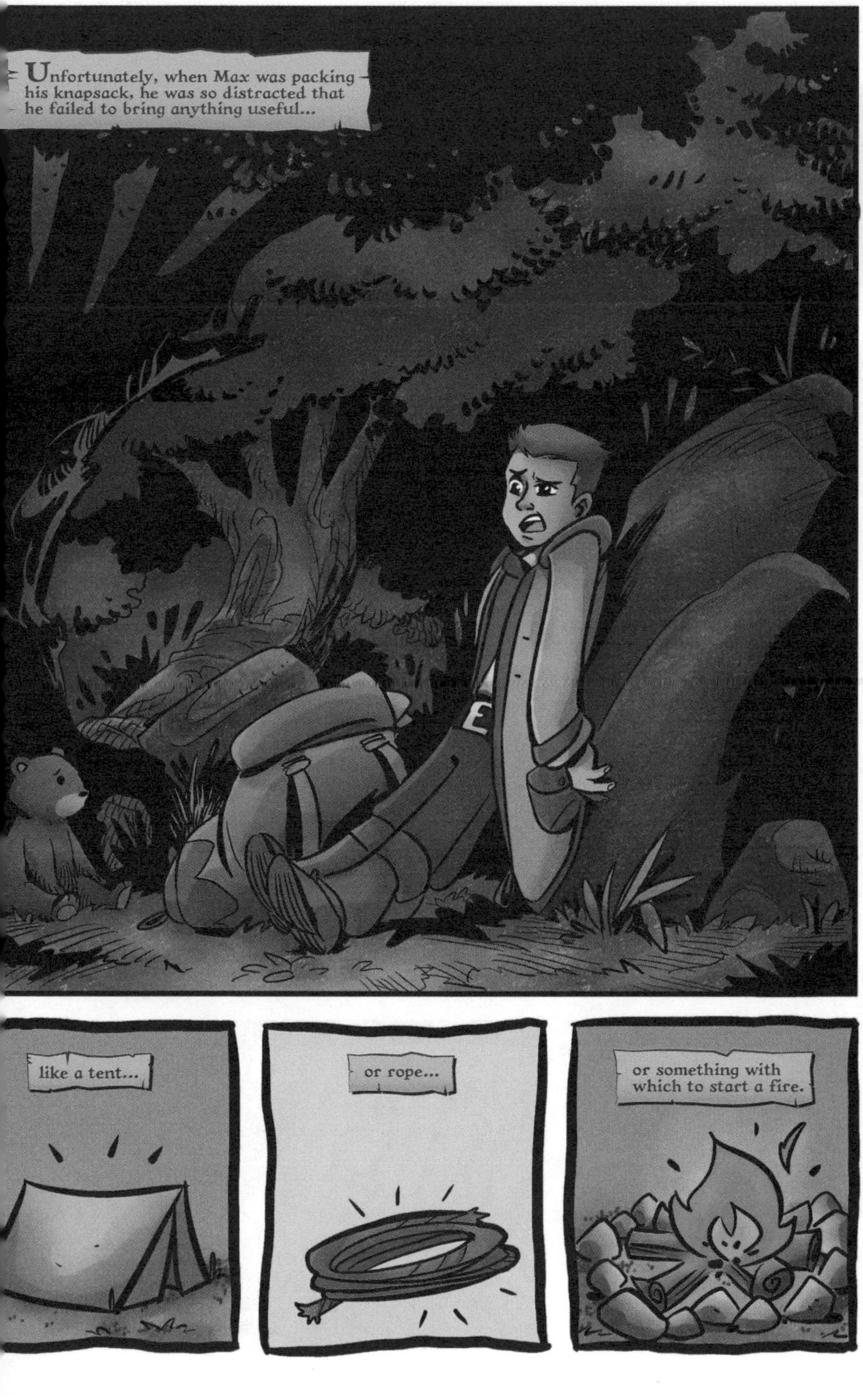
Unfortunately, when Max was packing his knapsack, he was so distracted that he failed to bring anything useful...
like a tent...
or rope...
or something with which to start a fire.

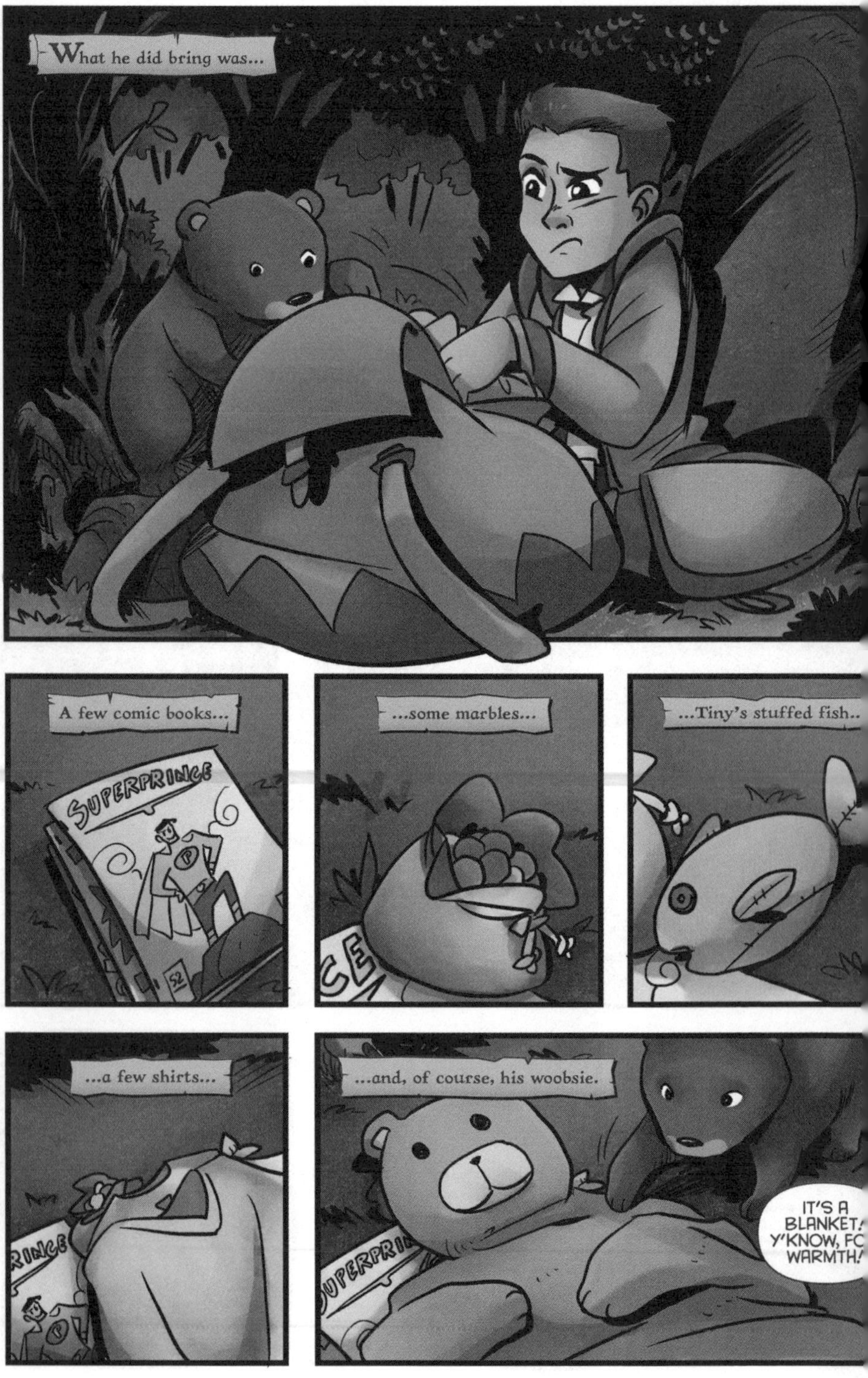
What he did bring was...
A few comic books...
SUPERPRINCE
52
...some marbles...
...Tiny's stuffed fish...
...a few shirts...
...and, of course, his woobsie.
IT'S A BLANKET! Y'KNOW, FO WARMTH!

But as the wind blew around them, Max realized the blanket didn't provide much warmth.

IT'S JUST Y TO GET SOME S-SLEEP, T-TINY.

AAAOOOOOHH

OLVES! WAS T WOLVES? WHERE ARE THEY?

OH, NO! WE'RE GOING TO GET EATEN BY WOLVES! I KNEW IT! IT'S ALL OVER!

MOM AND DAD WERE RIGHT. I NEVER SHOULD HAVE COME IN THESE WOODS ALONE.

I NEVER SHOULD HAVE—

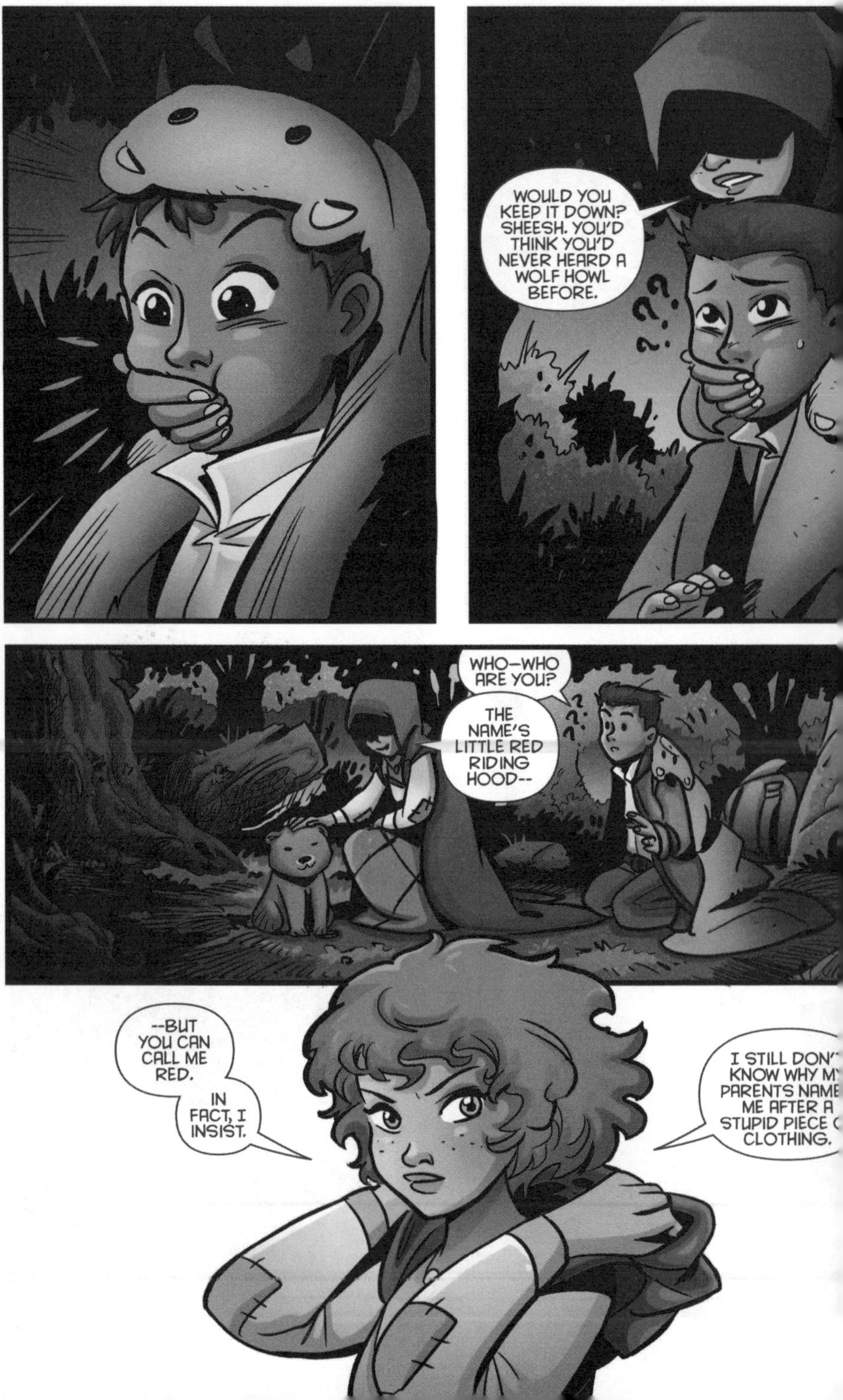
WOULD YOU KEEP IT DOWN? SHEESH. YOU'D THINK YOU'D NEVER HEARD A WOLF HOWL BEFORE.
WHO—WHO ARE YOU?
THE NAME'S LITTLE RED RIDING HOOD--
--BUT YOU CAN CALL ME RED.
IN FACT, I INSIST.
I STILL DON'T KNOW WHY MY PARENTS NAMED ME AFTER A STUPID PIECE OF CLOTHING.

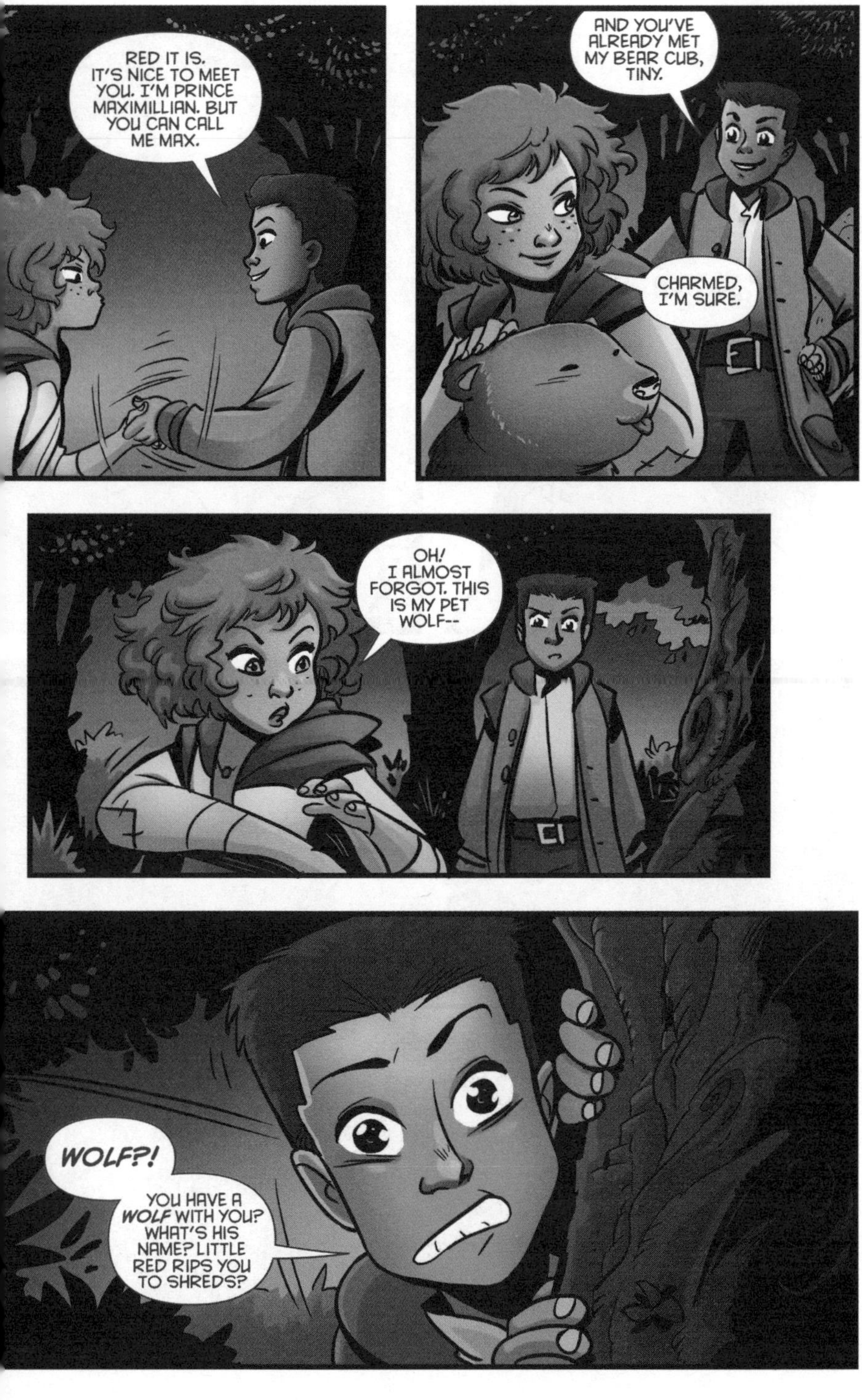
RED IT IS. IT'S NICE TO MEET YOU. I'M PRINCE MAXIMILLIAN. BUT YOU CAN CALL ME MAX.
AND YOU'VE ALREADY MET MY BEAR CUB, TINY.
CHARMED, I'M SURE.
OH! I ALMOST FORGOT. THIS IS MY PET WOLF--
WOLF?!
YOU HAVE A *WOLF* WITH YOU? WHAT'S HIS NAME? LITTLE RED RIPS YOU TO SHREDS?

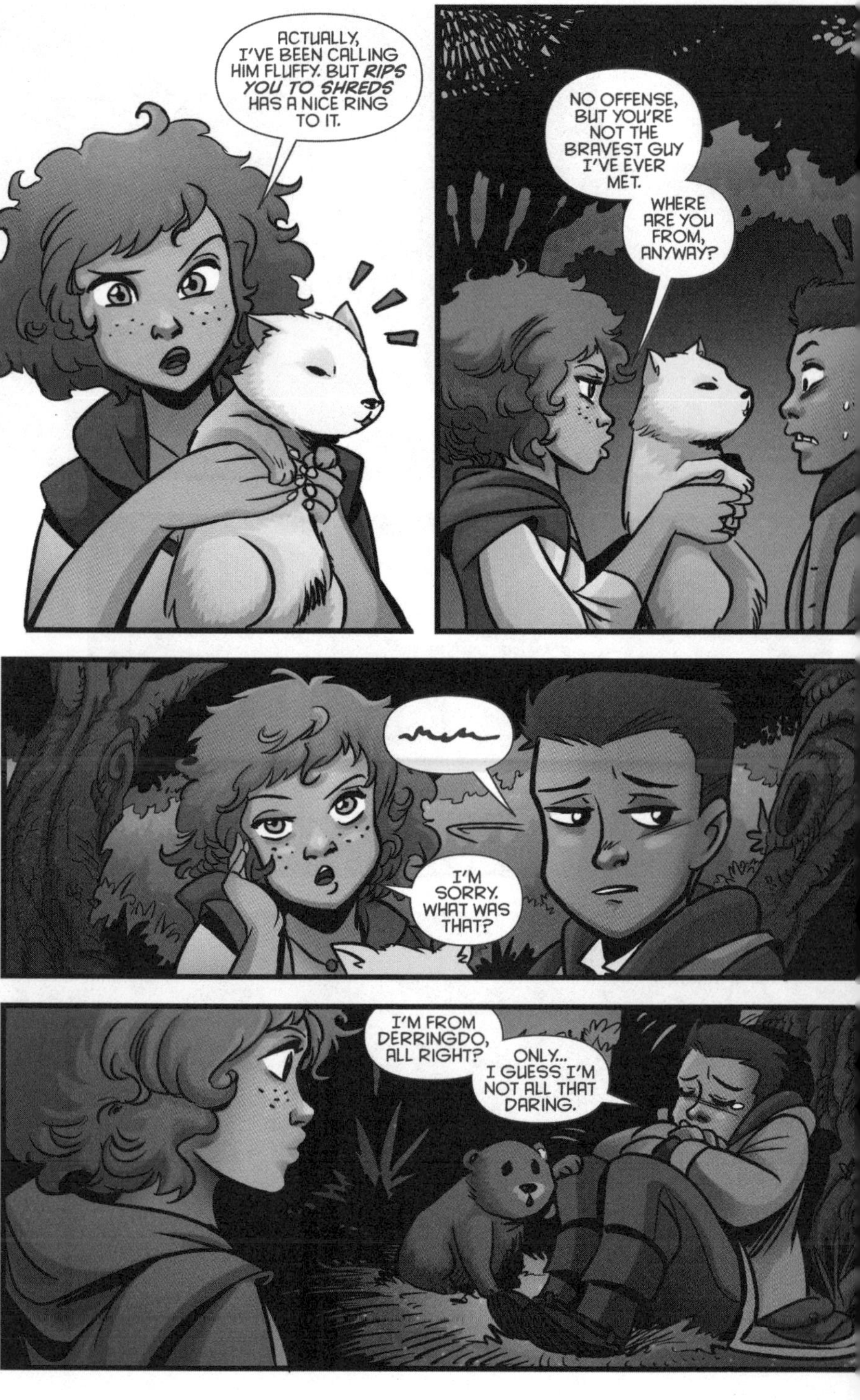
ACTUALLY, I'VE BEEN CALLING HIM FLUFFY. BUT *RIPS YOU TO SHREDS* HAS A NICE RING TO IT.
NO OFFENSE, BUT YOU'RE NOT THE BRAVEST GUY I'VE EVER MET.
WHERE ARE YOU FROM, ANYWAY?
I'M SORRY. WHAT WAS THAT?
I'M FROM DERRINGDO, ALL RIGHT?
ONLY... I GUESS I'M NOT ALL THAT DARING.

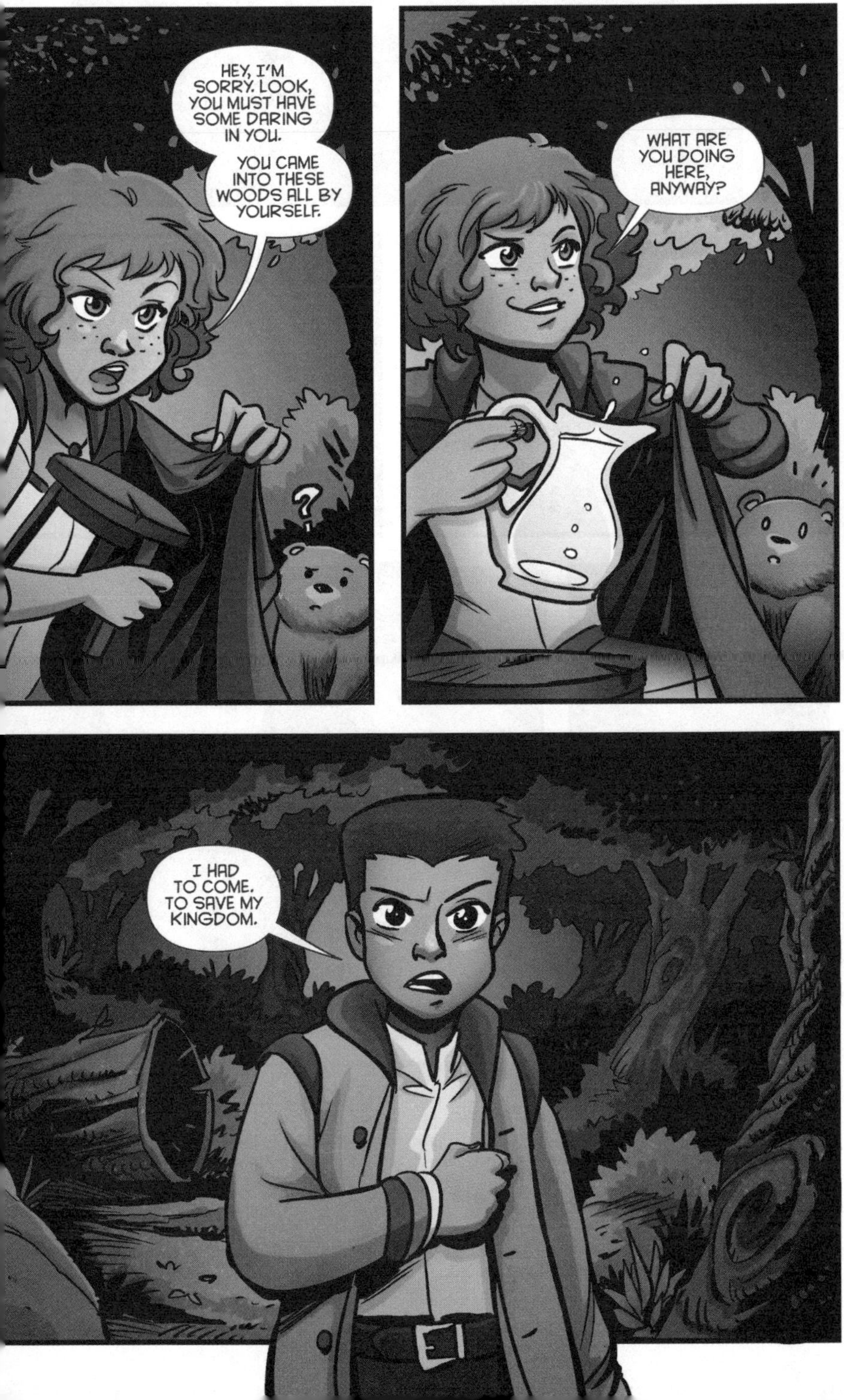
HEY, I'M SORRY. LOOK, YOU MUST HAVE SOME DARING IN YOU.
YOU CAME INTO THESE WOODS ALL BY YOURSELF.
?
WHAT ARE YOU DOING HERE, ANYWAY?
I HAD TO COME. TO SAVE MY KINGDOM.

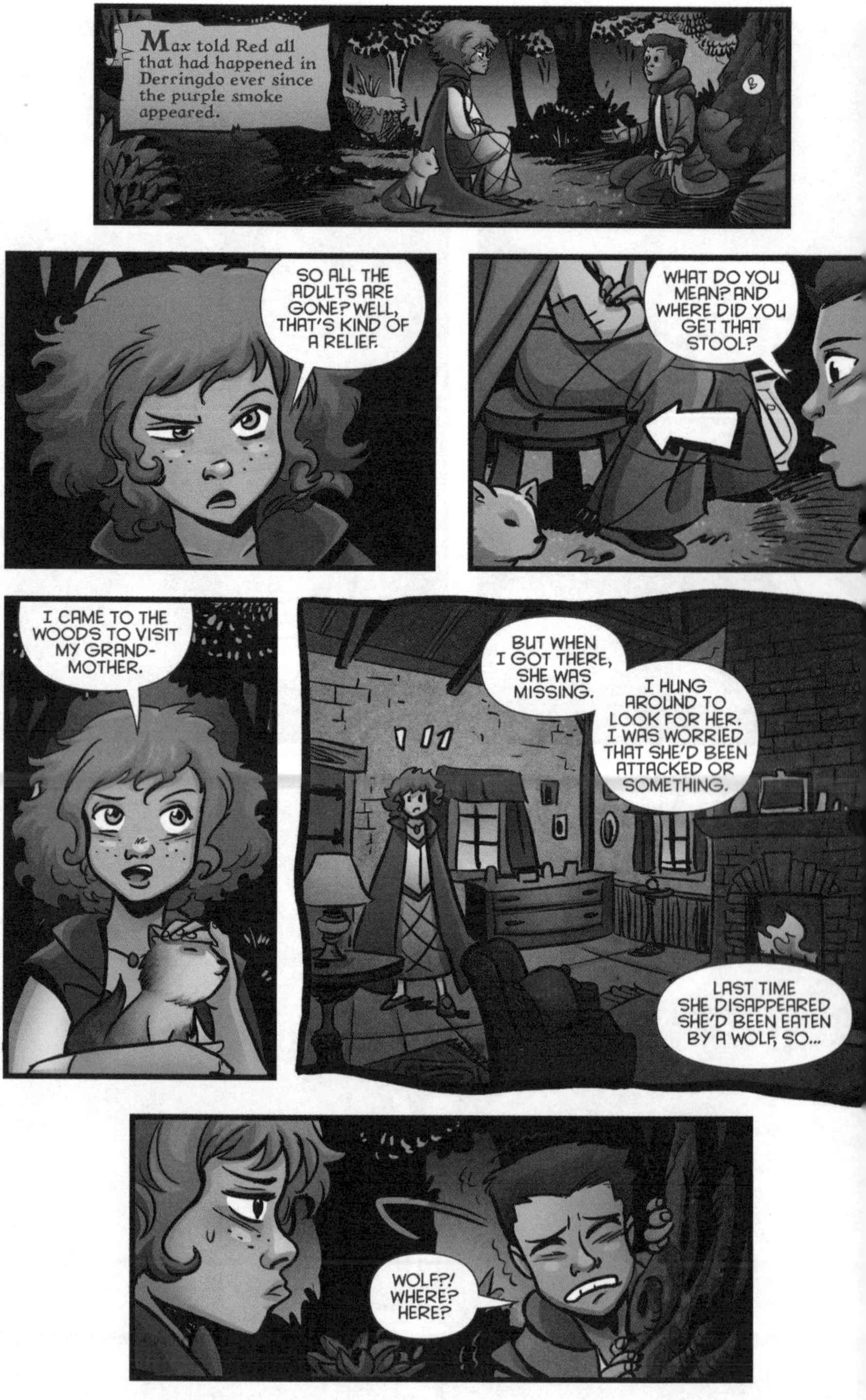
Max told Red all that had happened in Derringdo ever since the purple smoke appeared.
SO ALL THE ADULTS ARE GONE? WELL, THAT'S KIND OF A RELIEF.
WHAT DO YOU MEAN? AND WHERE DID YOU GET THAT STOOL?
I CAME TO THE WOODS TO VISIT MY GRAND-MOTHER.
BUT WHEN I GOT THERE, SHE WAS MISSING.
I HUNG AROUND TO LOOK FOR HER. I WAS WORRIED THAT SHE'D BEEN ATTACKED OR SOMETHING.
LAST TIME SHE DISAPPEARED SHE'D BEEN EATEN BY A WOLF, SO...
WOLF?! WHERE? HERE?

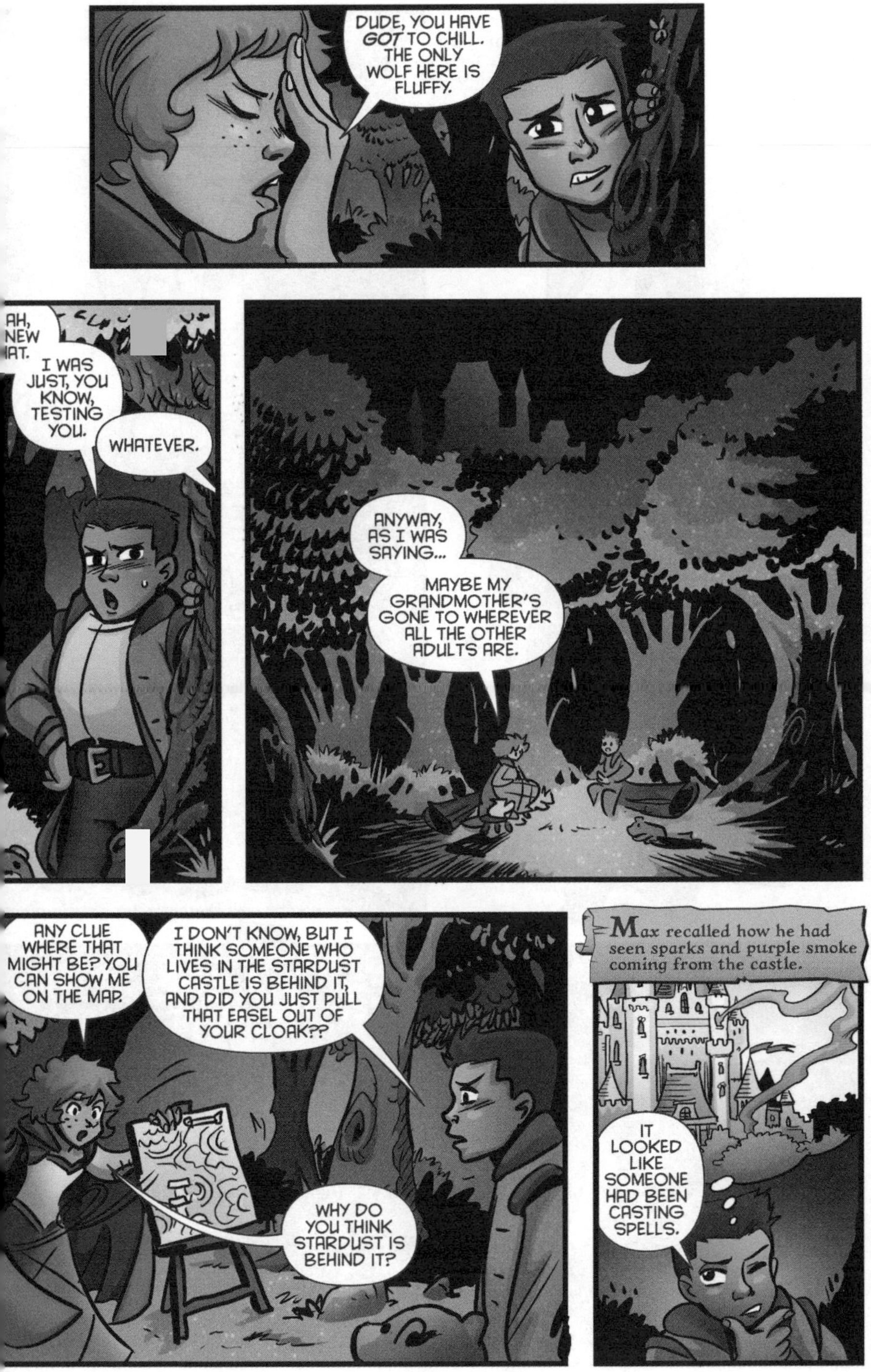
DUDE, YOU HAVE *GOT* TO CHILL. THE ONLY WOLF HERE IS FLUFFY.
AH, NEW
I WAS JUST, YOU KNOW, TESTING YOU.
WHATEVER.
ANYWAY, AS I WAS SAYING...
MAYBE MY GRANDMOTHER'S GONE TO WHEREVER ALL THE OTHER ADULTS ARE.
ANY CLUE WHERE THAT MIGHT BE? YOU CAN SHOW ME ON THE MAP.
I DON'T KNOW, BUT I THINK SOMEONE WHO LIVES IN THE STARDUST CASTLE IS BEHIND IT, AND DID YOU JUST PULL THAT EASEL OUT OF YOUR CLOAK??
WHY DO YOU THINK STARDUST IS BEHIND IT?
Max recalled how he had seen sparks and purple smoke coming from the castle.
IT LOOKED LIKE SOMEONE HAD BEEN CASTING SPELLS.

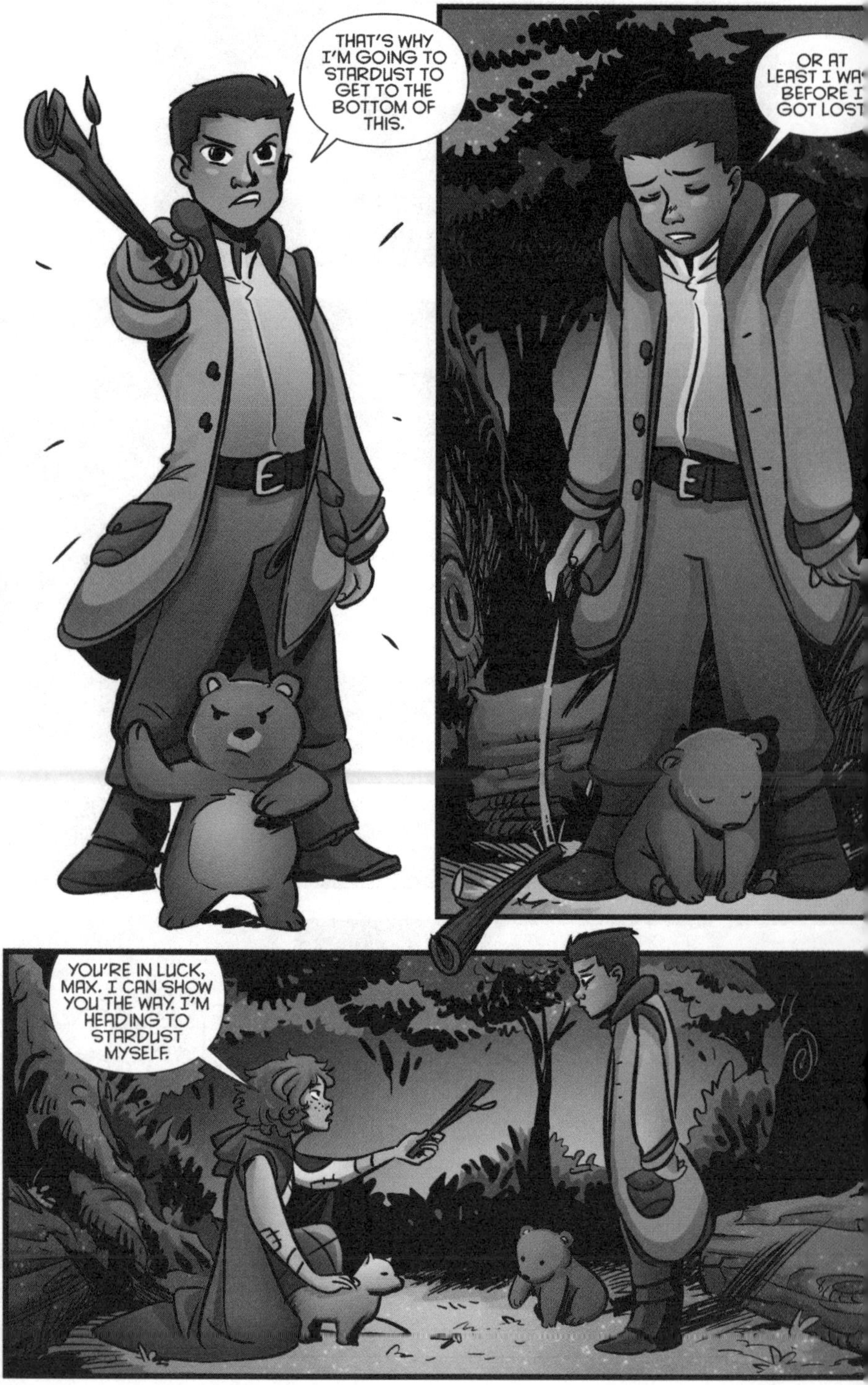
THAT'S WHY I'M GOING TO STARDUST TO GET TO THE BOTTOM OF THIS.
OR AT LEAST I WA BEFORE I GOT LOST
YOU'RE IN LUCK, MAX. I CAN SHOW YOU THE WAY. I'M HEADING TO STARDUST MYSELF.

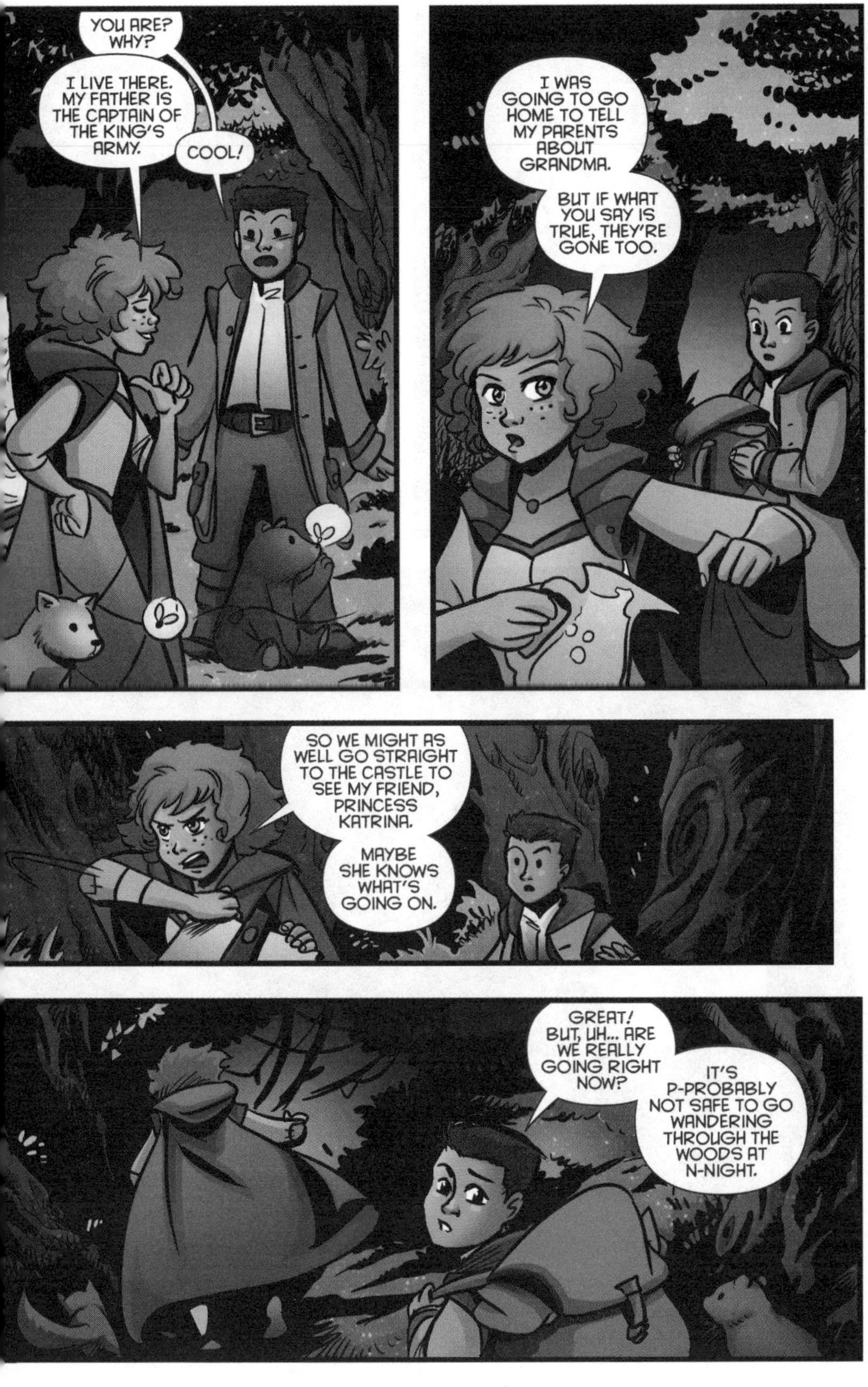
YOU ARE? WHY?
I LIVE THERE. MY FATHER IS THE CAPTAIN OF THE KING'S ARMY.
COOL!
I WAS GOING TO GO HOME TO TELL MY PARENTS ABOUT GRANDMA.
BUT IF WHAT YOU SAY IS TRUE, THEY'RE GONE TOO.
SO WE MIGHT AS WELL GO STRAIGHT TO THE CASTLE TO SEE MY FRIEND, PRINCESS KATRINA.
MAYBE SHE KNOWS WHAT'S GOING ON.
GREAT! BUT, UH... ARE WE REALLY GOING RIGHT NOW?
IT'S P-PROBABLY NOT SAFE TO GO WANDERING THROUGH THE WOODS AT N-NIGHT.

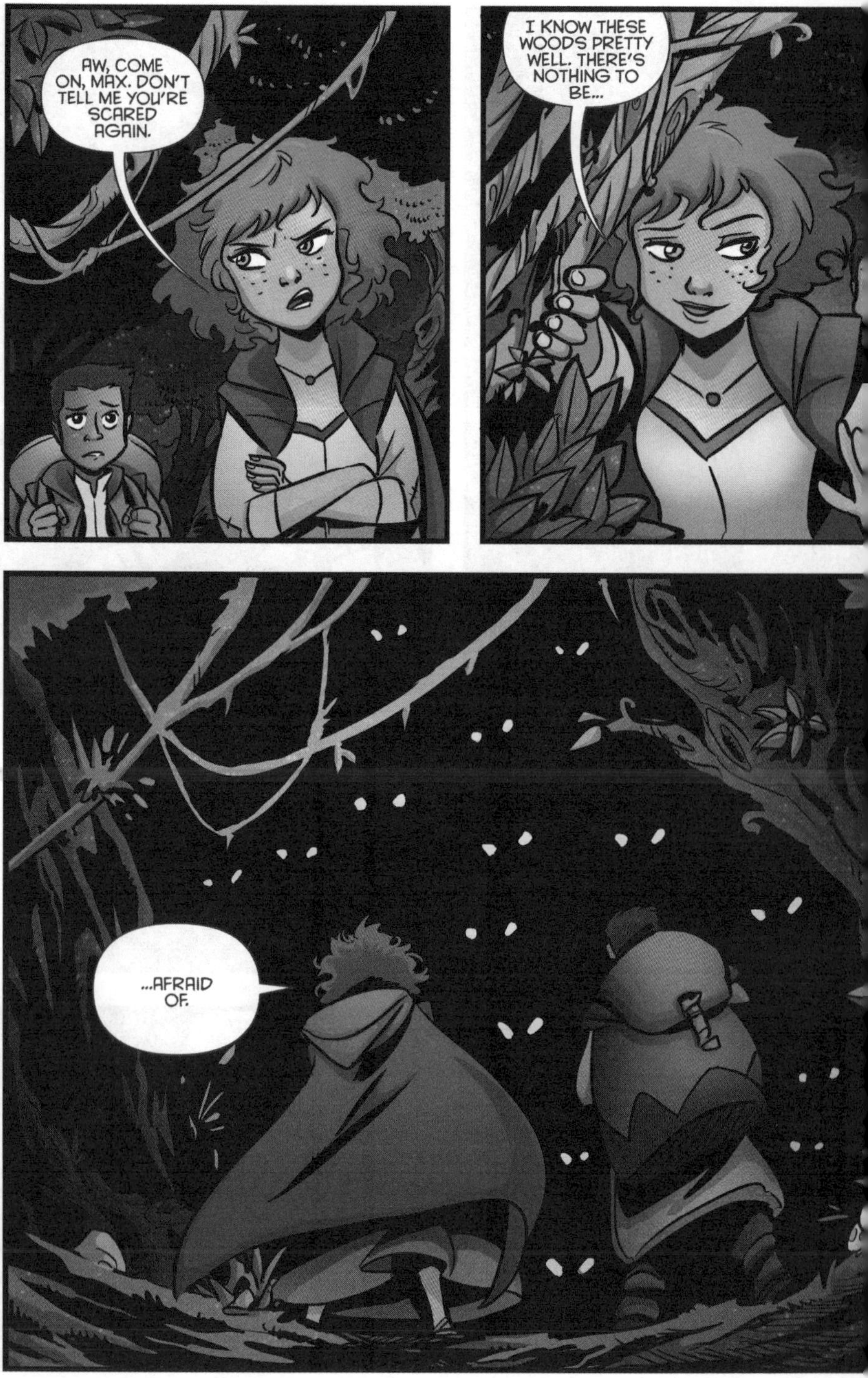
AW, COME ON, MAX. DON'T TELL ME YOU'RE SCARED AGAIN.
I KNOW THESE WOODS PRETTY WELL. THERE'S NOTHING TO BE...
...AFRAID OF.

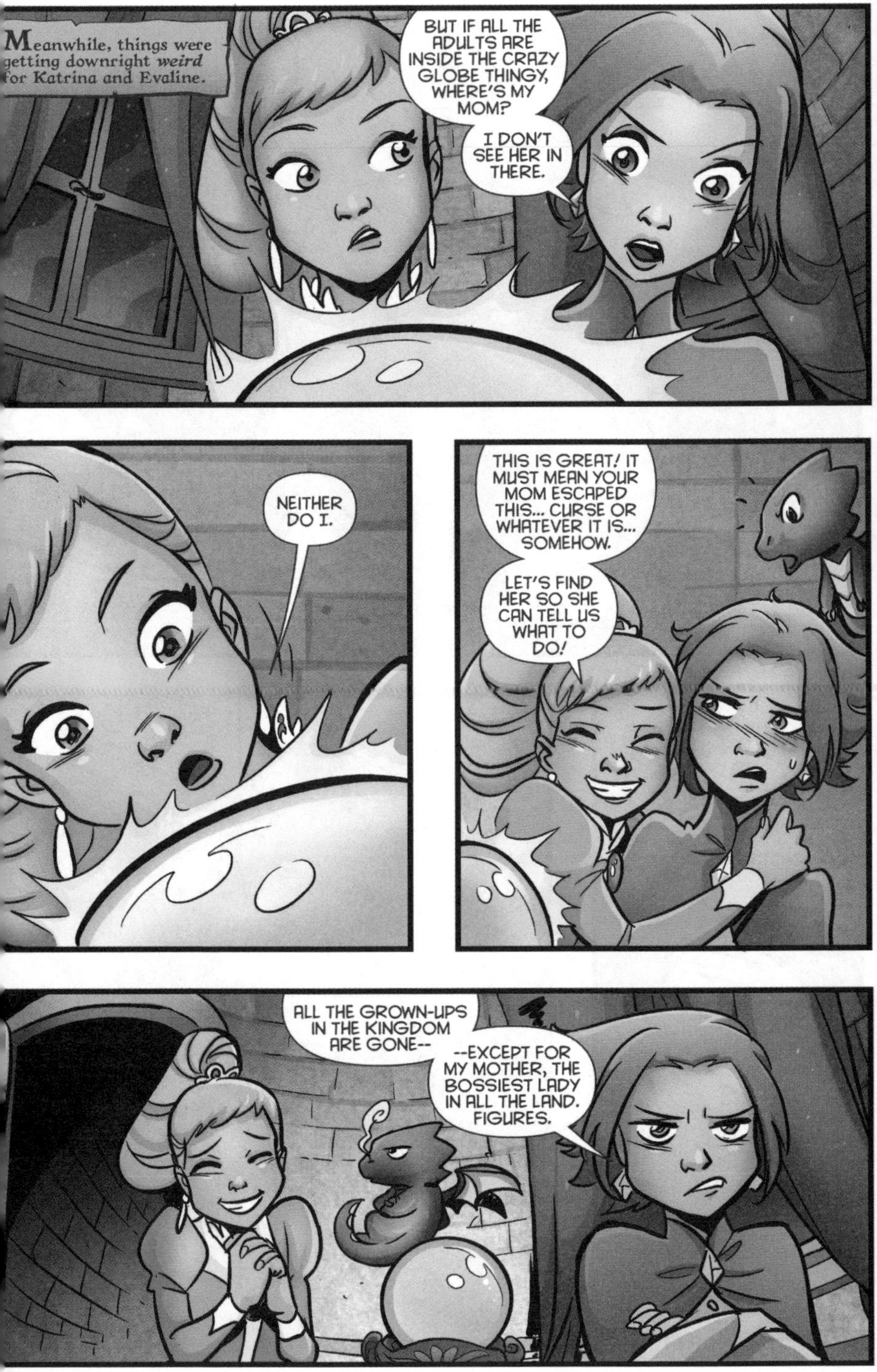
Meanwhile, things were getting downright *weird* for Katrina and Evaline.
BUT IF ALL THE ADULTS ARE INSIDE THE CRAZY GLOBE THINGY, WHERE'S MY MOM?
I DON'T SEE HER IN THERE.
NEITHER DO I.
THIS IS GREAT! IT MUST MEAN YOUR MOM ESCAPED THIS... CURSE OR WHATEVER IT IS... SOMEHOW.
LET'S FIND HER SO SHE CAN TELL US WHAT TO DO!
ALL THE GROWN-UPS IN THE KINGDOM ARE GONE--
--EXCEPT FOR MY MOTHER, THE BOSSIEST LADY IN ALL THE LAND. FIGURES.

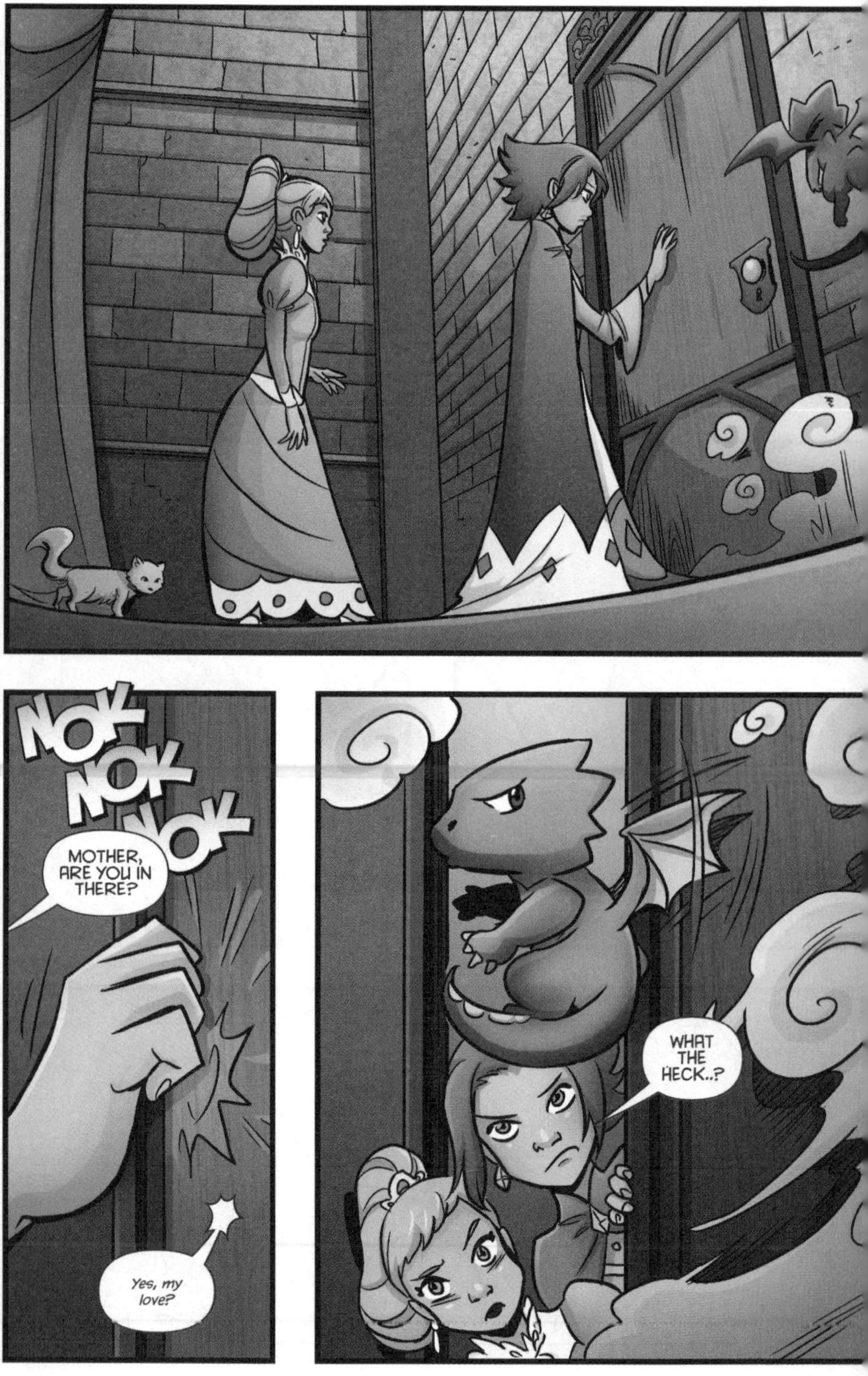
NOK
NOK
NOK
MOTHER, ARE YOU IN THERE?
Yes, my love?
WHAT THE HECK..?

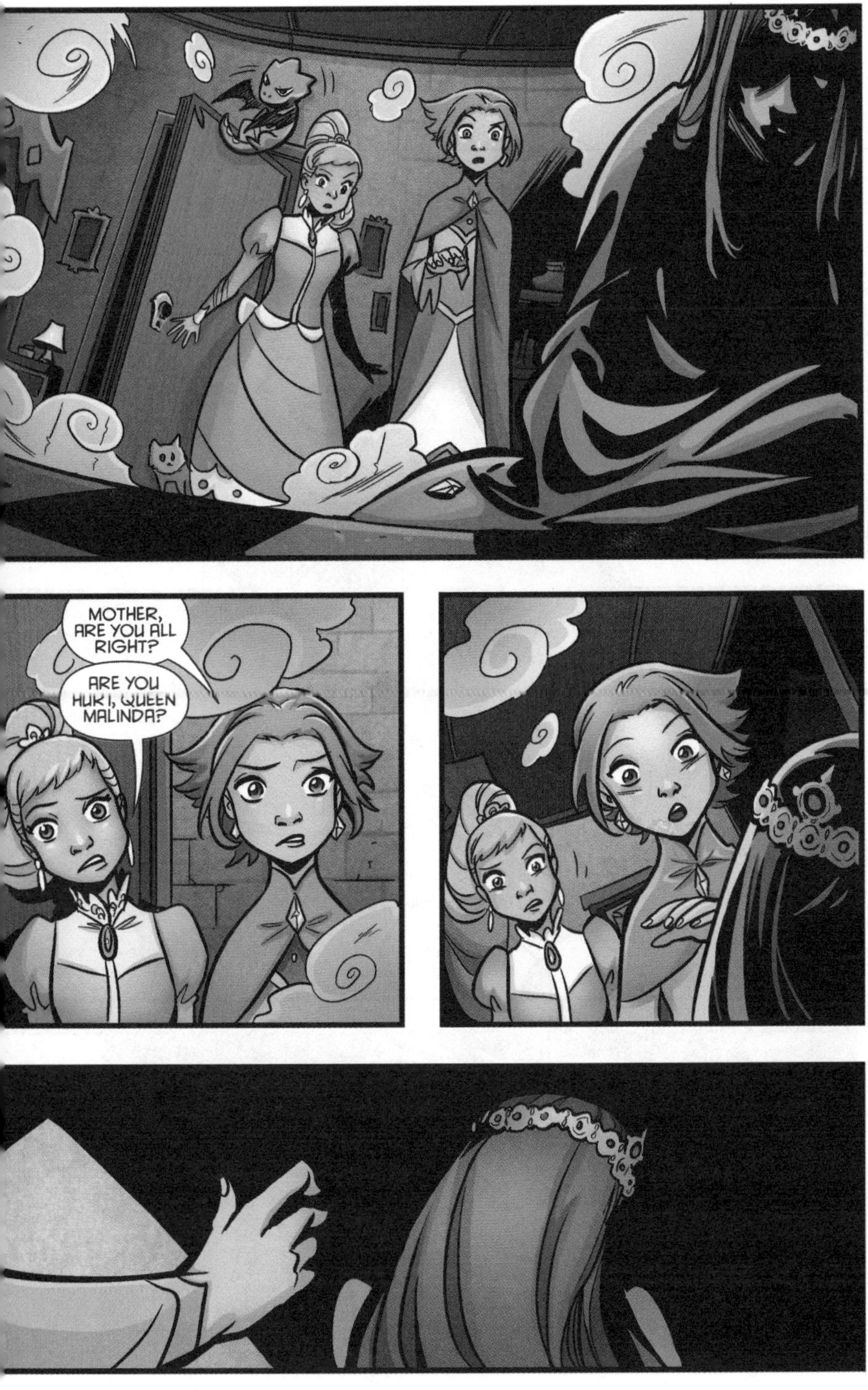
MOTHER, ARE YOU ALL RIGHT?
ARE YOU HURT, QUEEN MALINDA?

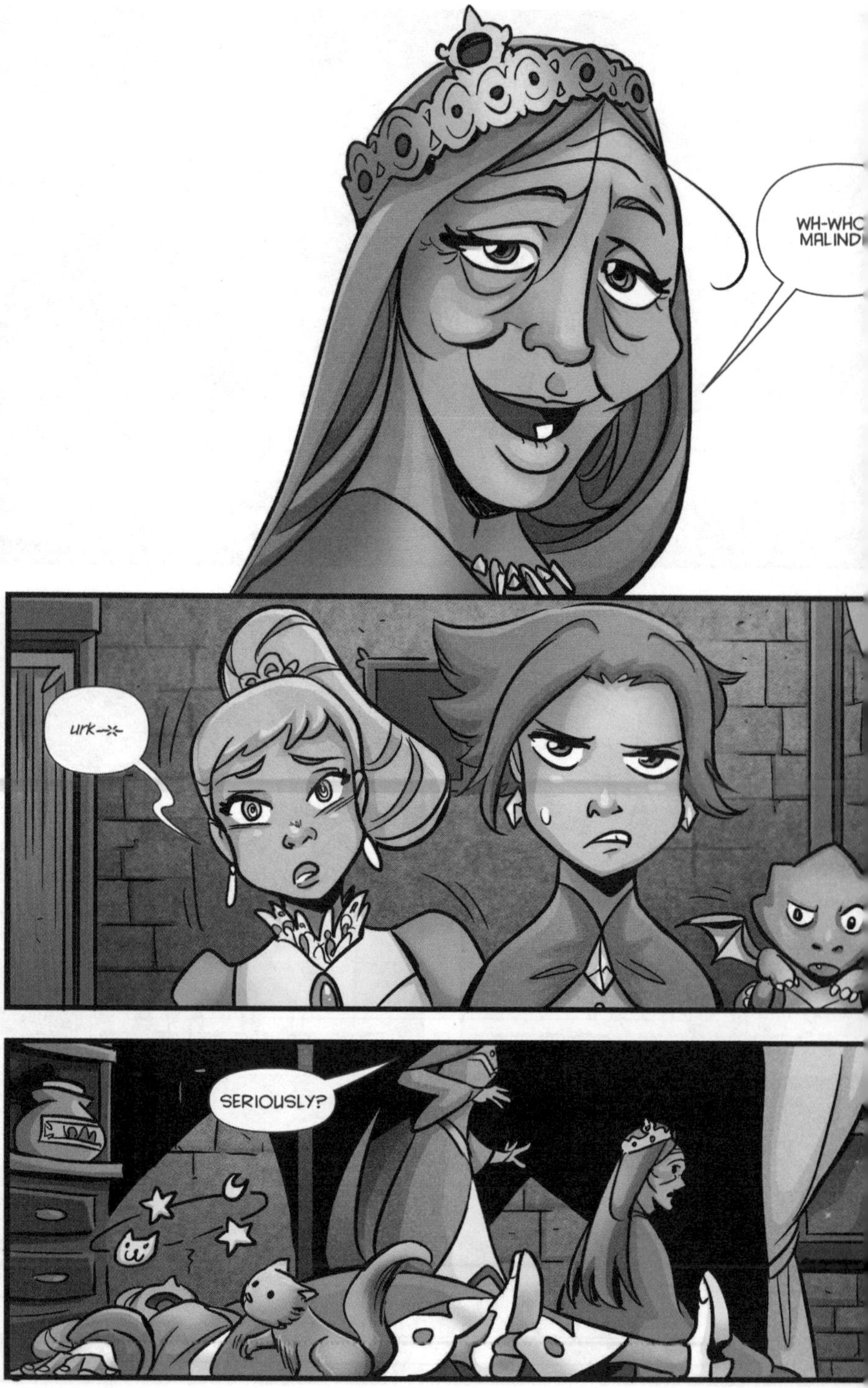
WH-WH
MALIND
urk—
SERIOUSLY?

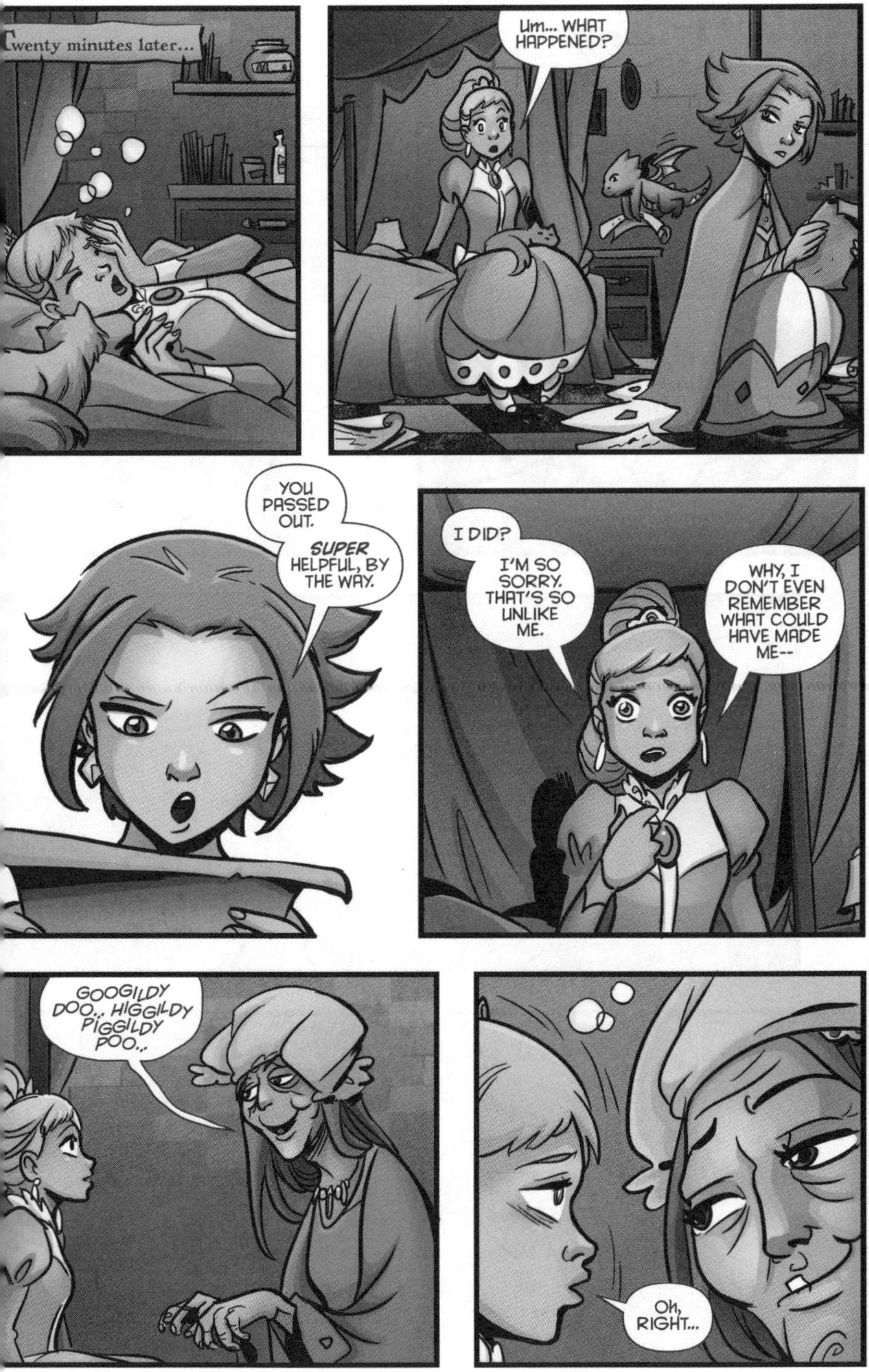
Twenty minutes later...
Um... WHAT HAPPENED?
YOU PASSED OUT.
SUPER HELPFUL, BY THE WAY.
I DID?
I'M SO SORRY. THAT'S SO UNLIKE ME.
WHY, I DON'T EVEN REMEMBER WHAT COULD HAVE MADE ME--
GOOGILDY DOO... HIGGILDY PIGGILDY POO...
Oh, RIGHT...

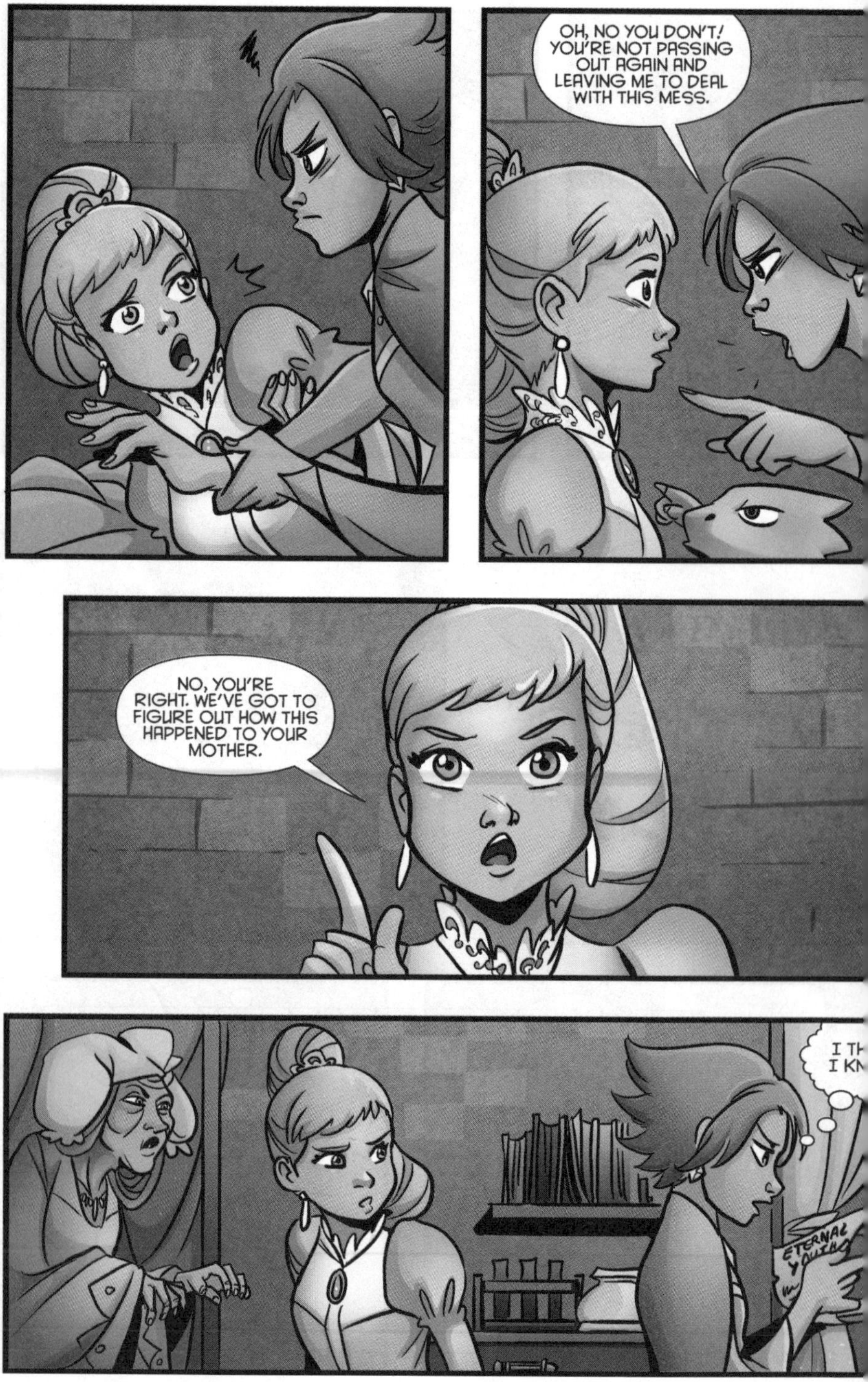
OH, NO YOU DON'T! YOU'RE NOT PASSING OUT AGAIN AND LEAVING ME TO DEAL WITH THIS MESS.
NO, YOU'RE RIGHT. WE'VE GOT TO FIGURE OUT HOW THIS HAPPENED TO YOUR MOTHER.
ETERNAL YOUTH

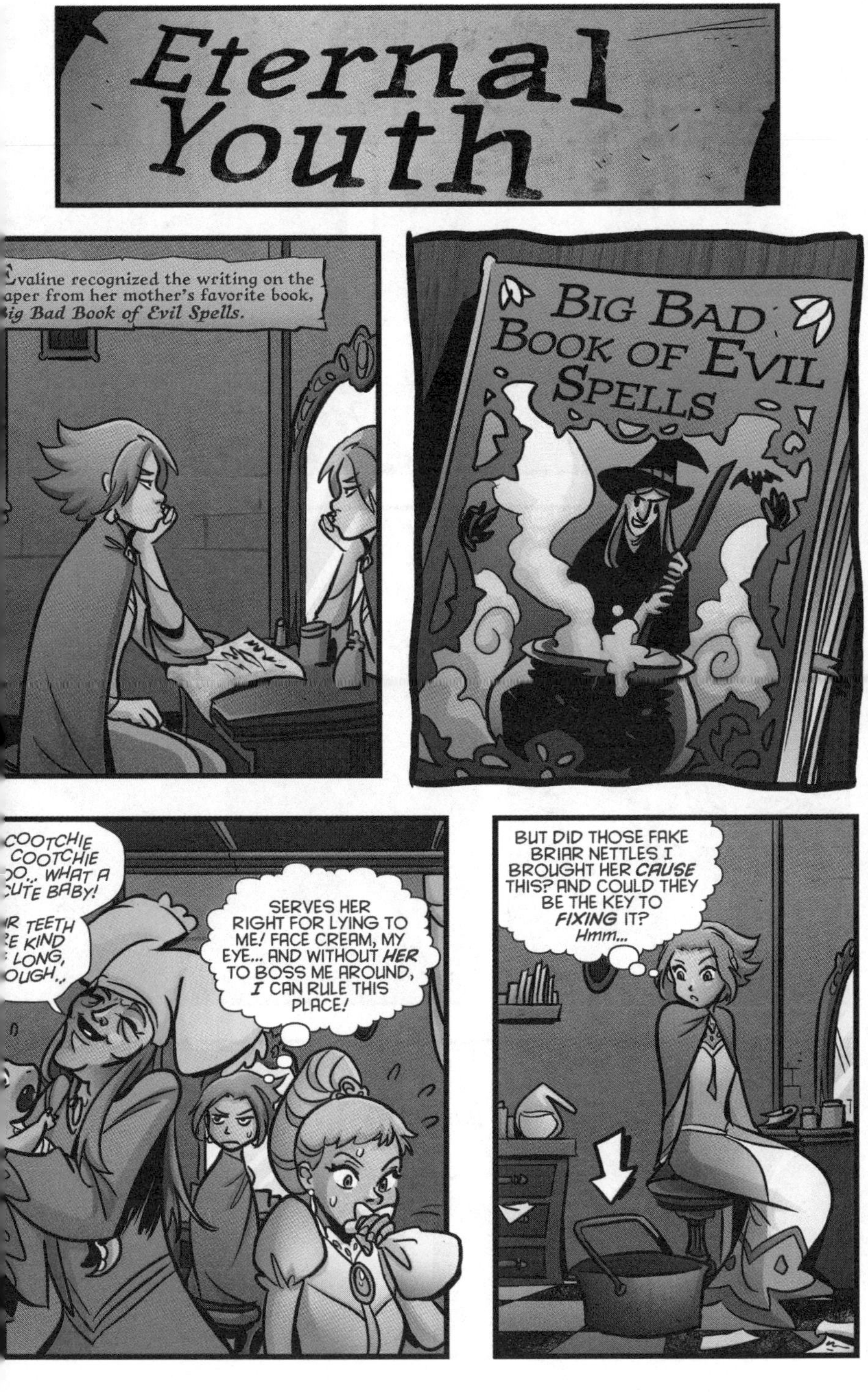
Eternal Youth
Evaline recognized the writing on the
aper from her mother's favorite book,
ig Bad Book of Evil Spells.
BIG BAD BOOK OF EVIL SPELLS
COOTCHIE COOTCHIE OO... WHAT A CUTE BABY!
R TEETH E KIND LONG, OUGH...
SERVES HER RIGHT FOR LYING TO ME! FACE CREAM, MY EYE... AND WITHOUT HER TO BOSS ME AROUND, I CAN RULE THIS PLACE!
BUT DID THOSE FAKE BRIAR NETTLES I BROUGHT HER CAUSE THIS? AND COULD THEY BE THE KEY TO FIXING IT? Hmm...

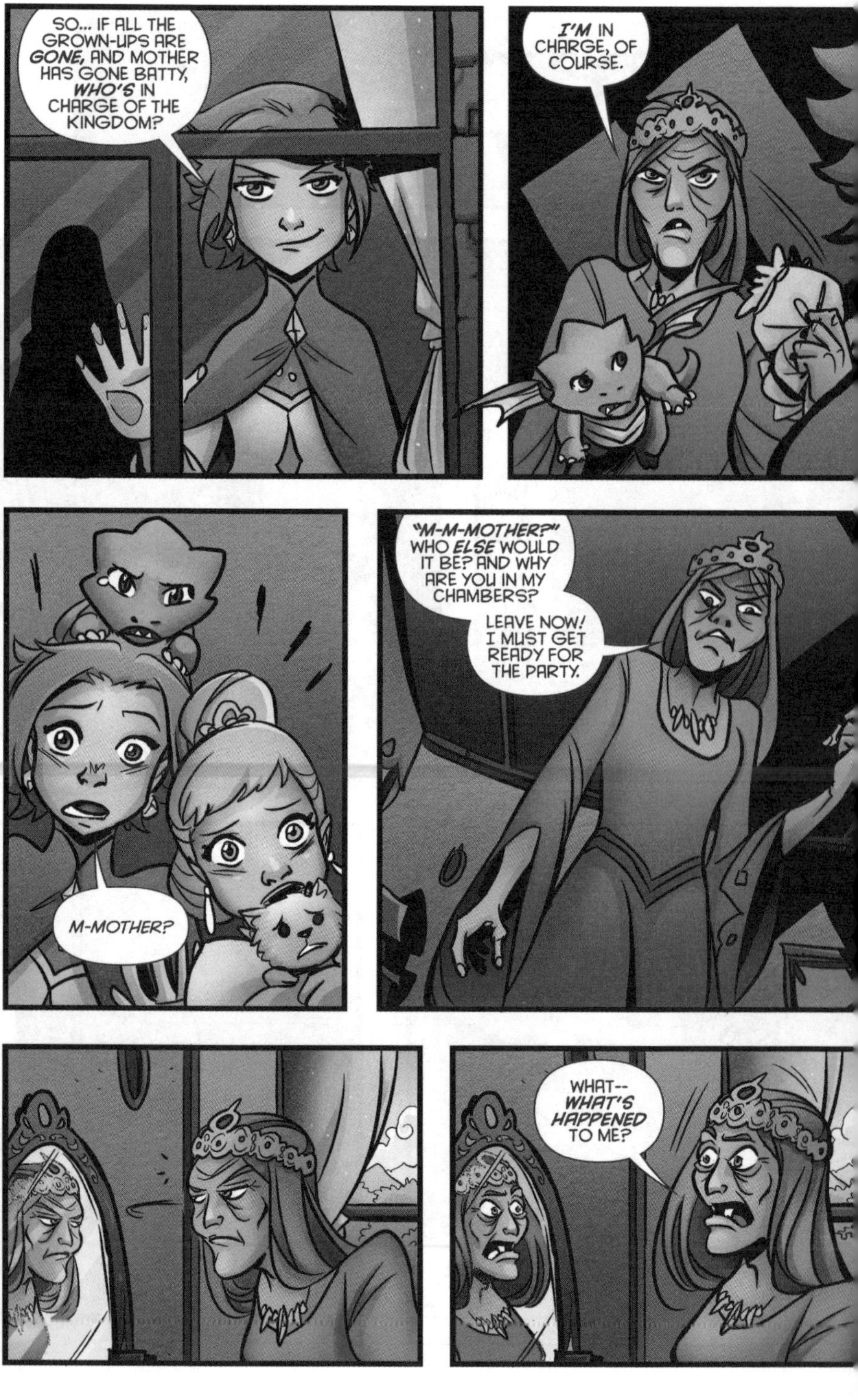
SO... IF ALL THE GROWN-UPS ARE GONE, AND MOTHER HAS GONE BATTY, WHO'S IN CHARGE OF THE KINGDOM?
I'M IN CHARGE, OF COURSE.
M-MOTHER?
"M-M-MOTHER?" WHO ELSE WOULD IT BE? AND WHY ARE YOU IN MY CHAMBERS?
LEAVE NOW! I MUST GET READY FOR THE PARTY.
WHAT-- WHAT'S HAPPENED TO ME?

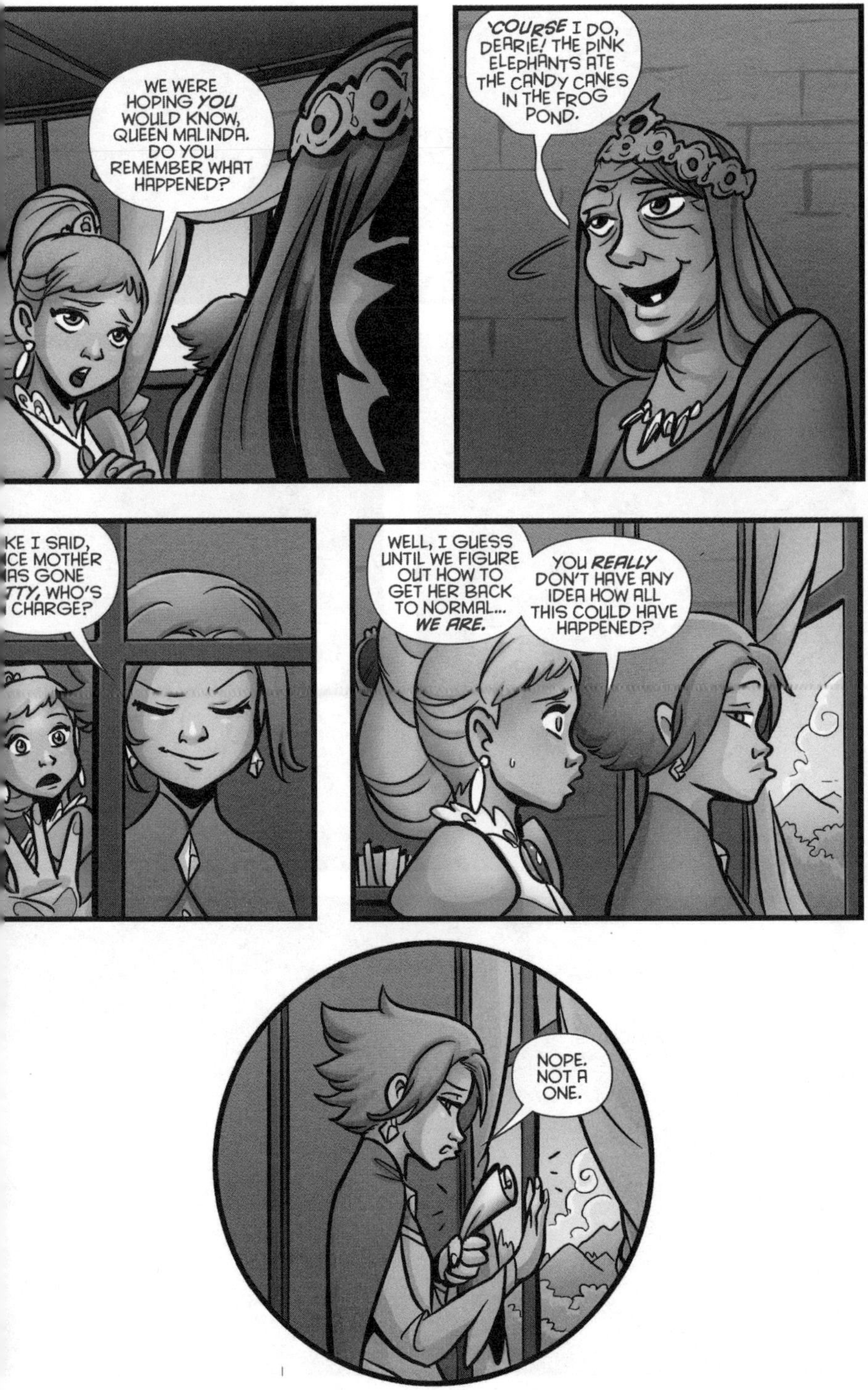
WE WERE HOPING *YOU* WOULD KNOW, QUEEN MALINDA. DO YOU REMEMBER WHAT HAPPENED?
'COURSE I DO, DEARIE! THE PINK ELEPHANTS ATE THE CANDY CANES IN THE FROG POND.
KE I SAID, CE MOTHER AS GONE *TTY*, WHO'S CHARGE?
WELL, I GUESS UNTIL WE FIGURE OUT HOW TO GET HER BACK TO NORMAL... *WE ARE.*
YOU *REALLY* DON'T HAVE ANY IDEA HOW ALL THIS COULD HAVE HAPPENED?
NOPE. NOT A ONE.

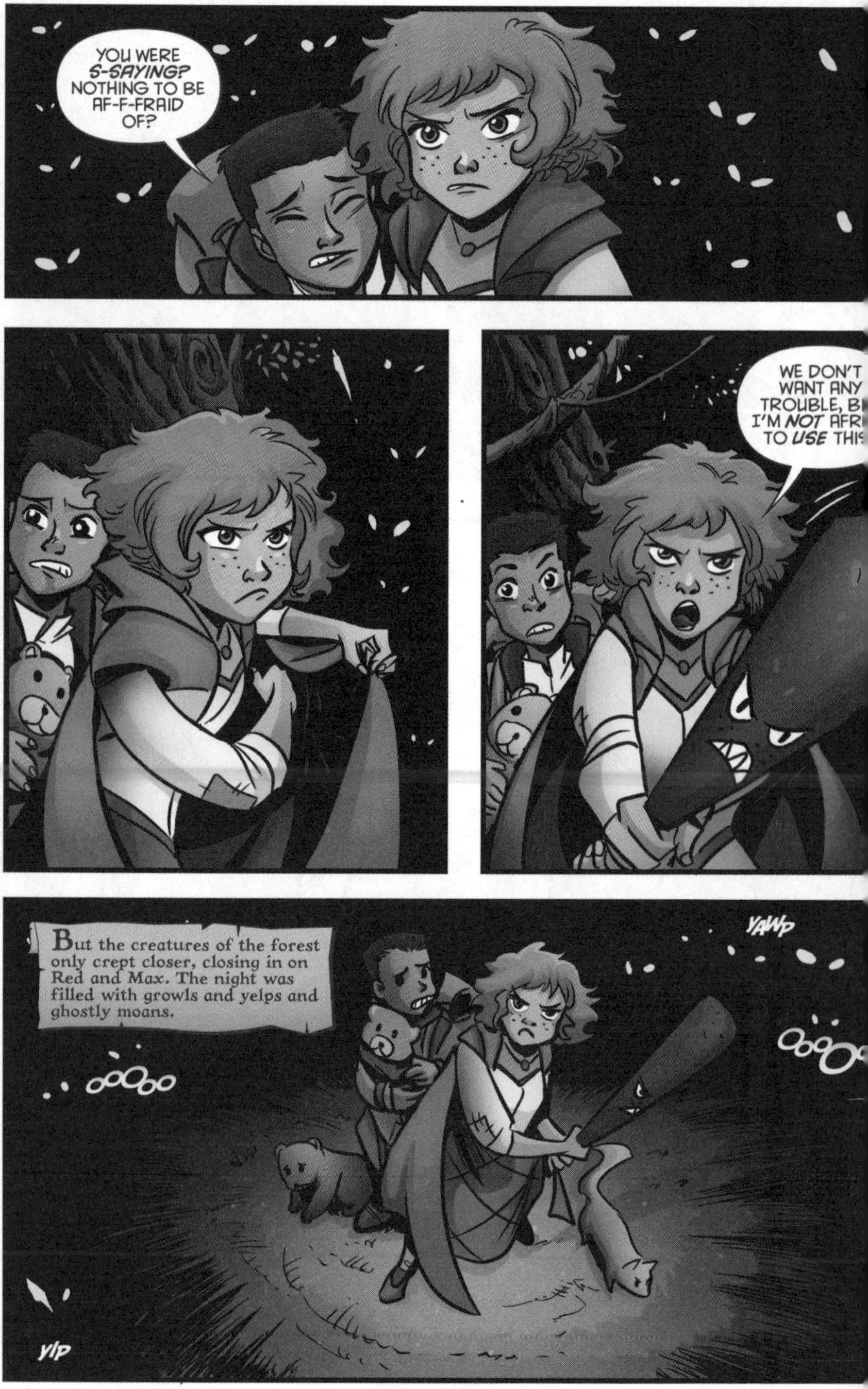
YOU WERE S-SAYING? NOTHING TO BE AF-F-FRAID OF?
WE DON'T WANT ANY TROUBLE, B
I'M NOT AFR
TO USE THIS
But the creatures of the forest only crept closer, closing in on Red and Max. The night was filled with growls and yelps and ghostly moans.
YAWP
OOOOO
OOOOO
YIP

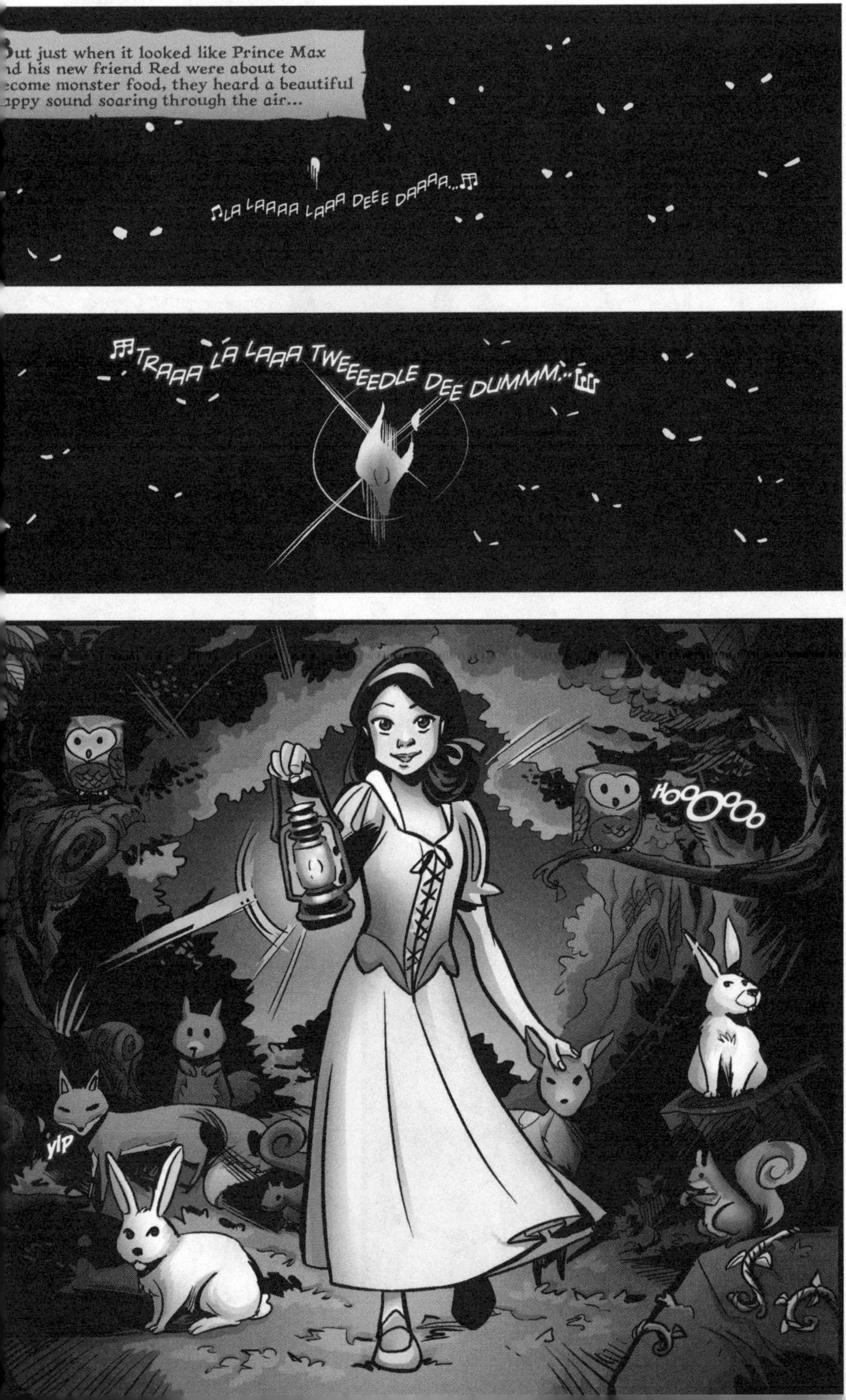
ut just when it looked like Prince Max
d his new friend Red were about to
ecome monster food, they heard a beautiful
appy sound soaring through the air...
LA LAAAA LAAA DEEE DAAAA...
TRAAA LA LAAA TWEEEEDLE DEE DUMMM...
HOOOOOO
YIP

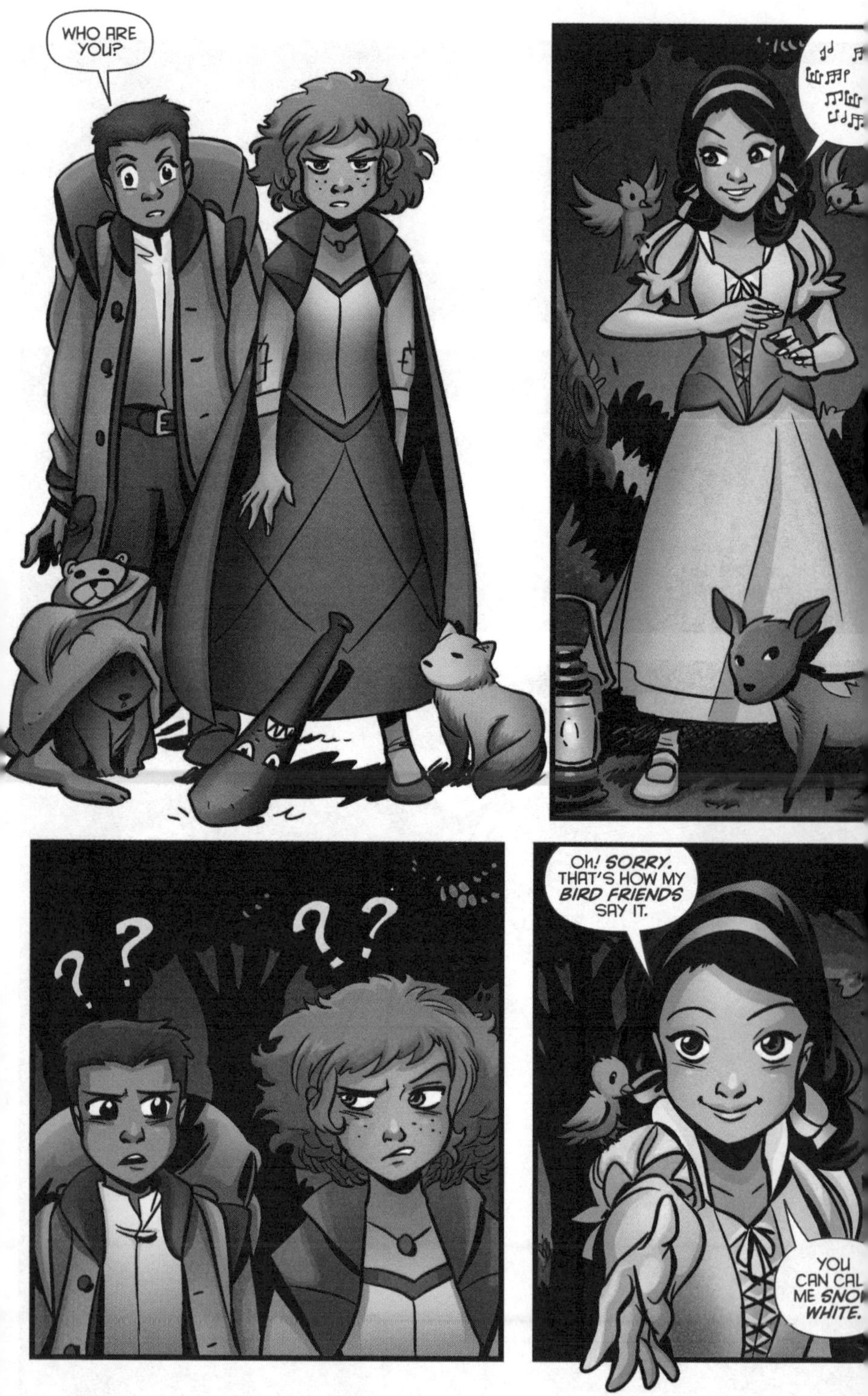
WHO ARE YOU?
Oh! SORRY. THAT'S HOW MY BIRD FRIENDS SAY IT.
YOU CAN CAL ME SNO WHITE.

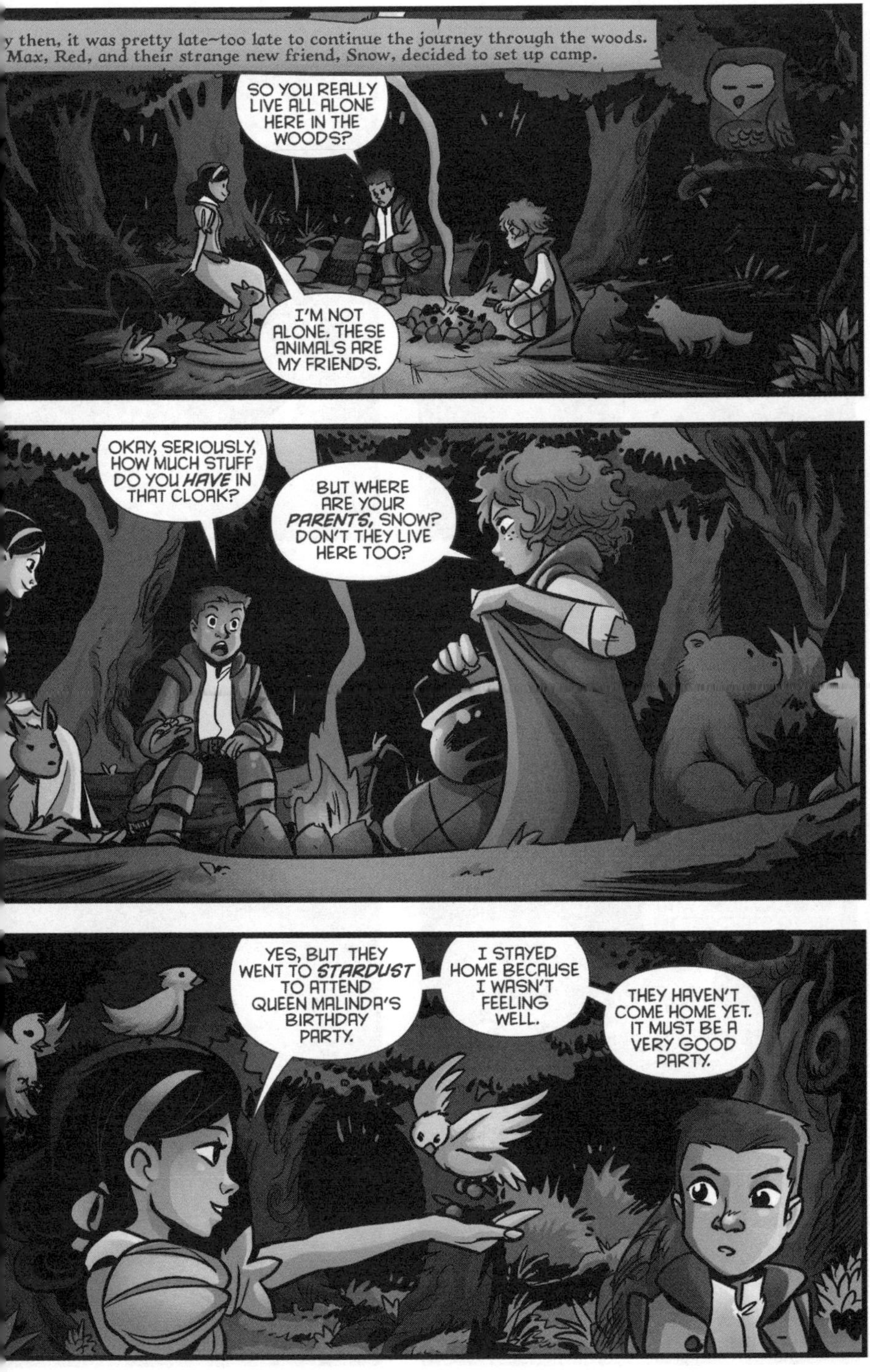
y then, it was pretty late~too late to continue the journey through the woods. Max, Red, and their strange new friend, Snow, decided to set up camp.
SO YOU REALLY LIVE ALL ALONE HERE IN THE WOODS?
I'M NOT ALONE. THESE ANIMALS ARE MY FRIENDS.
OKAY, SERIOUSLY, HOW MUCH STUFF DO YOU *HAVE* IN THAT CLOAK?
BUT WHERE ARE YOUR *PARENTS,* SNOW? DON'T THEY LIVE HERE TOO?
YES, BUT THEY WENT TO *STARDUST* TO ATTEND QUEEN MALINDA'S BIRTHDAY PARTY.
I STAYED HOME BECAUSE I WASN'T FEELING WELL.
THEY HAVEN'T COME HOME YET. IT MUST BE A VERY GOOD PARTY.

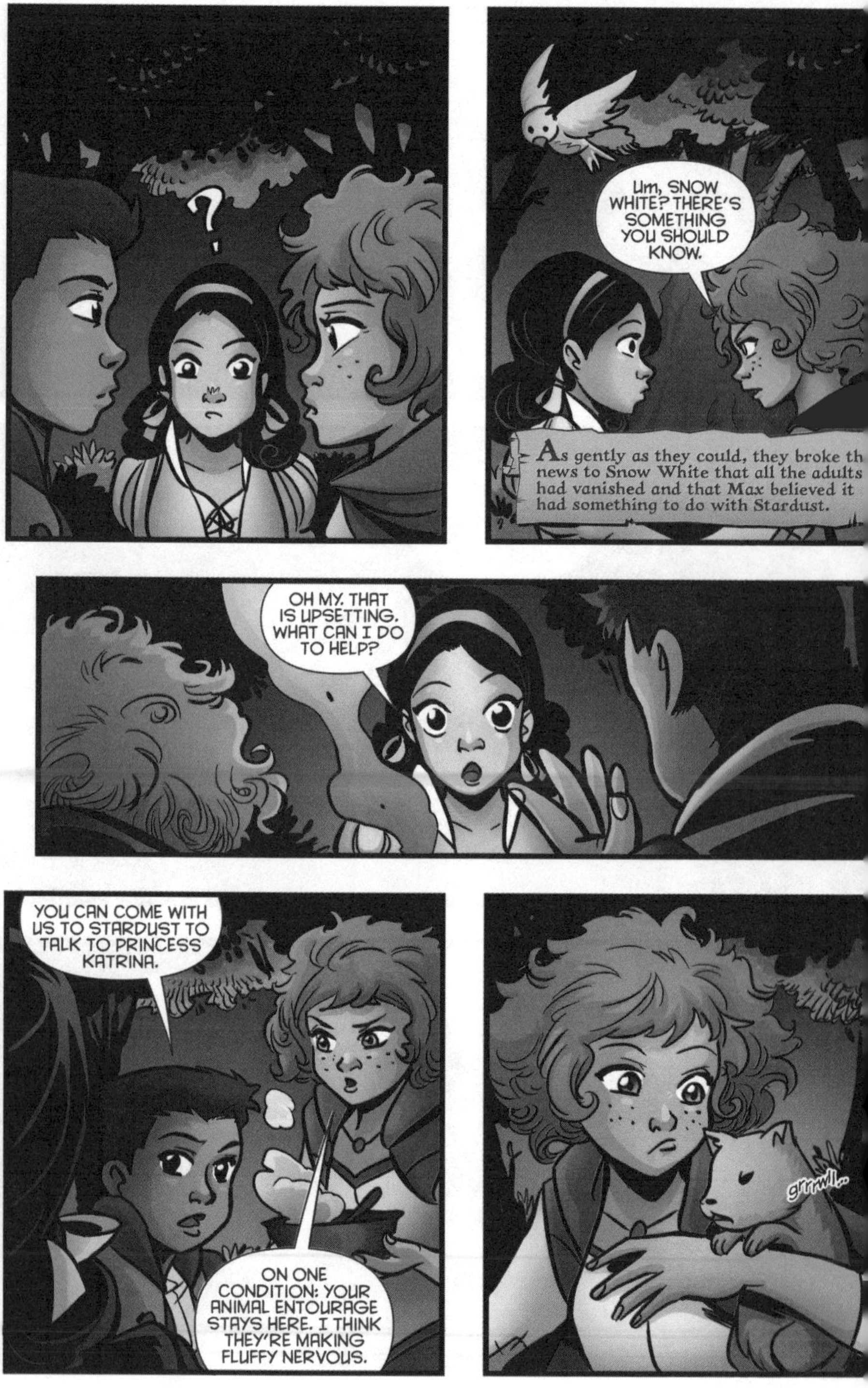
?
Um, SNOW WHITE? THERE'S SOMETHING YOU SHOULD KNOW.
As gently as they could, they broke th news to Snow White that all the adults had vanished and that Max believed it had something to do with Stardust.
OH MY. THAT IS UPSETTING. WHAT CAN I DO TO HELP?
YOU CAN COME WITH US TO STARDUST TO TALK TO PRINCESS KATRINA.
ON ONE CONDITION: YOUR ANIMAL ENTOURAGE STAYS HERE. I THINK THEY'RE MAKING FLUFFY NERVOUS.
grrrwll...

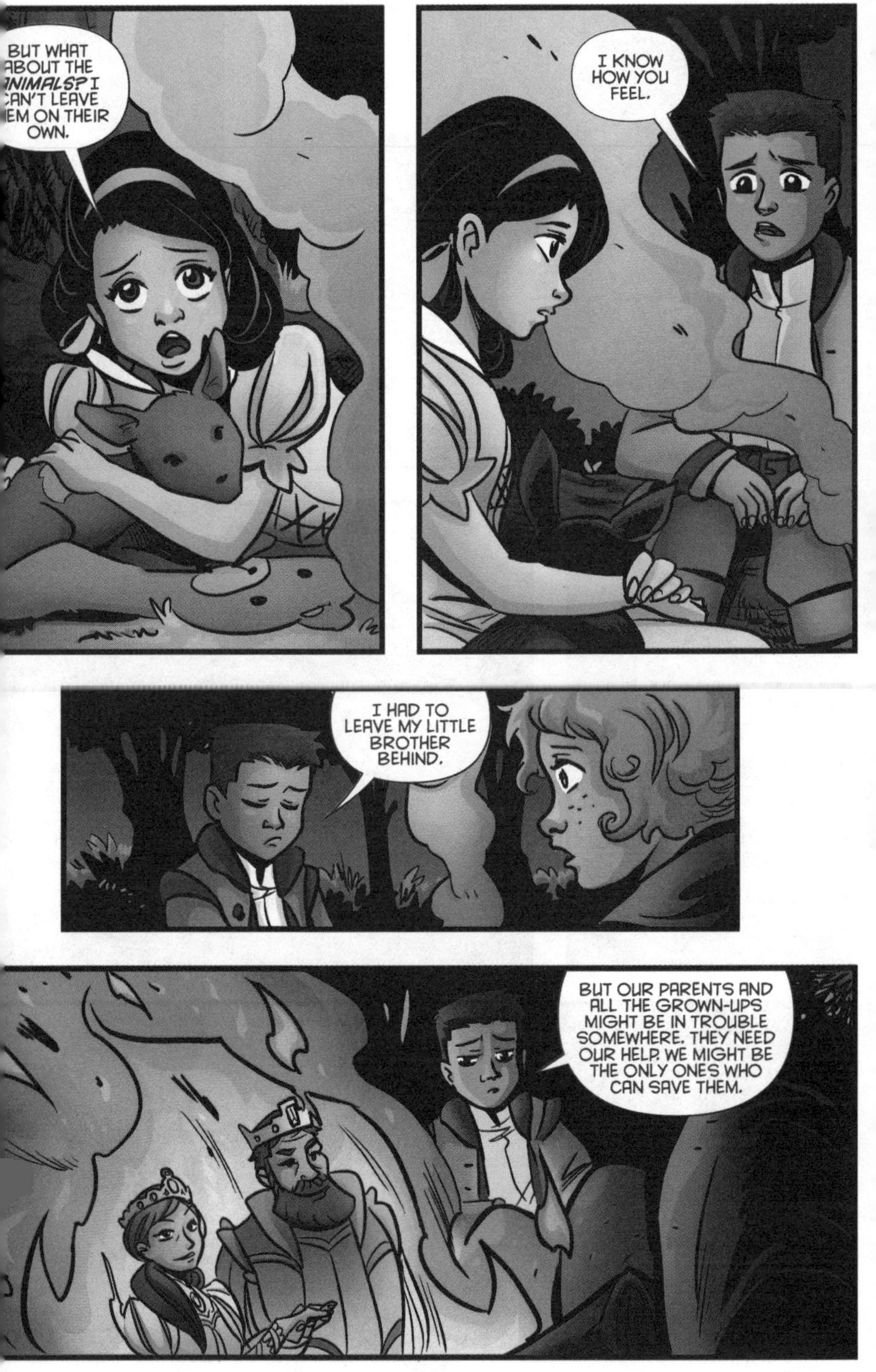
BUT WHAT ABOUT THE NIMALS? I CAN'T LEAVE EM ON THEIR OWN.
I KNOW HOW YOU FEEL.
I HAD TO LEAVE MY LITTLE BROTHER BEHIND.
BUT OUR PARENTS AND ALL THE GROWN-UPS MIGHT BE IN TROUBLE SOMEWHERE. THEY NEED OUR HELP. WE MIGHT BE THE ONLY ONES WHO CAN SAVE THEM.

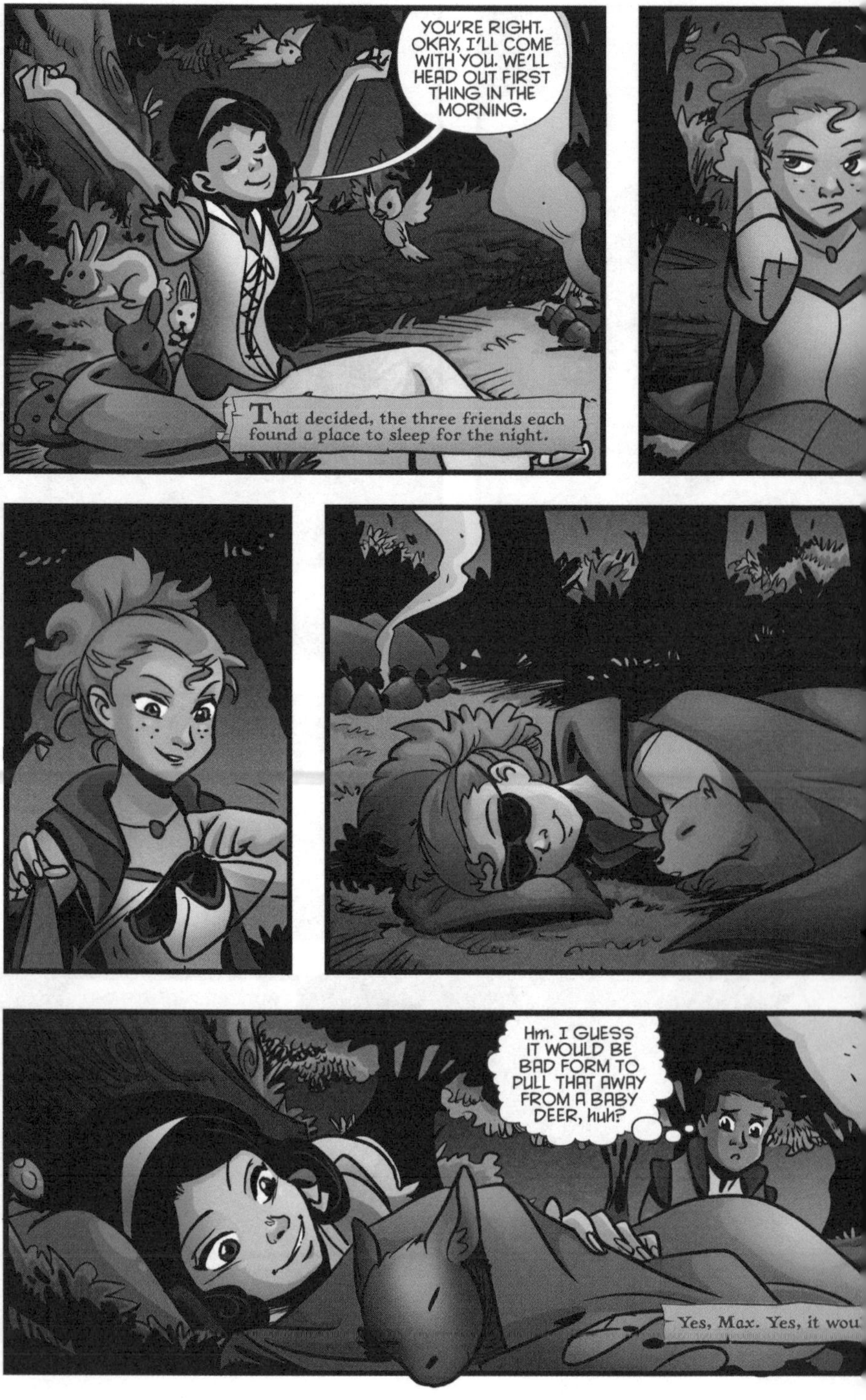
YOU'RE RIGHT. OKAY, I'LL COME WITH YOU. WE'LL HEAD OUT FIRST THING IN THE MORNING.
That decided, the three friends each found a place to sleep for the night.
Hm. I GUESS IT WOULD BE BAD FORM TO PULL THAT AWAY FROM A BABY DEER, huh?
Yes, Max. Yes, it wou

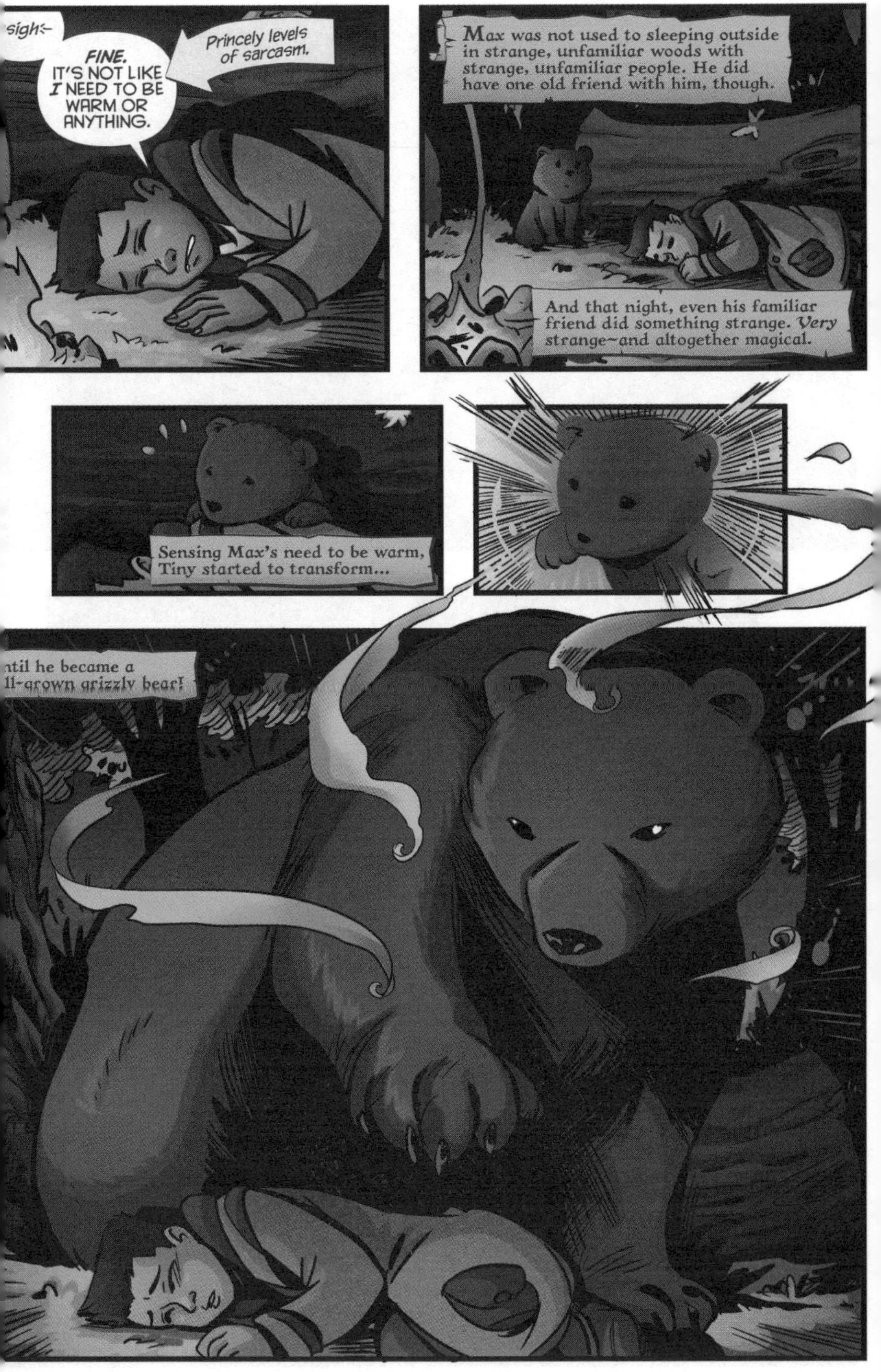

sigh~
FINE. IT'S NOT LIKE I NEED TO BE WARM OR ANYTHING.
Princely levels of sarcasm.
Max was not used to sleeping outside in strange, unfamiliar woods with strange, unfamiliar people. He did have one old friend with him, though.
And that night, even his familiar friend did something strange. Very strange~and altogether magical.
Sensing Max's need to be warm, Tiny started to transform...
ntil he became a
ll-grown grizzly bear!

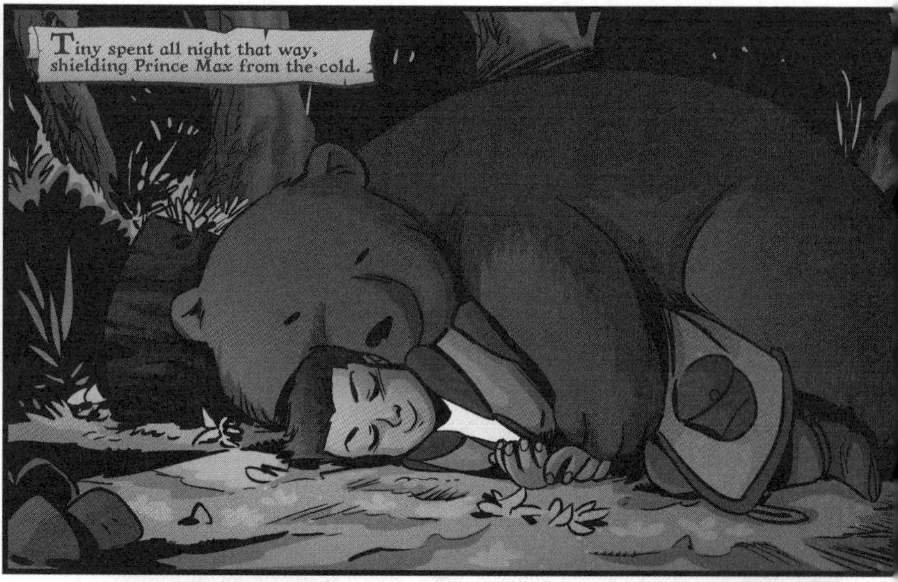
Tiny spent all night that way, shielding Prince Max from the cold.

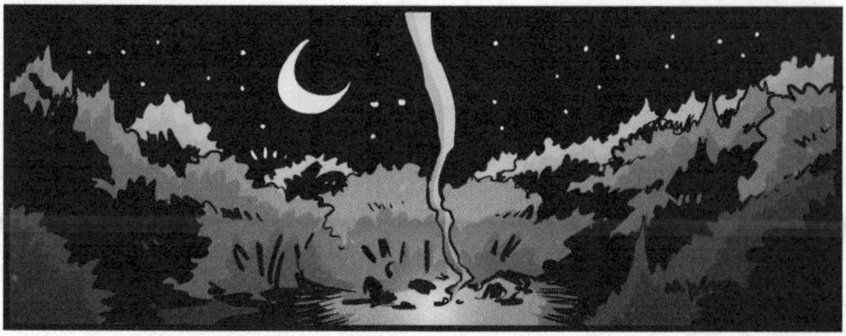

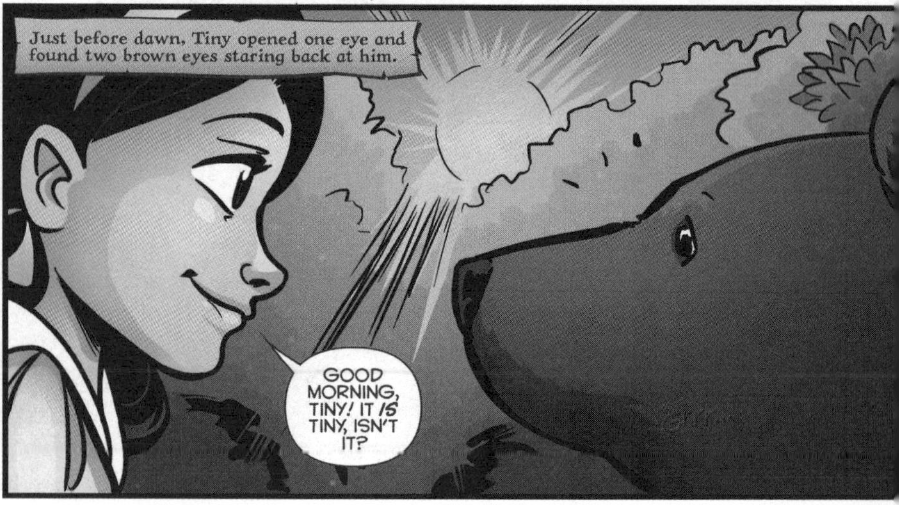
Just before dawn, Tiny opened one eye and found two brown eyes staring back at him.
GOOD MORNING, TINY! IT IS TINY, ISN'T IT?

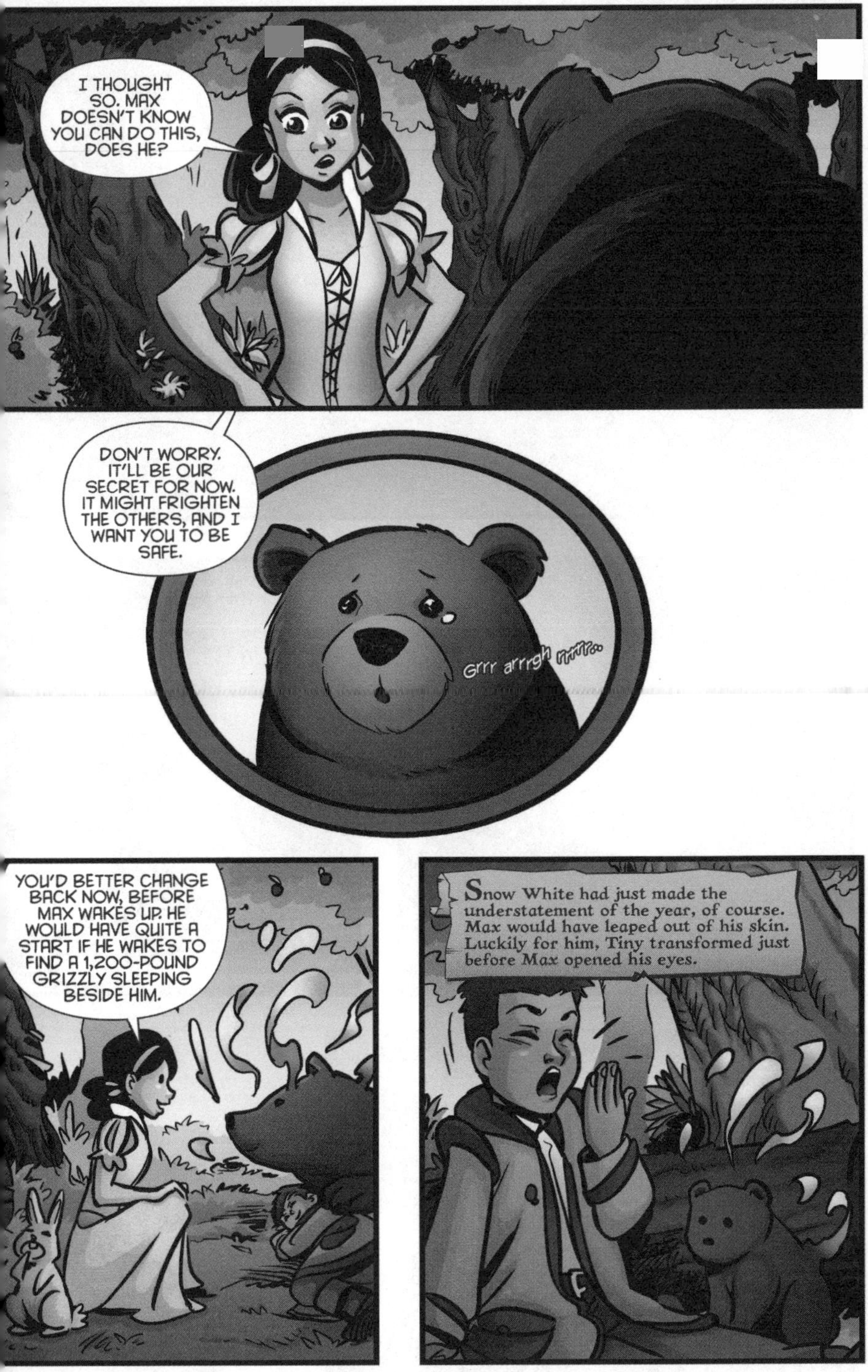
I THOUGHT SO. MAX DOESN'T KNOW YOU CAN DO THIS, DOES HE?
DON'T WORRY. IT'LL BE OUR SECRET FOR NOW. IT MIGHT FRIGHTEN THE OTHERS, AND I WANT YOU TO BE SAFE.
Grrr arrrgh rrrrr..
YOU'D BETTER CHANGE BACK NOW, BEFORE MAX WAKES UP. HE WOULD HAVE QUITE A START IF HE WAKES TO FIND A 1,200-POUND GRIZZLY SLEEPING BESIDE HIM.
Snow White had just made the understatement of the year, of course. Max would have leaped out of his skin. Luckily for him, Tiny transformed just before Max opened his eyes.

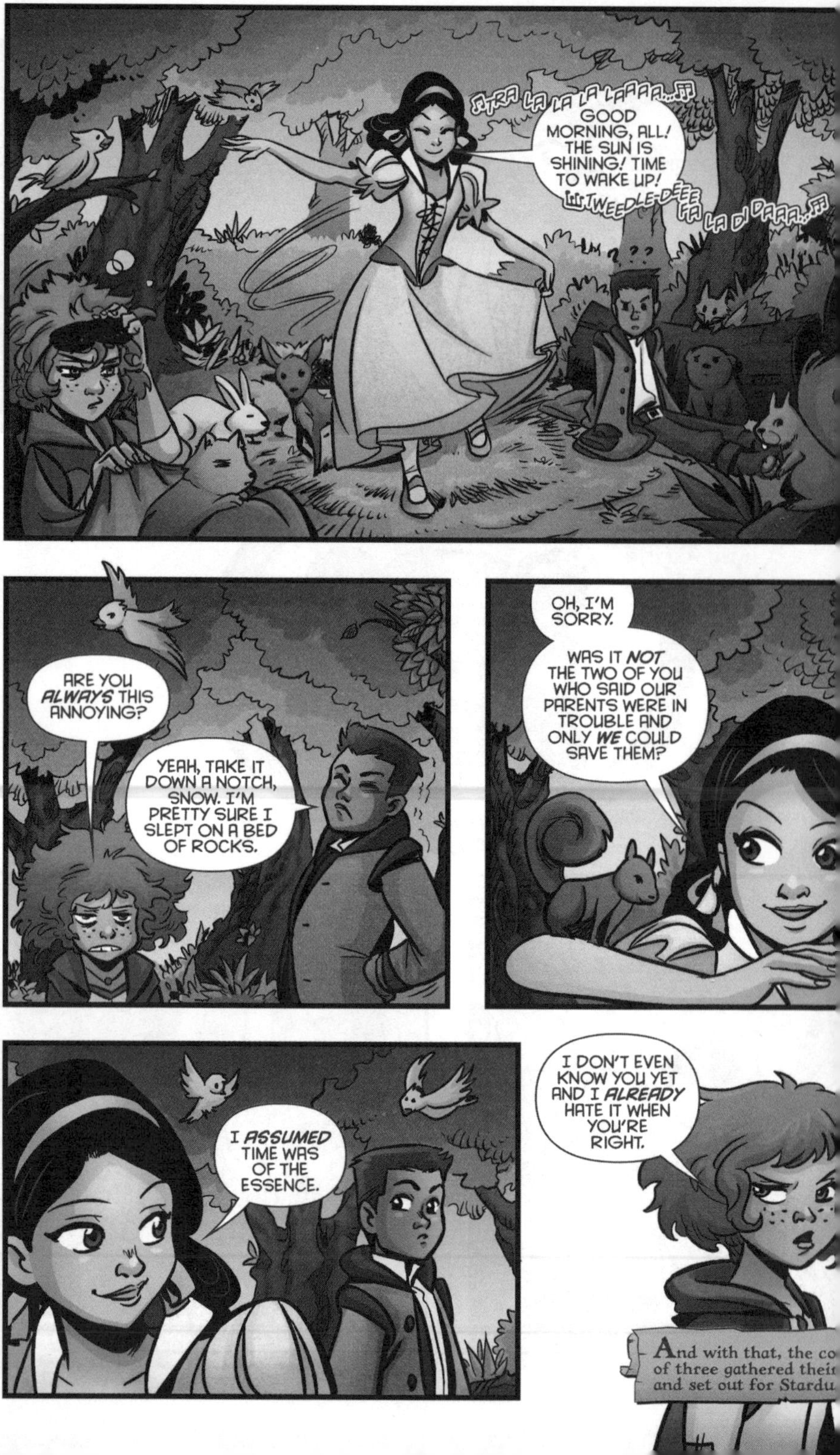
TRA LA LA LA LAAAA...
GOOD MORNING, ALL! THE SUN IS SHINING! TIME TO WAKE UP!
TWEEDLE-DEEE FA LA DI DAAA...
? ?
ARE YOU ALWAYS THIS ANNOYING?
YEAH, TAKE IT DOWN A NOTCH, SNOW. I'M PRETTY SURE I SLEPT ON A BED OF ROCKS.
OH, I'M SORRY.
WAS IT NOT THE TWO OF YOU WHO SAID OUR PARENTS WERE IN TROUBLE AND ONLY WE COULD SAVE THEM?
I ASSUMED TIME WAS OF THE ESSENCE.
I DON'T EVEN KNOW YOU YET AND I ALREADY HATE IT WHEN YOU'RE RIGHT.
And with that, the co
of three gathered their
and set out for Stardu

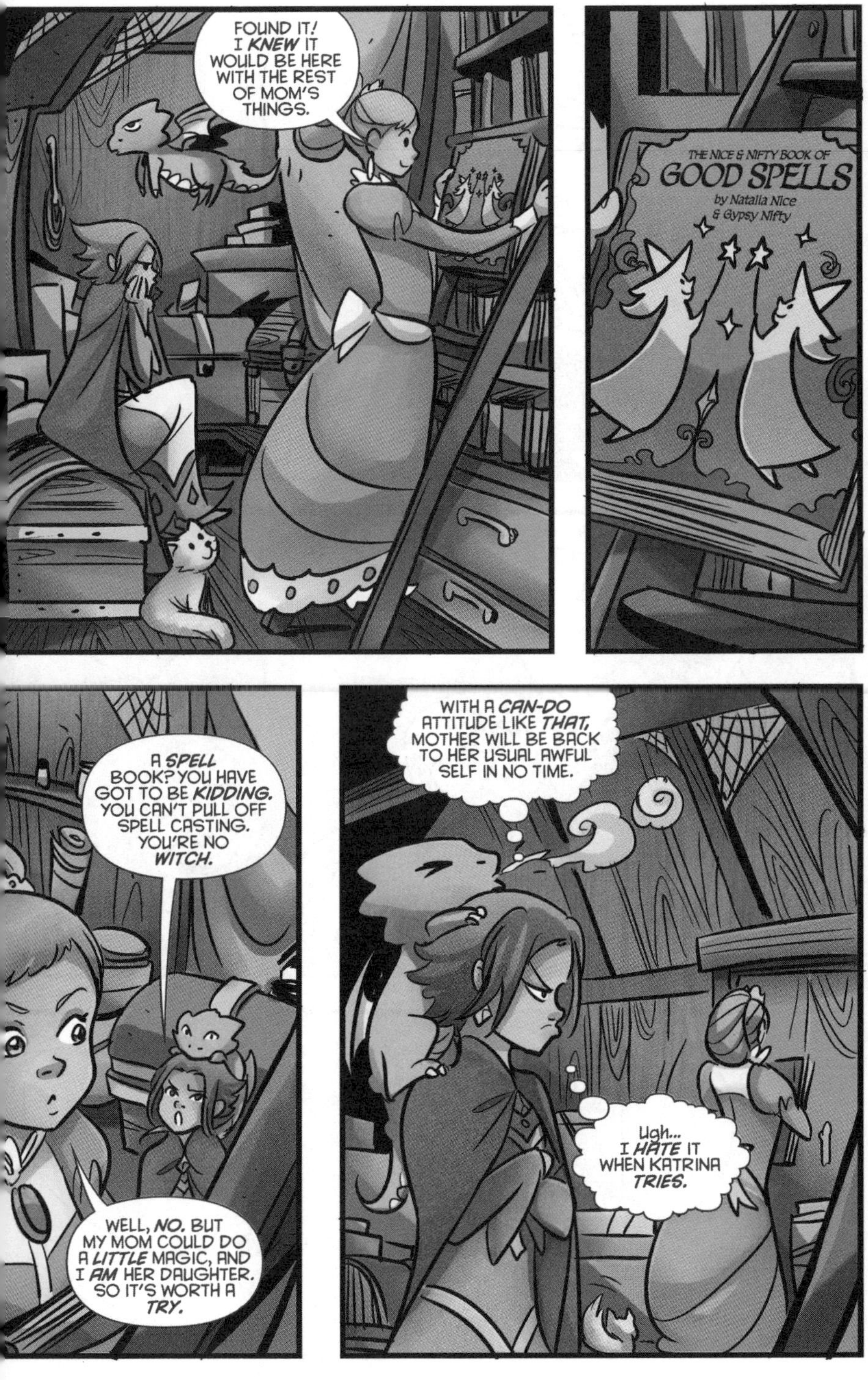

FOUND IT! I KNEW IT WOULD BE HERE WITH THE REST OF MOM'S THINGS.
THE NICE & NIFTY BOOK OF GOOD SPELLS
by Natalia Nice & Gypsy Nifty
A SPELL BOOK? YOU HAVE GOT TO BE KIDDING. YOU CAN'T PULL OFF SPELL CASTING. YOU'RE NO WITCH.
WELL, NO. BUT MY MOM COULD DO A LITTLE MAGIC, AND I AM HER DAUGHTER. SO IT'S WORTH A TRY.
WITH A CAN-DO ATTITUDE LIKE THAT, MOTHER WILL BE BACK TO HER USUAL AWFUL SELF IN NO TIME.
Ugh... I HATE IT WHEN KATRINA TRIES.

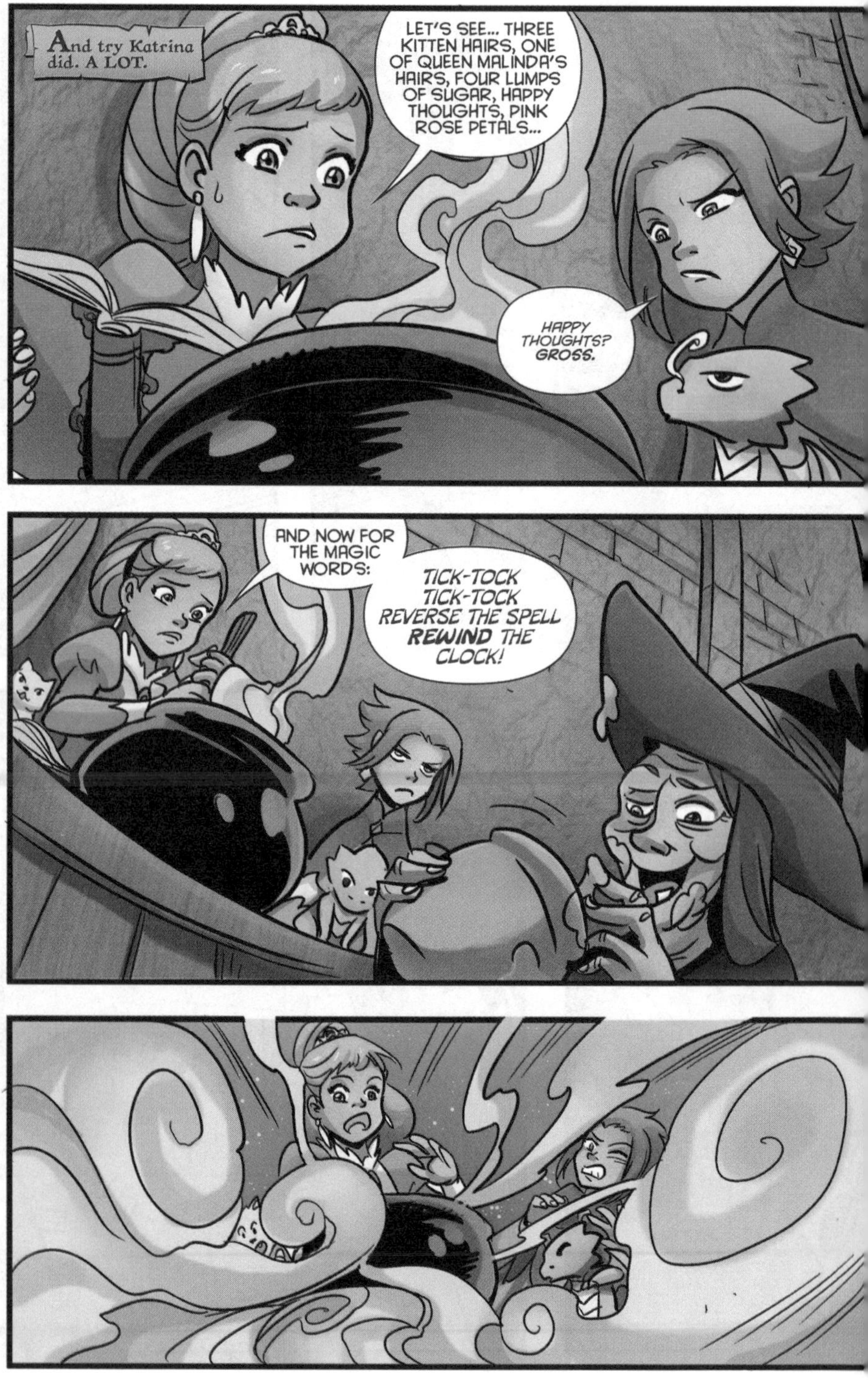
And try Katrina did. A LOT.
LET'S SEE... THREE KITTEN HAIRS, ONE OF QUEEN MALINDA'S HAIRS, FOUR LUMPS OF SUGAR, HAPPY THOUGHTS, PINK ROSE PETALS...
HAPPY THOUGHTS? GROSS.
AND NOW FOR THE MAGIC WORDS:
TICK-TOCK TICK-TOCK REVERSE THE SPELL REWIND THE CLOCK!

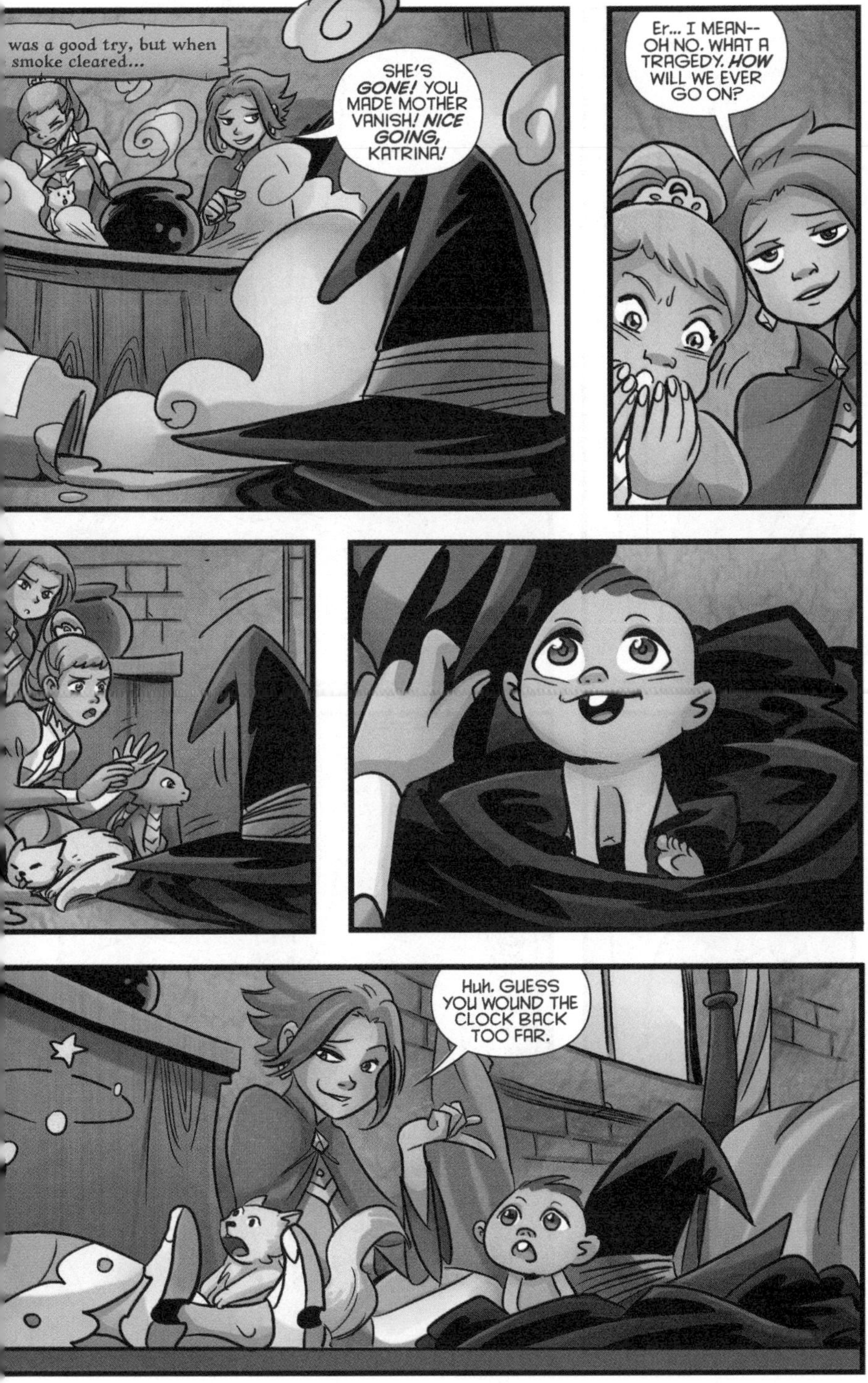
was a good try, but when smoke cleared...
SHE'S GONE! YOU MADE MOTHER VANISH! NICE GOING, KATRINA!
Er... I MEAN-- OH NO. WHAT A TRAGEDY. HOW WILL WE EVER GO ON?
Huh. GUESS YOU WOUND THE CLOCK BACK TOO FAR.

And so, when Katrina came to, she tried again.

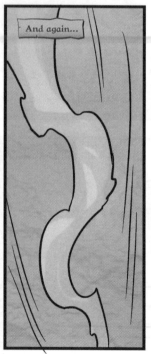

And again...

YOU'RE REALLY BAD AT THIS.

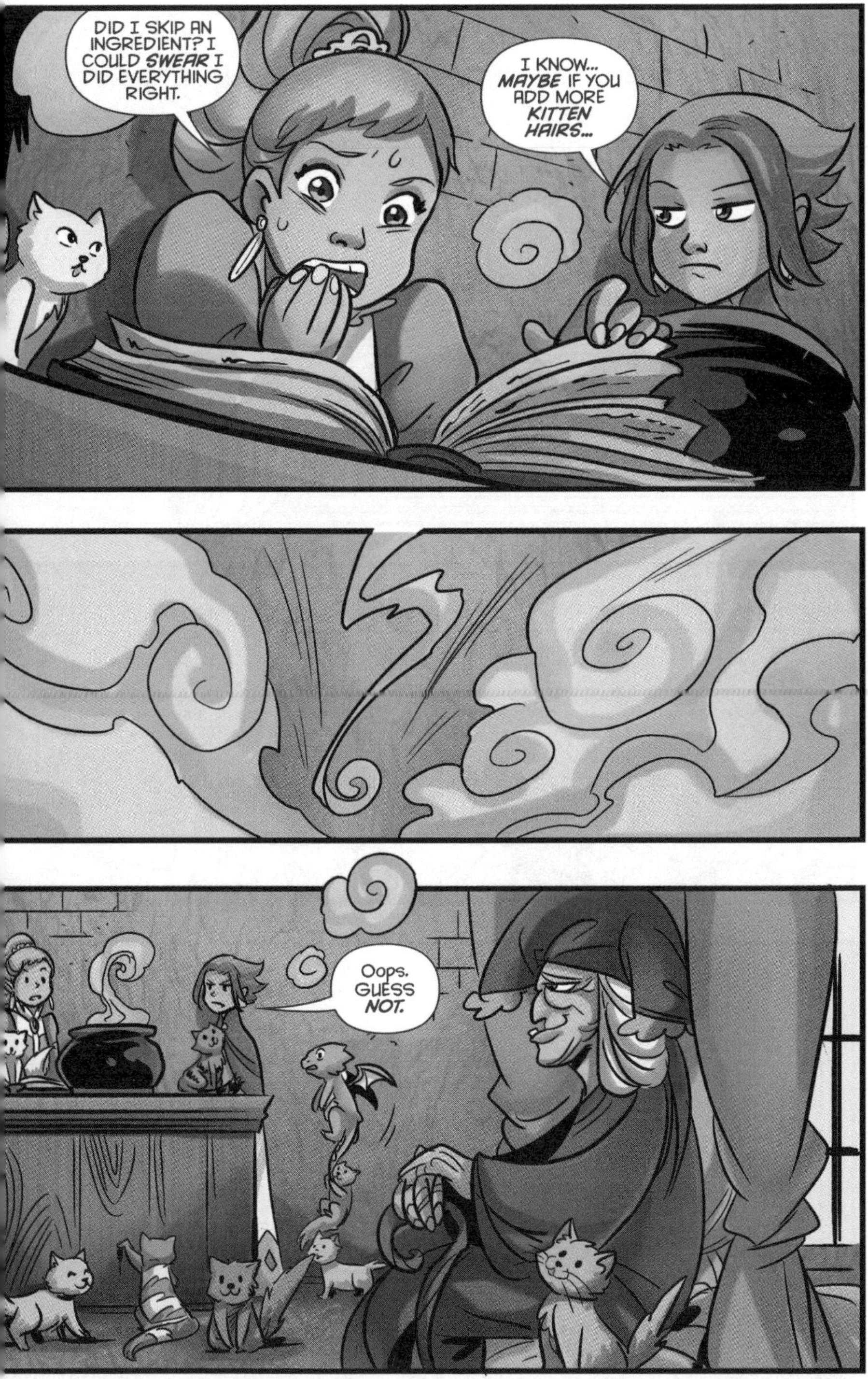
DID I SKIP AN INGREDIENT? I COULD *SWEAR* I DID EVERYTHING RIGHT.
I KNOW... *MAYBE* IF YOU ADD MORE *KITTEN HAIRS...*
Oops. GUESS *NOT.*

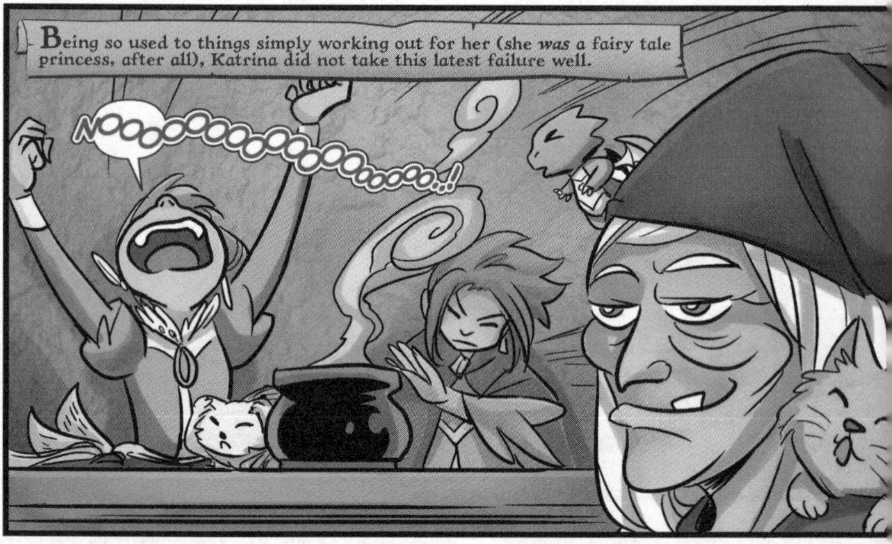

Being so used to things simply working out for her (she *was* a fairy tale princess, after all), Katrina did not take this latest failure well.
NOOOOOOOOOOOOOOOOOOOoooo..!

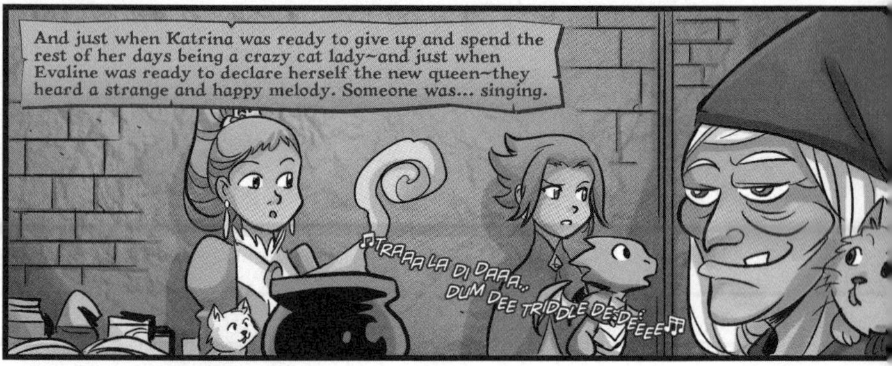

And just when Katrina was ready to give up and spend the rest of her days being a crazy cat lady~and just when Evaline was ready to declare herself the new queen~they heard a strange and happy melody. Someone was... singing.
♪TRAAA LA DI DAAA.. DUM DEE TRIDDLE DE DEEEE♪

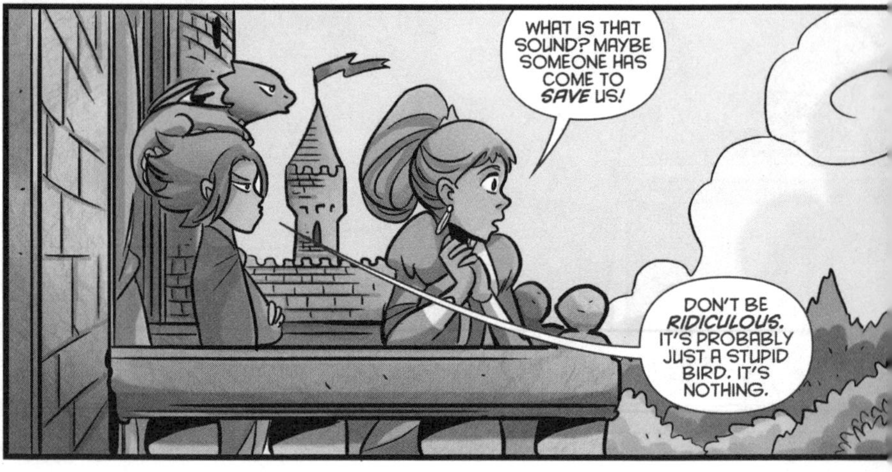

WHAT IS THAT SOUND? MAYBE SOMEONE HAS COME TO *SAVE* US!
DON'T BE *RIDICULOUS.* IT'S PROBABLY JUST A STUPID BIRD. IT'S NOTHING.

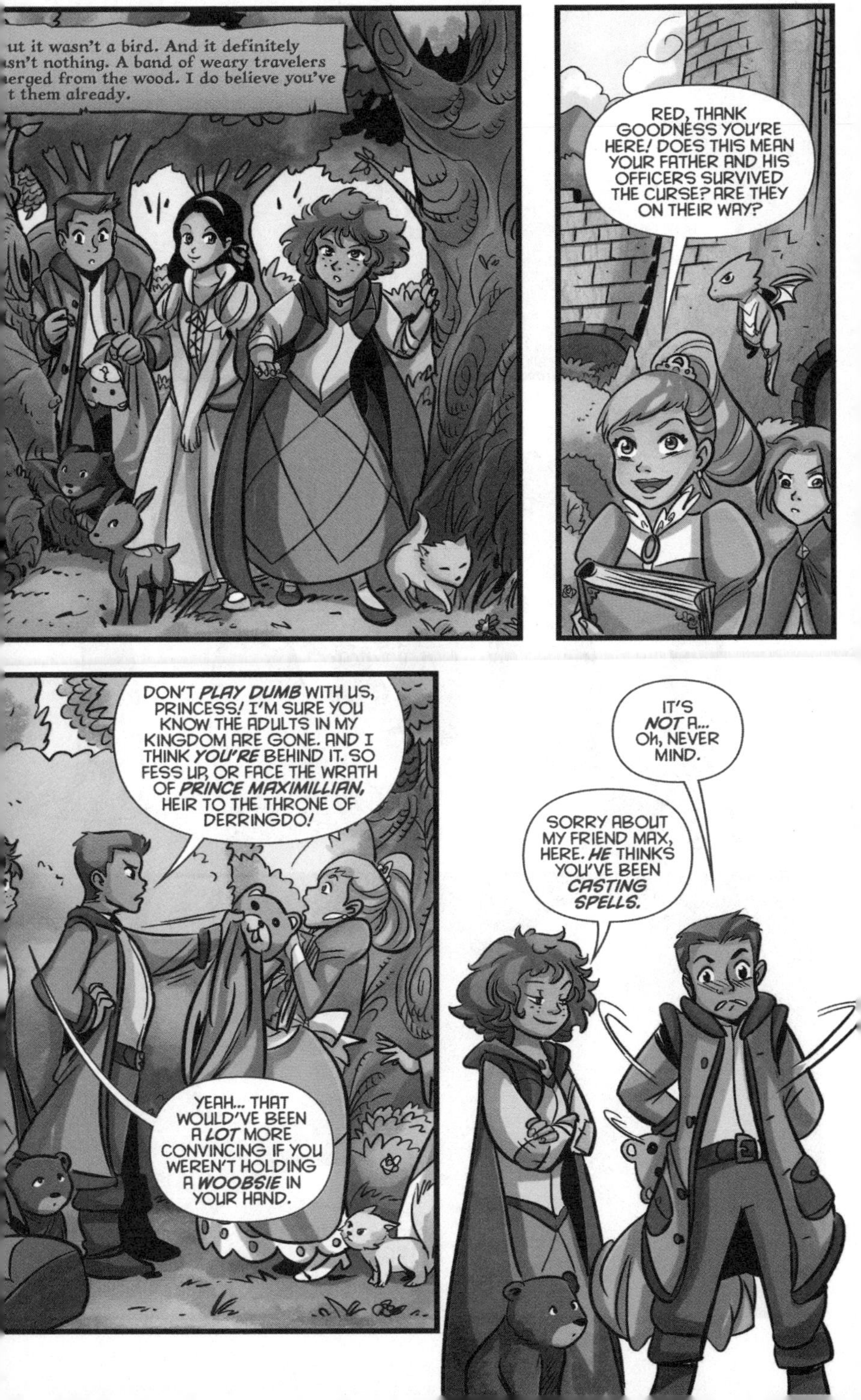
ut it wasn't a bird. And it definitely
sn't nothing. A band of weary travelers
erged from the wood. I do believe you've
t them already.
RED, THANK GOODNESS YOU'RE HERE! DOES THIS MEAN YOUR FATHER AND HIS OFFICERS SURVIVED THE CURSE? ARE THEY ON THEIR WAY?
DON'T PLAY DUMB WITH US, PRINCESS! I'M SURE YOU KNOW THE ADULTS IN MY KINGDOM ARE GONE. AND I THINK YOU'RE BEHIND IT. SO FESS UP, OR FACE THE WRATH OF PRINCE MAXIMILLIAN, HEIR TO THE THRONE OF DERRINGDO!
YEAH... THAT WOULD'VE BEEN A LOT MORE CONVINCING IF YOU WEREN'T HOLDING A WOOBSIE IN YOUR HAND.
SORRY ABOUT MY FRIEND MAX, HERE. HE THINKS YOU'VE BEEN CASTING SPELLS.
IT'S NOT A... Oh, NEVER MIND.

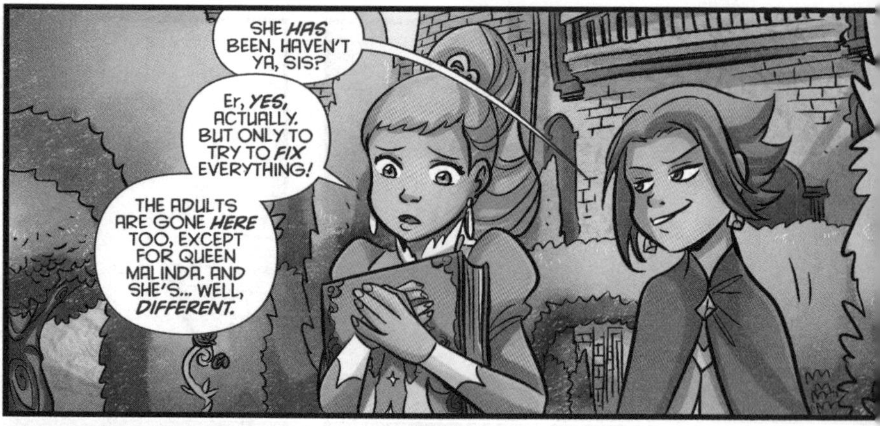
SHE *HAS* BEEN, HAVEN'T YA, SIS?
Er, *YES,* ACTUALLY. BUT ONLY TO TRY TO *FIX* EVERYTHING!
THE ADULTS ARE GONE *HERE* TOO, EXCEPT FOR QUEEN MALINDA. AND SHE'S... WELL, *DIFFERENT.*

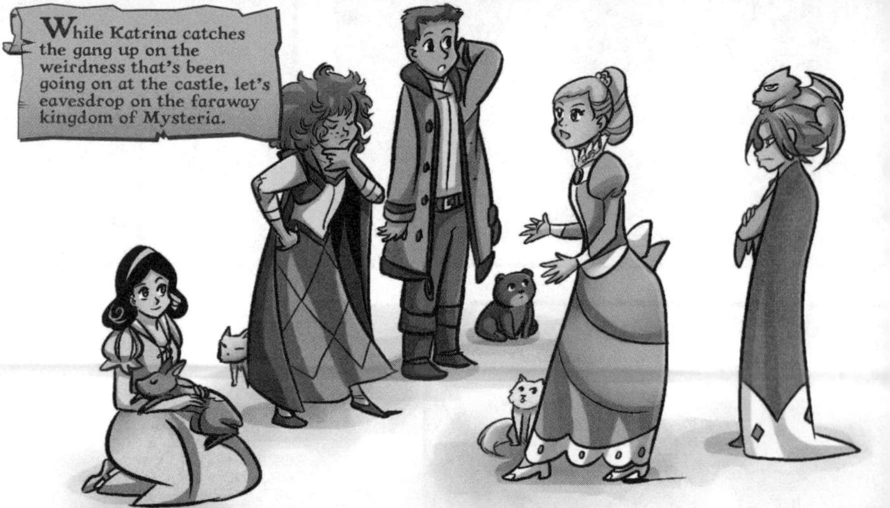
While Katrina catches the gang up on the weirdness that's been going on at the castle, let's eavesdrop on the faraway kingdom of Mysteria.

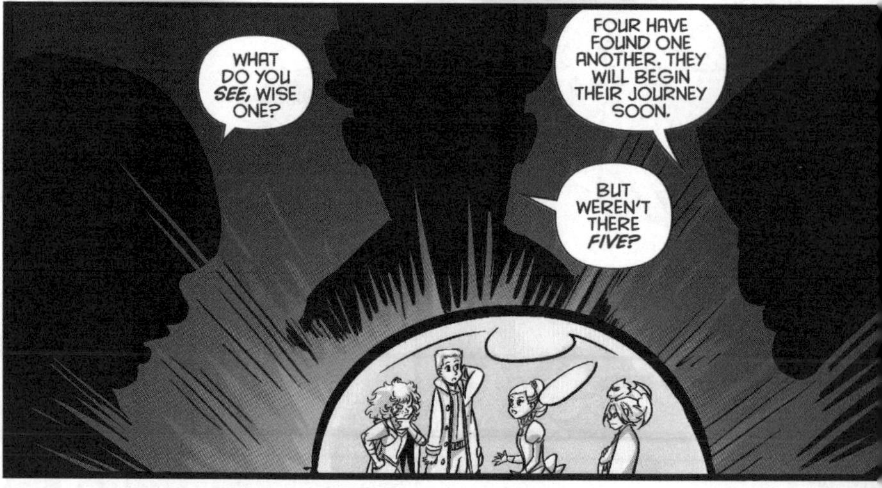
WHAT DO YOU *SEE,* WISE ONE?
FOUR HAVE FOUND ONE ANOTHER. THEY WILL BEGIN THEIR JOURNEY SOON.
BUT WEREN'T THERE *FIVE?*

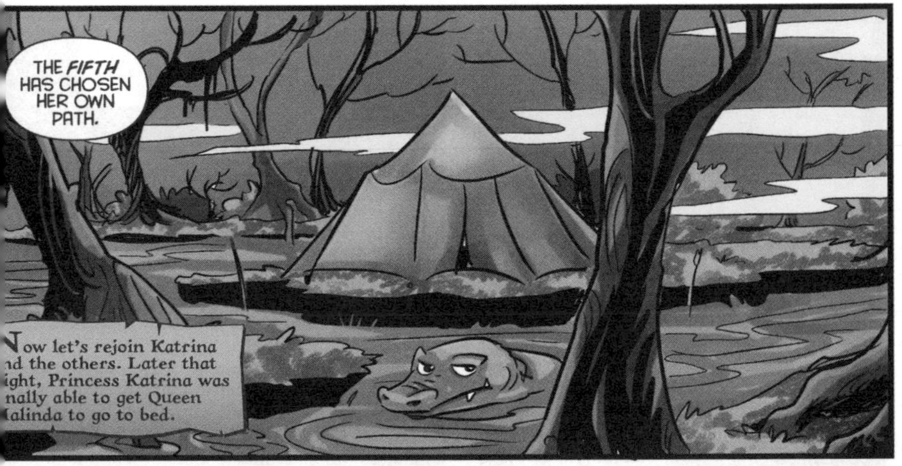
THE FIFTH HAS CHOSEN HER OWN PATH.
Now let's rejoin Katrina and the others. Later that night, Princess Katrina was finally able to get Queen Malinda to go to bed.

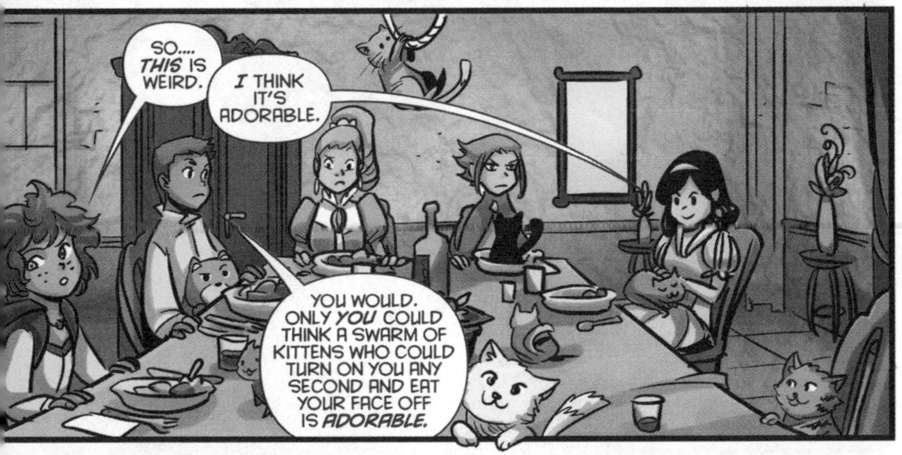
SO.... THIS IS WEIRD.
I THINK IT'S ADORABLE.
YOU WOULD. ONLY YOU COULD THINK A SWARM OF KITTENS WHO COULD TURN ON YOU ANY SECOND AND EAT YOUR FACE OFF IS ADORABLE.

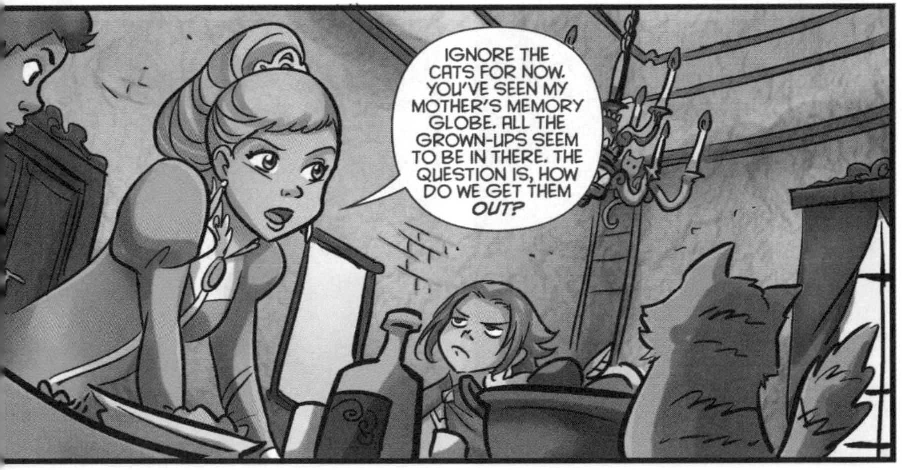
IGNORE THE CATS FOR NOW. YOU'VE SEEN MY MOTHER'S MEMORY GLOBE. ALL THE GROWN-UPS SEEM TO BE IN THERE. THE QUESTION IS, HOW DO WE GET THEM OUT?

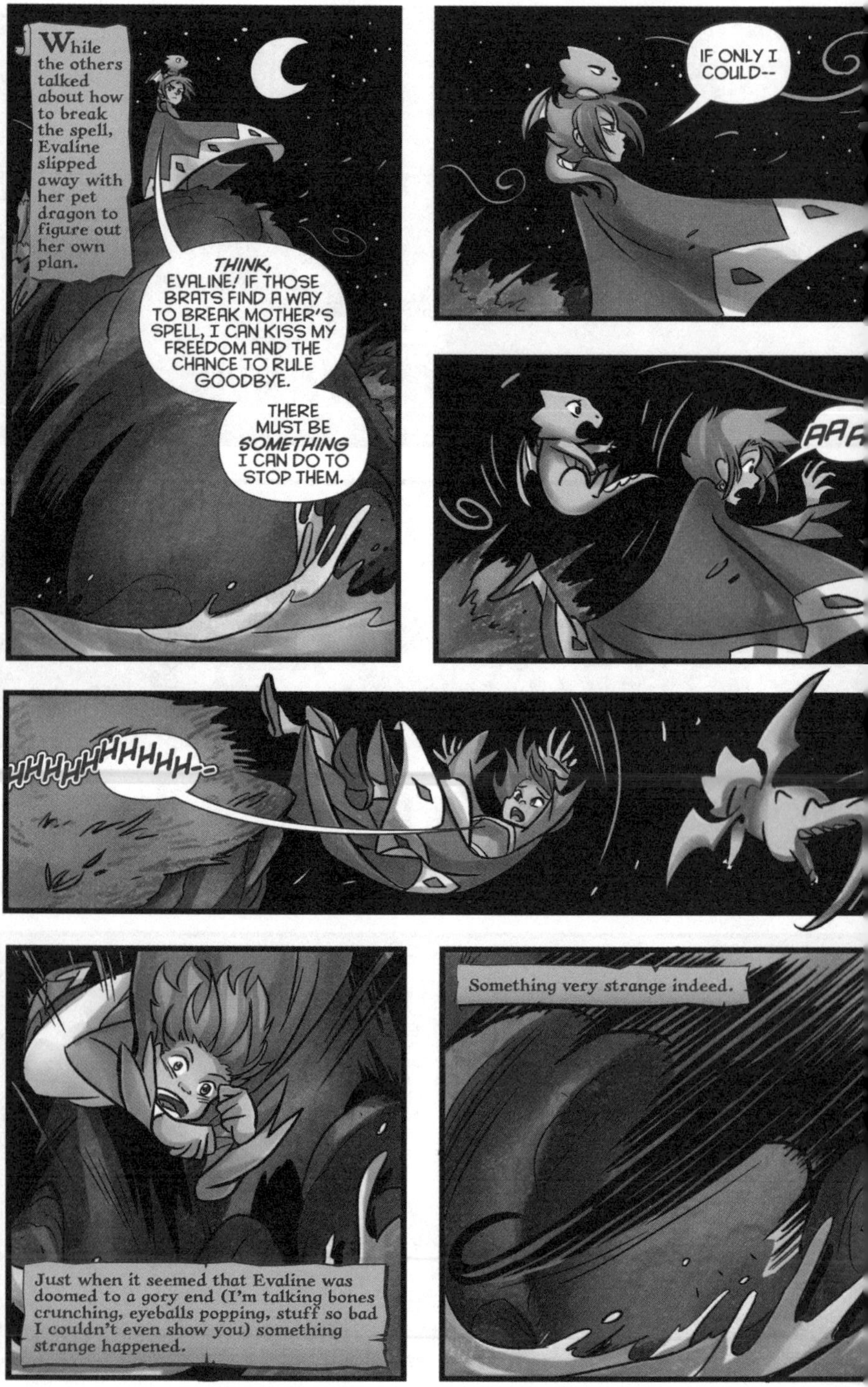
While the others talked about how to break the spell, Evaline slipped away with her pet dragon to figure out her own plan.
THINK, EVALINE! IF THOSE BRATS FIND A WAY TO BREAK MOTHER'S SPELL, I CAN KISS MY FREEDOM AND THE CHANCE TO RULE GOODBYE.
THERE MUST BE SOMETHING I CAN DO TO STOP THEM.
IF ONLY I COULD--
AAA
HHHHHHHHHHH--
Just when it seemed that Evaline was doomed to a gory end (I'm talking bones crunching, eyeballs popping, stuff so bad I couldn't even show you) something strange happened.
Something very strange indeed.

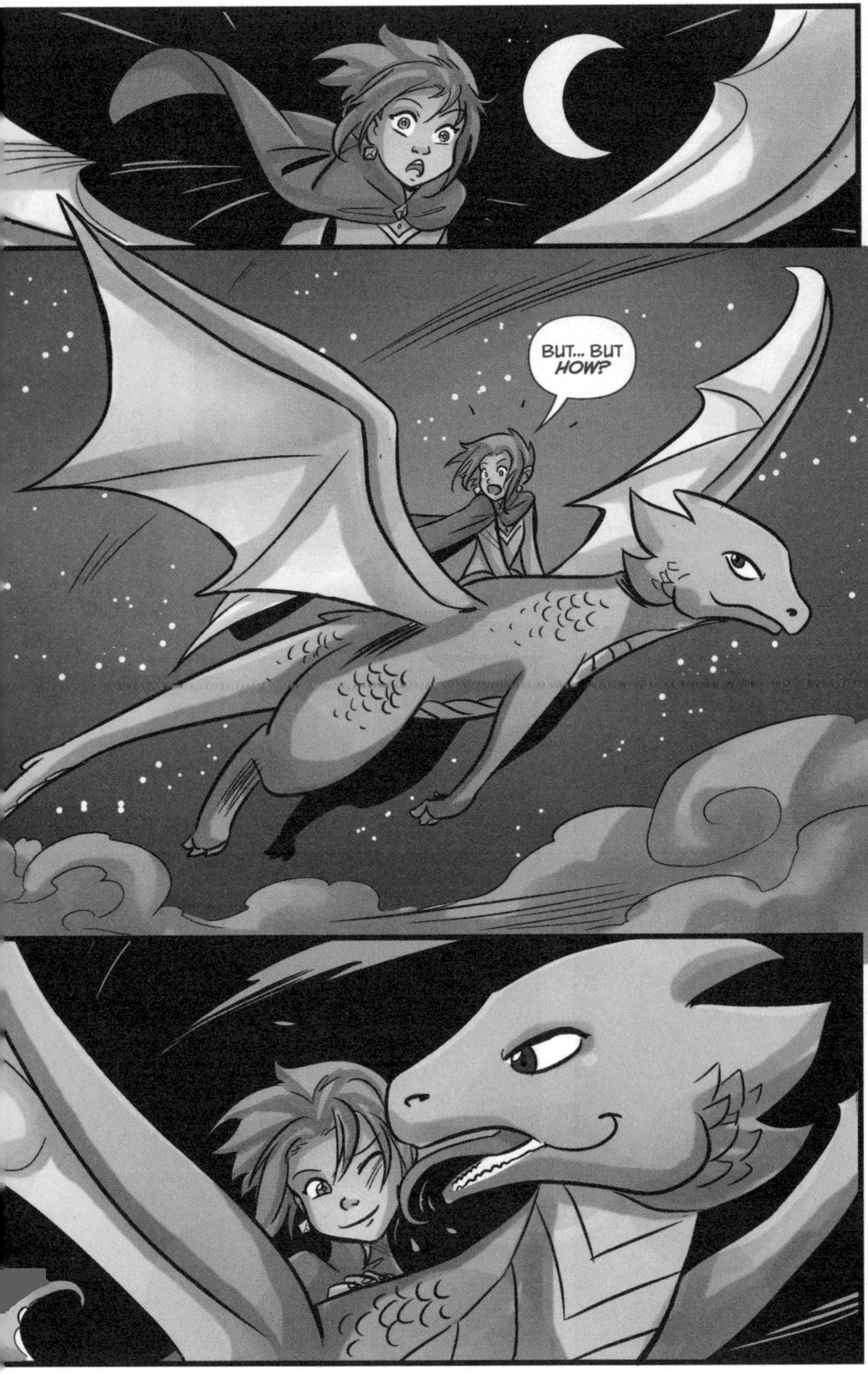
BUT... BUT HOW?

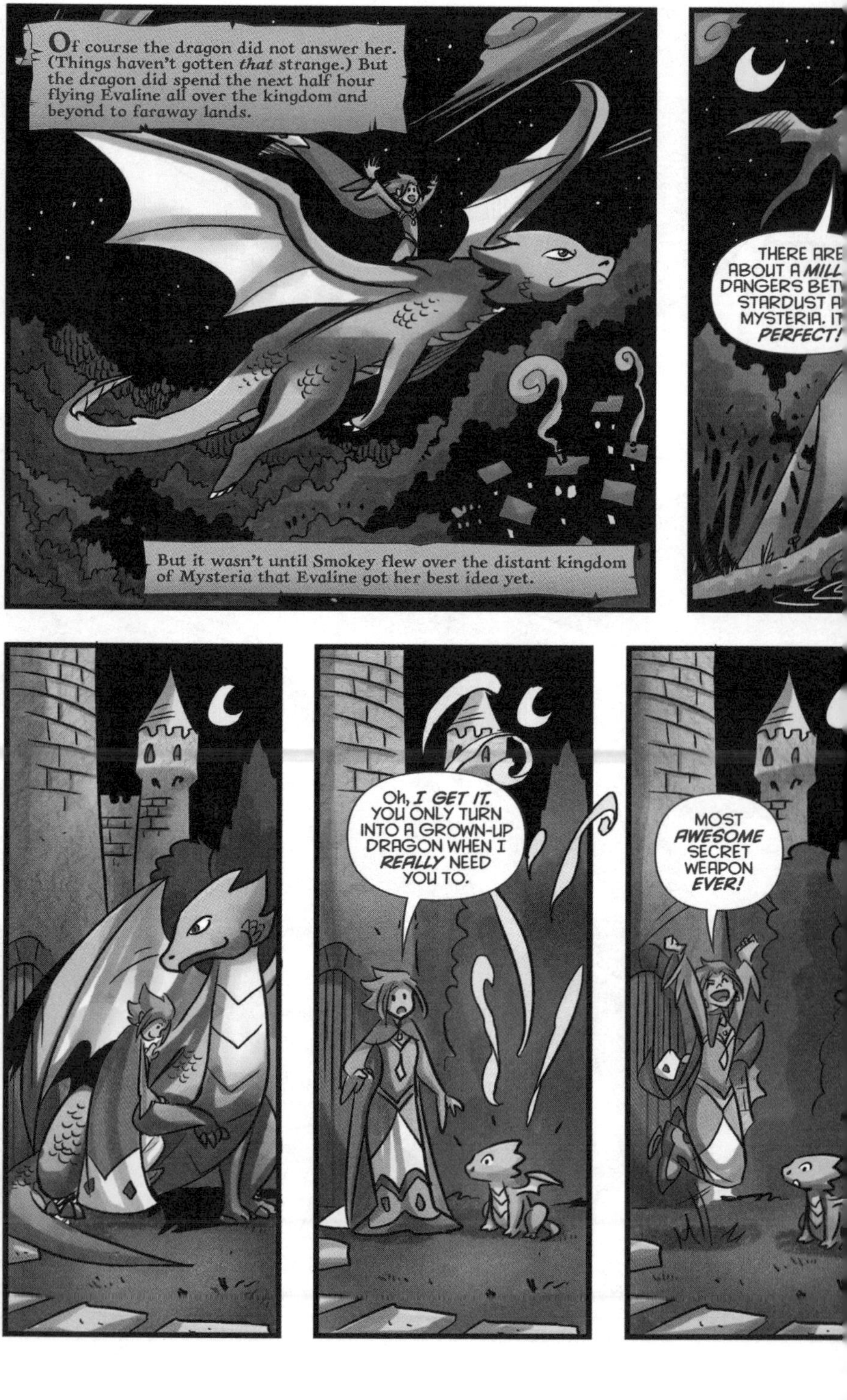
Of course the dragon did not answer her. (Things haven't gotten *that* strange.) But the dragon did spend the next half hour flying Evaline all over the kingdom and beyond to faraway lands.
But it wasn't until Smokey flew over the distant kingdom of Mysteria that Evaline got her best idea yet.
THERE ARE ABOUT A *MILL* DANGERS BET STARDUST A MYSTERIA. IT *PERFECT!*
Oh, *I GET IT.* YOU ONLY TURN INTO A GROWN-UP DRAGON WHEN I *REALLY* NEED YOU TO.
MOST *AWESOME* SECRET WEAPON *EVER!*

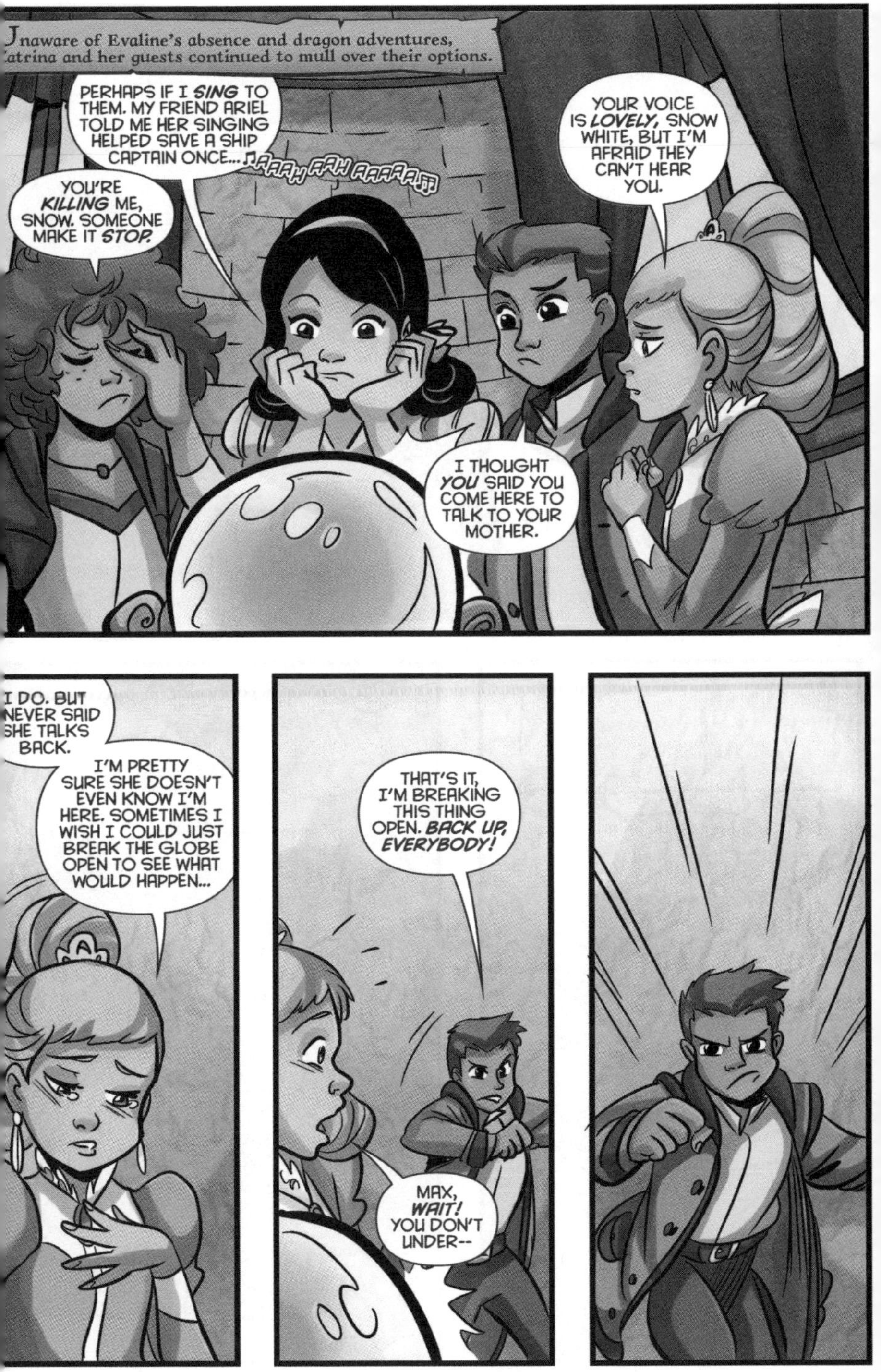
Unaware of Evaline's absence and dragon adventures, Catrina and her guests continued to mull over their options.
PERHAPS IF I SING TO THEM. MY FRIEND ARIEL TOLD ME HER SINGING HELPED SAVE A SHIP CAPTAIN ONCE...♫AAAAH AAH AAAAAA♫
YOU'RE KILLING ME, SNOW. SOMEONE MAKE IT STOP.
YOUR VOICE IS LOVELY, SNOW WHITE, BUT I'M AFRAID THEY CAN'T HEAR YOU.
I THOUGHT YOU SAID YOU COME HERE TO TALK TO YOUR MOTHER.
I DO. BUT I NEVER SAID SHE TALKS BACK.
I'M PRETTY SURE SHE DOESN'T EVEN KNOW I'M HERE. SOMETIMES I WISH I COULD JUST BREAK THE GLOBE OPEN TO SEE WHAT WOULD HAPPEN...
THAT'S IT, I'M BREAKING THIS THING OPEN. BACK UP, EVERYBODY!
MAX, WAIT! YOU DON'T UNDER--

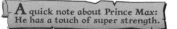
A quick note about Prince Max: He has a touch of super strength.

All right, I know he doesn't look it. But ever since he was a child, he was oddly strong for his age.

That night at the castle, Max used every bit of strength he had to push the globe off the pedestal. He pushed and he shoved. But no matter how hard he tried, well...

Um... PRINCE MAX?

THE THING IS, THE GLOBE IS *ENCHANTED.* IT CAN'T BE MOVED OR BROKEN.

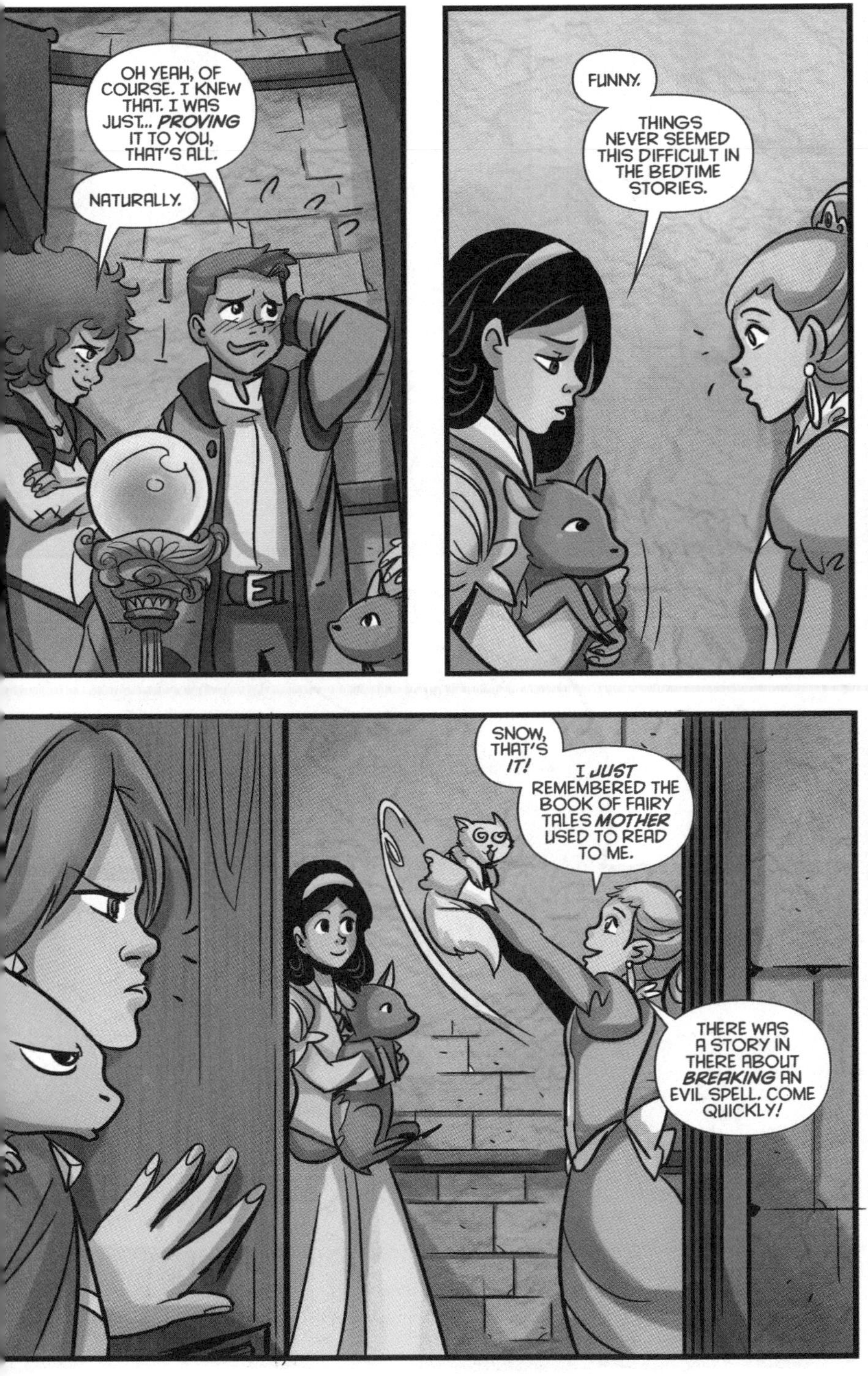
OH YEAH, OF COURSE. I KNEW THAT. I WAS JUST... *PROVING* IT TO YOU, THAT'S ALL.
NATURALLY.
FUNNY.
THINGS NEVER SEEMED THIS DIFFICULT IN THE BEDTIME STORIES.
SNOW, THAT'S *IT!*
I *JUST* REMEMBERED THE BOOK OF FAIRY TALES *MOTHER* USED TO READ TO ME.
THERE WAS A STORY IN THERE ABOUT *BREAKING* AN EVIL SPELL. COME QUICKLY*!*

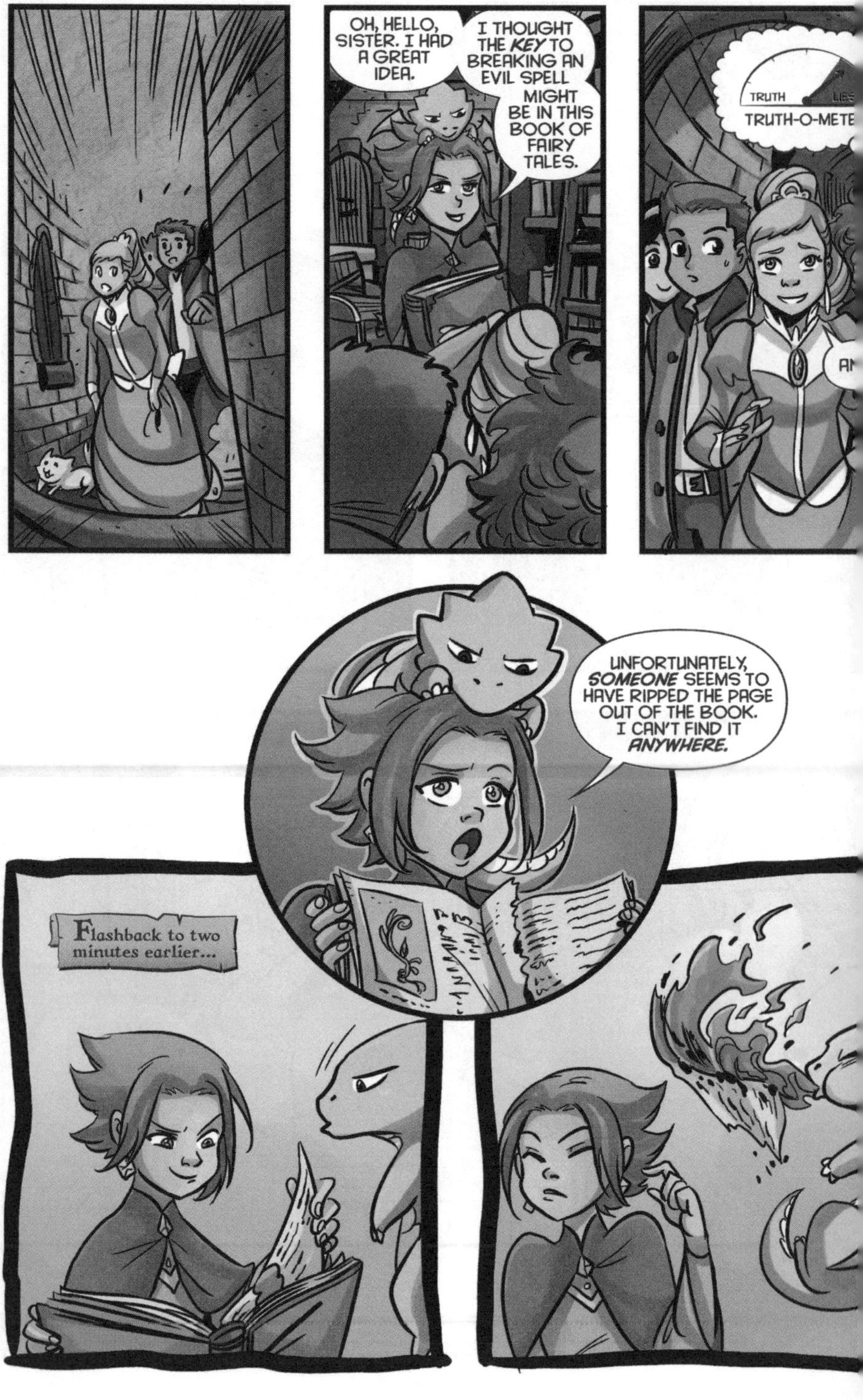
OH, HELLO, SISTER. I HAD A GREAT IDEA.
I THOUGHT THE KEY TO BREAKING AN EVIL SPELL
MIGHT BE IN THIS BOOK OF FAIRY TALES.
TRUTH
TRUTH-O-METE
UNFORTUNATELY, SOMEONE SEEMS TO HAVE RIPPED THE PAGE OUT OF THE BOOK. I CAN'T FIND IT ANYWHERE.
Flashback to two minutes earlier...

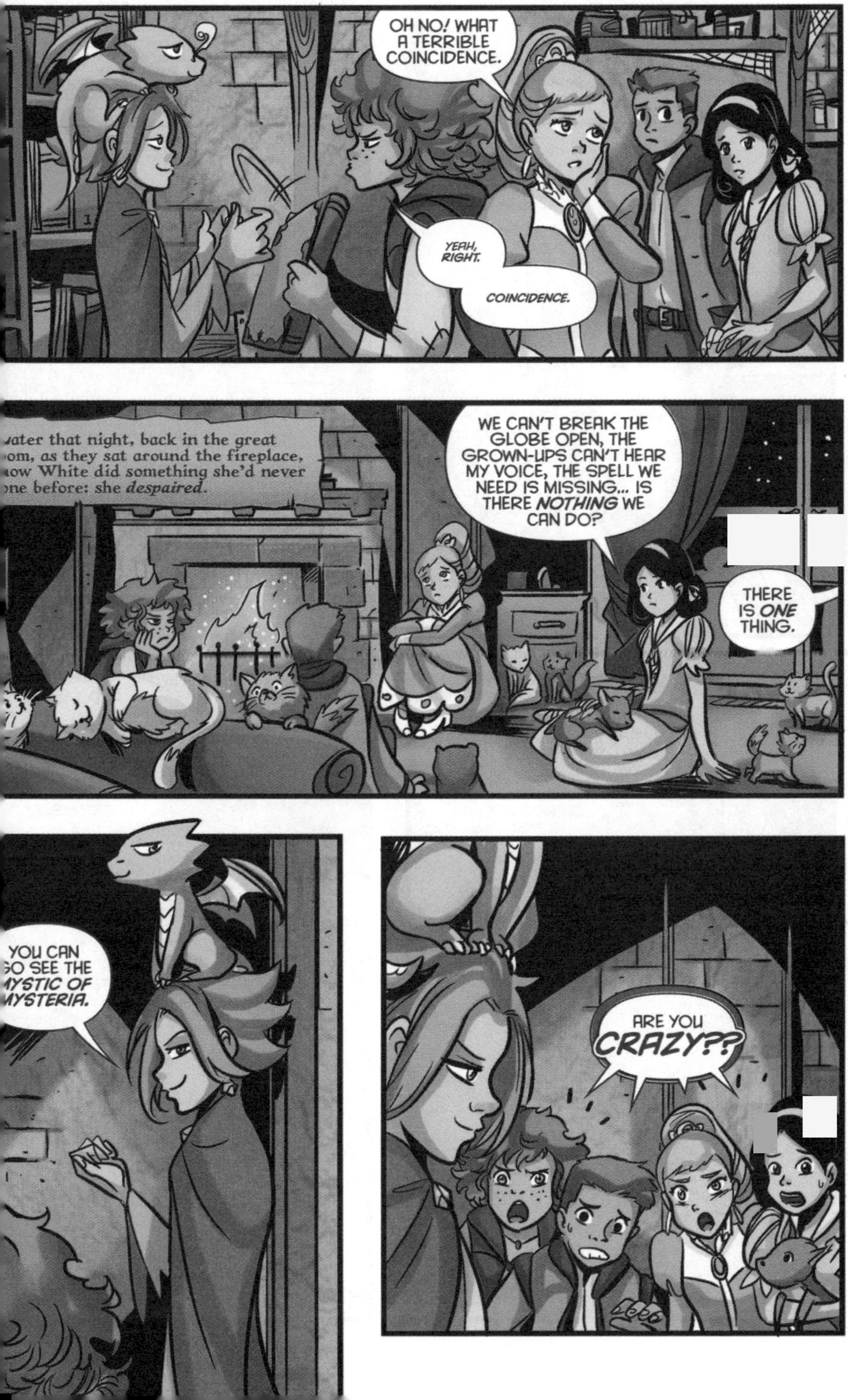
OH NO! WHAT A TERRIBLE COINCIDENCE.
YEAH, RIGHT.
COINCIDENCE.
ater that night, back in the great
om, as they sat around the fireplace,
ow White did something she'd never
ne before: she *despaired*.
WE CAN'T BREAK THE GLOBE OPEN, THE GROWN-UPS CAN'T HEAR MY VOICE, THE SPELL WE NEED IS MISSING... IS THERE *NOTHING* WE CAN DO?
THERE IS *ONE* THING.
YOU CAN O SEE THE YSTIC OF YSTERIA.
ARE YOU CRAZY??

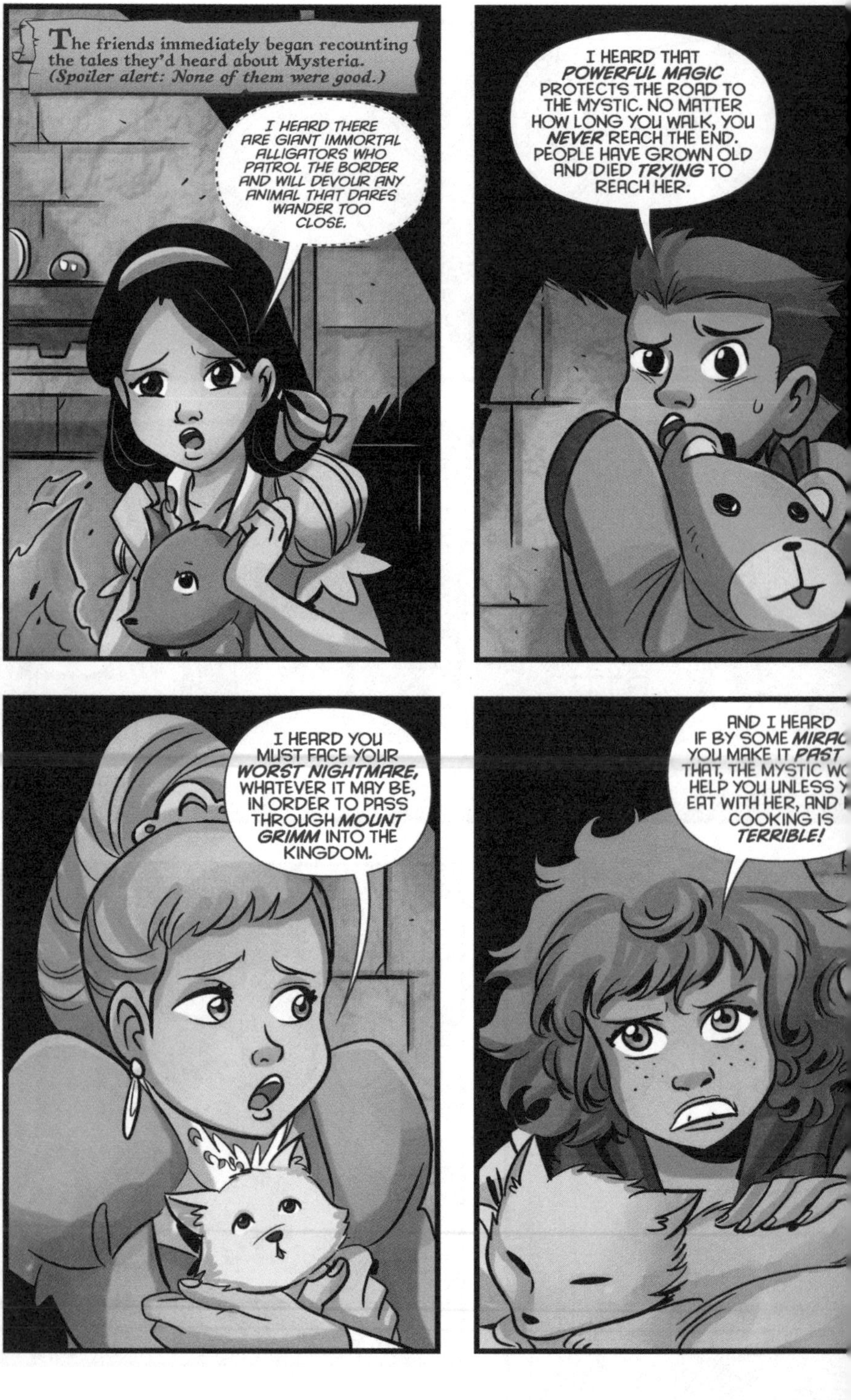
The friends immediately began recounting the tales they'd heard about Mysteria. *(Spoiler alert: None of them were good.)*
I HEARD THERE ARE GIANT IMMORTAL ALLIGATORS WHO PATROL THE BORDER AND WILL DEVOUR ANY ANIMAL THAT DARES WANDER TOO CLOSE.
I HEARD THAT **POWERFUL MAGIC** PROTECTS THE ROAD TO THE MYSTIC. NO MATTER HOW LONG YOU WALK, YOU **NEVER** REACH THE END. PEOPLE HAVE GROWN OLD AND DIED **TRYING** TO REACH HER.
I HEARD YOU MUST FACE YOUR **WORST NIGHTMARE,** WHATEVER IT MAY BE, IN ORDER TO PASS THROUGH **MOUNT GRIMM** INTO THE KINGDOM.
AND I HEARD
IF BY SOME MIRAC
YOU MAKE IT PAST
THAT, THE MYSTIC WO
HELP YOU UNLESS Y
EAT WITH HER, AND
COOKING IS
TERRIBLE!

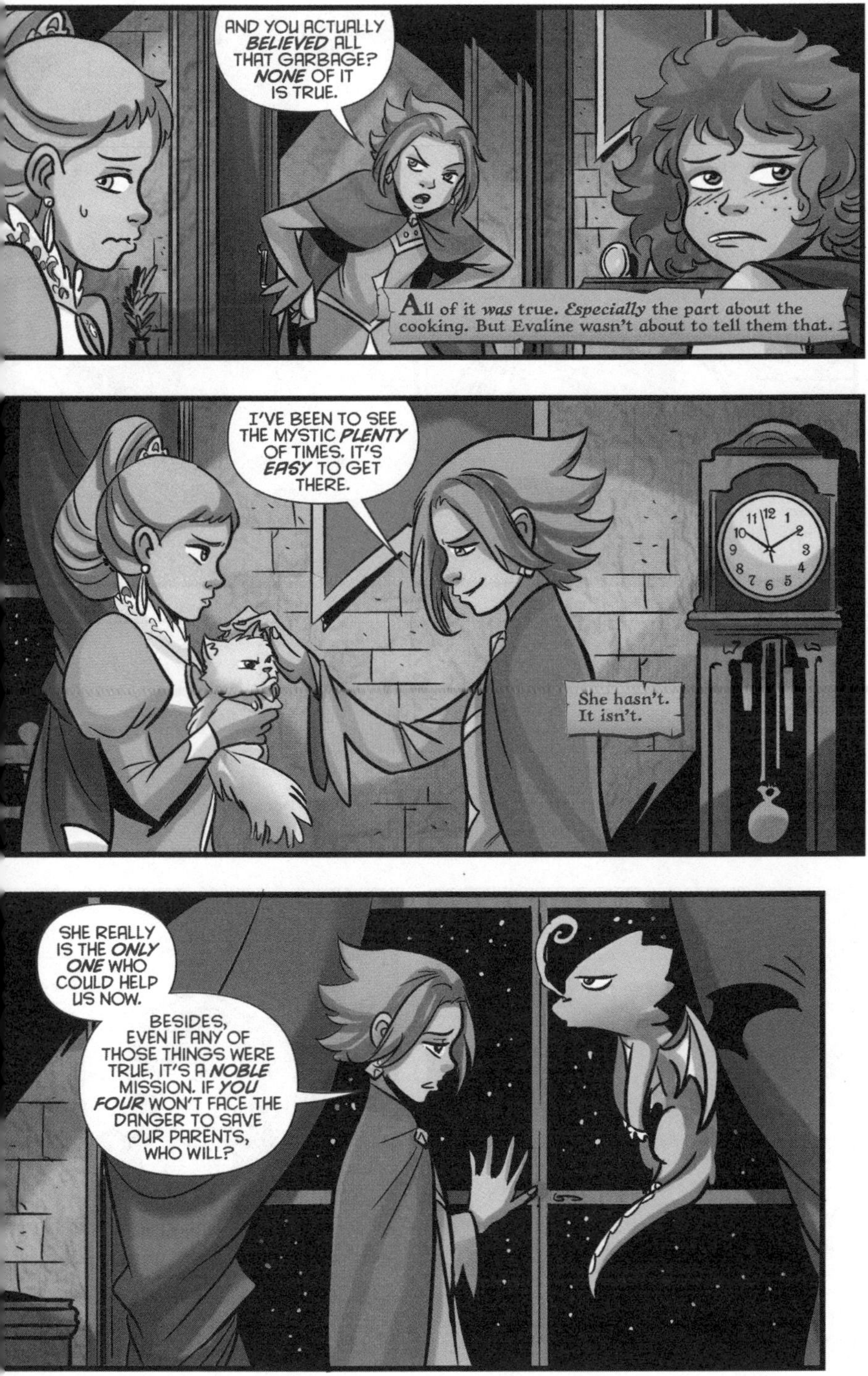
AND YOU ACTUALLY BELIEVED ALL THAT GARBAGE? NONE OF IT IS TRUE.
All of it *was* true. *Especially* the part about the cooking. But Evaline wasn't about to tell them that.
I'VE BEEN TO SEE THE MYSTIC PLENTY OF TIMES. IT'S EASY TO GET THERE.
She hasn't. It isn't.
SHE REALLY IS THE ONLY ONE WHO COULD HELP US NOW.
BESIDES, EVEN IF ANY OF THOSE THINGS WERE TRUE, IT'S A NOBLE MISSION. IF YOU FOUR WON'T FACE THE DANGER TO SAVE OUR PARENTS, WHO WILL?

WAIT JUST A SECOND. *"YOU FOUR"*?

YOU'RE NOT COMING WITH US ON THIS *"NOBLE MISSION,"* HUH?

I WOULD. REALLY. BUT *SOMEONE* HAS TO STAY AND TAKE CARE OF MY ELDERLY MOTHER.

AND WITH KING VICTOR GONE AND MY DEAR SISTER AWAY, I SUPPOSE *I'LL* HAVE TO STAY AND RULE THE KINGDOM.

IT ISN PLACE I'M HAF *HE*

R̶ed, who had been lied to before, had a very good nose for when she was being deceived.

YEAH, I'LL BET.

The five kids argued into the wee hours of the morning about what they should do instead, but Evaline was clever and shot each plan down. For example...

PERHAPS IF WE SENT THIS MYSTIC WOMAN A NICELY WORDED *LETTER* EXPLAINING OUR DIFFICULTIES...

MYSTIC SWAMP WITCHES *DON'T* HAVE MAILBOXES.

See what I me

inally, after exhausting
emselves discussing their
tions all night, they
reed to Evaline's plan
r *the worst reason of all:*
o one had a better idea.

FINE.

SURE.

AS LONG AS I CAN TAKE FAWN.

EXCELLENT.

WHATEVER.

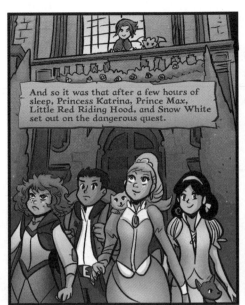

And so it was that after a few hours of
sleep, Princess Katrina, Prince Max,
Little Red Riding Hood, and Snow White
set out on the dangerous quest.

But even though Evaline
suspected her sister would
never survive the journey,
she wanted nothing left to
chance.

HEY, TWEEDLE-DEE, TWEEDLE-DUM--

--FORGET THE *HORSES.* I HAVE MORE *IMPORTANT* JOBS FOR THE TWO OF YOU.

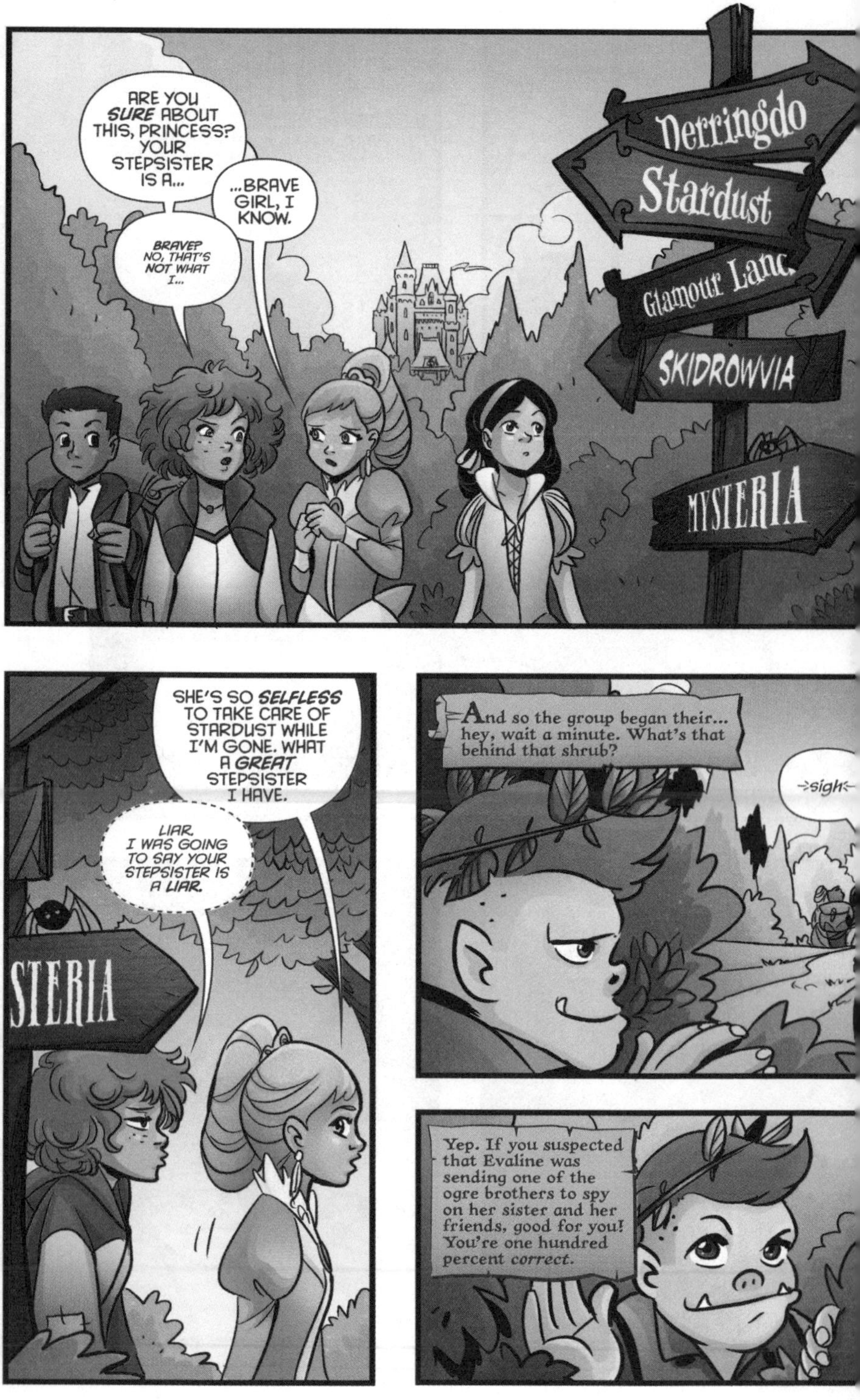

ARE YOU *SURE* ABOUT THIS, PRINCESS? YOUR STEPSISTER IS A...
...BRAVE GIRL, I KNOW.
BRAVE? NO, THAT'S NOT WHAT I...
Derringdo
Stardust
Glamour Land
SKIDROWVIA
MYSTERIA
SHE'S SO *SELFLESS* TO TAKE CARE OF STARDUST WHILE I'M GONE. WHAT A *GREAT* STEPSISTER I HAVE.
LIAR. I WAS GOING TO SAY YOUR STEPSISTER IS A *LIAR.*
STERIA
And so the group began their... hey, wait a minute. What's that behind that shrub?
sigh
Yep. If you suspected that Evaline was sending one of the ogre brothers to spy on her sister and her friends, good for you! You're one hundred percent *correct*.

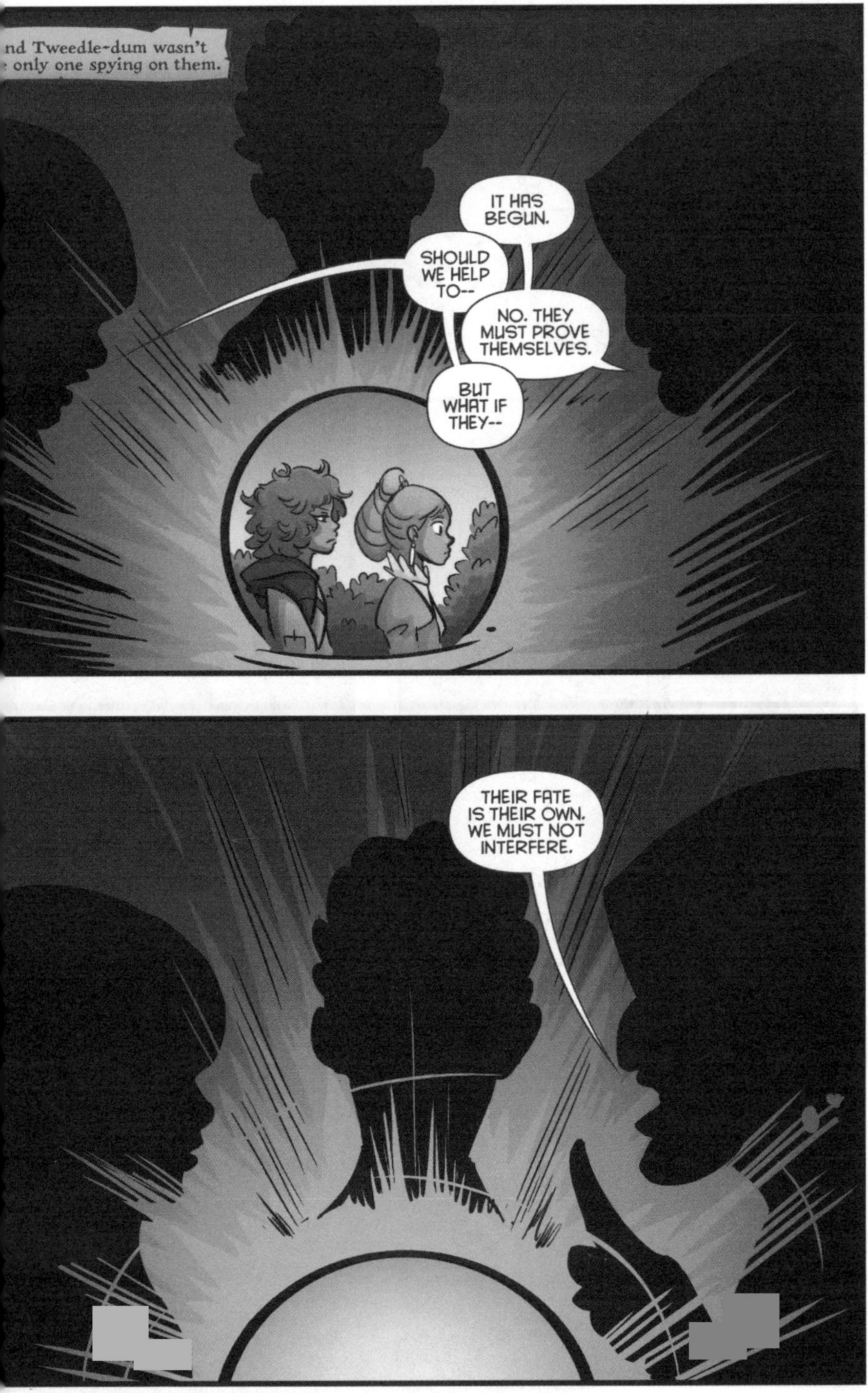
nd Tweedle-dum wasn't
only one spying on them.
IT HAS BEGUN.
SHOULD WE HELP TO--
NO. THEY MUST PROVE THEMSELVES.
BUT WHAT IF THEY--
THEIR FATE IS THEIR OWN. WE MUST NOT INTERFERE.

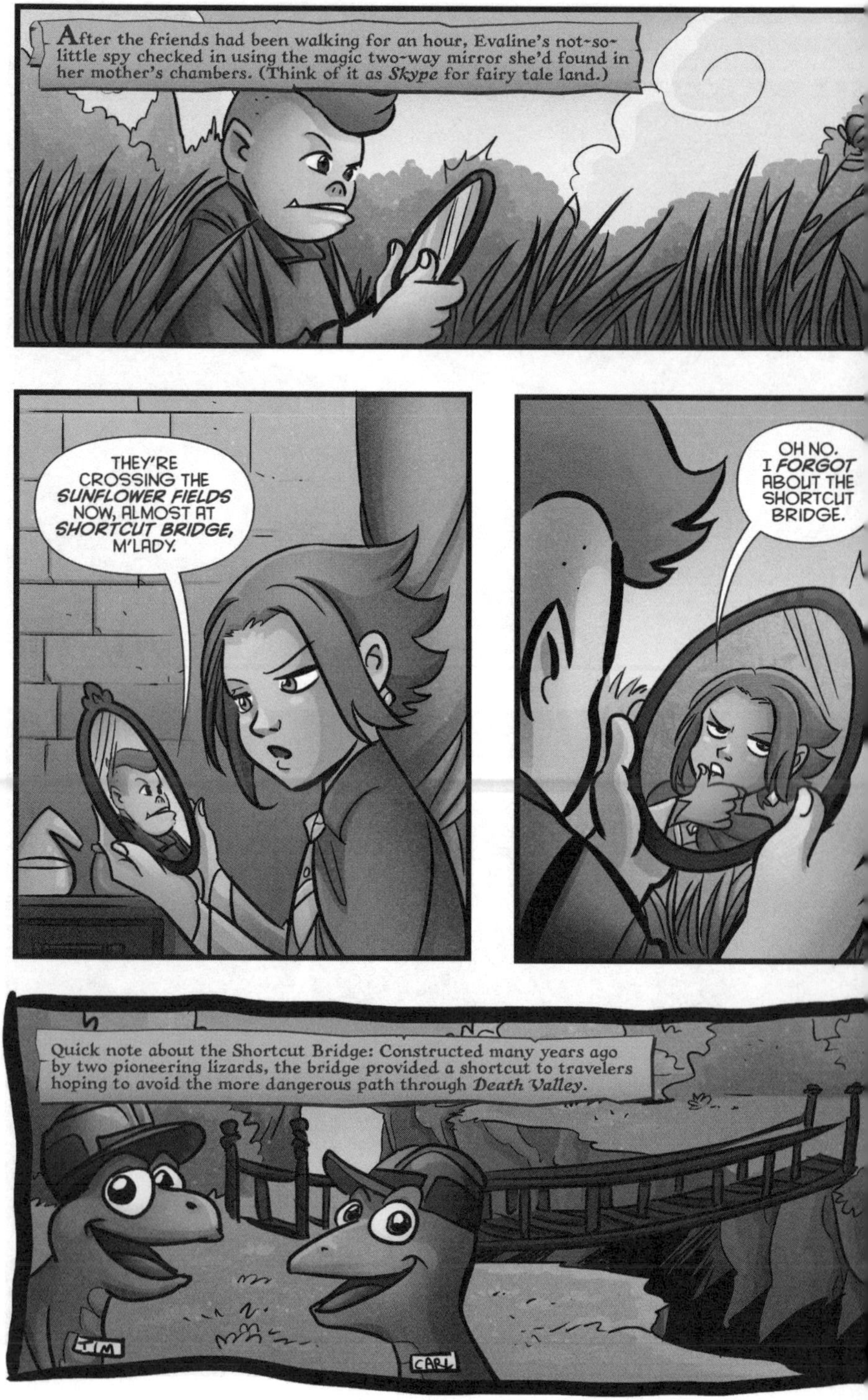
After the friends had been walking for an hour, Evaline's not-so-little spy checked in using the magic two-way mirror she'd found in her mother's chambers. (Think of it as *Skype* for fairy tale land.)
THEY'RE CROSSING THE *SUNFLOWER FIELDS* NOW, ALMOST AT *SHORTCUT BRIDGE,* M'LADY.
OH NO. I *FORGOT* ABOUT THE SHORTCUT BRIDGE.
Quick note about the Shortcut Bridge: Constructed many years ago by two pioneering lizards, the bridge provided a shortcut to travelers hoping to avoid the more dangerous path through *Death Valley*.
TIM
CARL

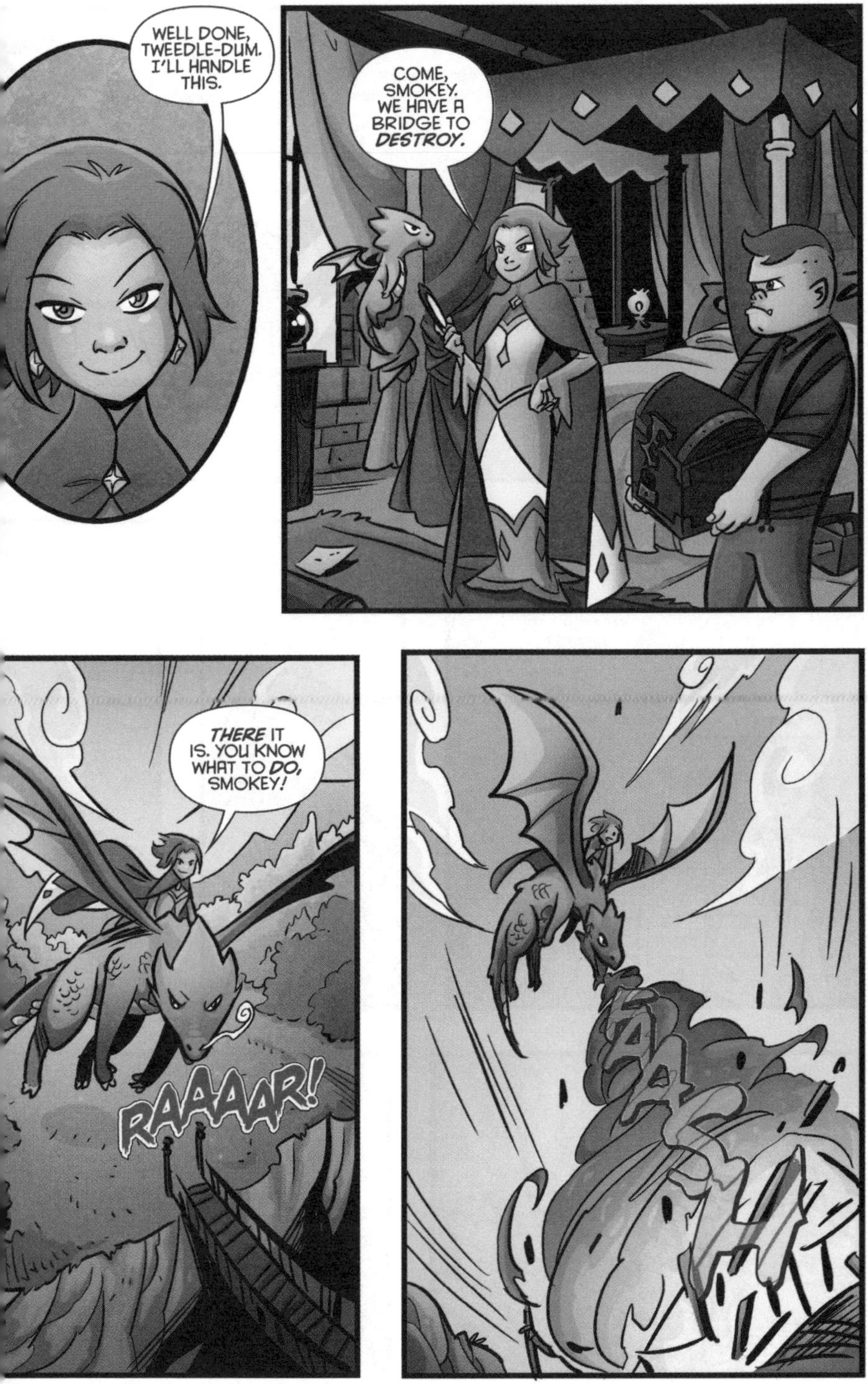
WELL DONE, TWEEDLE-DUM. I'LL HANDLE THIS.
COME, SMOKEY. WE HAVE A BRIDGE TO *DESTROY*.
THERE IT IS. YOU KNOW WHAT TO *DO*, SMOKEY!
RAAAAR!

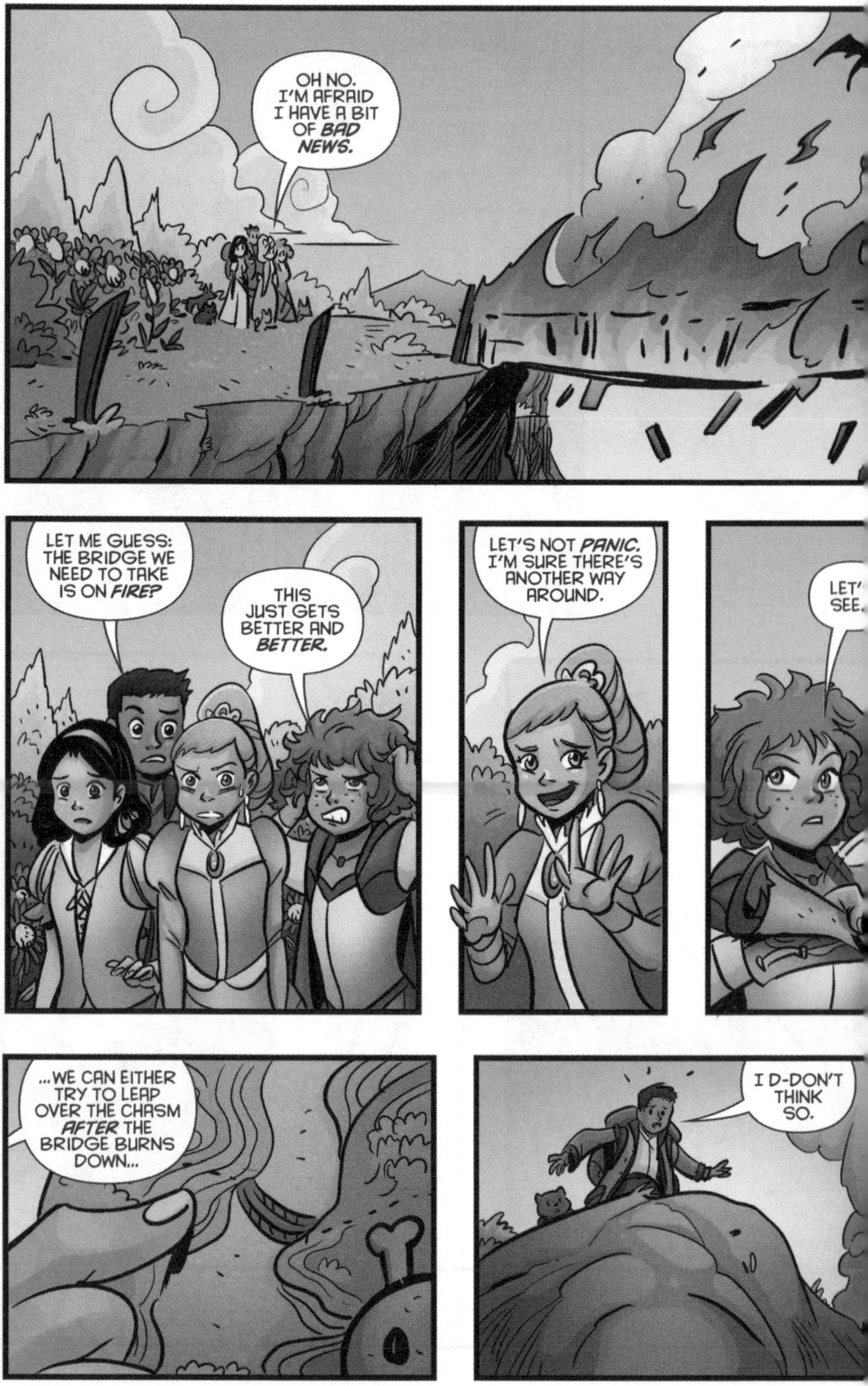
OH NO. I'M AFRAID I HAVE A BIT OF *BAD NEWS.*
LET ME GUESS: THE BRIDGE WE NEED TO TAKE IS ON *FIRE?*
THIS JUST GETS BETTER AND *BETTER.*
LET'S NOT *PANIC.* I'M SURE THERE'S ANOTHER WAY AROUND.
...WE CAN EITHER TRY TO LEAP OVER THE CHASM *AFTER* THE BRIDGE BURNS DOWN...
I D-DON'T THINK SO.

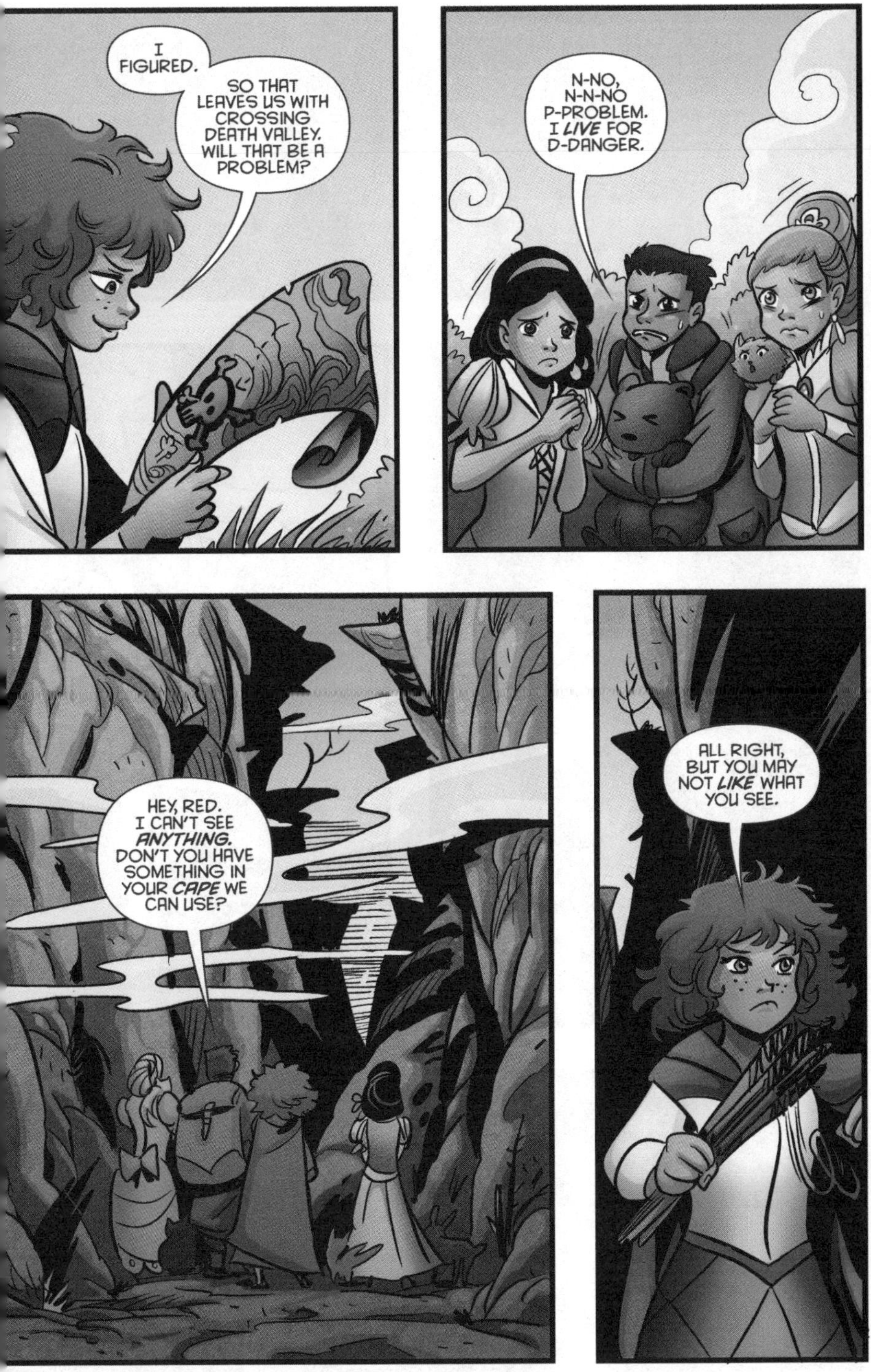
I FIGURED.
SO THAT LEAVES US WITH CROSSING DEATH VALLEY. WILL THAT BE A PROBLEM?
N-NO, N-N-NO P-PROBLEM. I *LIVE* FOR D-DANGER.
HEY, RED. I CAN'T SEE *ANYTHING*. DON'T YOU HAVE SOMETHING IN YOUR *CAPE* WE CAN USE?
ALL RIGHT, BUT YOU MAY NOT *LIKE* WHAT YOU SEE.

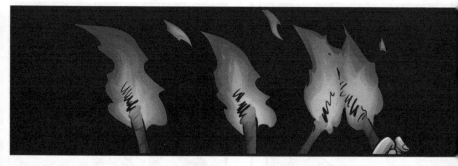

eep!

YOU WERE RIGHT.
I DIDN'T NEED
TO SEE THAT.

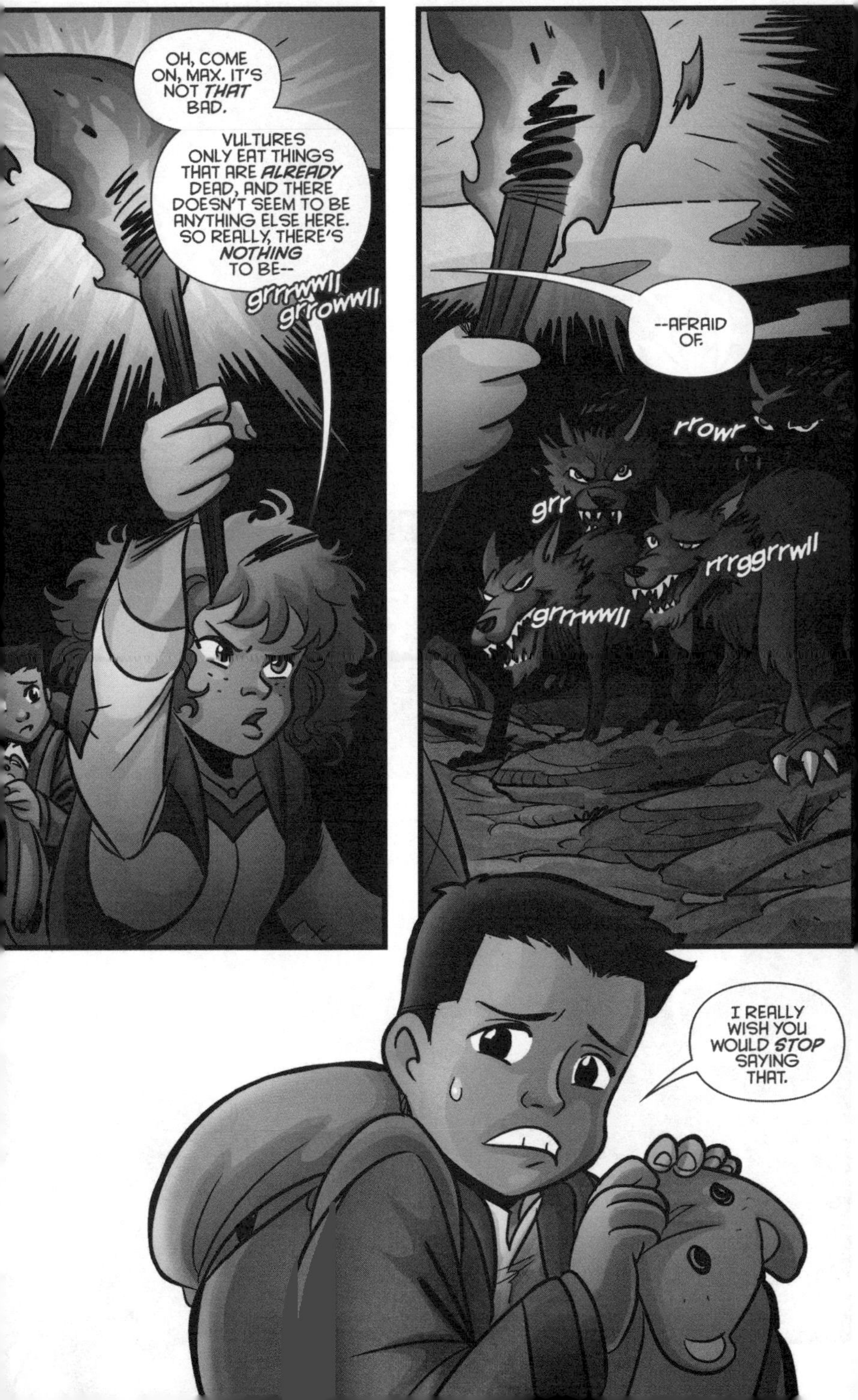
OH, COME ON, MAX. IT'S NOT *THAT* BAD.
VULTURES ONLY EAT THINGS THAT ARE *ALREADY* DEAD, AND THERE DOESN'T SEEM TO BE ANYTHING ELSE HERE. SO REALLY, THERE'S ***NOTHING*** TO BE--
grrrwwll
grrowwll
--AFRAID OF.
rrowr
grr
rrrggrrwll
grrrwwll
I REALLY WISH YOU WOULD ***STOP*** SAYING THAT.

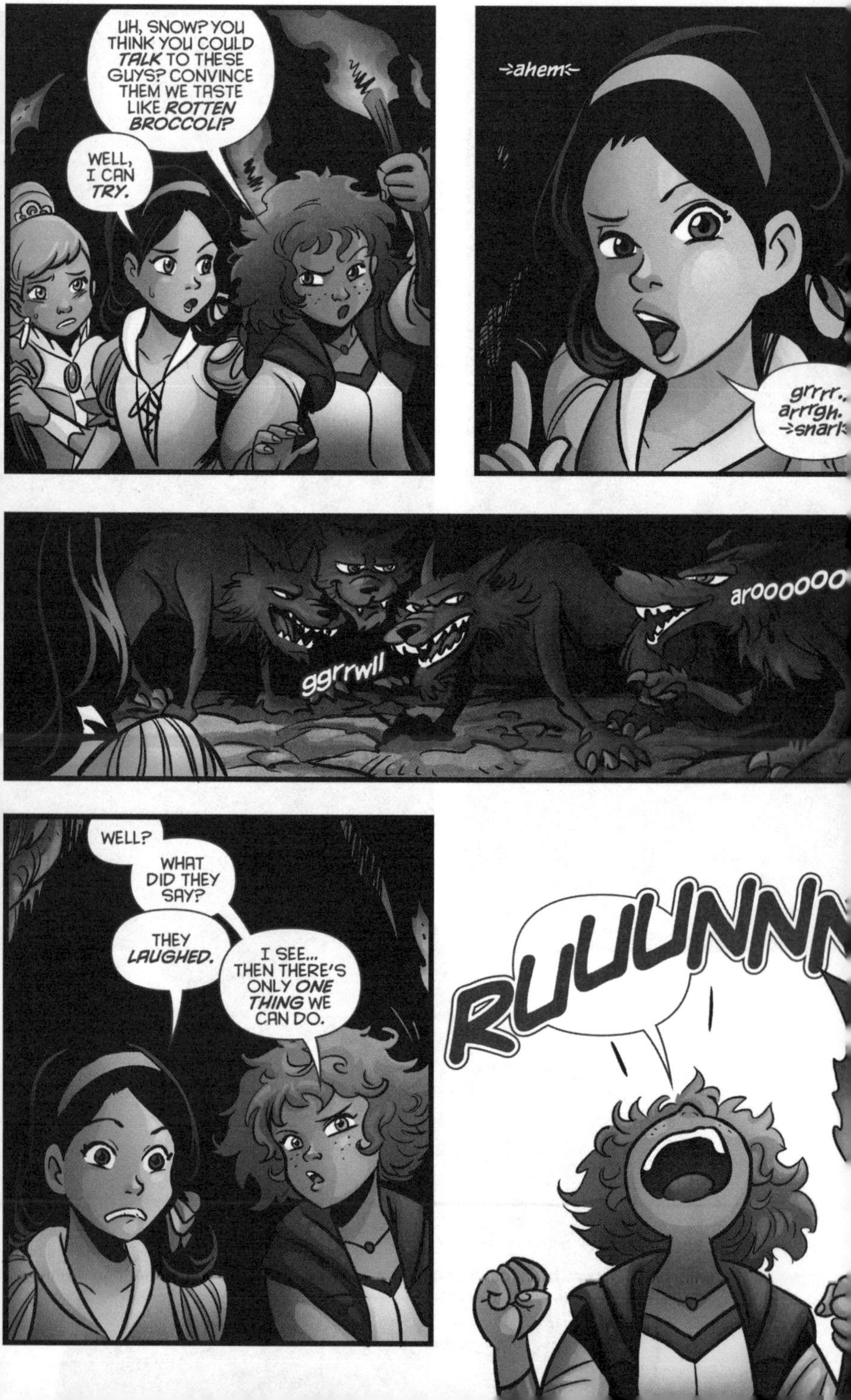
UH, SNOW? YOU THINK YOU COULD TALK TO THESE GUYS? CONVINCE THEM WE TASTE LIKE ROTTEN BROCCOLI?
WELL, I CAN TRY.
ahem
grrrr.. arrrgh. snarl
ggrrwll
arooooooo
WELL?
WHAT DID THEY SAY?
THEY LAUGHED.
I SEE... THEN THERE'S ONLY ONE THING WE CAN DO.
RUUUNNN

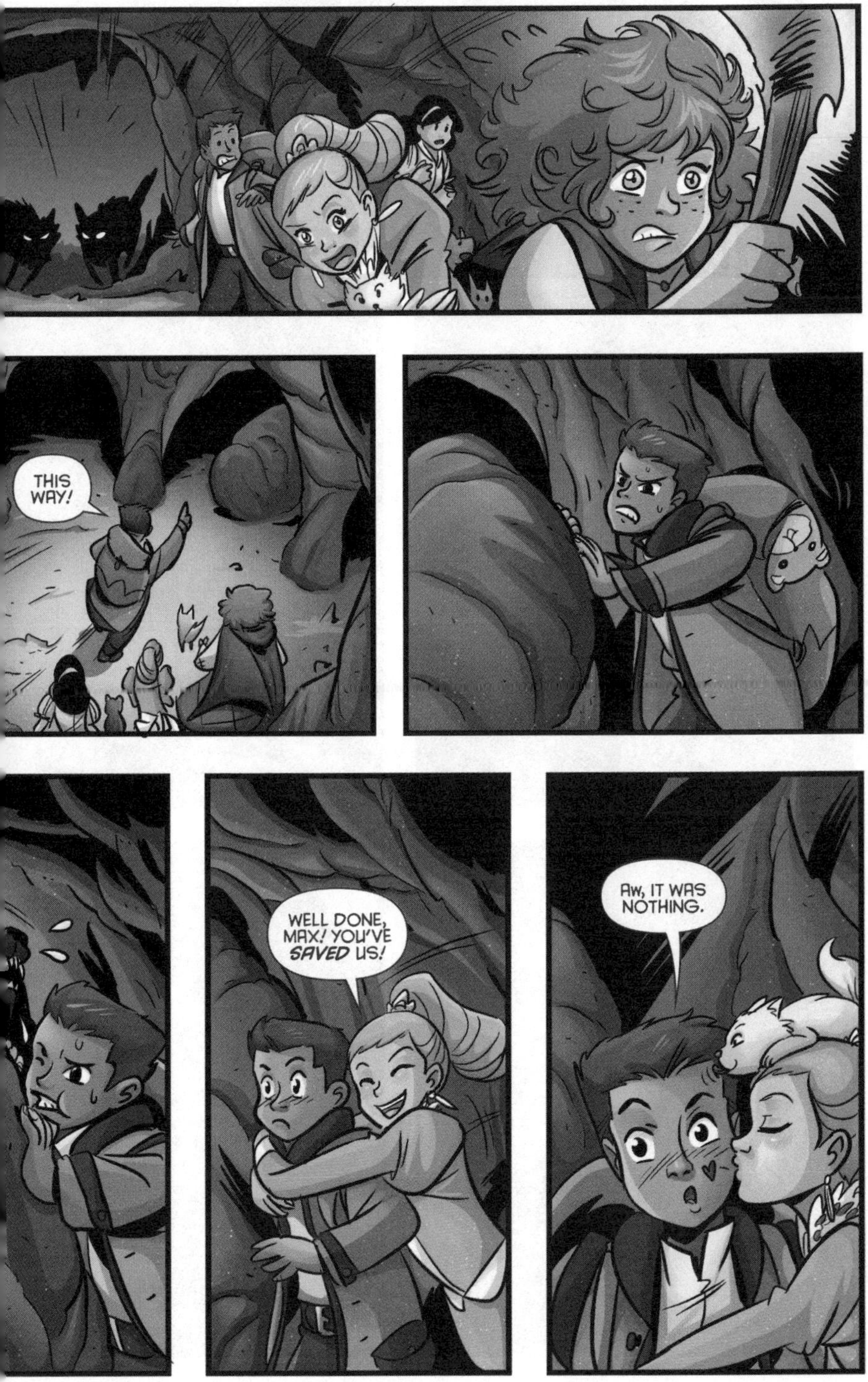
THIS WAY!
WELL DONE, MAX! YOU'VE *SAVED* US!
AW, IT WAS NOTHING.

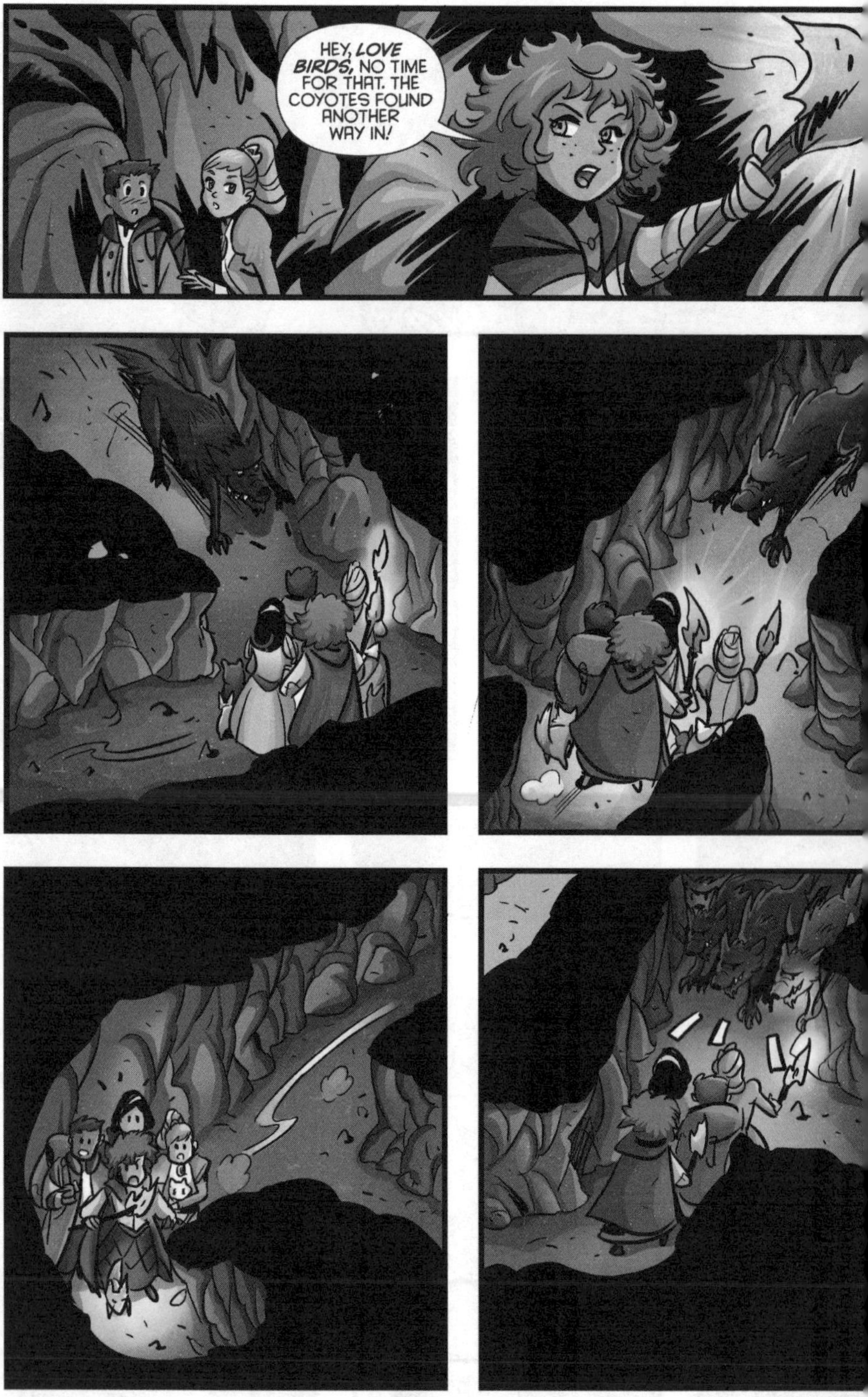
HEY, ***LOVE BIRDS,*** NO TIME FOR THAT. THE COYOTES FOUND ANOTHER WAY IN!

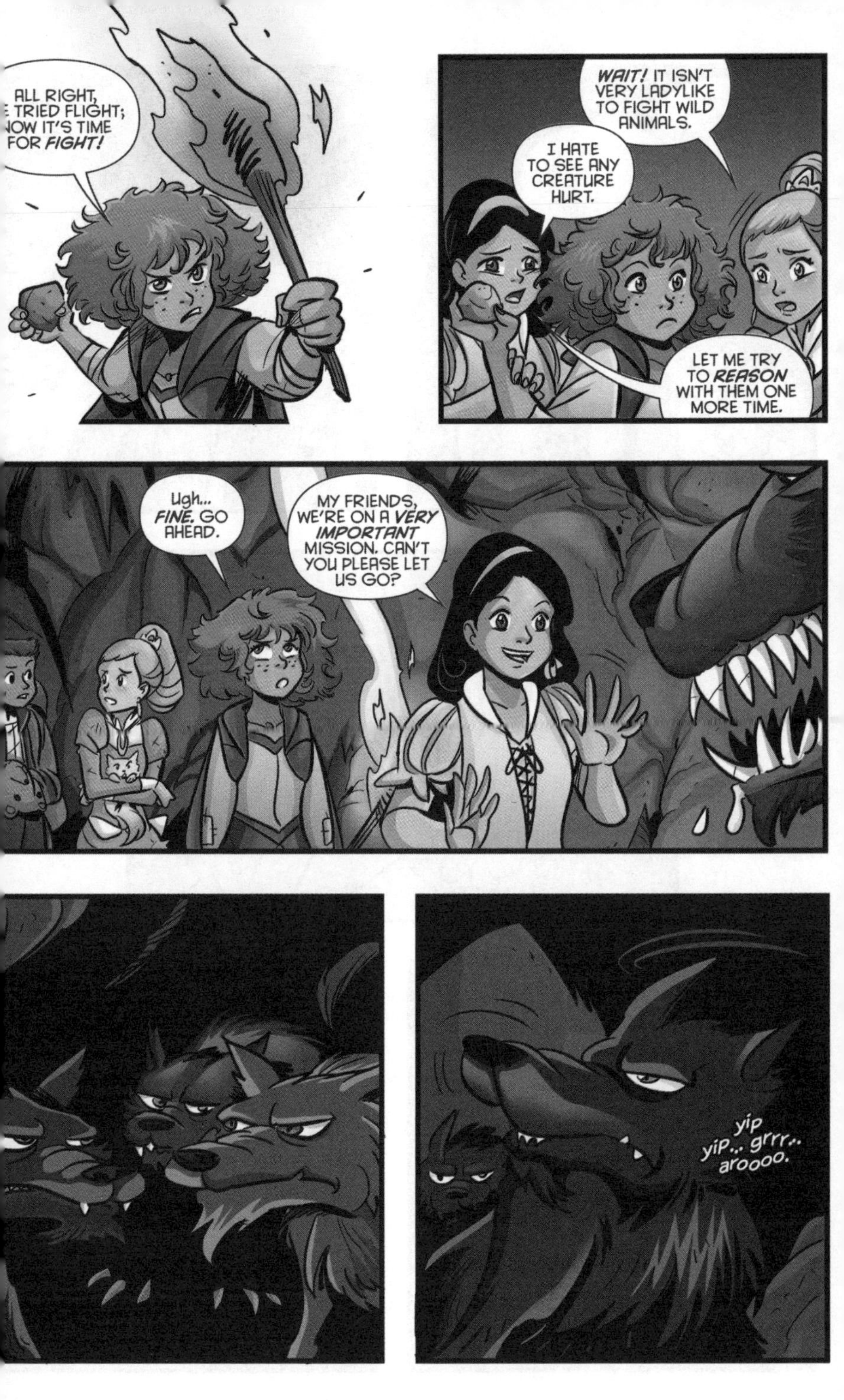

ALL RIGHT, E TRIED FLIGHT; NOW IT'S TIME FOR *FIGHT!*
WAIT! IT ISN'T VERY LADYLIKE TO FIGHT WILD ANIMALS.
I HATE TO SEE ANY CREATURE HURT.
LET ME TRY TO *REASON* WITH THEM ONE MORE TIME.
Ugh... *FINE.* GO AHEAD.
MY FRIENDS, WE'RE ON A *VERY IMPORTANT* MISSION. CAN'T YOU PLEASE LET US GO?
yip yip... grrr... aroooo.

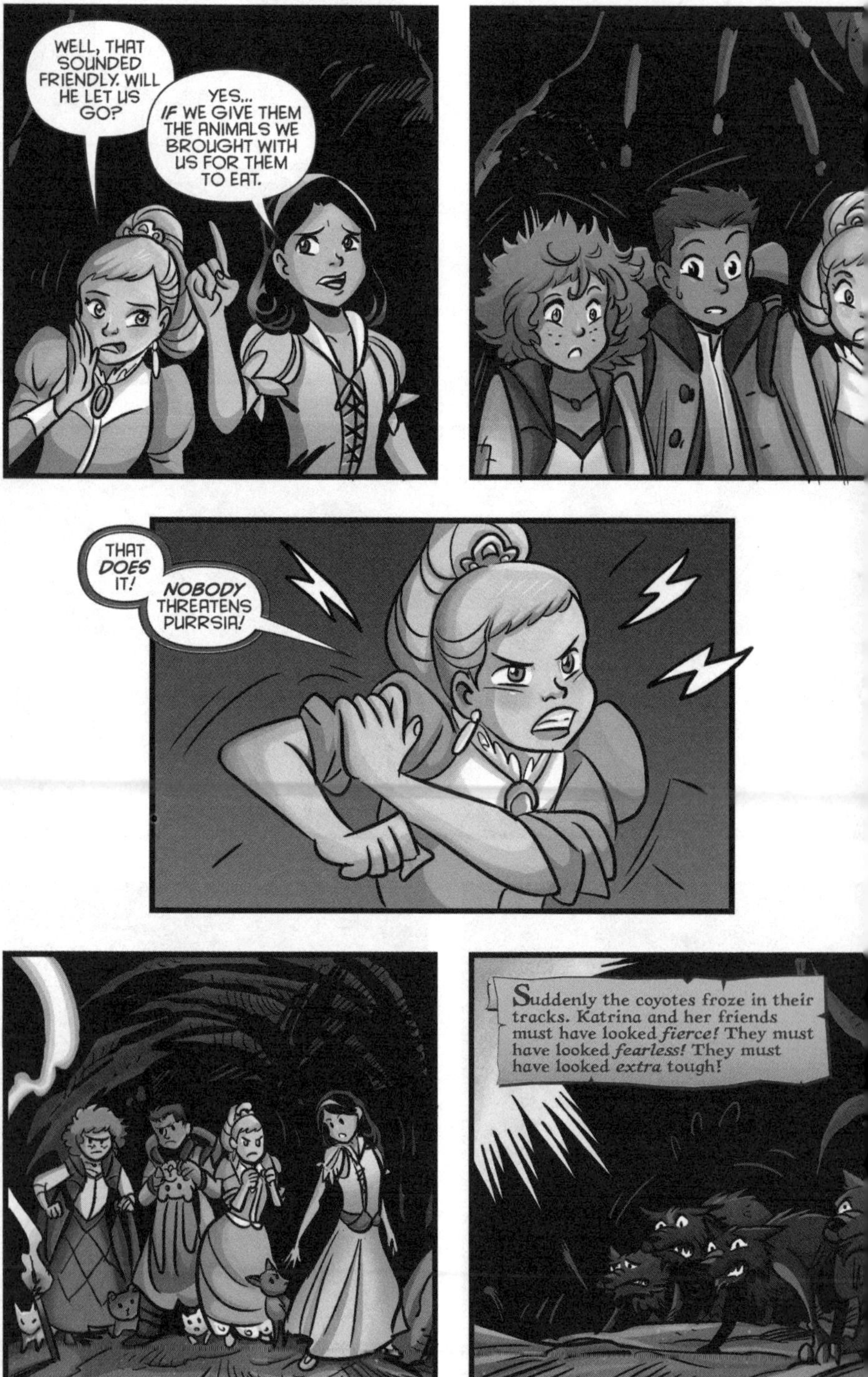
WELL, THAT SOUNDED FRIENDLY. WILL HE LET US GO?
YES... *IF* WE GIVE THEM THE ANIMALS WE BROUGHT WITH US FOR THEM TO EAT.
THAT *DOES* IT!
NOBODY THREATENS PURRSIA!
Suddenly the coyotes froze in their tracks. Katrina and her friends must have looked *fierce!* They must have looked *fearless!* They must have looked *extra* tough!

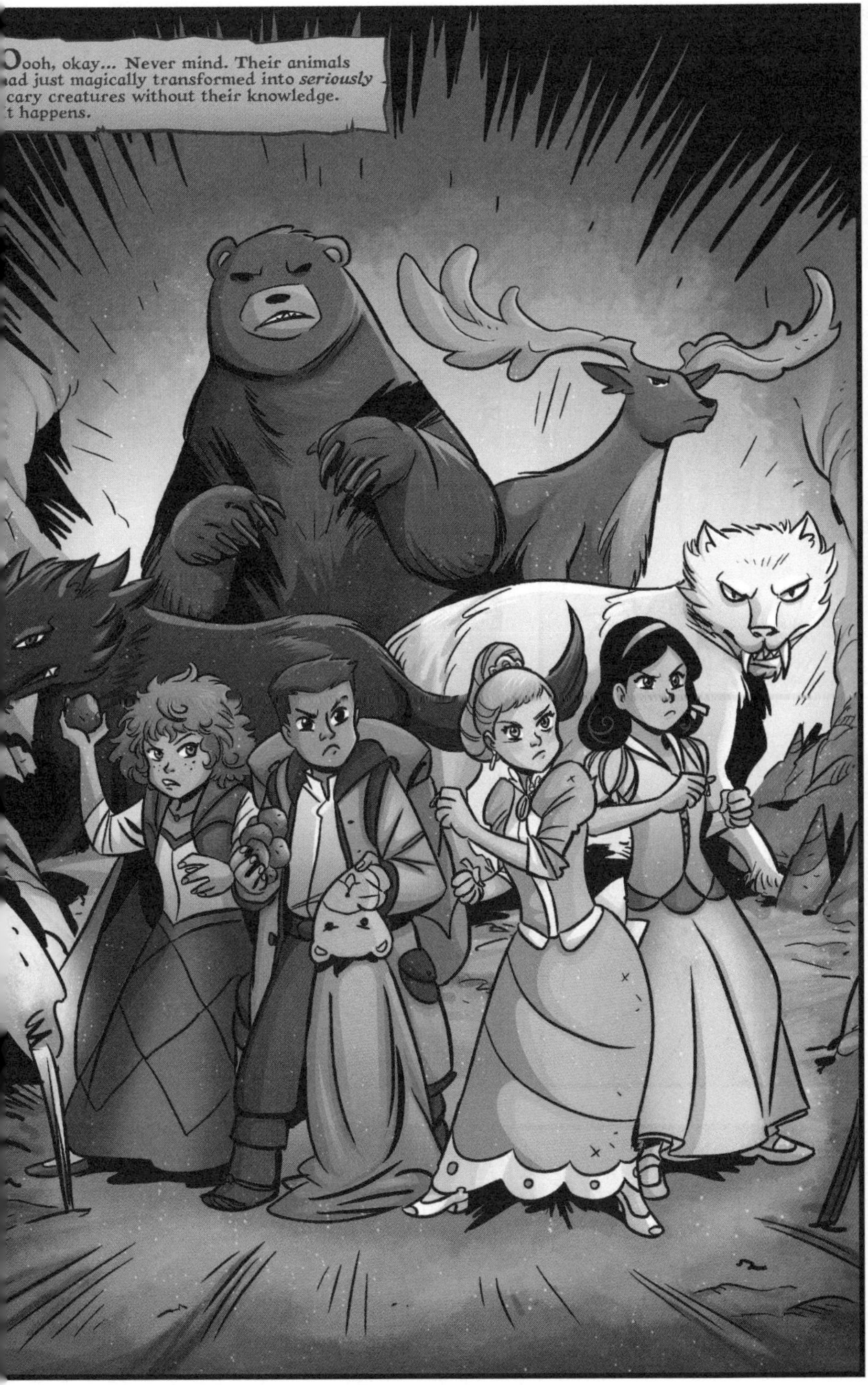
Oooh, okay... Never mind. Their animals
ad just magically transformed into *seriously*
cary creatures without their knowledge.
t happens.

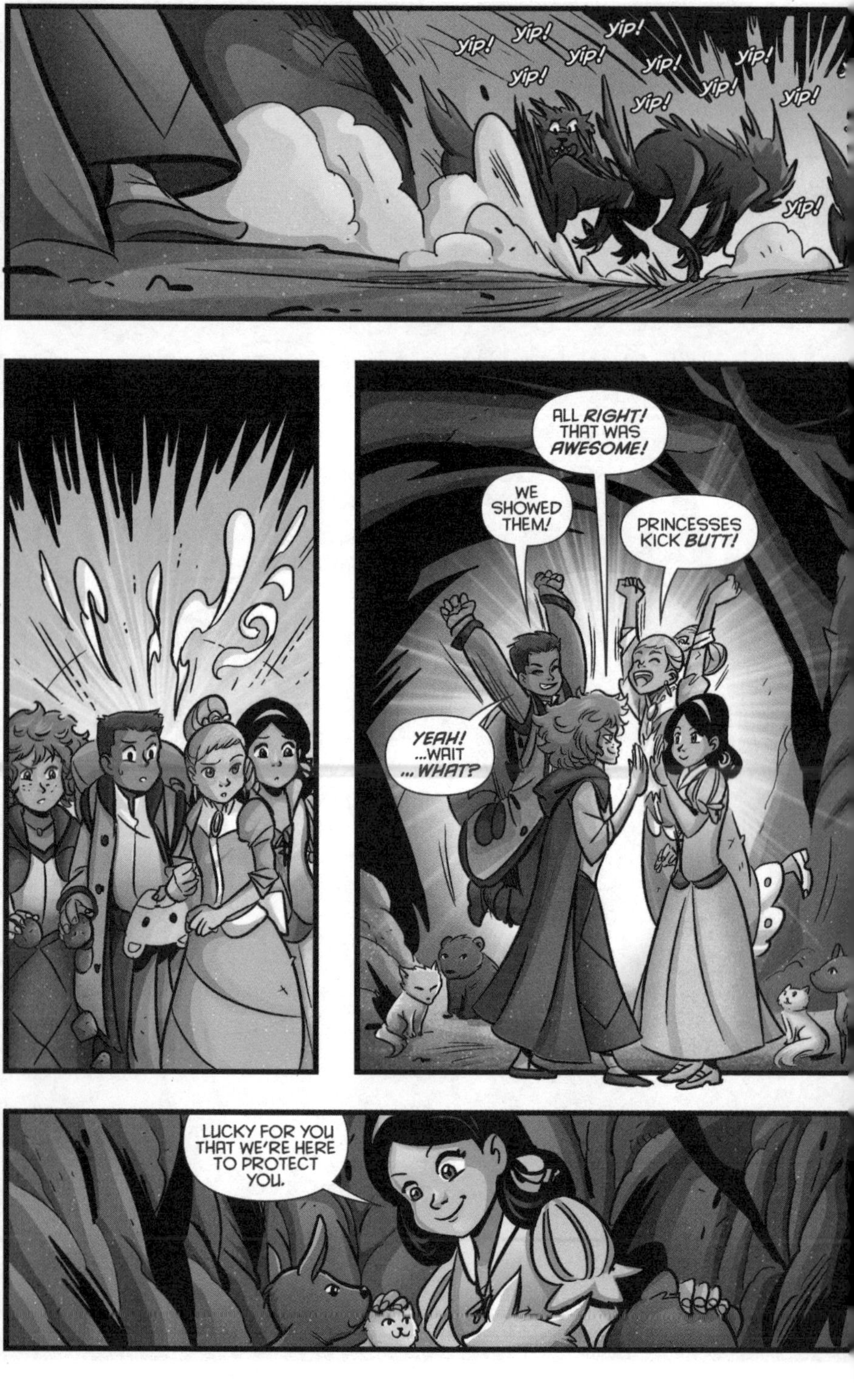

yip!
yip!
yip!
yip!
yip!
yip!
yip!
yip!
yip!
yip!
yip!
ALL RIGHT! THAT WAS AWESOME!
WE SHOWED THEM!
PRINCESSES KICK BUTT!
YEAH! ...WAIT ...WHAT?
LUCKY FOR YOU THAT WE'RE HERE TO PROTECT YOU.

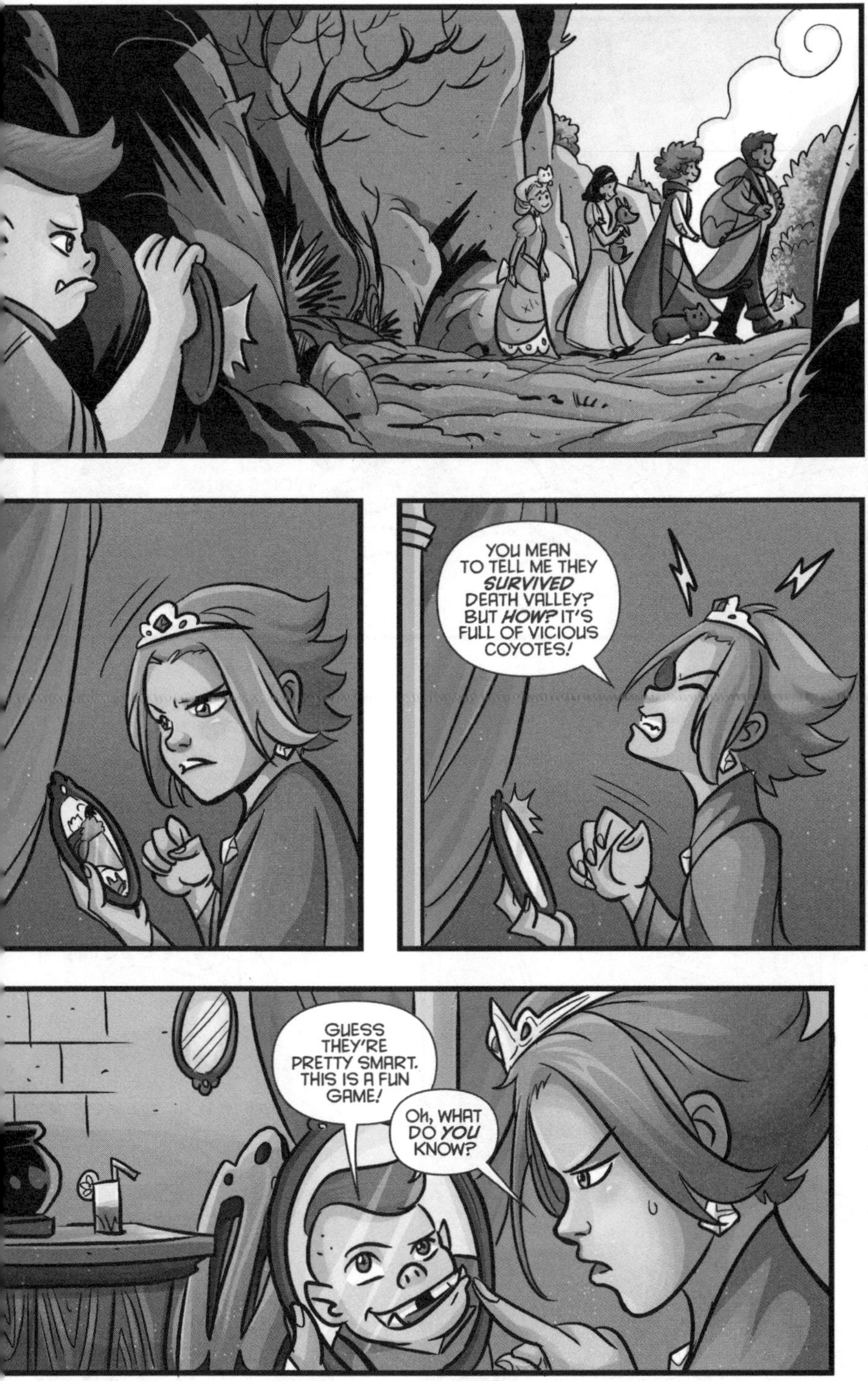
YOU MEAN TO TELL ME THEY *SURVIVED* DEATH VALLEY? BUT *HOW?* IT'S FULL OF VICIOUS COYOTES!
GUESS THEY'RE PRETTY SMART. THIS IS A FUN GAME!
Oh, WHAT DO *YOU* KNOW?

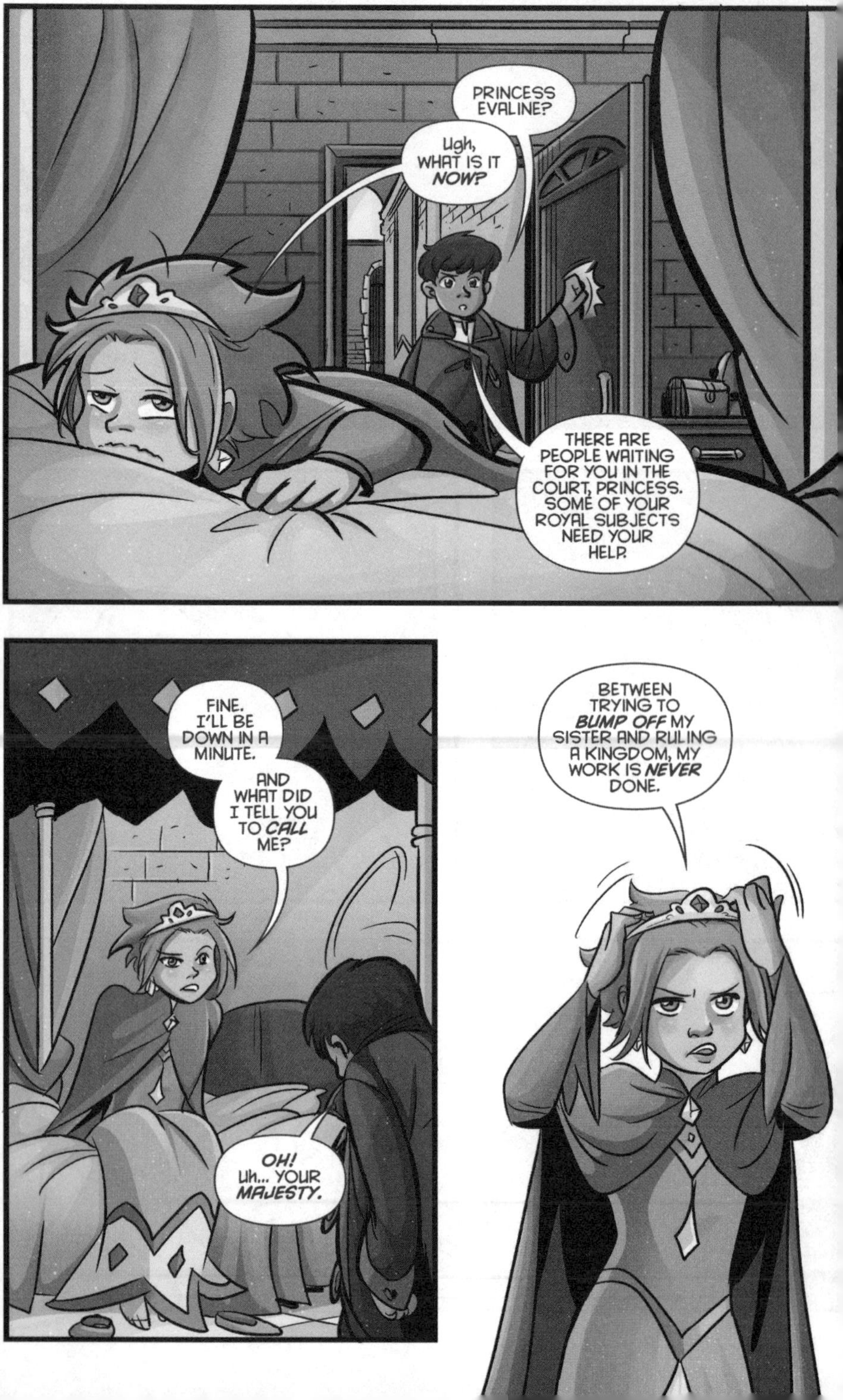
PRINCESS EVALINE?
Ugh, WHAT IS IT NOW?
THERE ARE PEOPLE WAITING FOR YOU IN THE COURT, PRINCESS. SOME OF YOUR ROYAL SUBJECTS NEED YOUR HELP.
FINE. I'LL BE DOWN IN A MINUTE.
AND WHAT DID I TELL YOU TO CALL ME?
OH! Uh... YOUR MAJESTY.
BETWEEN TRYING TO BUMP OFF MY SISTER AND RULING A KINGDOM, MY WORK IS NEVER DONE.

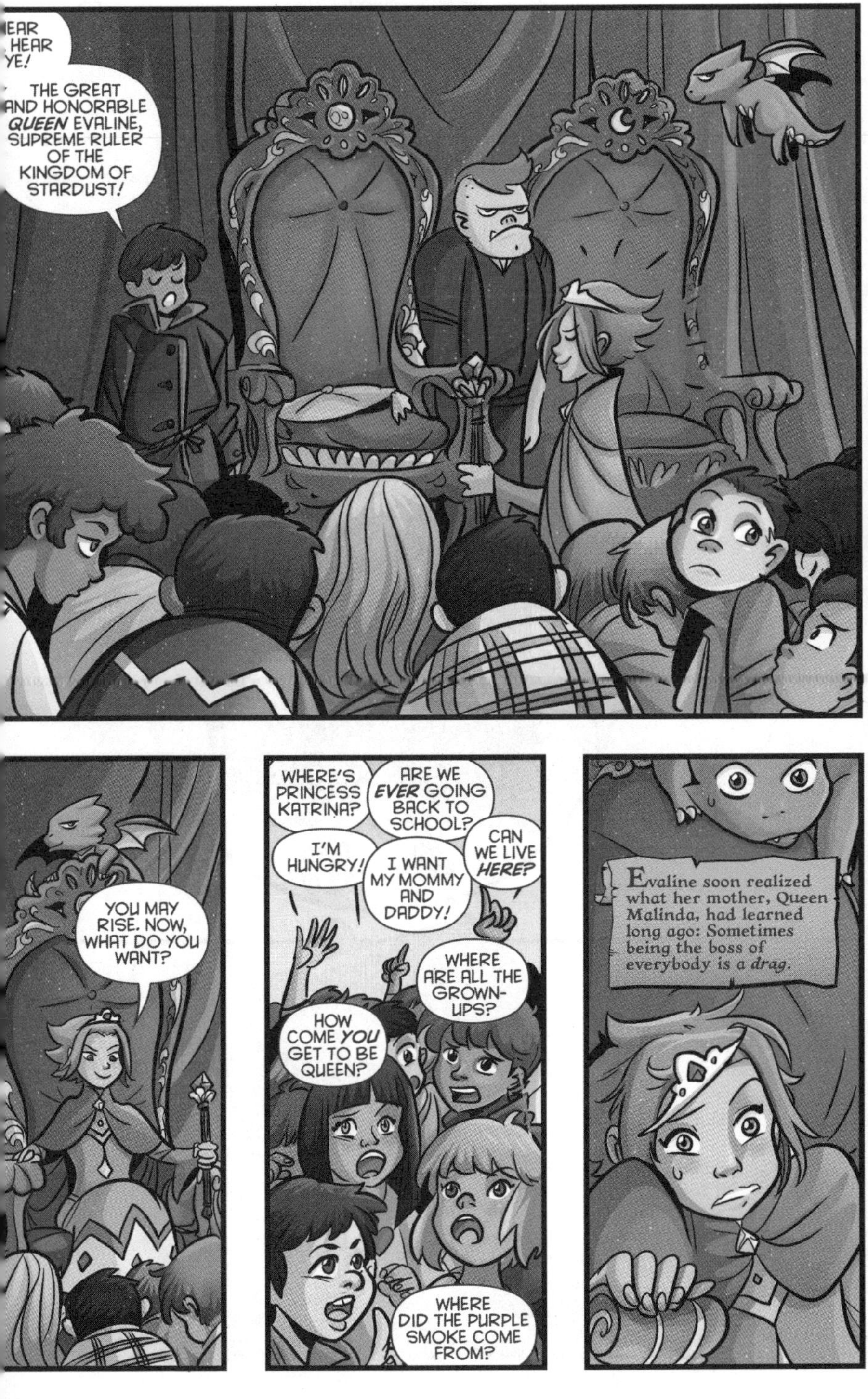

EAR HEAR YE!
THE GREAT AND HONORABLE QUEEN EVALINE, SUPREME RULER OF THE KINGDOM OF STARDUST!
YOU MAY RISE. NOW, WHAT DO YOU WANT?
WHERE'S PRINCESS KATRINA?
ARE WE EVER GOING BACK TO SCHOOL?
I'M HUNGRY!
I WANT MY MOMMY AND DADDY!
CAN WE LIVE HERE?
WHERE ARE ALL THE GROWN-UPS?
HOW COME YOU GET TO BE QUEEN?
WHERE DID THE PURPLE SMOKE COME FROM?
Evaline soon realized what her mother, Queen Malinda, had learned long ago: Sometimes being the boss of everybody is a drag.

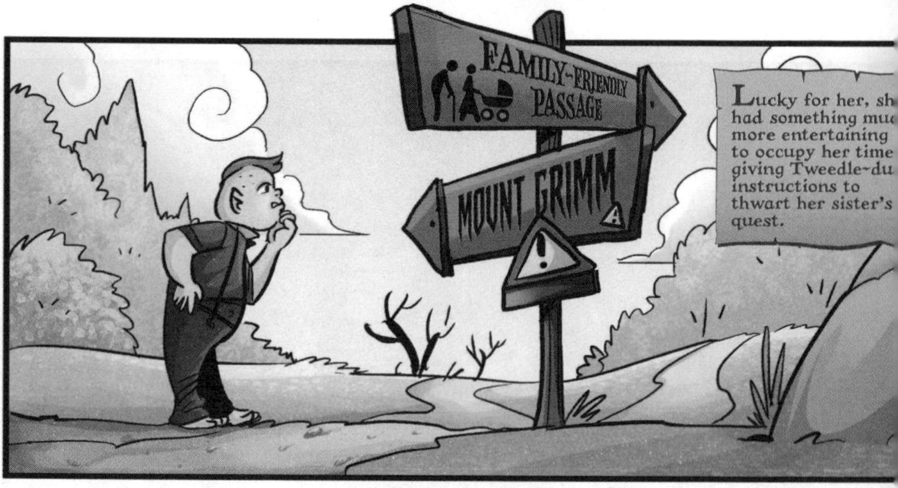
FAMILY-FRIENDLY
PASSAGE
MOUNT GRIMM
Lucky for her, sh
had something muc
more entertaining
to occupy her time
giving Tweedle-du
instructions to
thwart her sister's
quest.

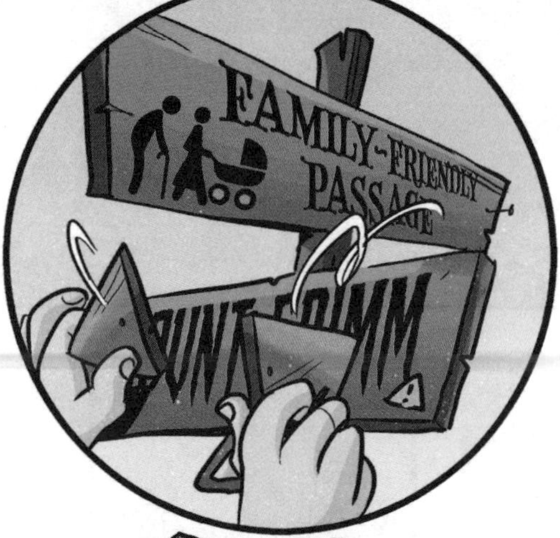
FAMILY-FRIENDLY

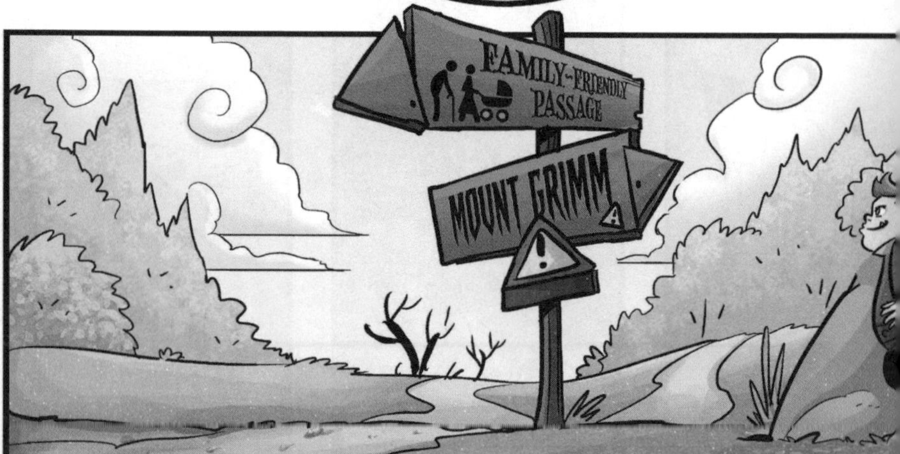
FAMILY-FRIENDLY
PASSAGE
MOUNT GRIMM

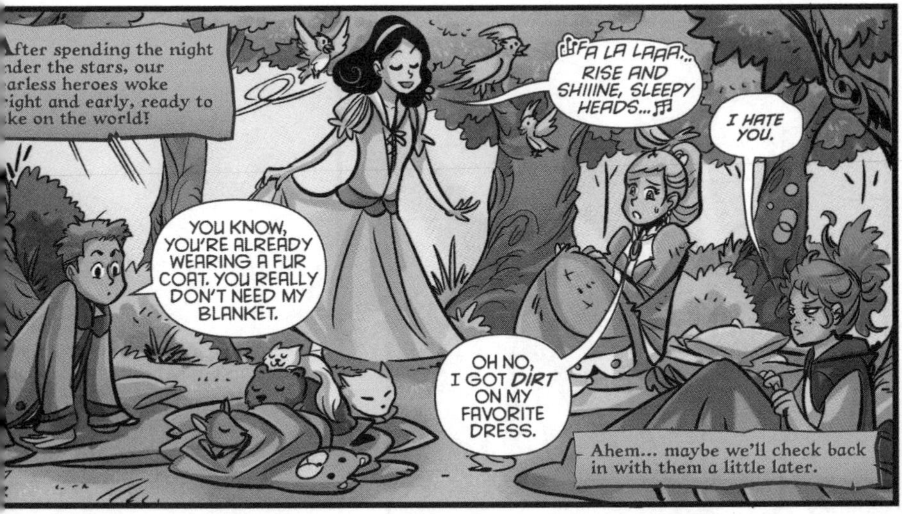
After spending the night
under the stars, our
fearless heroes woke
bright and early, ready to
take on the world!
A LA LAAA... RISE AND SHIIINE, SLEEPY HEADS...
YOU KNOW, YOU'RE ALREADY WEARING A FUR COAT. YOU REALLY DON'T NEED MY BLANKET.
I HATE YOU.
OH NO, I GOT DIRT ON MY FAVORITE DRESS.
Ahem... maybe we'll check back in with them a little later.

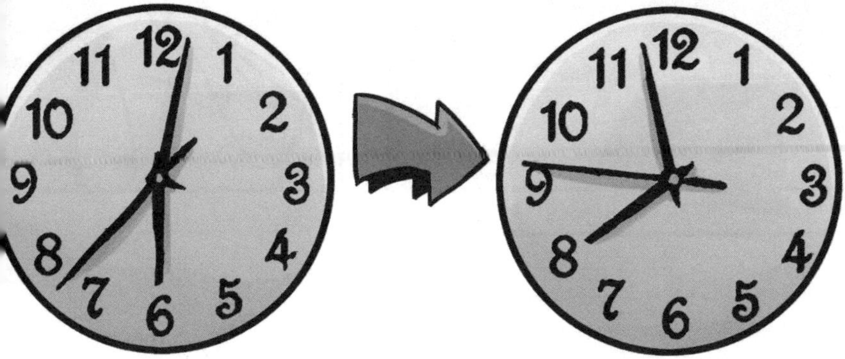
12 1 2 3 4 5 6 7 8 9 10 11
12 1 2 3 4 5 6 7 8 9 10 11

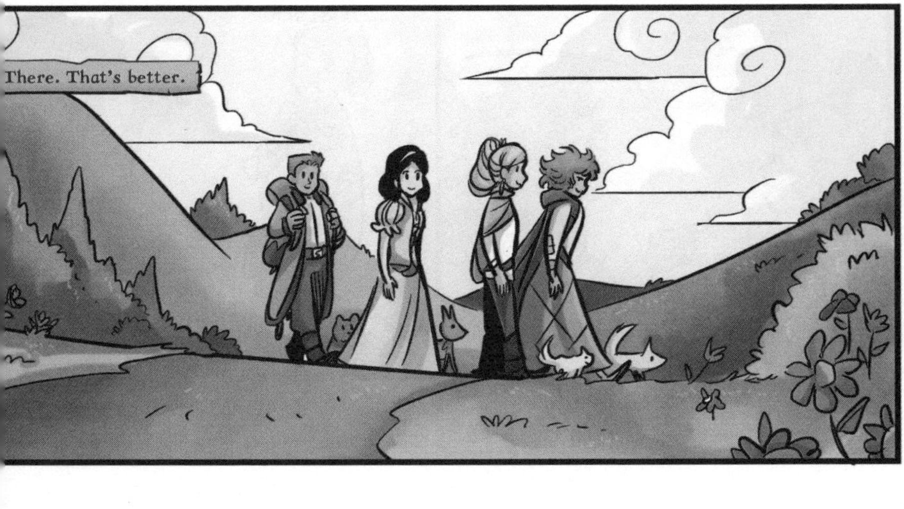
There. That's better.

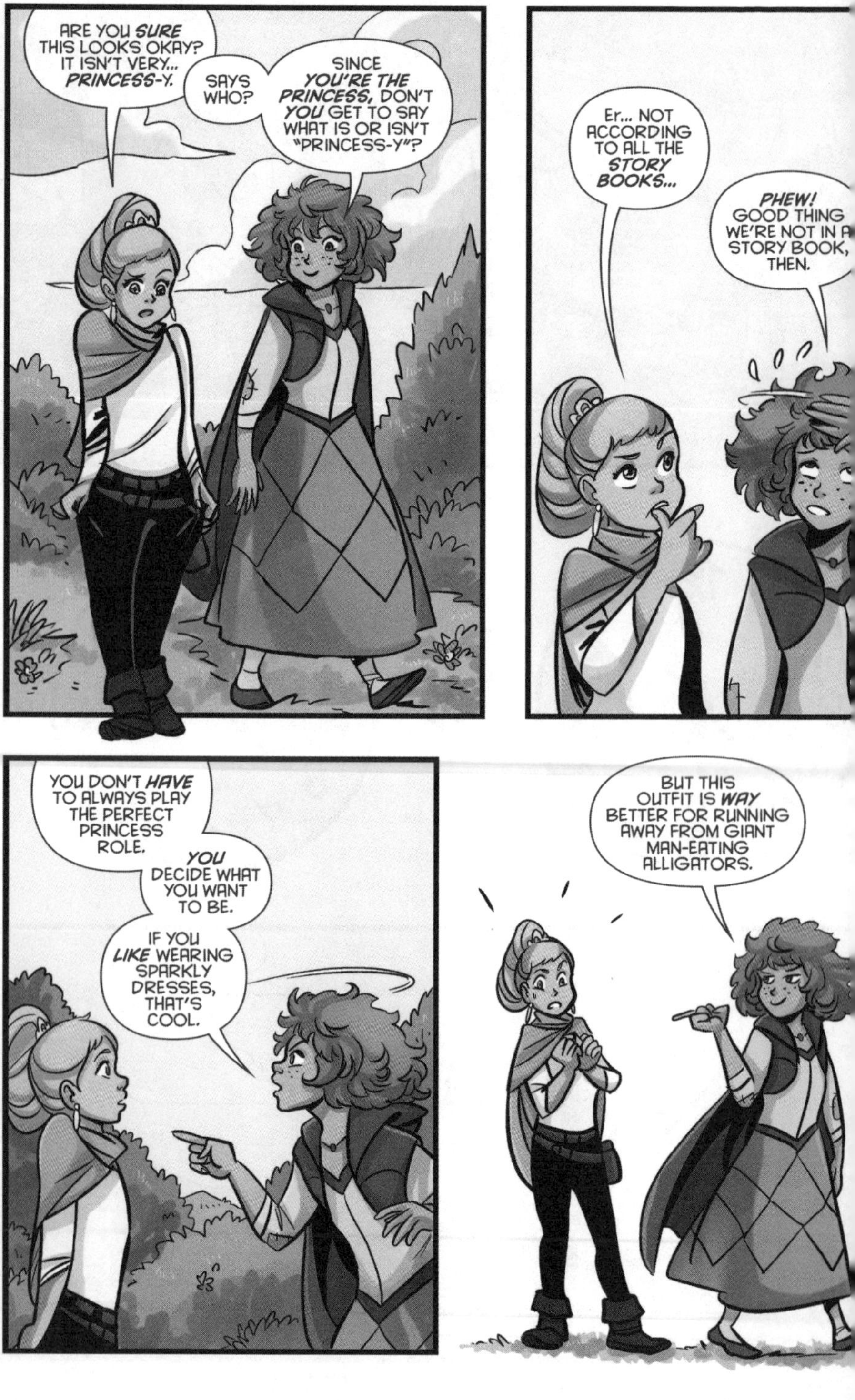
ARE YOU SURE THIS LOOKS OKAY? IT ISN'T VERY... PRINCESS-Y.
SAYS WHO?
SINCE YOU'RE THE PRINCESS, DON'T YOU GET TO SAY WHAT IS OR ISN'T "PRINCESS-Y"?
Er... NOT ACCORDING TO ALL THE STORY BOOKS...
PHEW! GOOD THING WE'RE NOT IN A STORY BOOK, THEN.
YOU DON'T HAVE TO ALWAYS PLAY THE PERFECT PRINCESS ROLE.
YOU DECIDE WHAT YOU WANT TO BE.
IF YOU LIKE WEARING SPARKLY DRESSES, THAT'S COOL.
BUT THIS OUTFIT IS WAY BETTER FOR RUNNING AWAY FROM GIANT MAN-EATING ALLIGATORS.

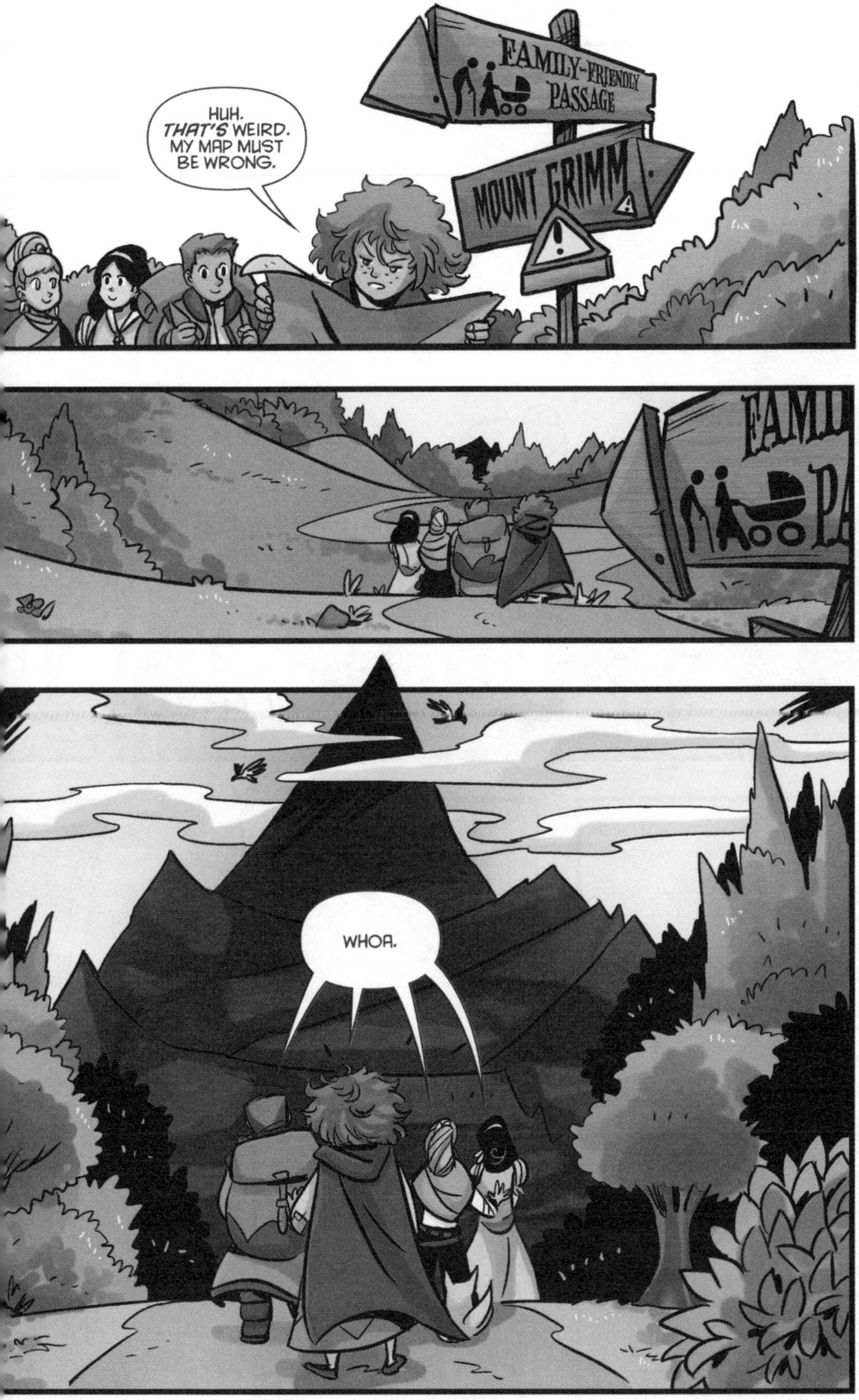
FAMILY-FRIENDLY PASSAGE
MOUNT GRIMM
HUH. THAT'S WEIRD. MY MAP MUST BE WRONG.
WHOA.

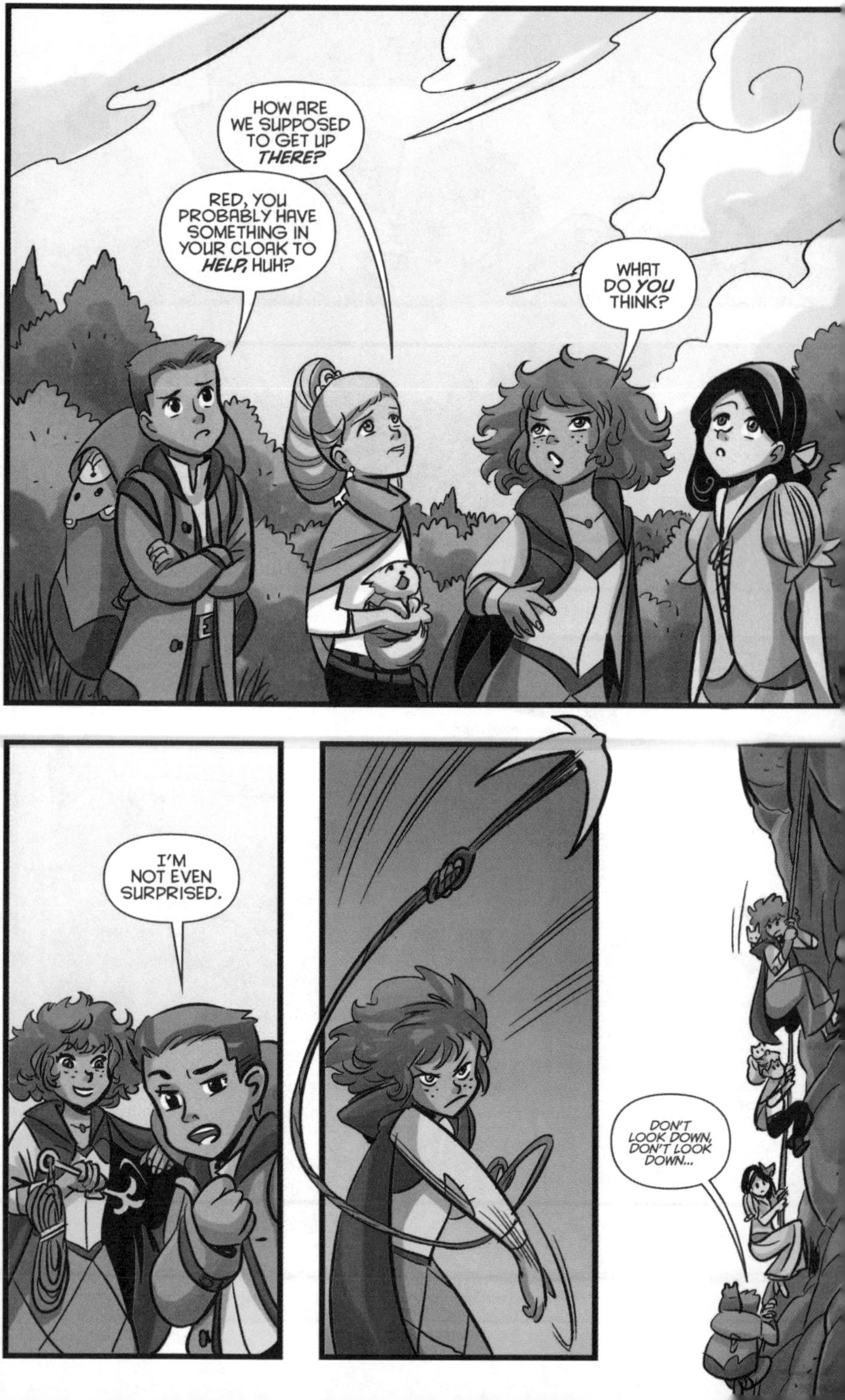
RED, YOU PROBABLY HAVE SOMETHING IN YOUR CLOAK TO *HELP,* HUH?
HOW ARE WE SUPPOSED TO GET UP *THERE?*
WHAT DO *YOU* THINK?
I'M NOT EVEN SURPRISED.
DON'T LOOK DOWN, DON'T LOOK DOWN...

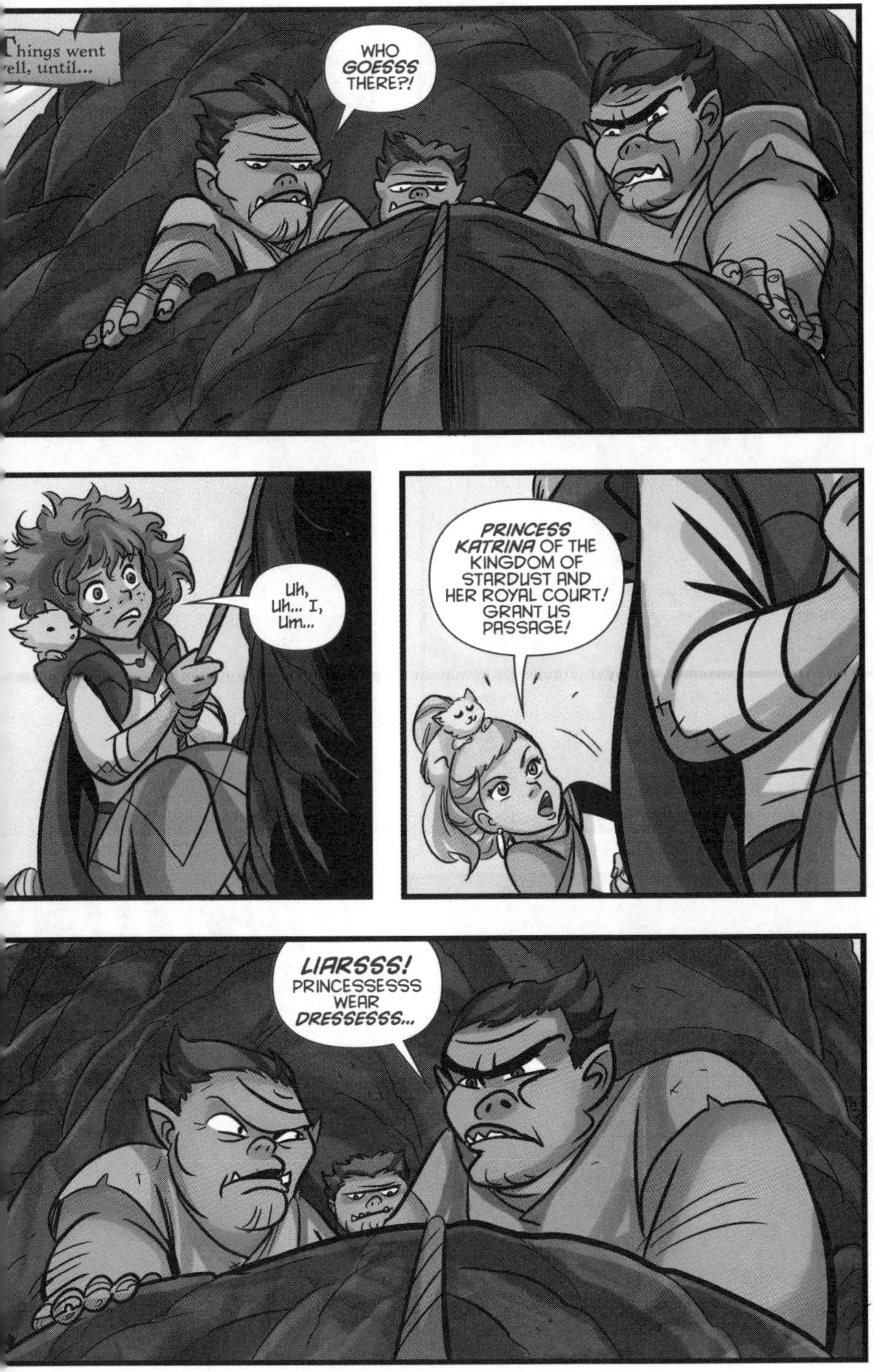

Things went
well, until...
WHO GOESSS THERE?!
Uh, uh... I, um...
PRINCESS KATRINA OF THE KINGDOM OF STARDUST AND HER ROYAL COURT! GRANT US PASSAGE!
LIARSSS! PRINCESSESSS WEAR DRESSESSS...

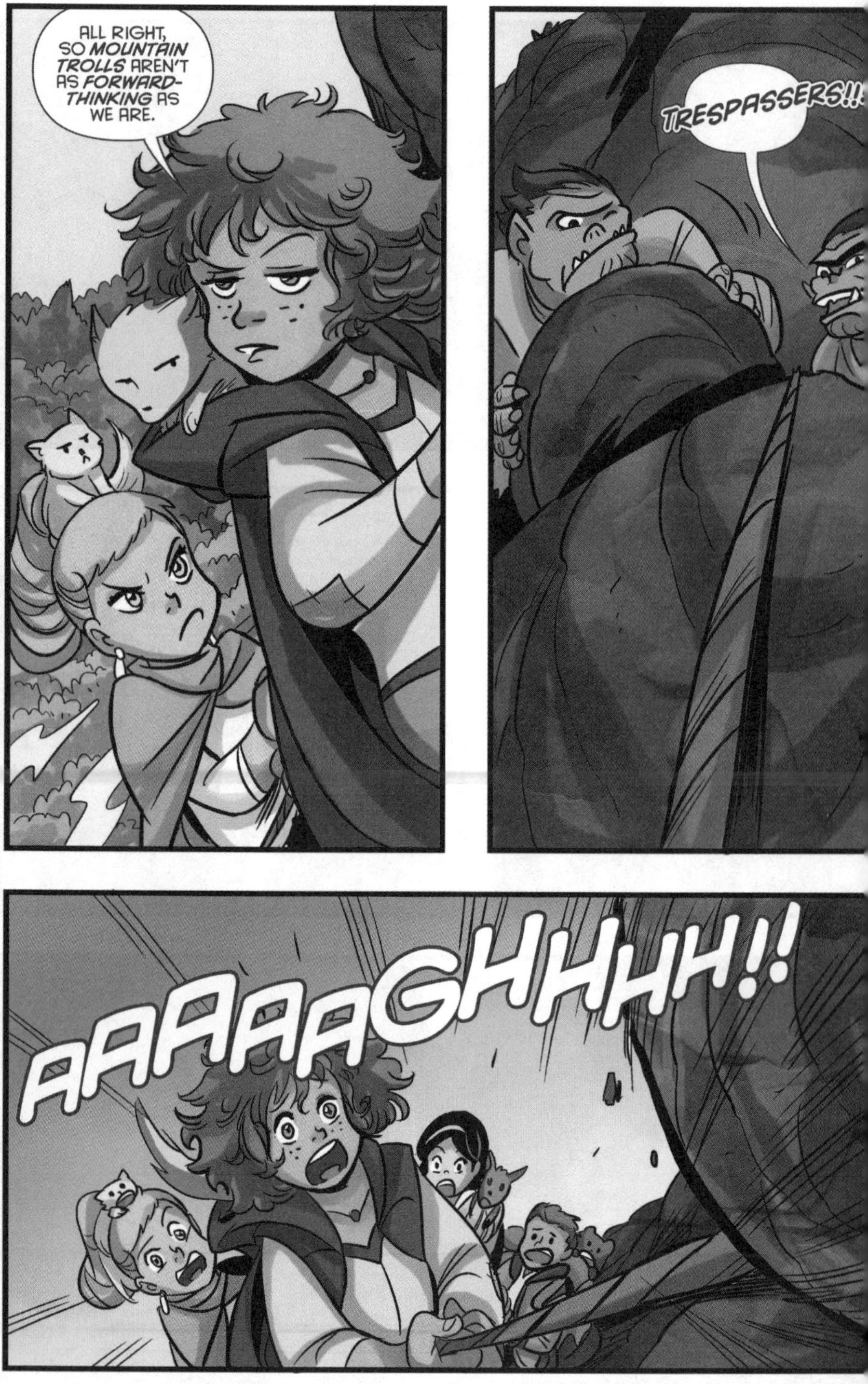
ALL RIGHT, SO MOUNTAIN TROLLS AREN'T AS FORWARD-THINKING AS WE ARE.
TRESPASSERS!!
AAAAAAGHHHHH!!

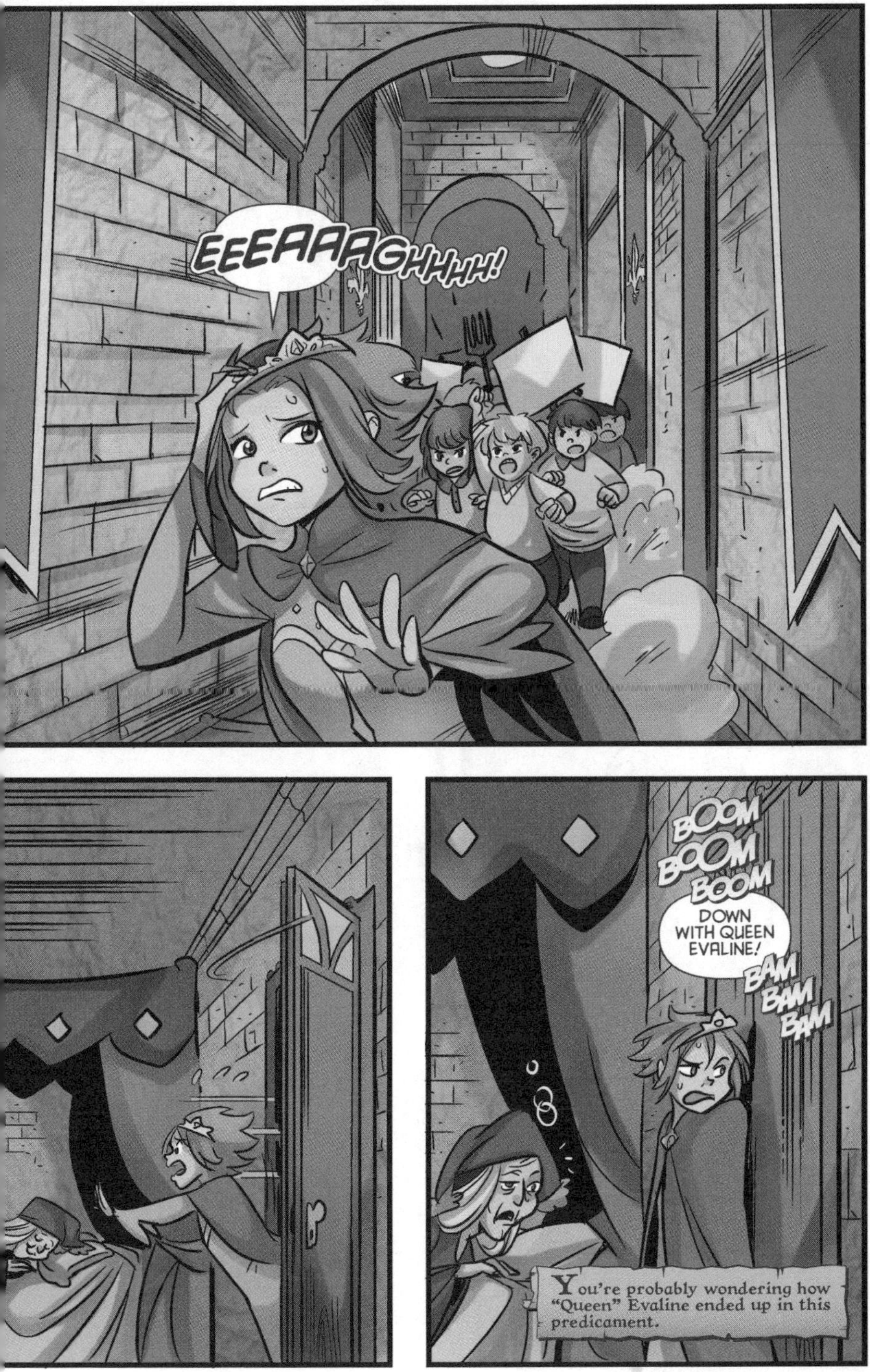
EEEAAAAGHHHH!
BOOM
BOOM
BOOM
DOWN WITH QUEEN EVALINE!
BAM
BAM
BAM
You're probably wondering how "Queen" Evaline ended up in this predicament.

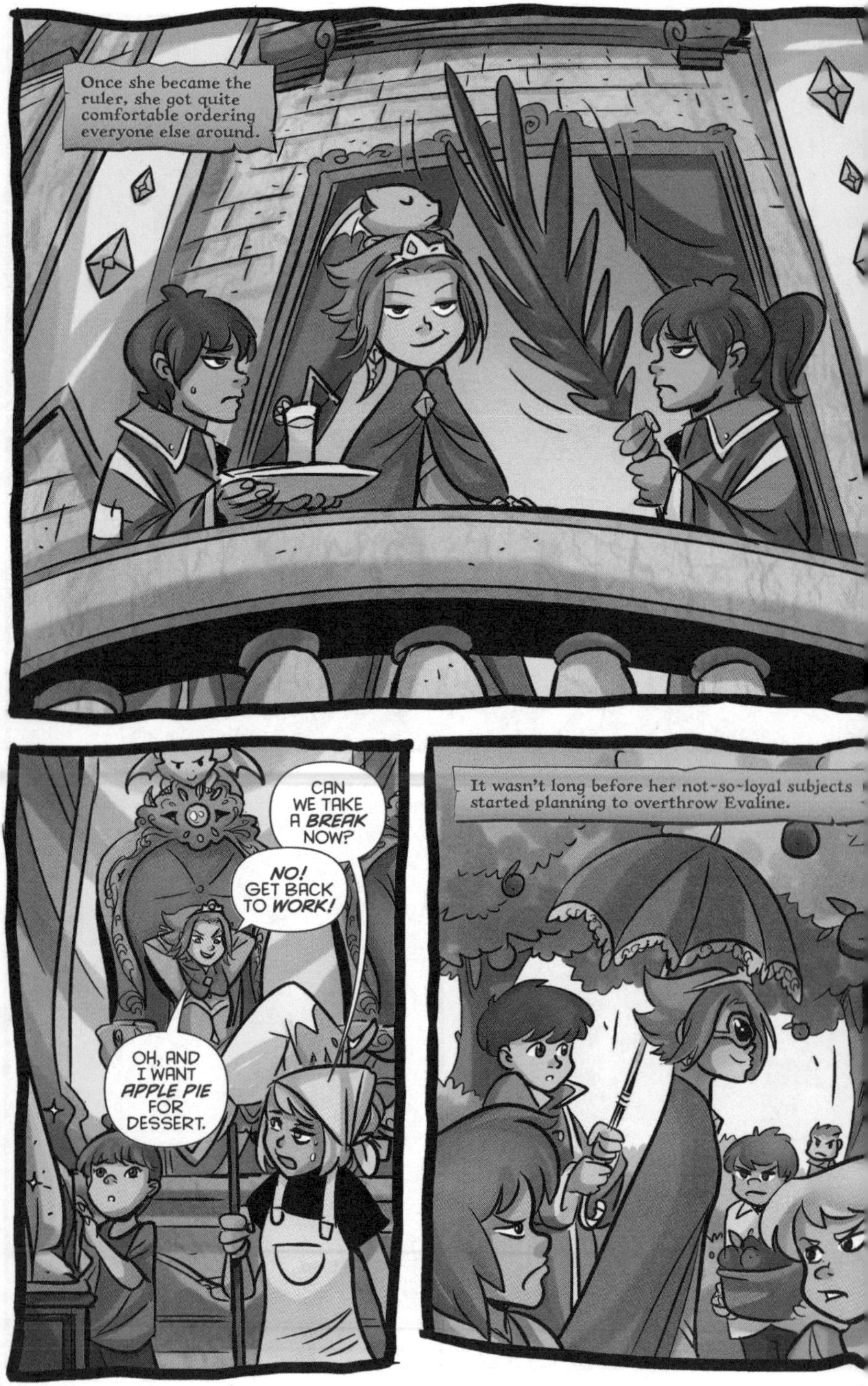

Once she became the ruler, she got quite comfortable ordering everyone else around.
CAN WE TAKE A BREAK NOW?
NO! GET BACK TO WORK!
OH, AND I WANT APPLE PIE FOR DESSERT.
It wasn't long before her not-so-loyal subjects started planning to overthrow Evaline.

EVERYBODY SWING LEFT...
NOW!

HERE COMES ANOTHER ONE. TO THE RIGHT...
NOW!

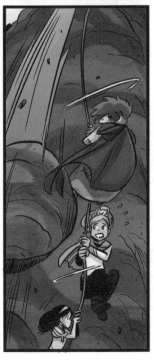

NOOOO!

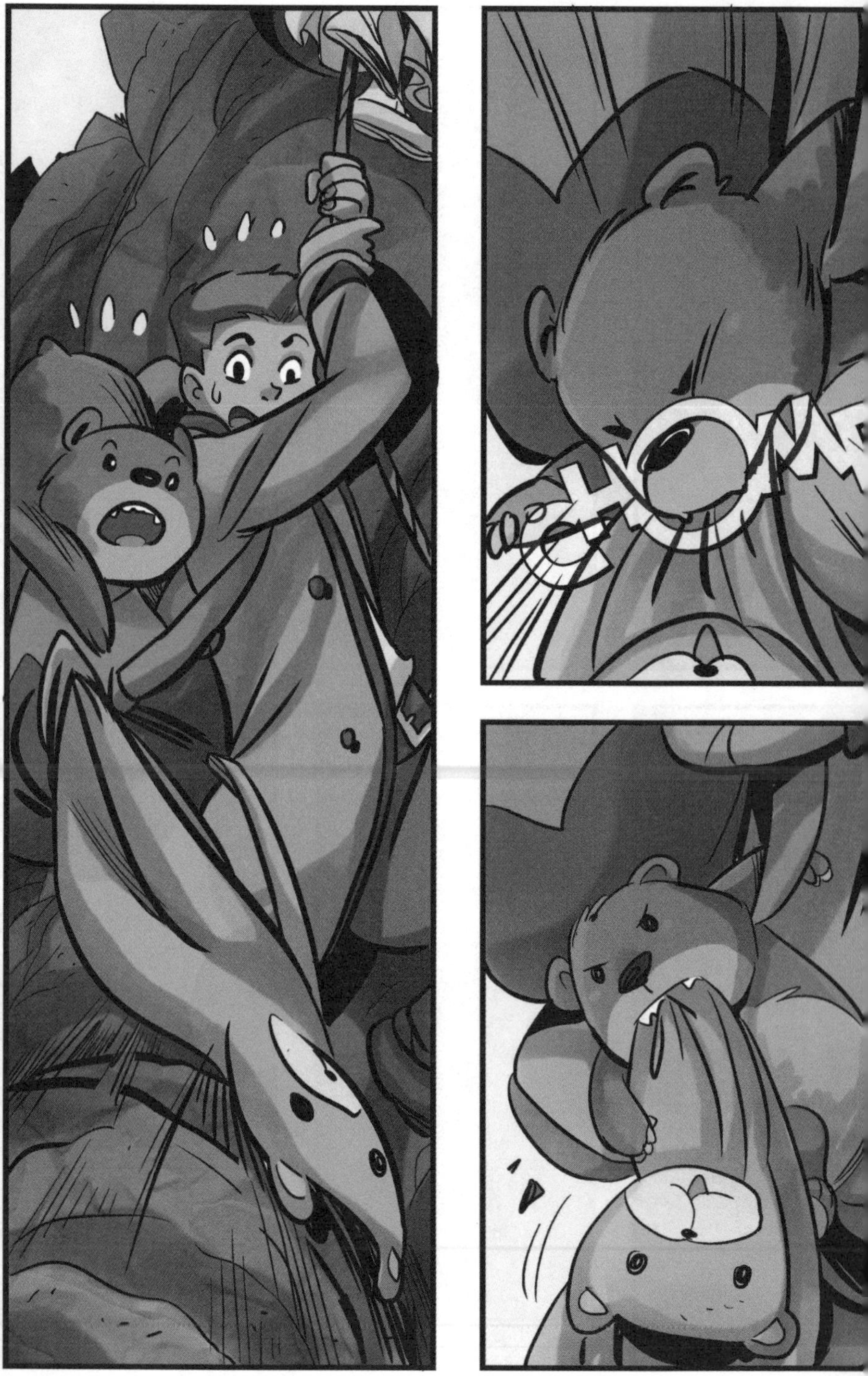
CHOM

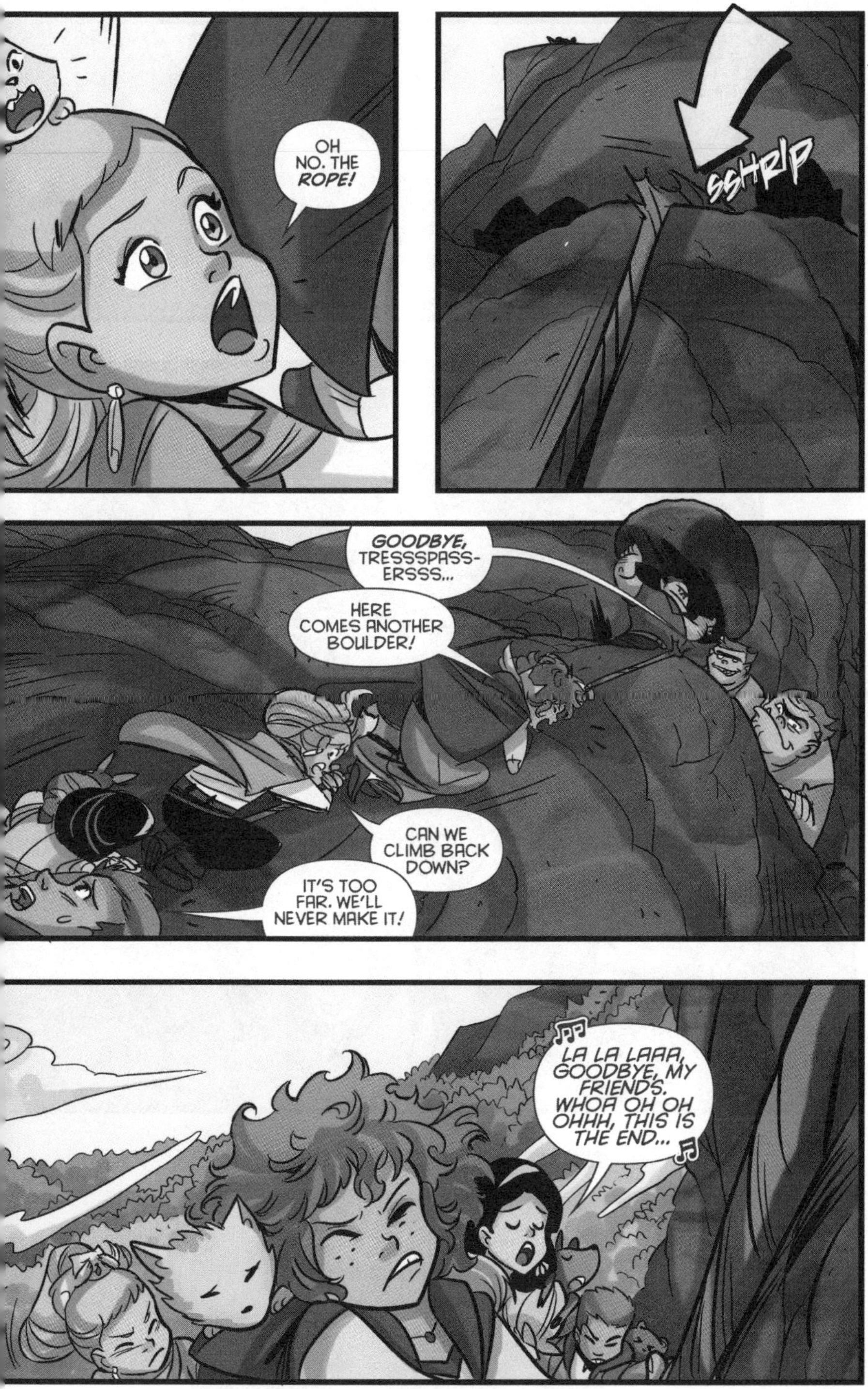

OH NO. THE *ROPE!*
SSHRIP
GOODBYE, TRESSSPASS-ERSSS...
HERE COMES ANOTHER BOULDER!
CAN WE CLIMB BACK DOWN?
IT'S TOO FAR. WE'LL NEVER MAKE IT!
LA LA LAAA, GOODBYE, MY FRIENDS. WHOA OH OH OHHH, THIS IS THE END...

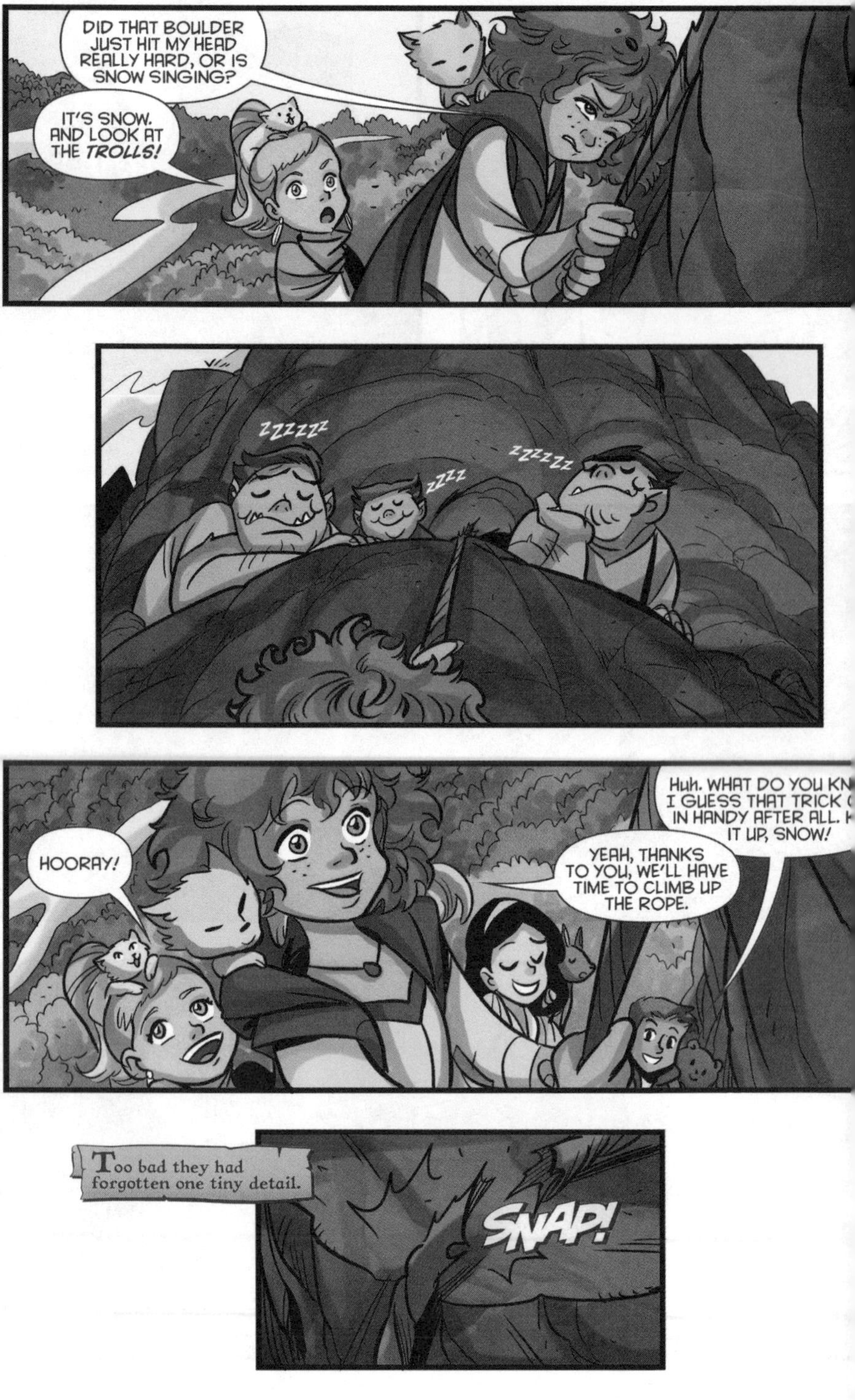
DID THAT BOULDER JUST HIT MY HEAD REALLY HARD, OR IS SNOW SINGING?
IT'S SNOW. AND LOOK AT THE *TROLLS!*
ZZZZZZ
ZZZZ
ZZZZZZ
HOORAY!
Huh. WHAT DO YOU KN
I GUESS THAT TRICK
IN HANDY AFTER ALL.
IT UP, SNOW!
YEAH, THANKS TO YOU, WE'LL HAVE TIME TO CLIMB UP THE ROPE.
Too bad they had forgotten one tiny detail.
SNAP!

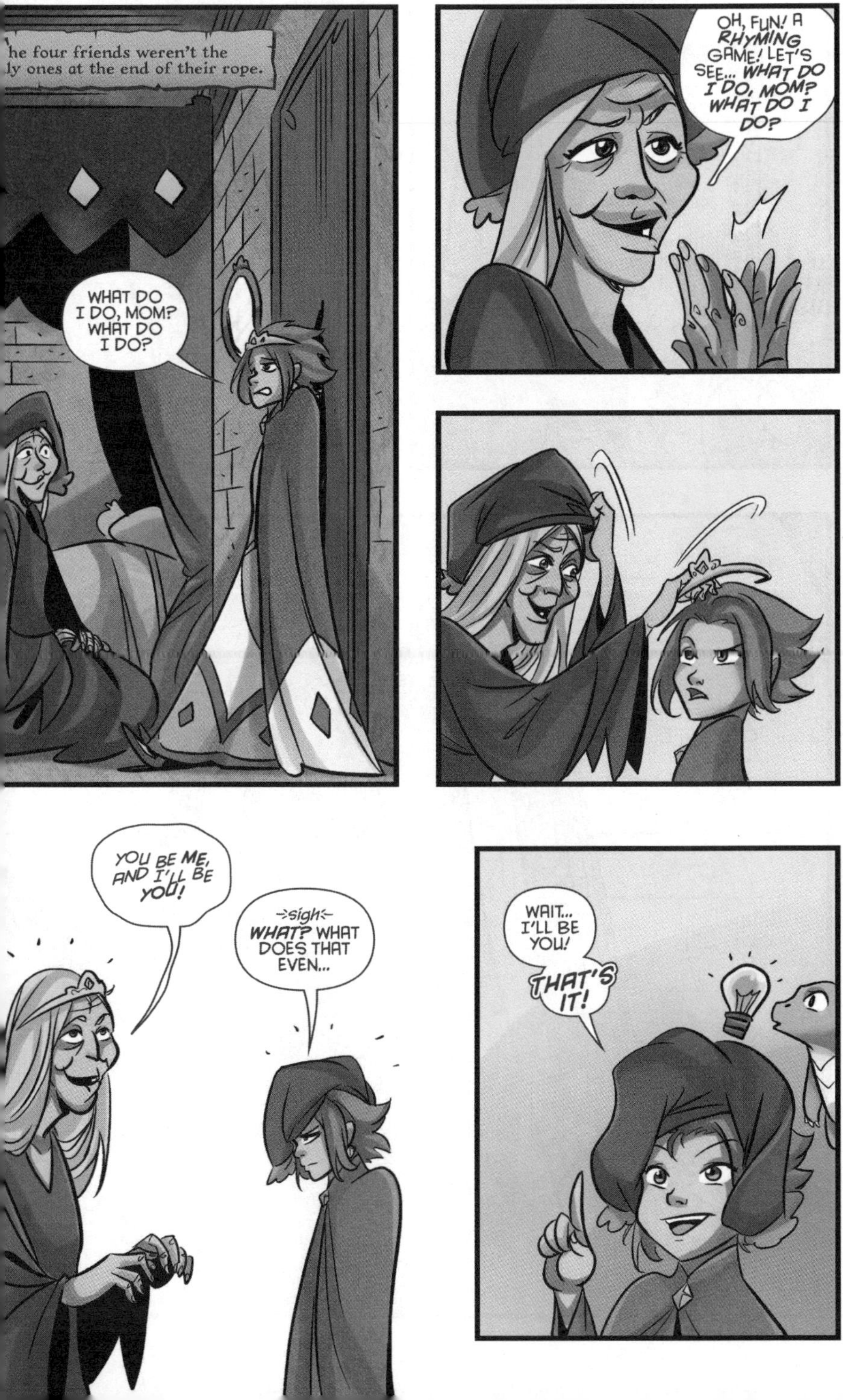
he four friends weren't the
ly ones at the end of their rope.
WHAT DO I DO, MOM? WHAT DO I DO?
OH, FUN! A RHYMING GAME! LET'S SEE... WHAT DO I DO, MOM? WHAT DO I DO?
YOU BE ME, AND I'LL BE YOU!
~sigh~ WHAT? WHAT DOES THAT EVEN...
WAIT... I'LL BE YOU!
THAT'S IT!

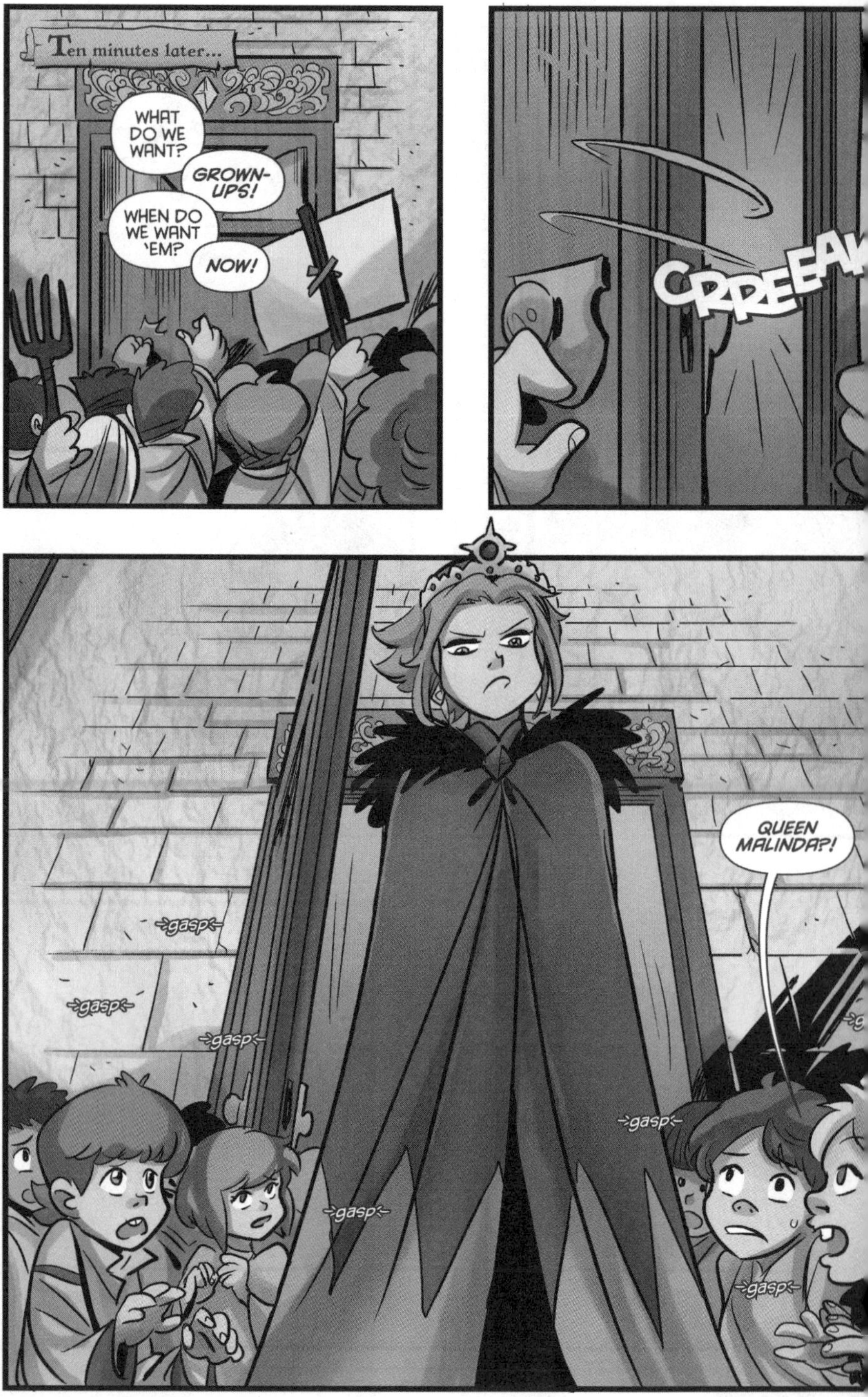
Ten minutes later...
WHAT DO WE WANT?
GROWN-UPS!
WHEN DO WE WANT 'EM?
NOW!
CRREEAK
~gasp~
~gasp~
~gasp~
~gasp~
~gasp~
QUEEN MALINDA?!
~gasp~

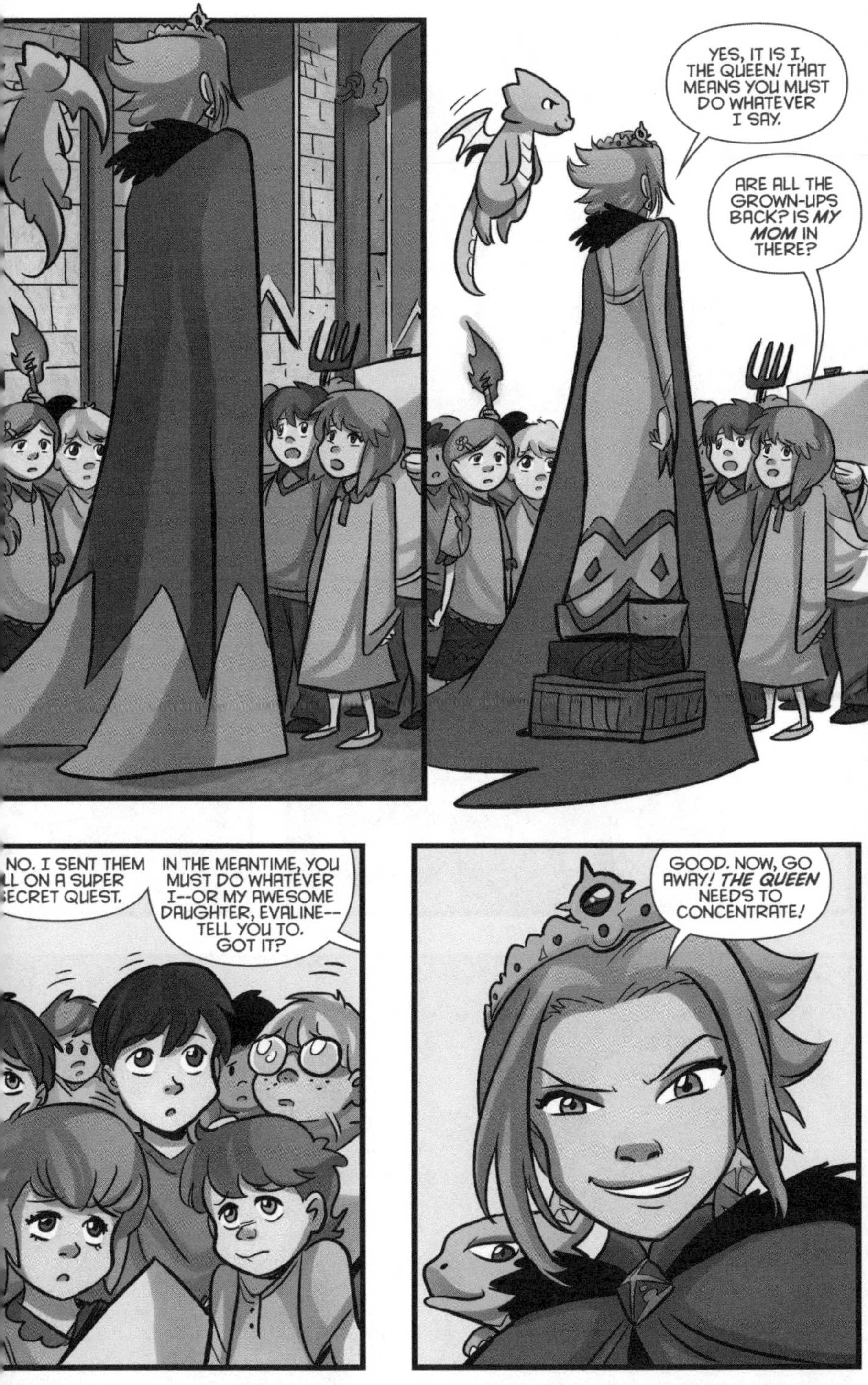
YES, IT IS I, THE QUEEN! THAT MEANS YOU MUST DO WHATEVER I SAY.
ARE ALL THE GROWN-UPS BACK? IS *MY MOM* IN THERE?
NO. I SENT THEM
LL ON A SUPER
ECRET QUEST.
IN THE MEANTIME, YOU MUST DO WHATEVER I--OR MY AWESOME DAUGHTER, EVALINE--TELL YOU TO. GOT IT?
GOOD. NOW, GO AWAY! *THE QUEEN* NEEDS TO CONCENTRATE!

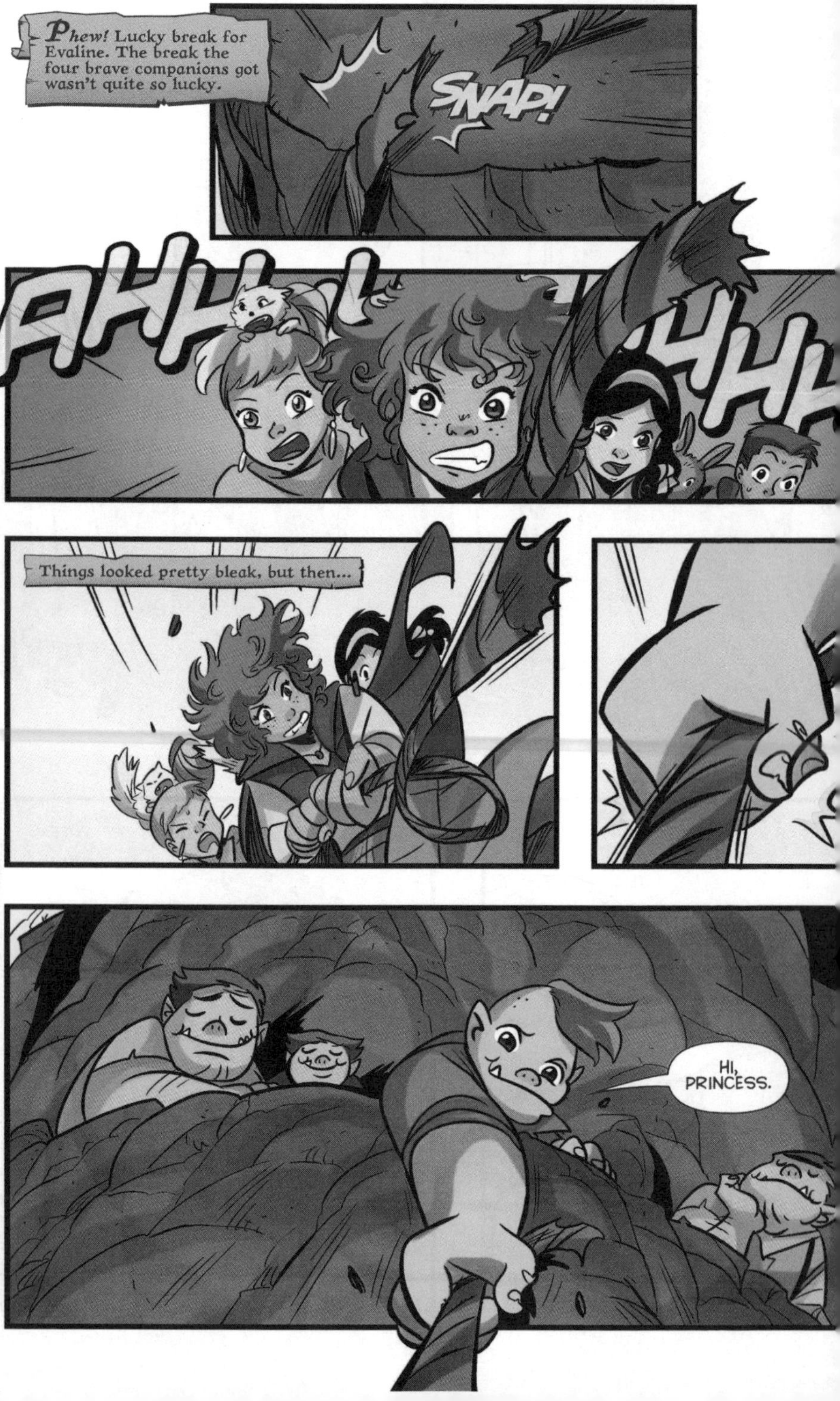
Phew! Lucky break for Evaline. The break the four brave companions got wasn't quite so lucky.
SNAP!
AHH...HHHH
Things looked pretty bleak, but then...
HI, PRINCESS.

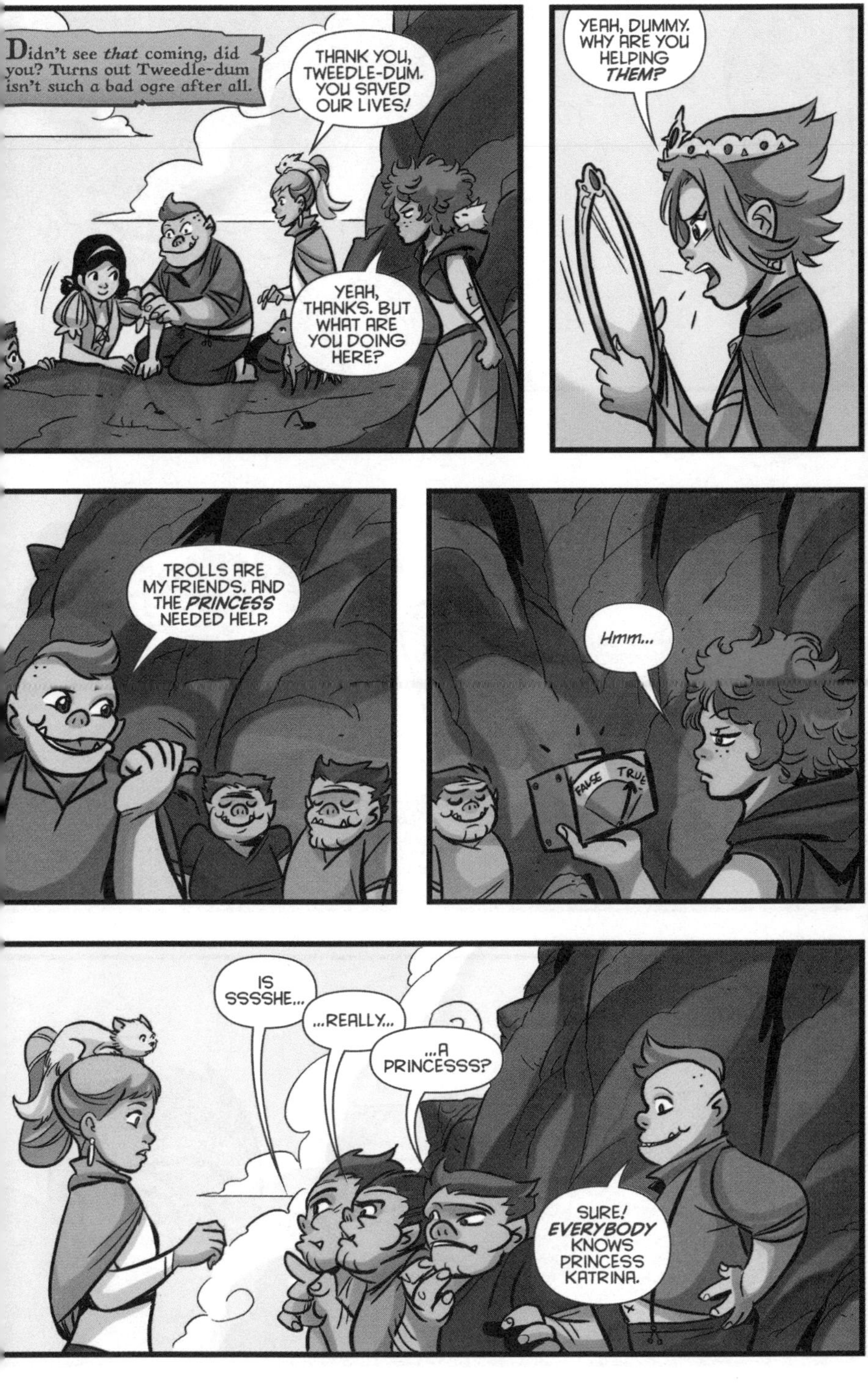

Didn't see *that* coming, did you? Turns out Tweedle-dum isn't such a bad ogre after all.
THANK YOU, TWEEDLE-DUM. YOU SAVED OUR LIVES!
YEAH, THANKS. BUT WHAT ARE YOU DOING HERE?
YEAH, DUMMY. WHY ARE YOU HELPING *THEM?*
TROLLS ARE MY FRIENDS. AND THE *PRINCESS* NEEDED HELP.
Hmm...
FALSE TRUE
IS SSSSHE...
...REALLY...
...A PRINCESSS?
SURE! *EVERYBODY* KNOWS PRINCESS KATRINA.

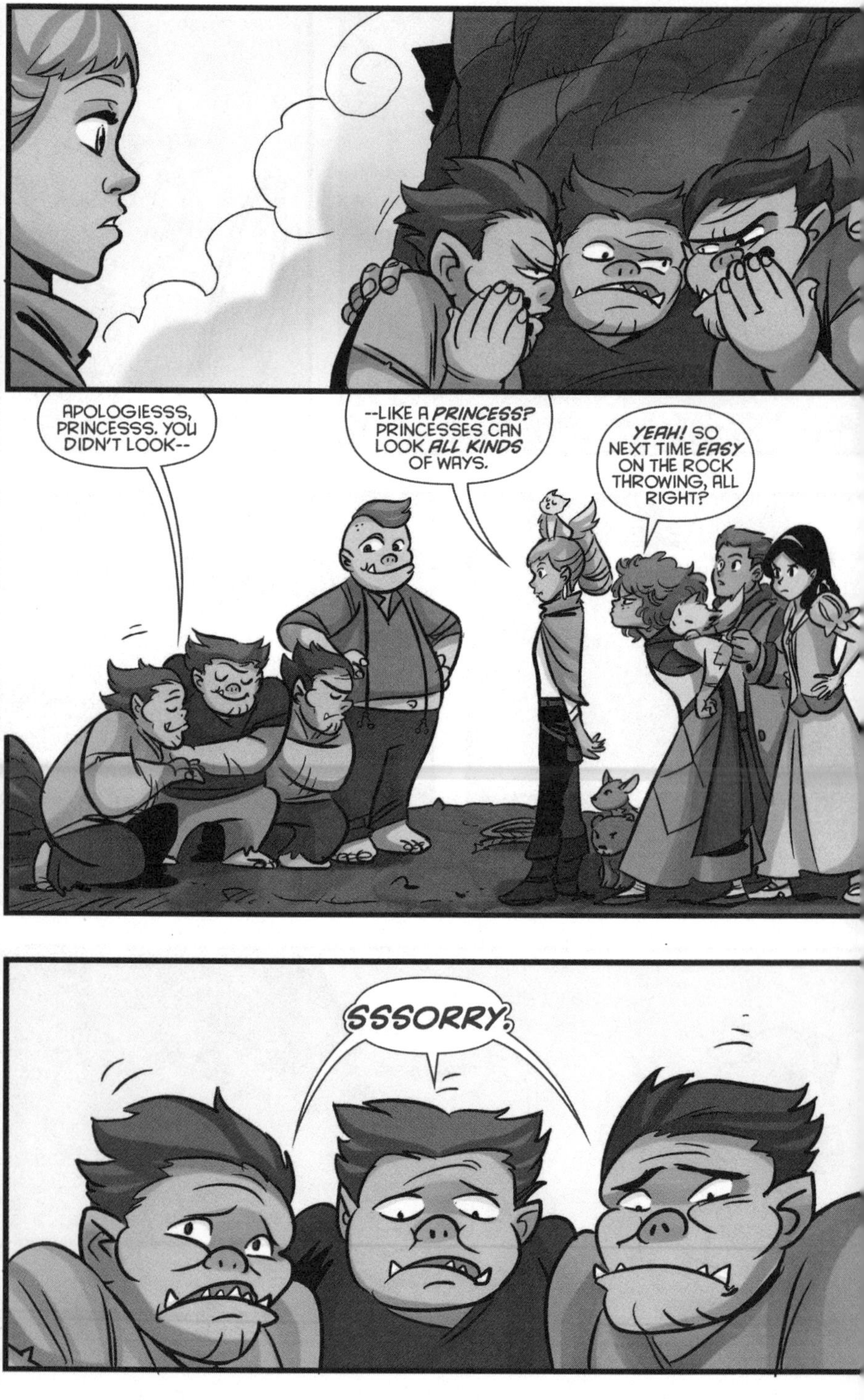
APOLOGIESSS, PRINCESSS. YOU DIDN'T LOOK--
--LIKE A PRINCESS? PRINCESSES CAN LOOK ALL KINDS OF WAYS.
YEAH! SO NEXT TIME EASY ON THE ROCK THROWING, ALL RIGHT?
SSSORRY.

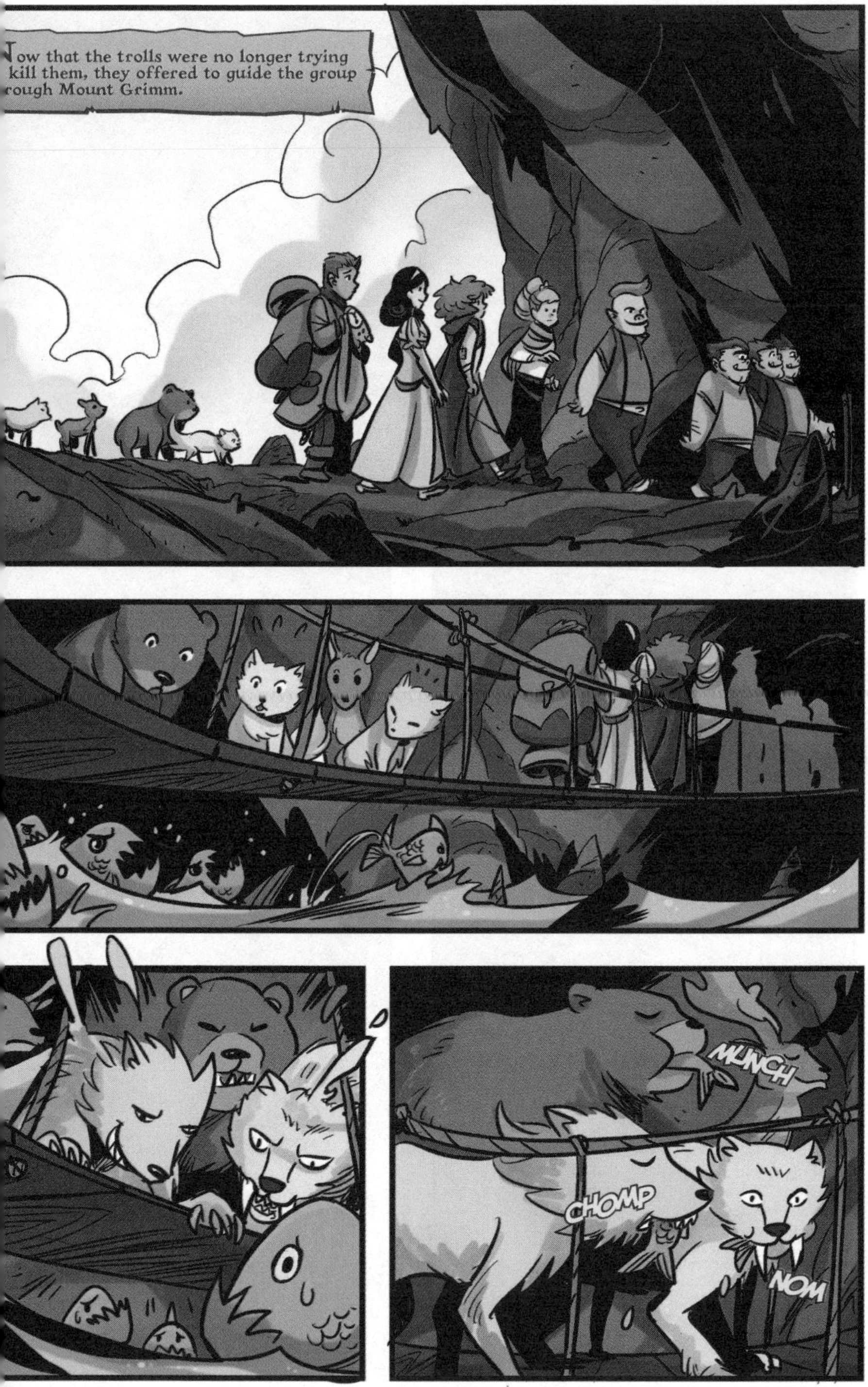

Now that the trolls were no longer trying
kill them, they offered to guide the group
rough Mount Grimm.
MUNCH
CHOMP
NOM

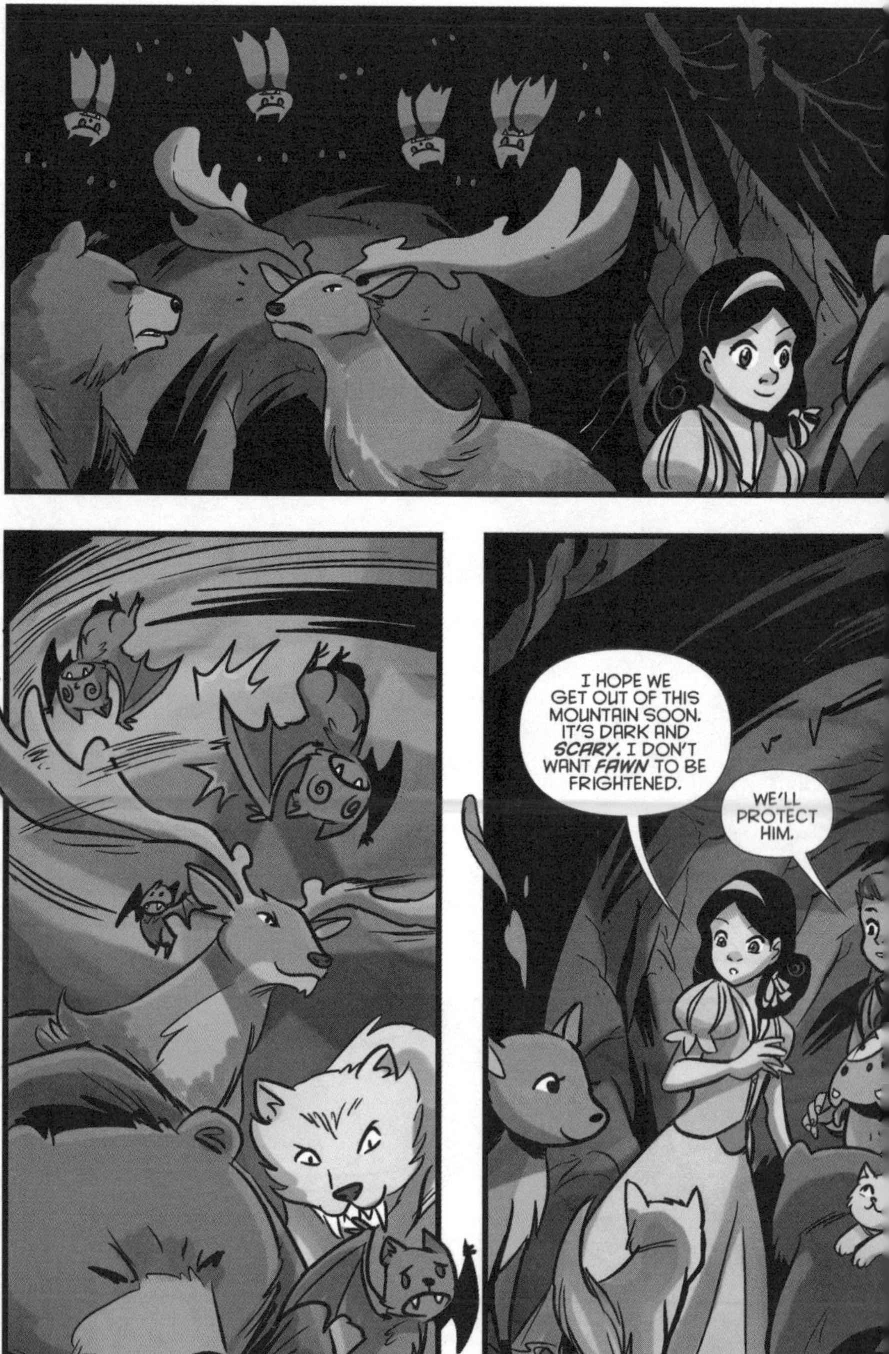
I HOPE WE GET OUT OF THIS MOUNTAIN SOON. IT'S DARK AND SCARY. I DON'T WANT FAWN TO BE FRIGHTENED.
WE'LL PROTECT HIM.

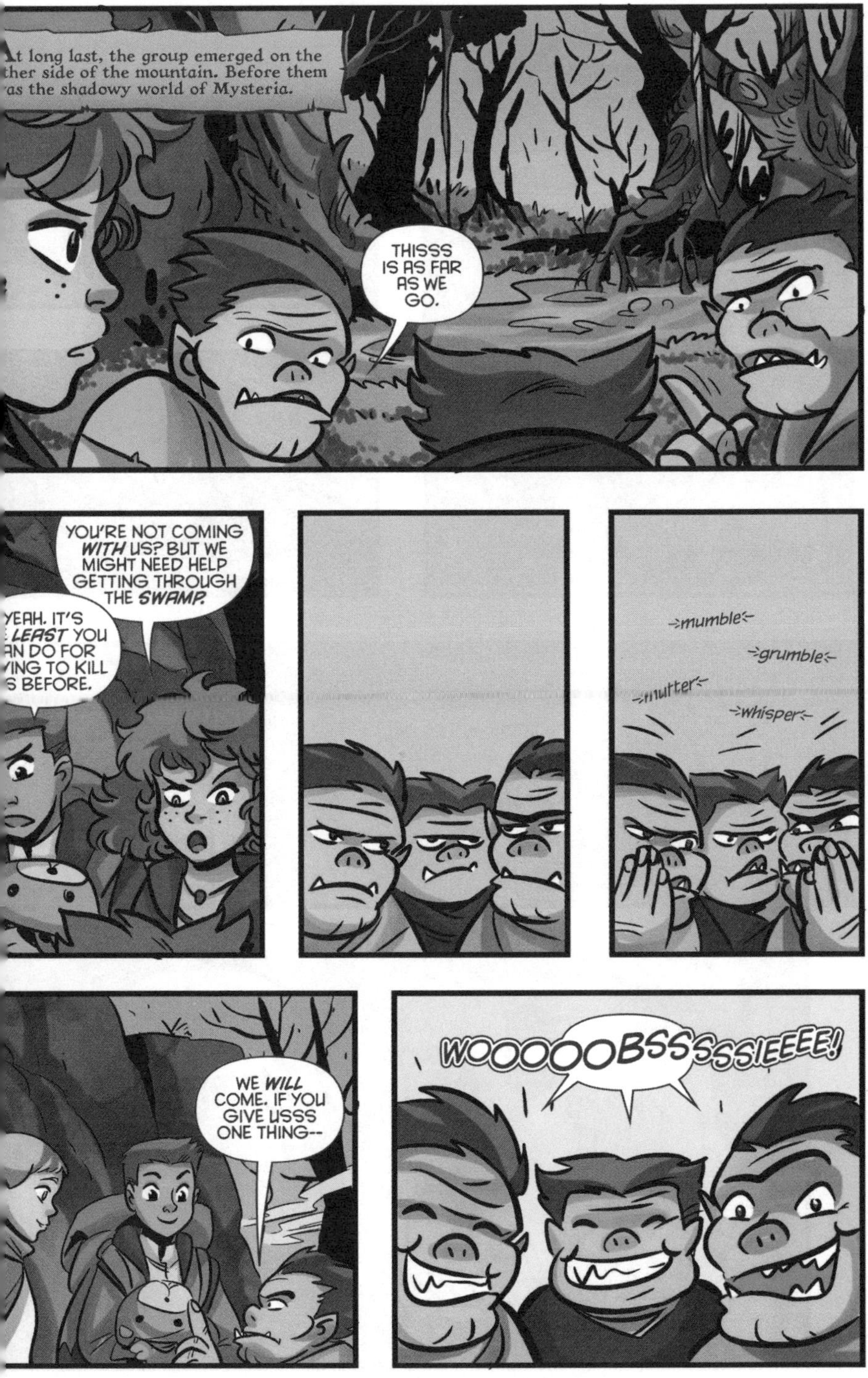
At long last, the group emerged on the
ther side of the mountain. Before them
as the shadowy world of Mysteria.
THISSS IS AS FAR AS WE GO.
YOU'RE NOT COMING *WITH* US? BUT WE MIGHT NEED HELP GETTING THROUGH THE *SWAMP*?
YEAH. IT'S *LEAST* YOU AN DO FOR ING TO KILL S BEFORE.
mumble
grumble
mutter
whisper
WE *WILL* COME. IF YOU GIVE USSS ONE THING--
WOOOOOOBSSSSSSIEEEEE!

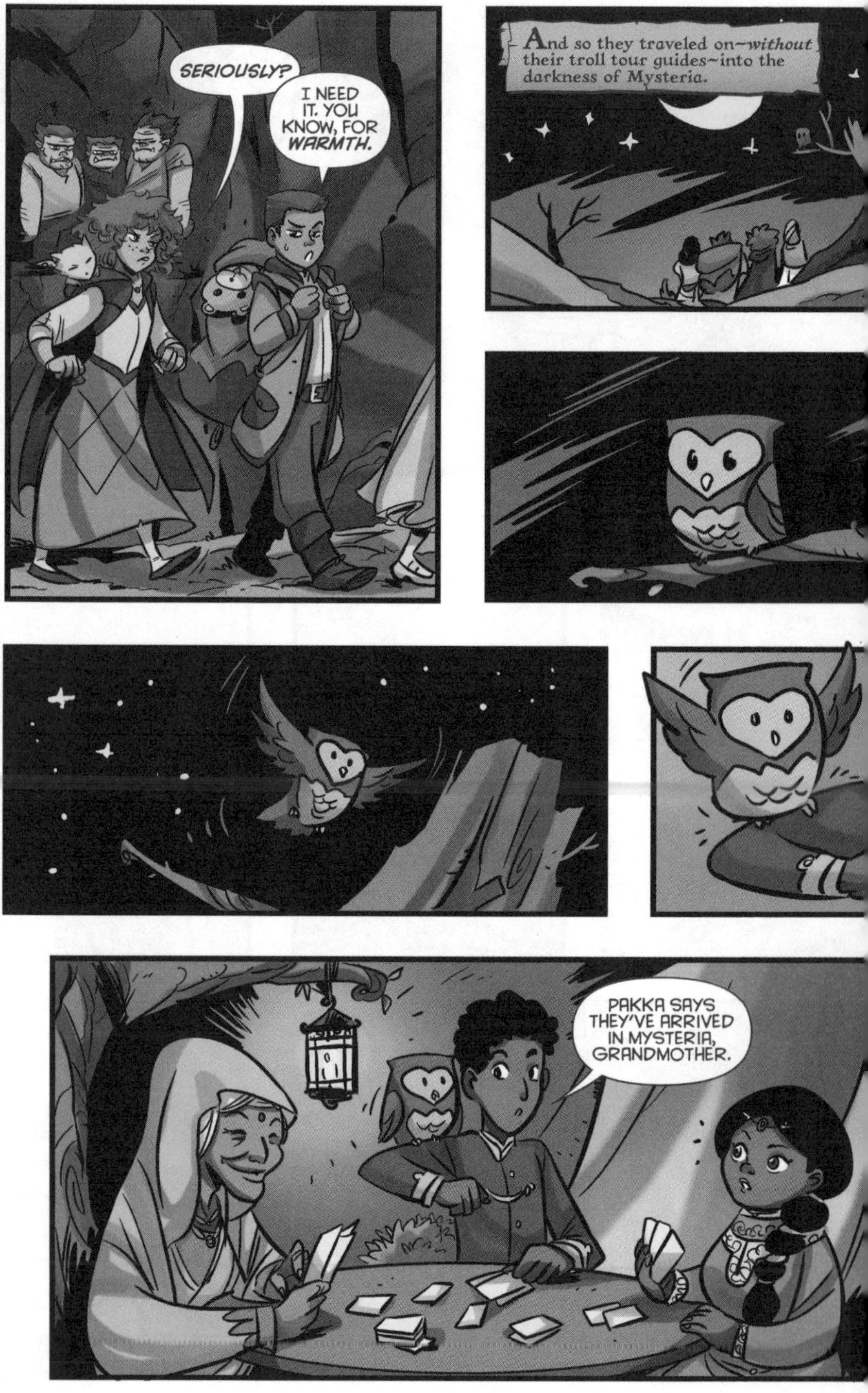
SERIOUSLY?
I NEED IT. YOU KNOW, FOR WARMTH.
And so they traveled on~*without* their troll tour guides~into the darkness of Mysteria.
PAKKA SAYS THEY'VE ARRIVED IN MYSTERIA, GRANDMOTHER.

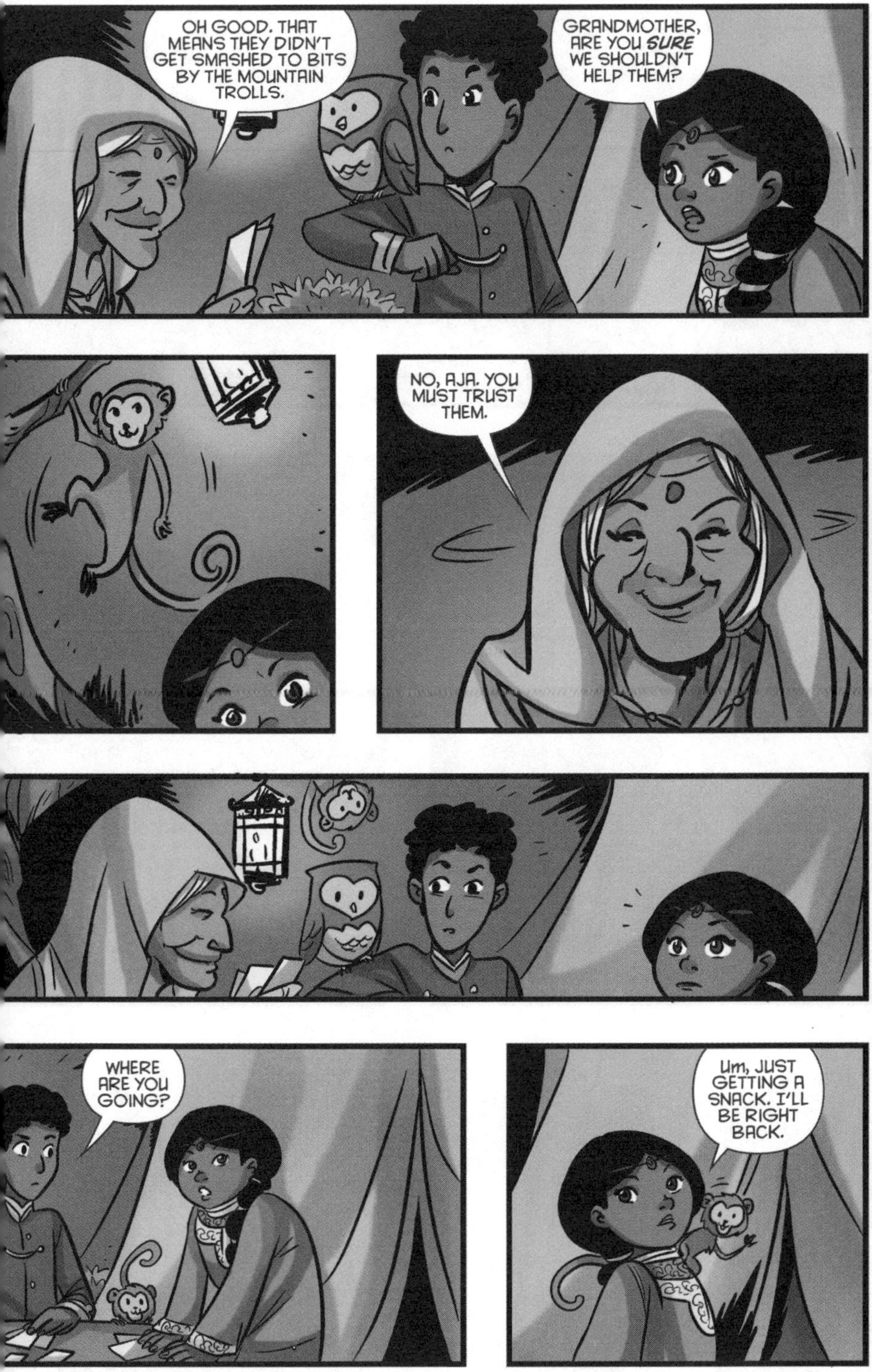
OH GOOD. THAT MEANS THEY DIDN'T GET SMASHED TO BITS BY THE MOUNTAIN TROLLS.
GRANDMOTHER, ARE YOU *SURE* WE SHOULDN'T HELP THEM?
NO, AJA. YOU MUST TRUST THEM.
WHERE ARE YOU GOING?
UM, JUST GETTING A SNACK. I'LL BE RIGHT BACK.

Meanwhile...

SLEEPY SHALLOWS

GUYS, ISN'T THERE SOME *OTHER* WAY AROUND?

SURE, MAX. TAKE YOUR PICK.

ANGRY ALLIGATOR ALLEY

TARANTULA TERRACE

LIKE I SAID, SLEEPY SHALLOWS SOUNDS GREAT

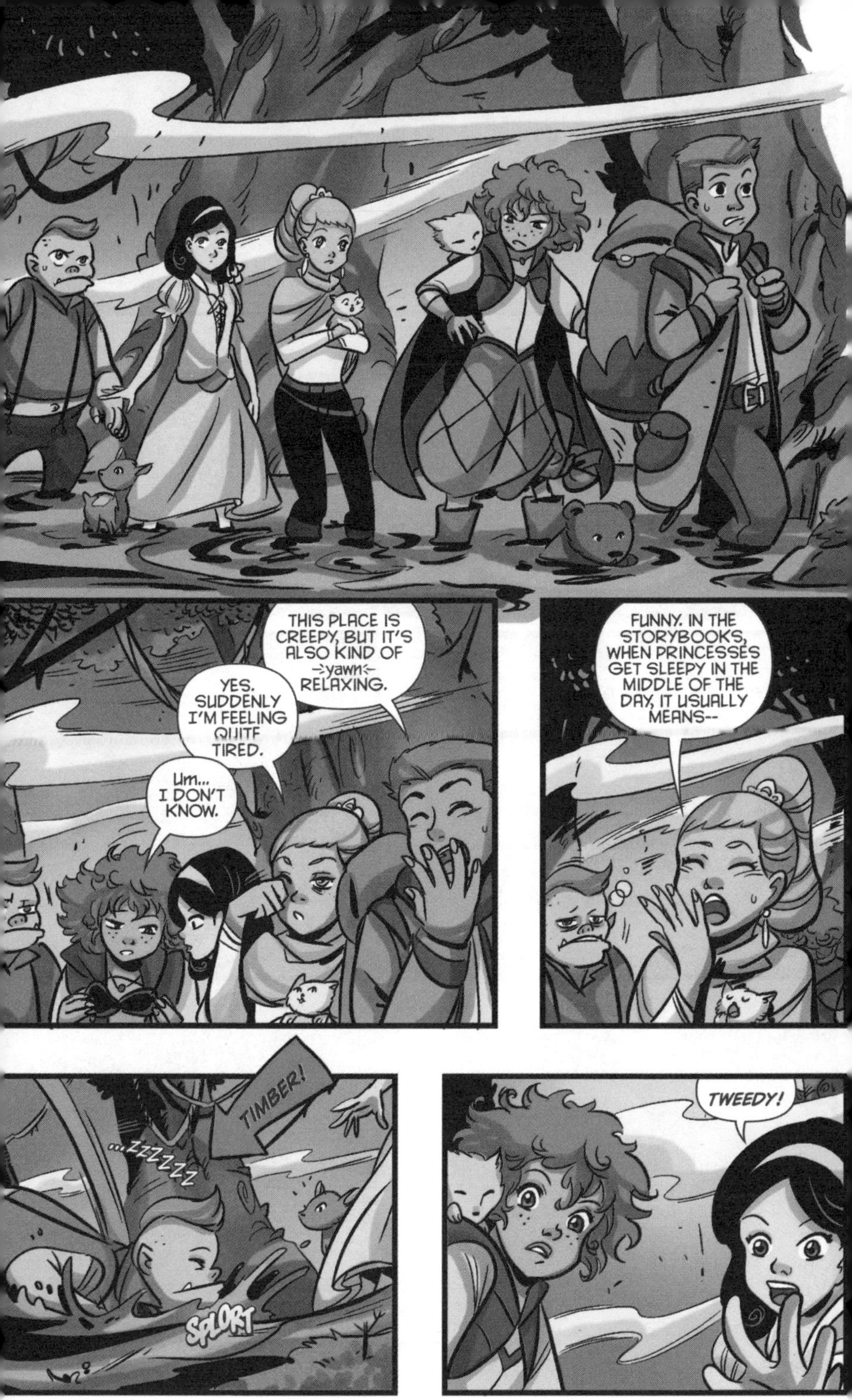

THIS PLACE IS CREEPY, BUT IT'S ALSO KIND OF -yawn- RELAXING.
YES. SUDDENLY I'M FEELING QUITE TIRED.
Um... I DON'T KNOW.
FUNNY. IN THE STORYBOOKS, WHEN PRINCESSES GET SLEEPY IN THE MIDDLE OF THE DAY, IT USUALLY MEANS--
TIMBER!
...ZZZZZZ
SPLORT
TWEEDY!

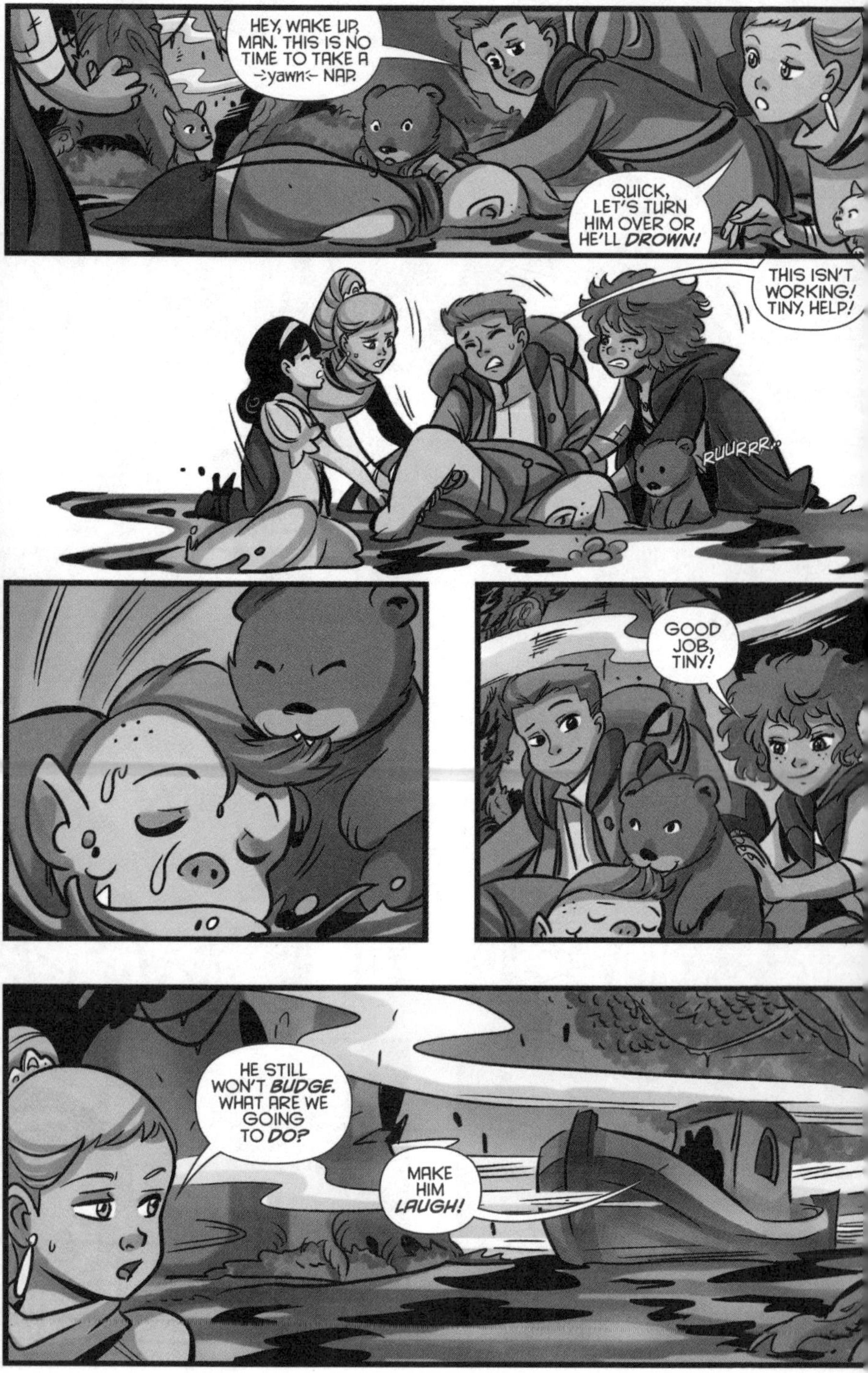
HEY, WAKE UP, MAN. THIS IS NO TIME TO TAKE A ~yawn~ NAP.
QUICK, LET'S TURN HIM OVER OR HE'LL *DROWN!*
THIS ISN'T WORKING! TINY, HELP!
RUURRR...
GOOD JOB, TINY!
HE STILL WON'T *BUDGE*. WHAT ARE WE GOING TO *DO?*
MAKE HIM *LAUGH!*

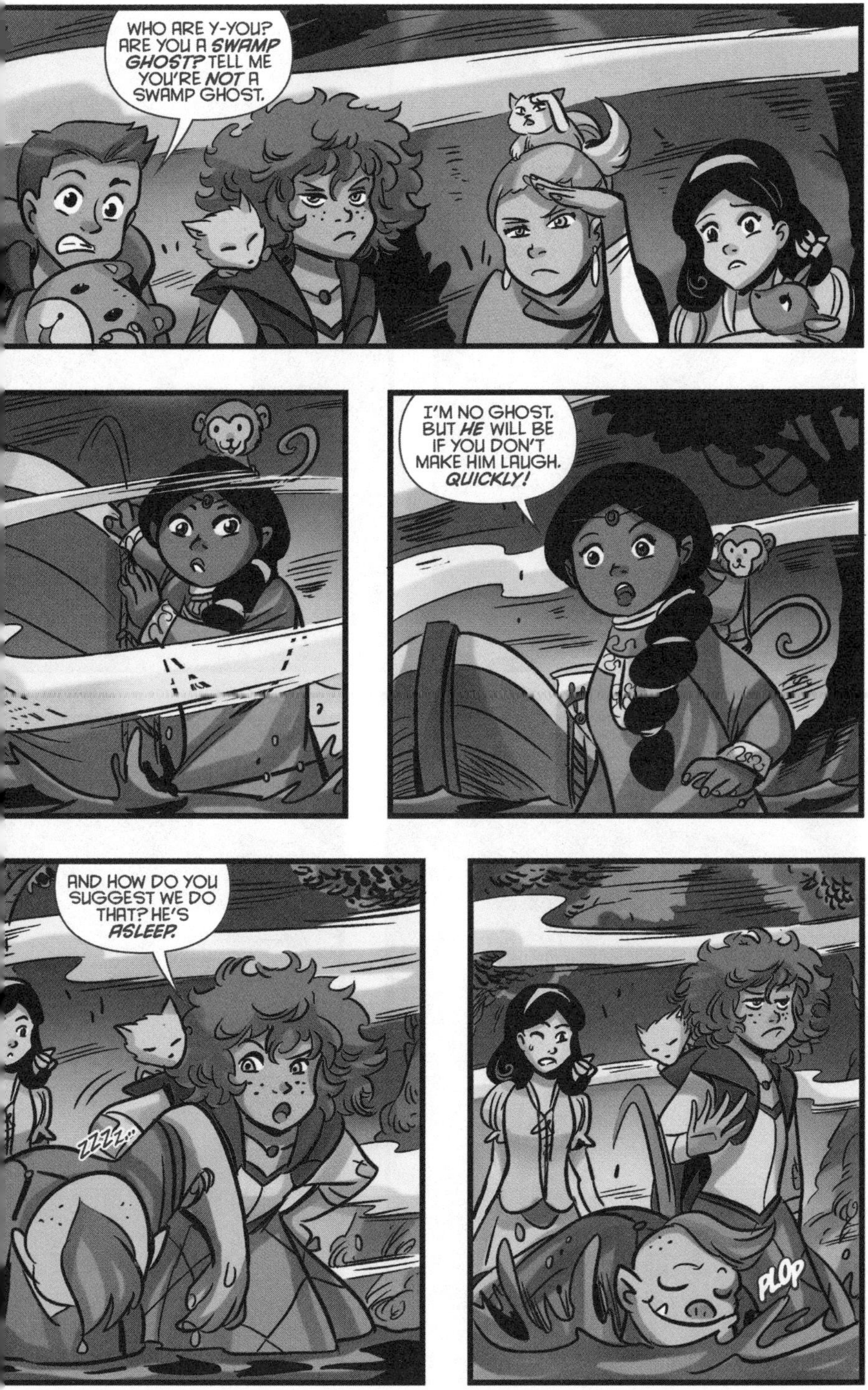
WHO ARE Y-YOU? ARE YOU A SWAMP GHOST? TELL ME YOU'RE NOT A SWAMP GHOST.
I'M NO GHOST. BUT HE WILL BE IF YOU DON'T MAKE HIM LAUGH. QUICKLY!
AND HOW DO YOU SUGGEST WE DO THAT? HE'S ASLEEP.
ZZZZ...
PLOP

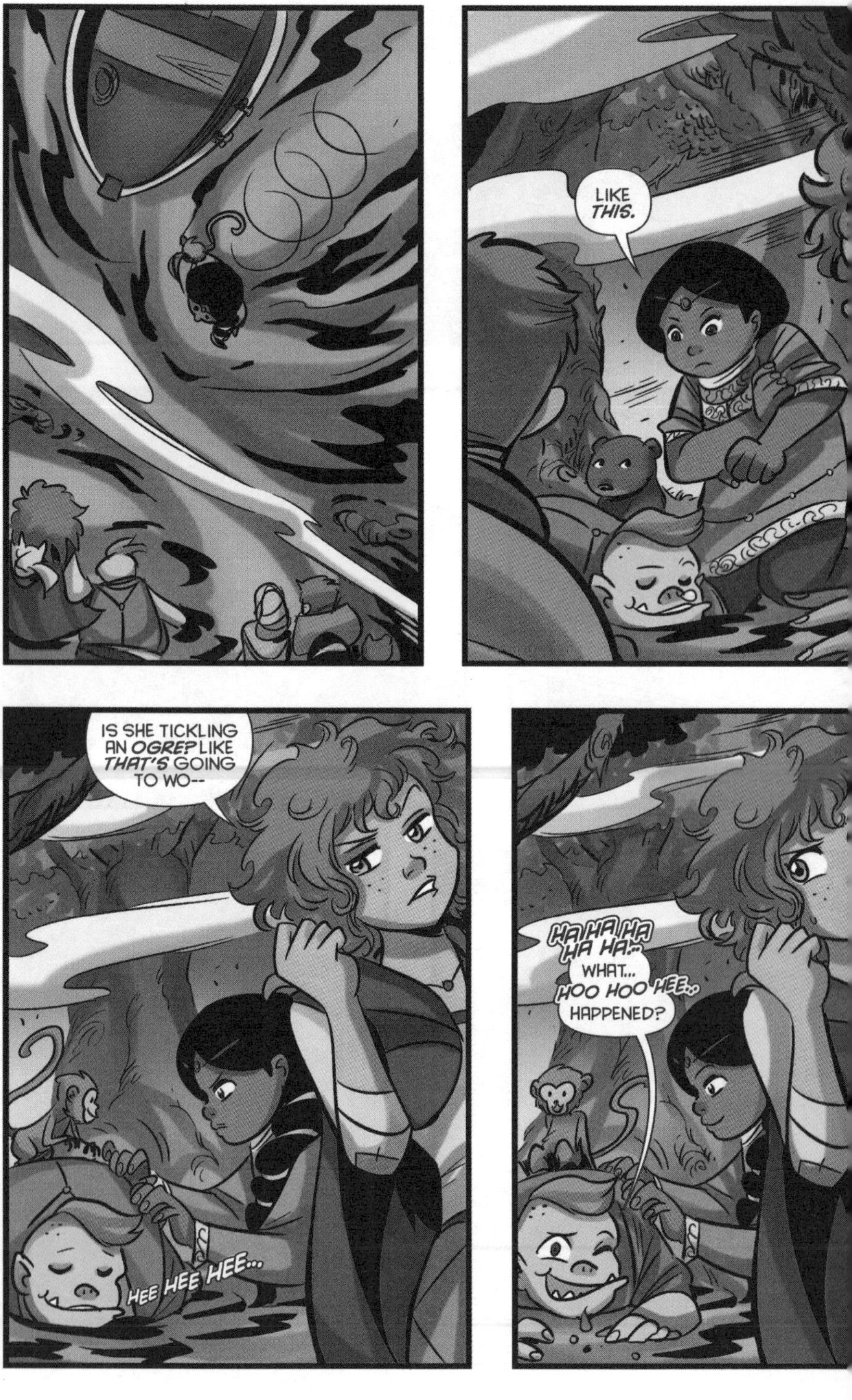
LIKE *THIS.*
IS SHE TICKLING AN *OGRE?* LIKE *THAT'S* GOING TO WO--
HEE HEE HEE...
HA HA HA HA HA...
WHAT...
HOO HOO HEE...
HAPPENED?

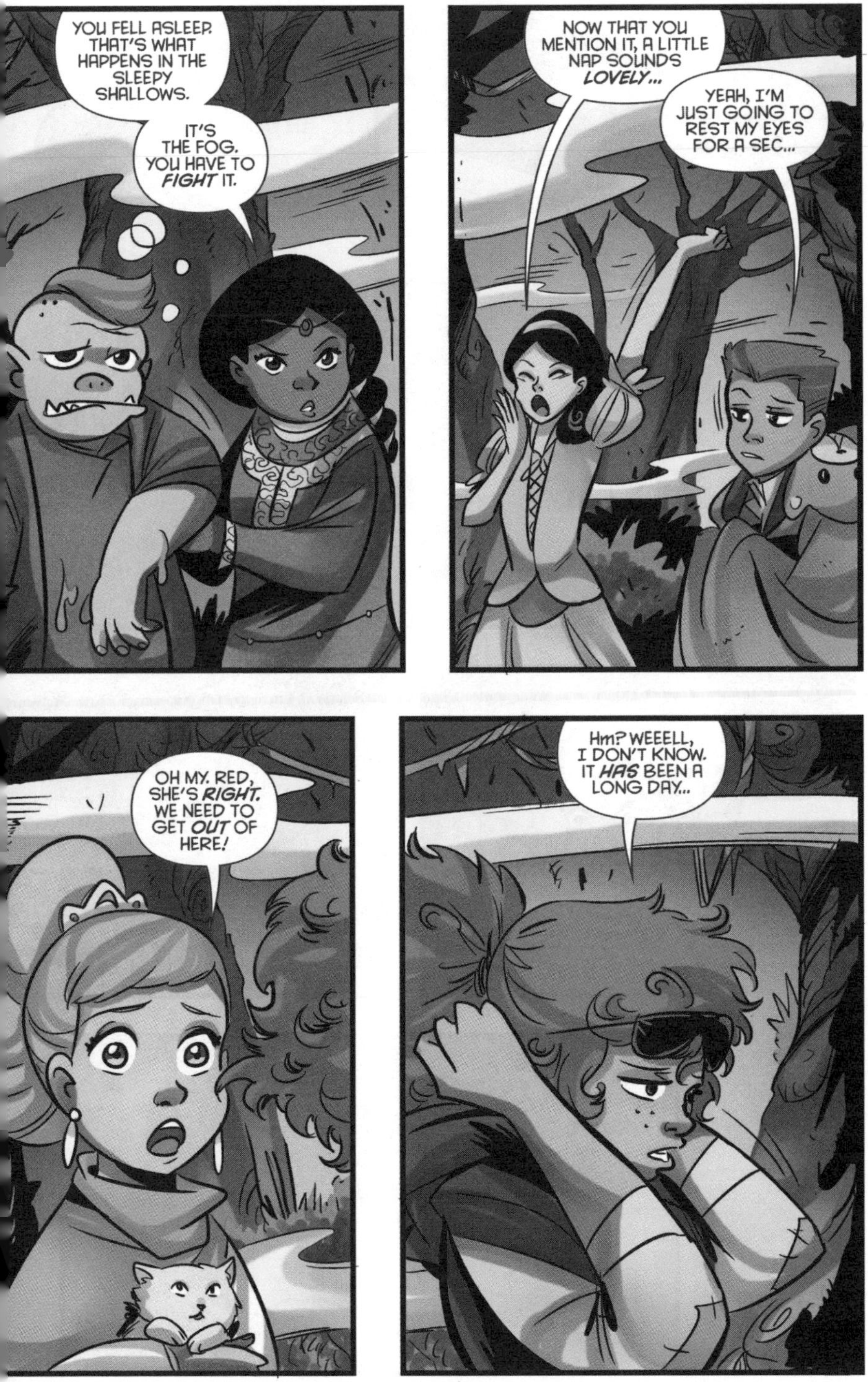
YOU FELL ASLEEP. THAT'S WHAT HAPPENS IN THE SLEEPY SHALLOWS.
IT'S THE FOG. YOU HAVE TO FIGHT IT.
NOW THAT YOU MENTION IT, A LITTLE NAP SOUNDS LOVELY...
YEAH, I'M JUST GOING TO REST MY EYES FOR A SEC...
OH MY. RED, SHE'S RIGHT. WE NEED TO GET OUT OF HERE!
Hm? WEEELL, I DON'T KNOW. IT HAS BEEN A LONG DAY...

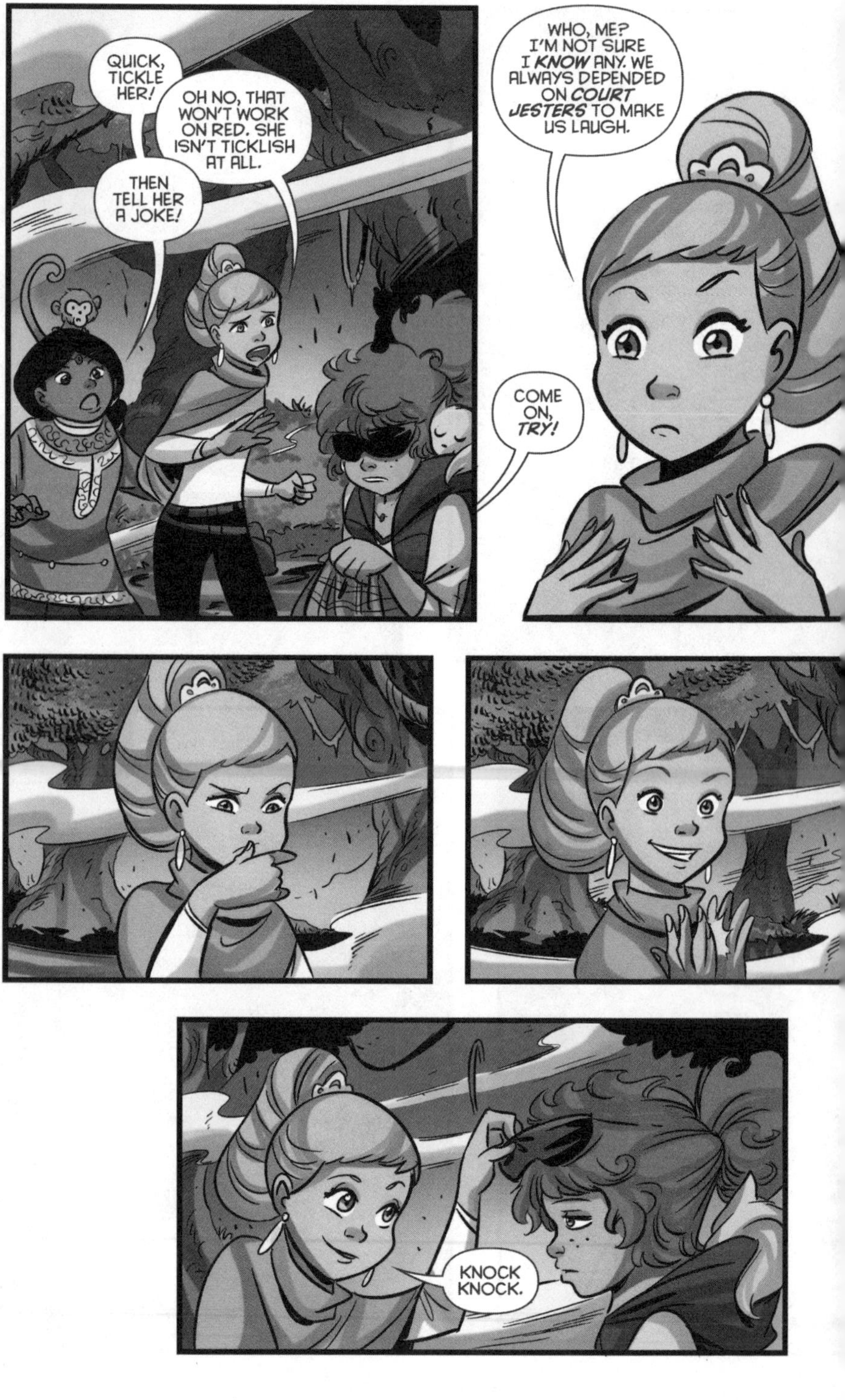
QUICK, TICKLE HER!
OH NO, THAT WON'T WORK ON RED. SHE ISN'T TICKLISH AT ALL.
THEN TELL HER A JOKE!
WHO, ME? I'M NOT SURE I **KNOW** ANY. WE ALWAYS DEPENDED ON **COURT JESTERS** TO MAKE US LAUGH.
COME ON, **TRY!**
KNOCK KNOCK.

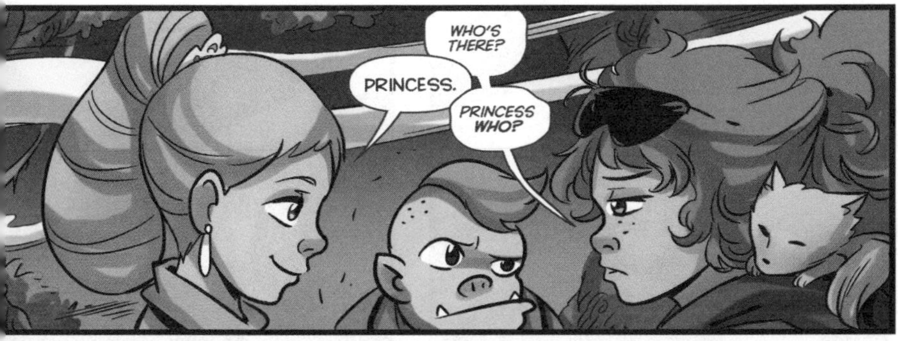
WHO'S THERE?
PRINCESS.
PRINCESS WHO?

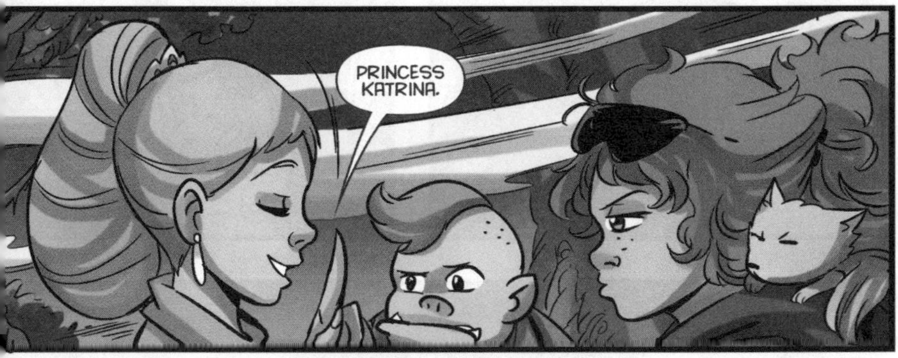
PRINCESS KATRINA.

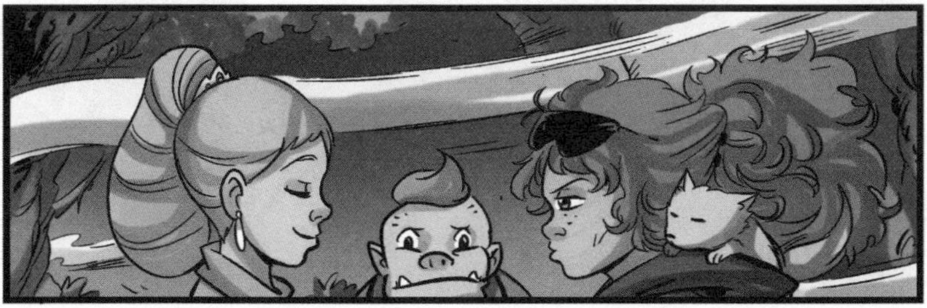

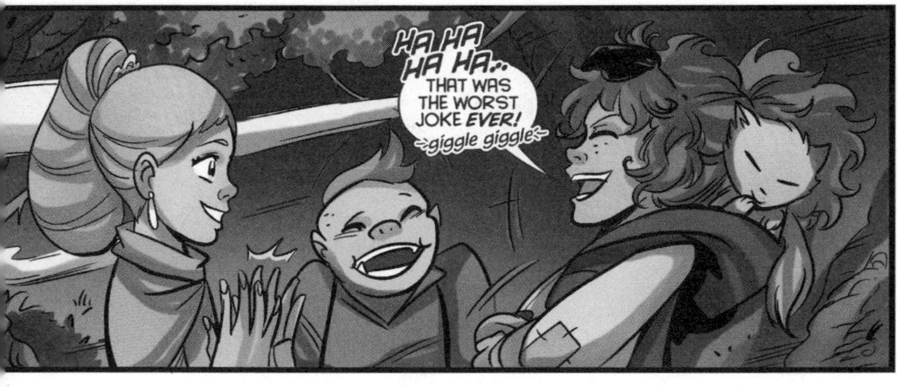
HA HA HA HA... THAT WAS THE WORST JOKE EVER!
giggle giggle

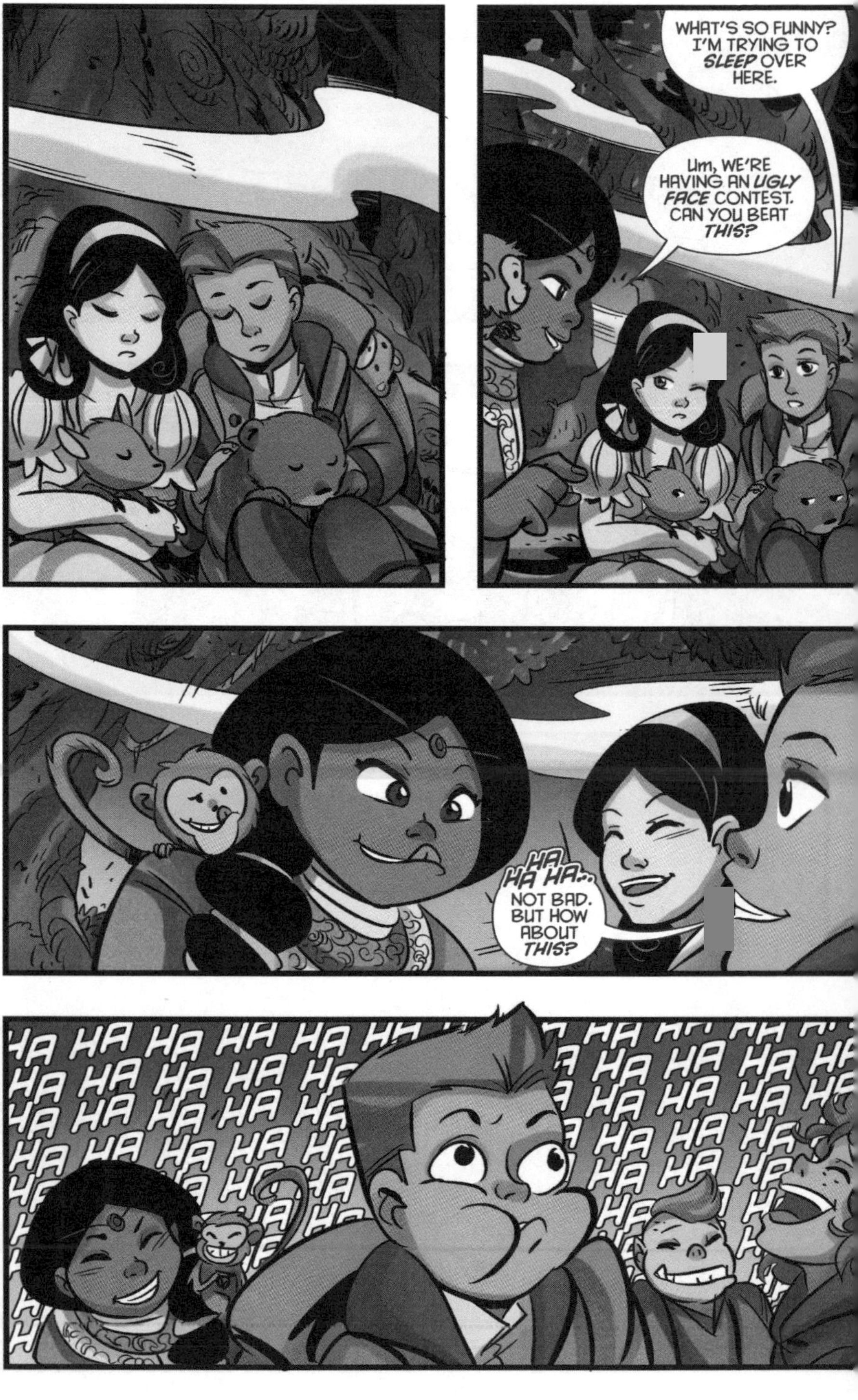
WHAT'S SO FUNNY? I'M TRYING TO *SLEEP* OVER HERE.
Um, WE'RE HAVING AN *UGLY FACE* CONTEST. CAN YOU BEAT *THIS?*
HA HA HA...
NOT BAD. BUT HOW ABOUT *THIS?*
HA HA HA HA HA HA

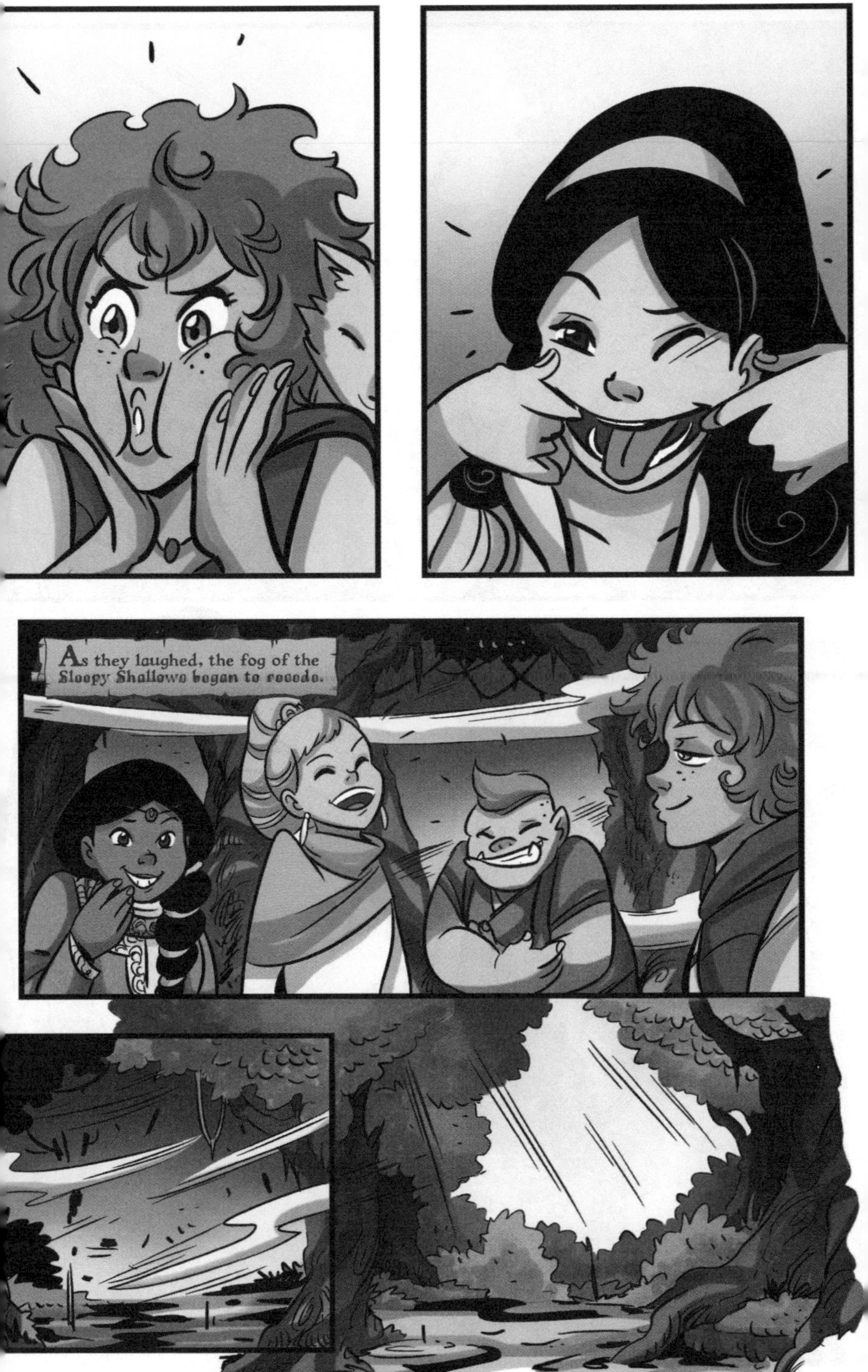
As they laughed, the fog of the Sleepy Shallows began to recede.

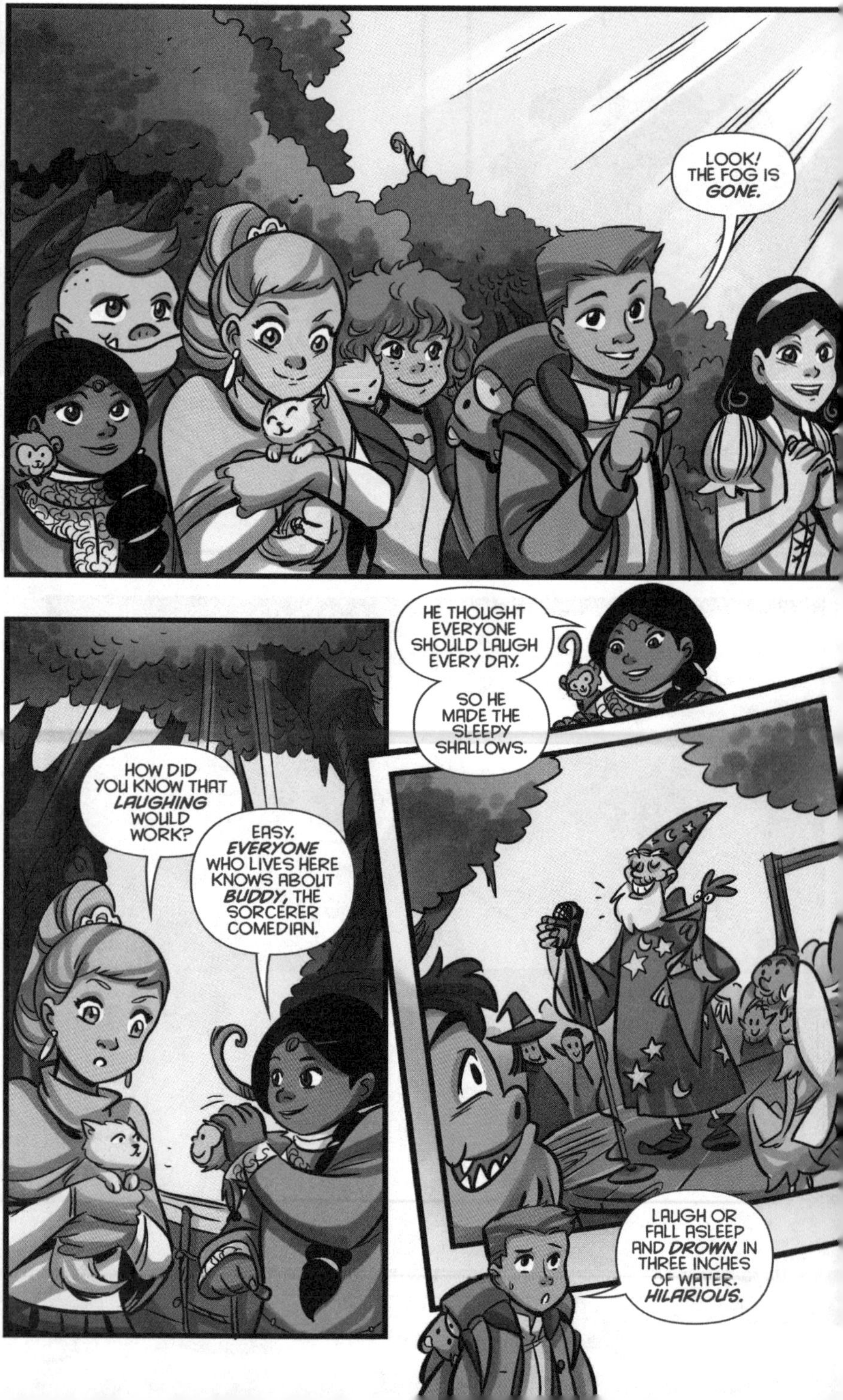
LOOK! THE FOG IS GONE.
HE THOUGHT EVERYONE SHOULD LAUGH EVERY DAY.
SO HE MADE THE SLEEPY SHALLOWS.
HOW DID YOU KNOW THAT LAUGHING WOULD WORK?
EASY. EVERYONE WHO LIVES HERE KNOWS ABOUT BUDDY, THE SORCERER COMEDIAN.
LAUGH OR FALL ASLEEP AND DROWN IN THREE INCHES OF WATER. HILARIOUS.

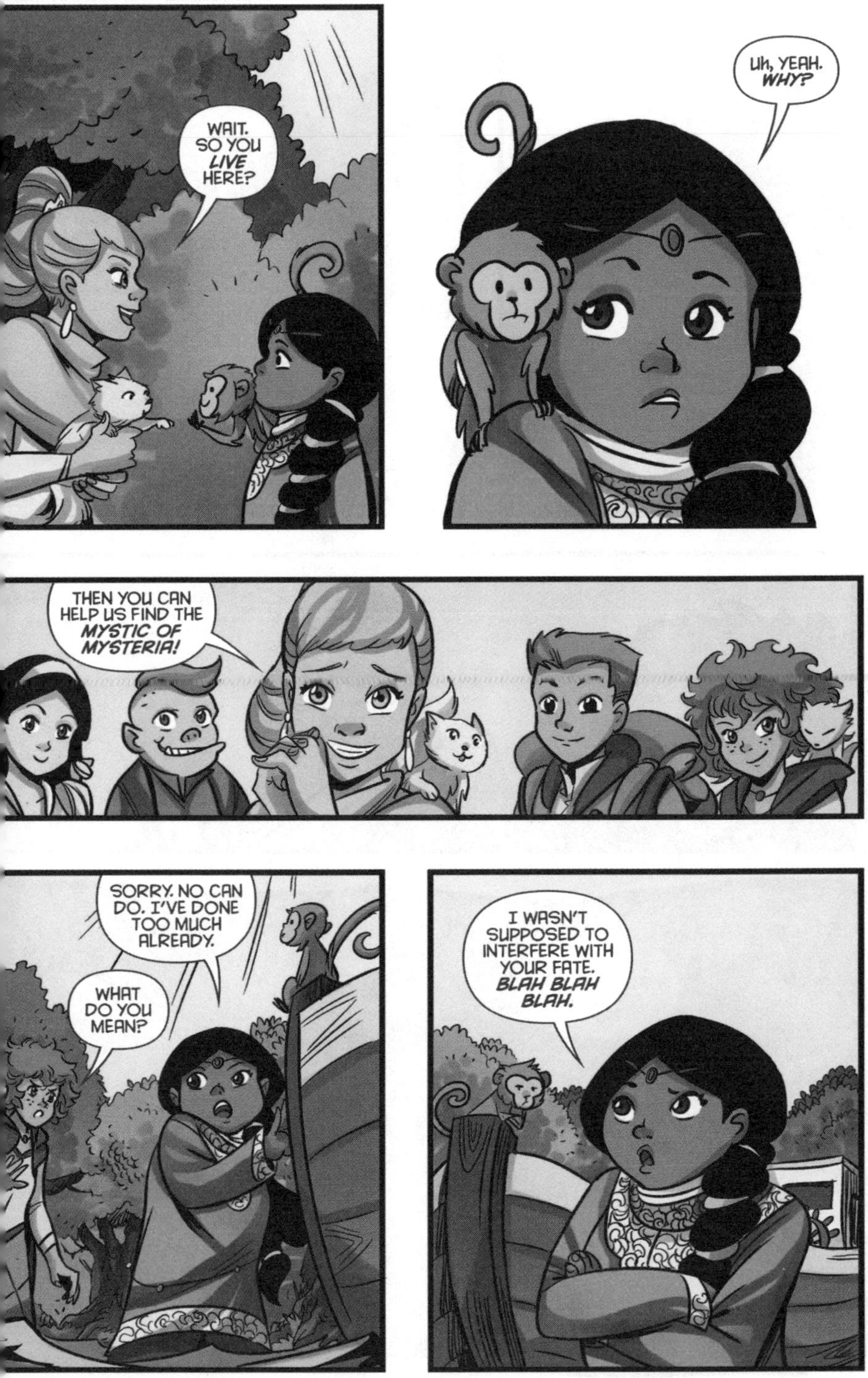
WAIT. SO YOU *LIVE* HERE?
Uh, YEAH. *WHY?*
THEN YOU CAN HELP US FIND THE *MYSTIC OF MYSTERIA!*
SORRY. NO CAN DO. I'VE DONE TOO MUCH ALREADY.
WHAT DO YOU MEAN?
I WASN'T SUPPOSED TO INTERFERE WITH YOUR FATE. *BLAH BLAH BLAH.*

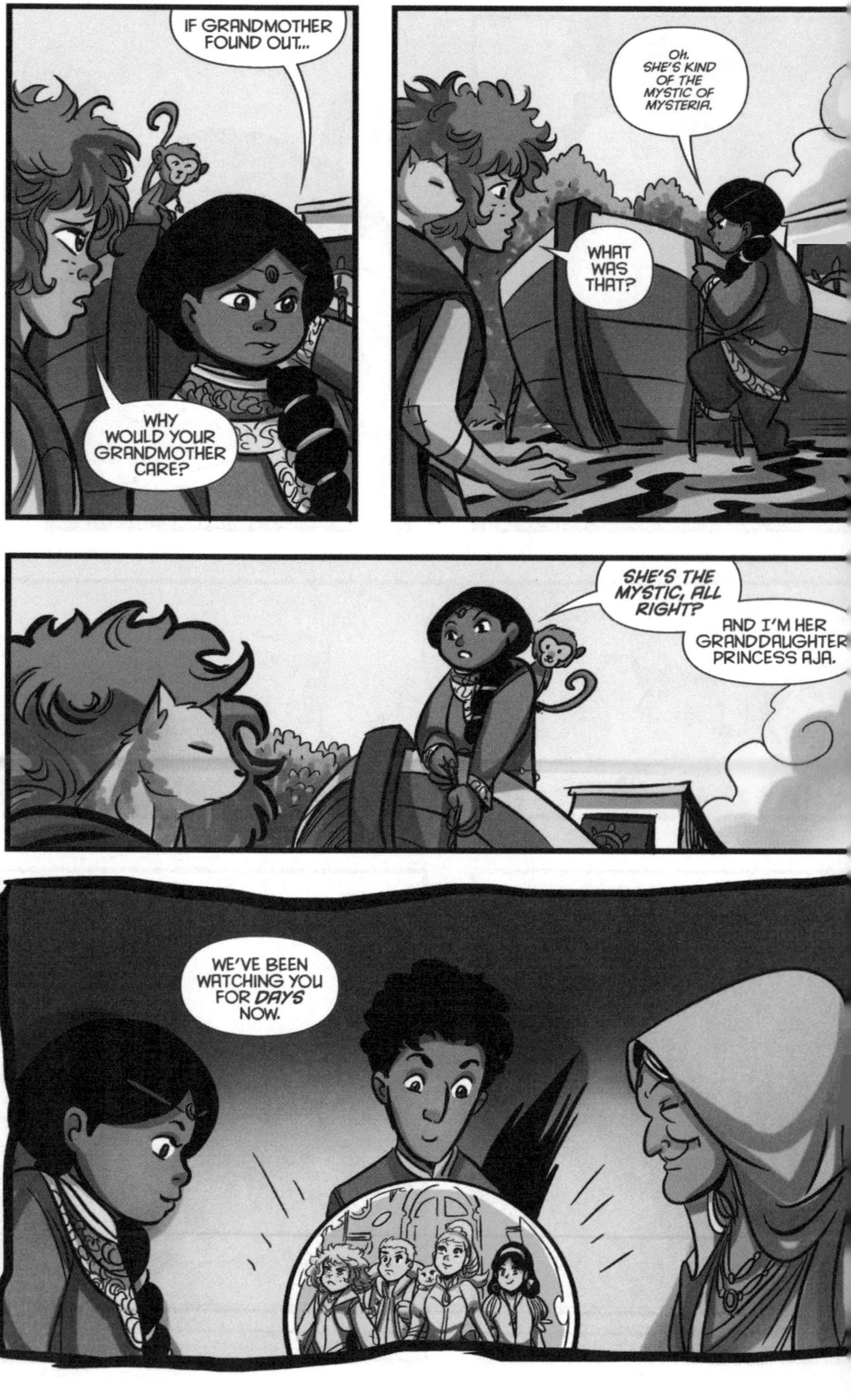
IF GRANDMOTHER FOUND OUT...
WHY WOULD YOUR GRANDMOTHER CARE?
OH. SHE'S KIND OF THE MYSTIC OF MYSTERIA.
WHAT WAS THAT?
SHE'S THE MYSTIC, ALL RIGHT?
AND I'M HER GRANDDAUGHTER PRINCESS AJA.
WE'VE BEEN WATCHING YOU FOR DAYS NOW.

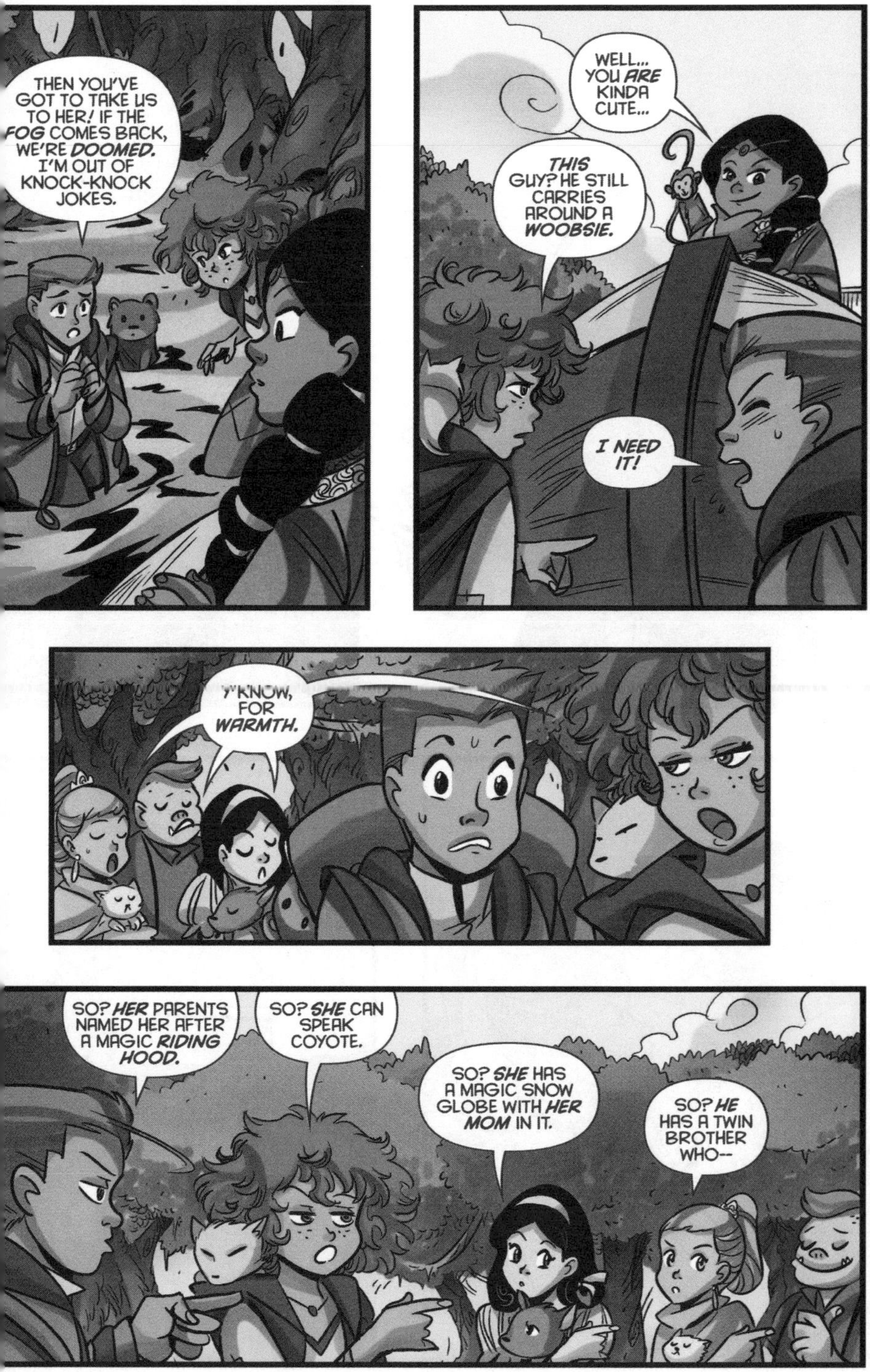

THEN YOU'VE GOT TO TAKE US TO HER! IF THE FOG COMES BACK, WE'RE DOOMED. I'M OUT OF KNOCK-KNOCK JOKES.
WELL... YOU ARE KINDA CUTE...
THIS GUY? HE STILL CARRIES AROUND A WOOBSIE.
I NEED IT!
Y'KNOW, FOR WARMTH.
SO? HER PARENTS NAMED HER AFTER A MAGIC RIDING HOOD.
SO? SHE CAN SPEAK COYOTE.
SO? SHE HAS A MAGIC SNOW GLOBE WITH HER MOM IN IT.
SO? HE HAS A TWIN BROTHER WHO--

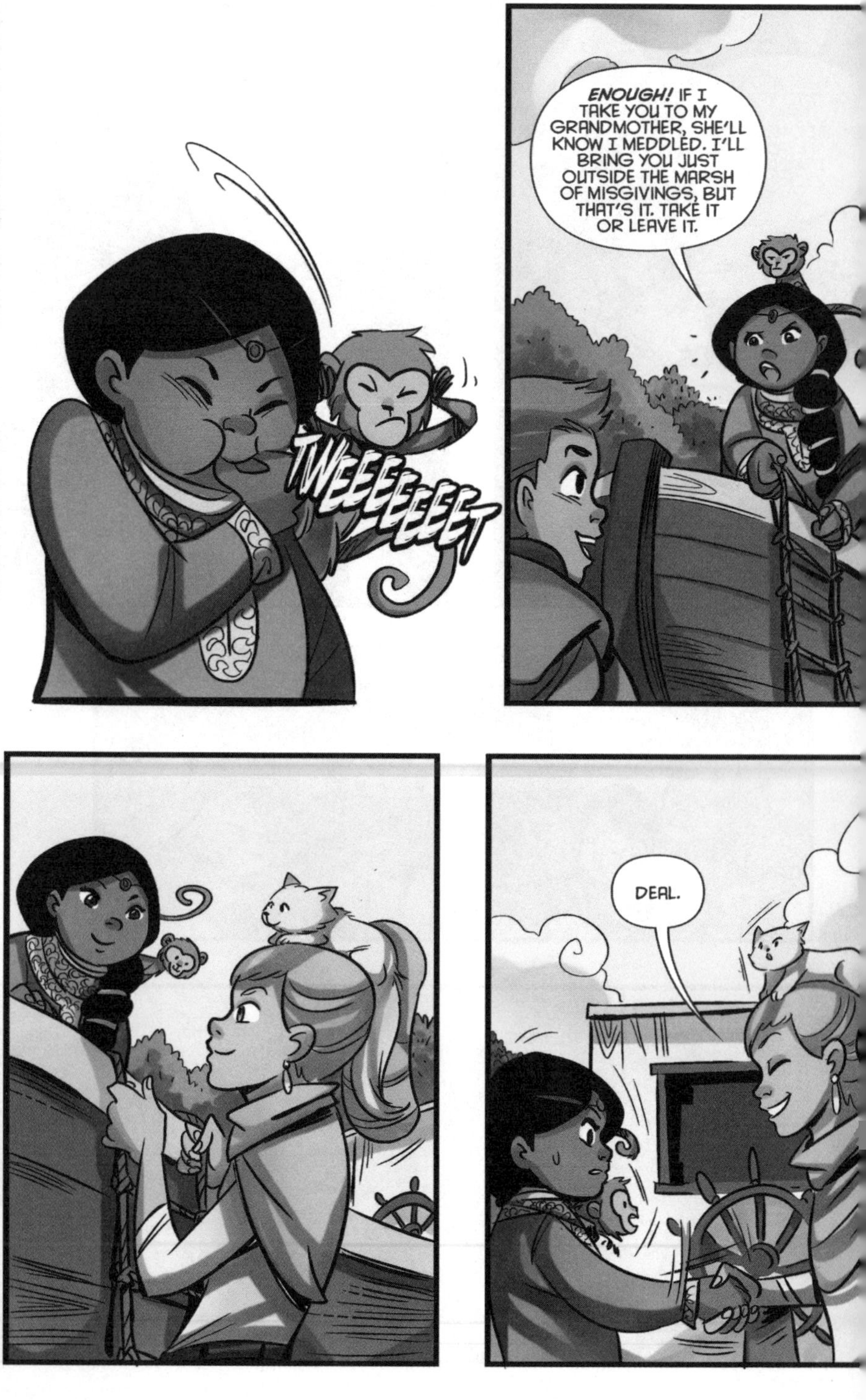
TWEEEEEEEET
ENOUGH! IF I TAKE YOU TO MY GRANDMOTHER, SHE'LL KNOW I MEDDLED. I'LL BRING YOU JUST OUTSIDE THE MARSH OF MISGIVINGS, BUT THAT'S IT. TAKE IT OR LEAVE IT.
DEAL.

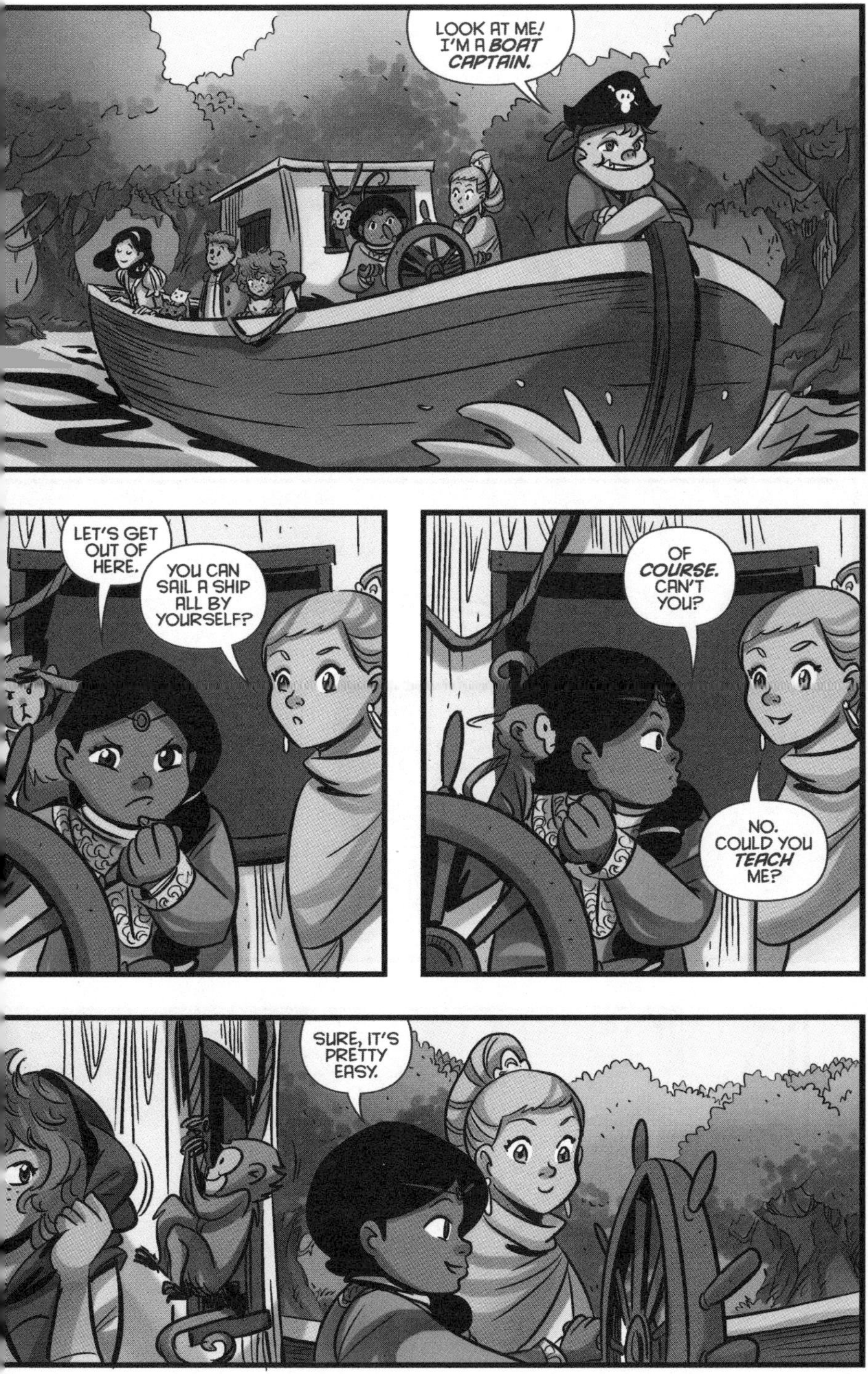
LOOK AT ME! I'M A BOAT CAPTAIN.
LET'S GET OUT OF HERE.
YOU CAN SAIL A SHIP ALL BY YOURSELF?
OF COURSE. CAN'T YOU?
NO. COULD YOU TEACH ME?
SURE, IT'S PRETTY EASY.

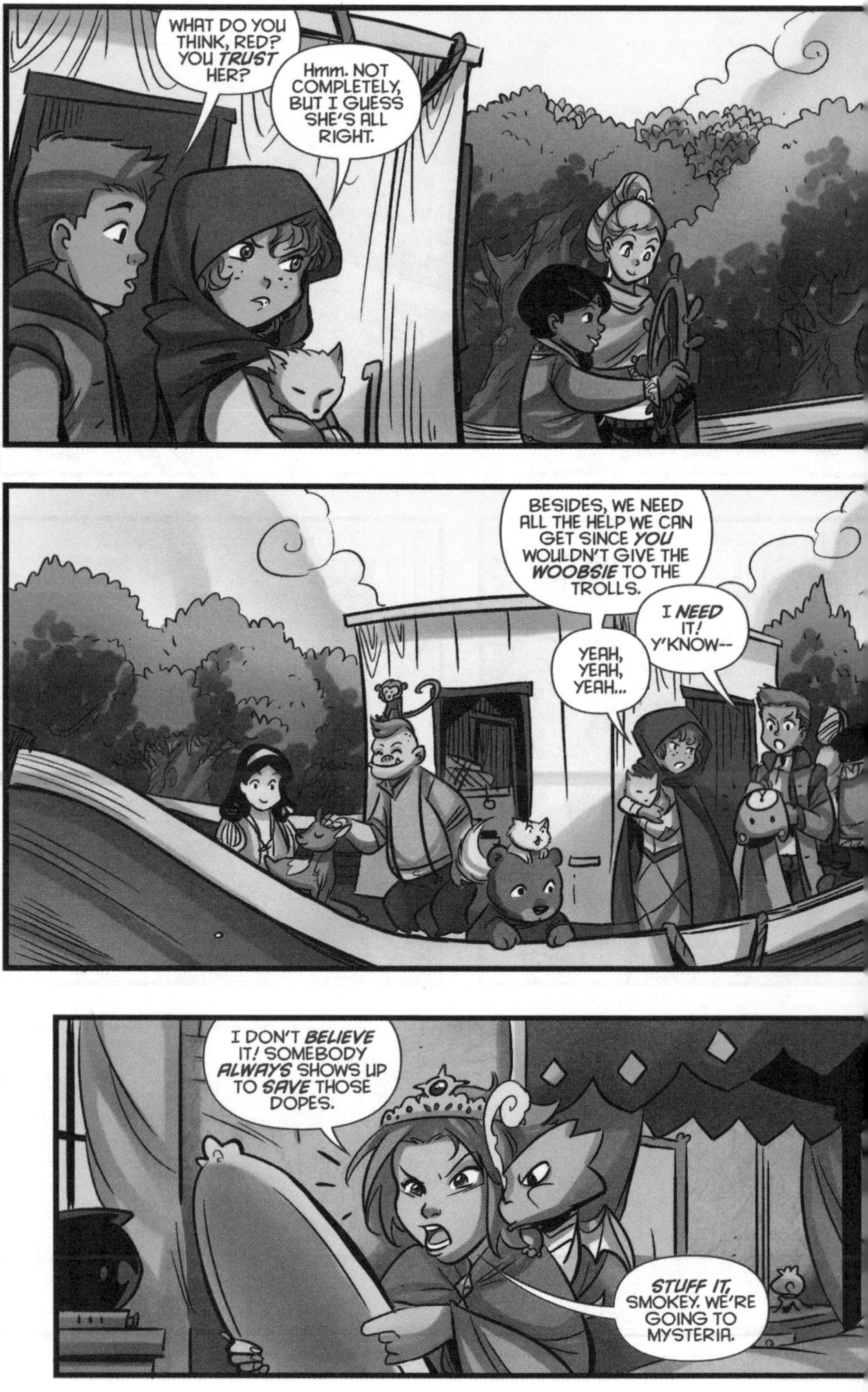
WHAT DO YOU THINK, RED? YOU *TRUST* HER?
Hmm. NOT COMPLETELY, BUT I GUESS SHE'S ALL RIGHT.
BESIDES, WE NEED ALL THE HELP WE CAN GET SINCE *YOU* WOULDN'T GIVE THE *WOOBSIE* TO THE TROLLS.
YEAH, YEAH, YEAH...
I *NEED* IT! Y'KNOW--
I DON'T *BELIEVE* IT! SOMEBODY *ALWAYS* SHOWS UP TO *SAVE* THOSE DOPES.
STUFF IT, SMOKEY. WE'RE GOING TO MYSTERIA.

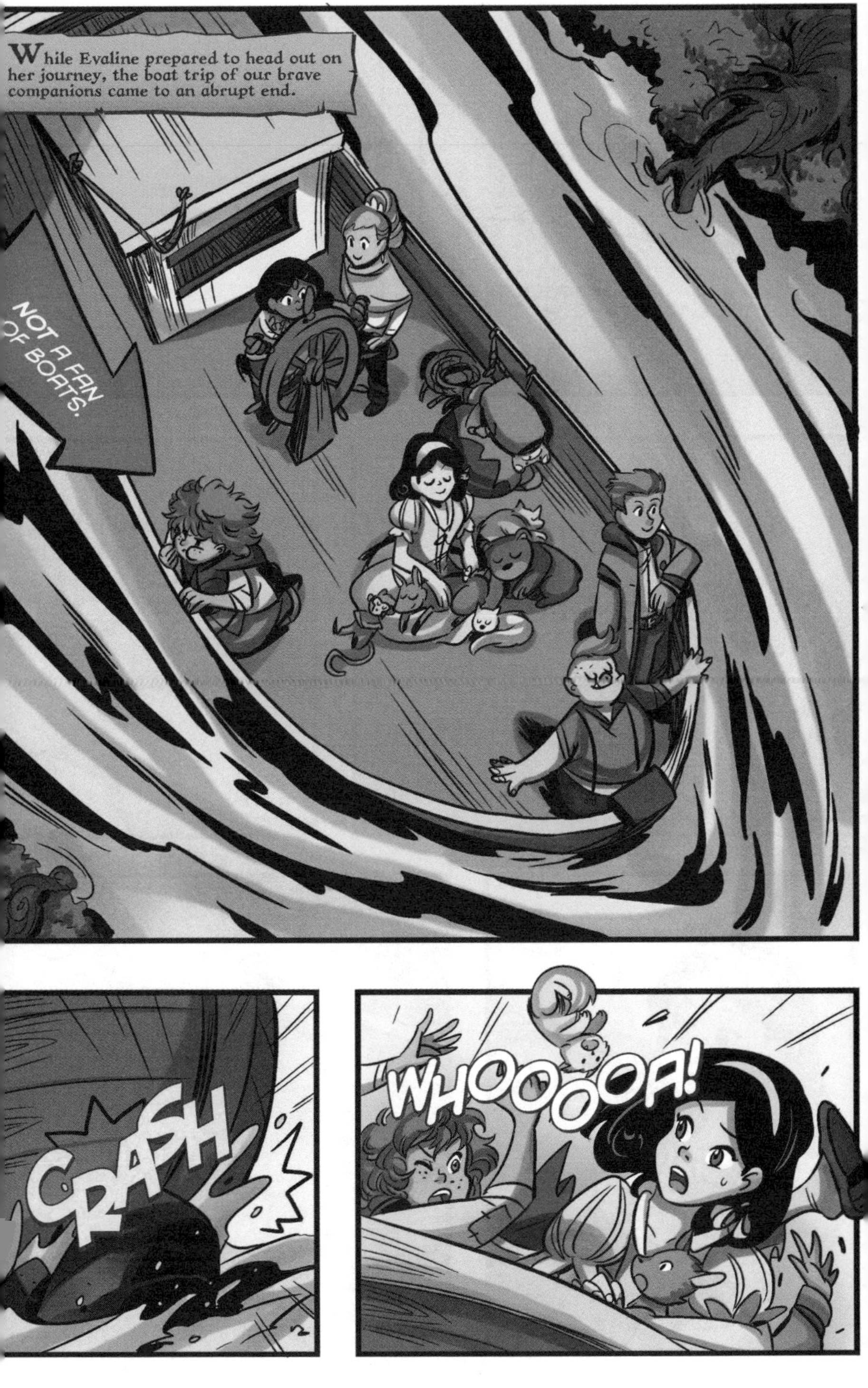
While Evaline prepared to head out on her journey, the boat trip of our brave companions came to an abrupt end.
NOT A FAN OF BOATS.
CRASH
WHOOOOOA!

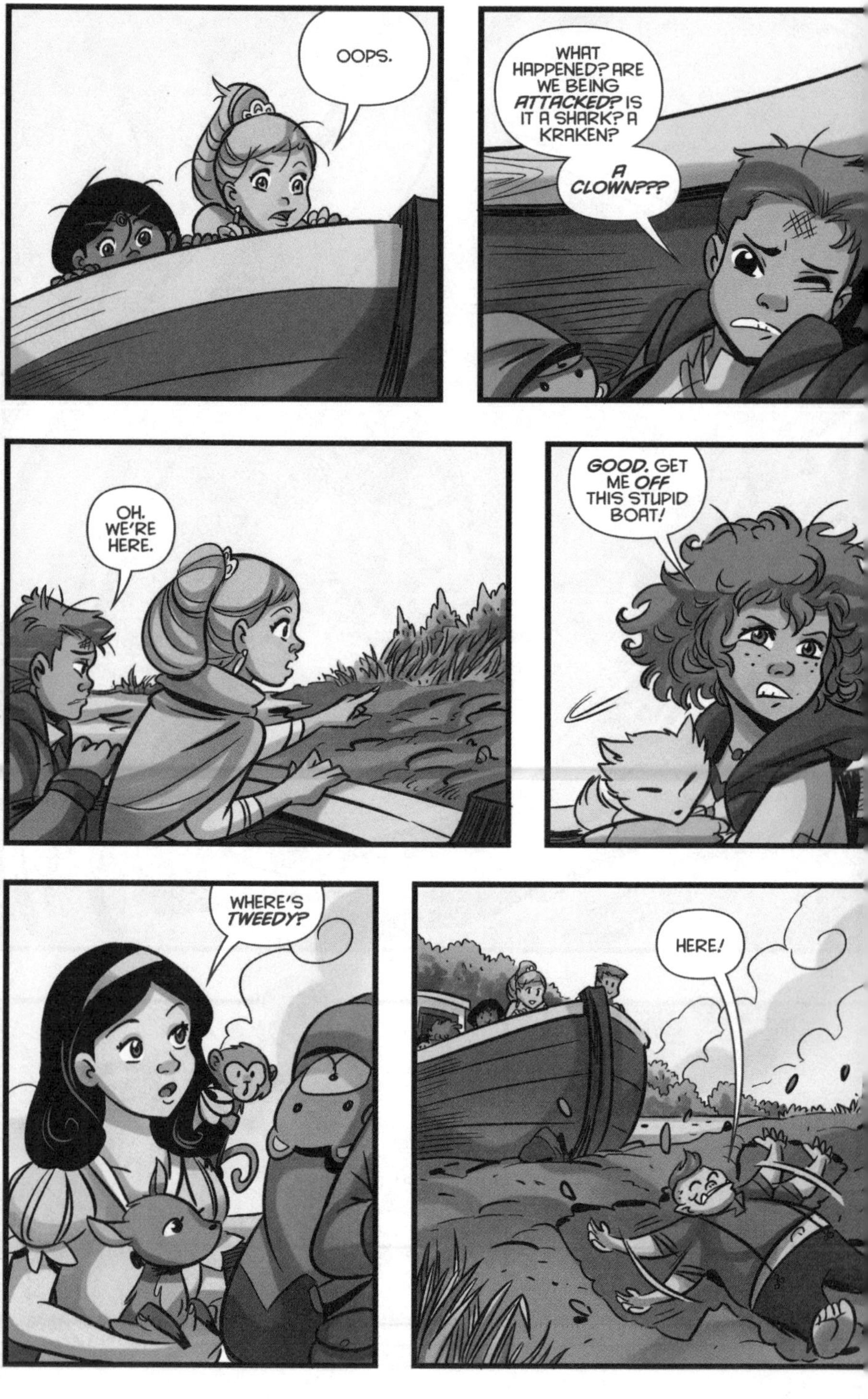
OOPS.
WHAT HAPPENED? ARE WE BEING ATTACKED? IS IT A SHARK? A KRAKEN?
A CLOWN???
OH. WE'RE HERE.
GOOD. GET ME OFF THIS STUPID BOAT!
WHERE'S TWEEDY?
HERE!

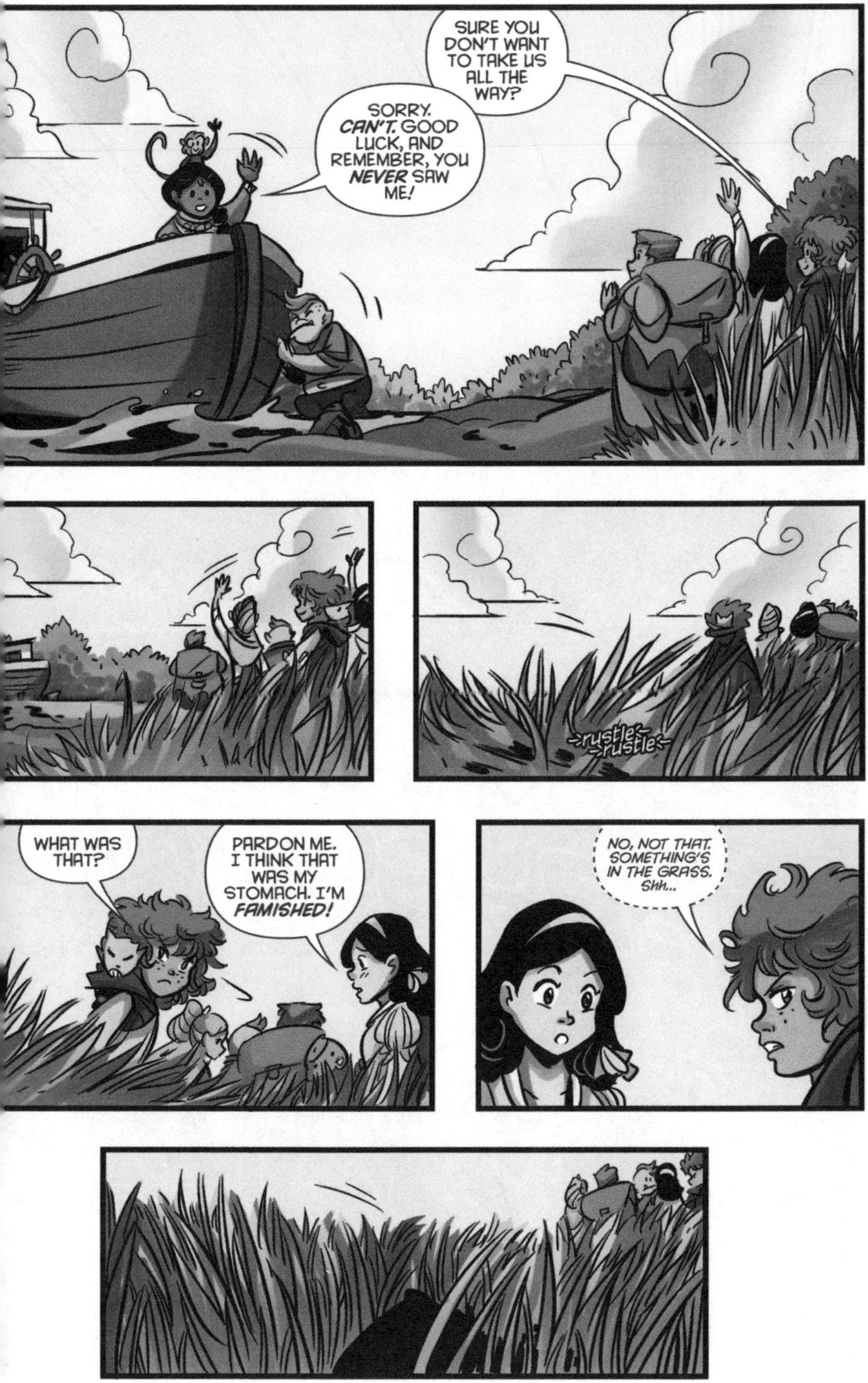
SURE YOU DON'T WANT TO TAKE US ALL THE WAY?
SORRY. CAN'T. GOOD LUCK, AND REMEMBER, YOU NEVER SAW ME!
rustle rustle
WHAT WAS THAT?
PARDON ME. I THINK THAT WAS MY STOMACH. I'M FAMISHED!
NO, NOT THAT. SOMETHING'S IN THE GRASS. Shh...

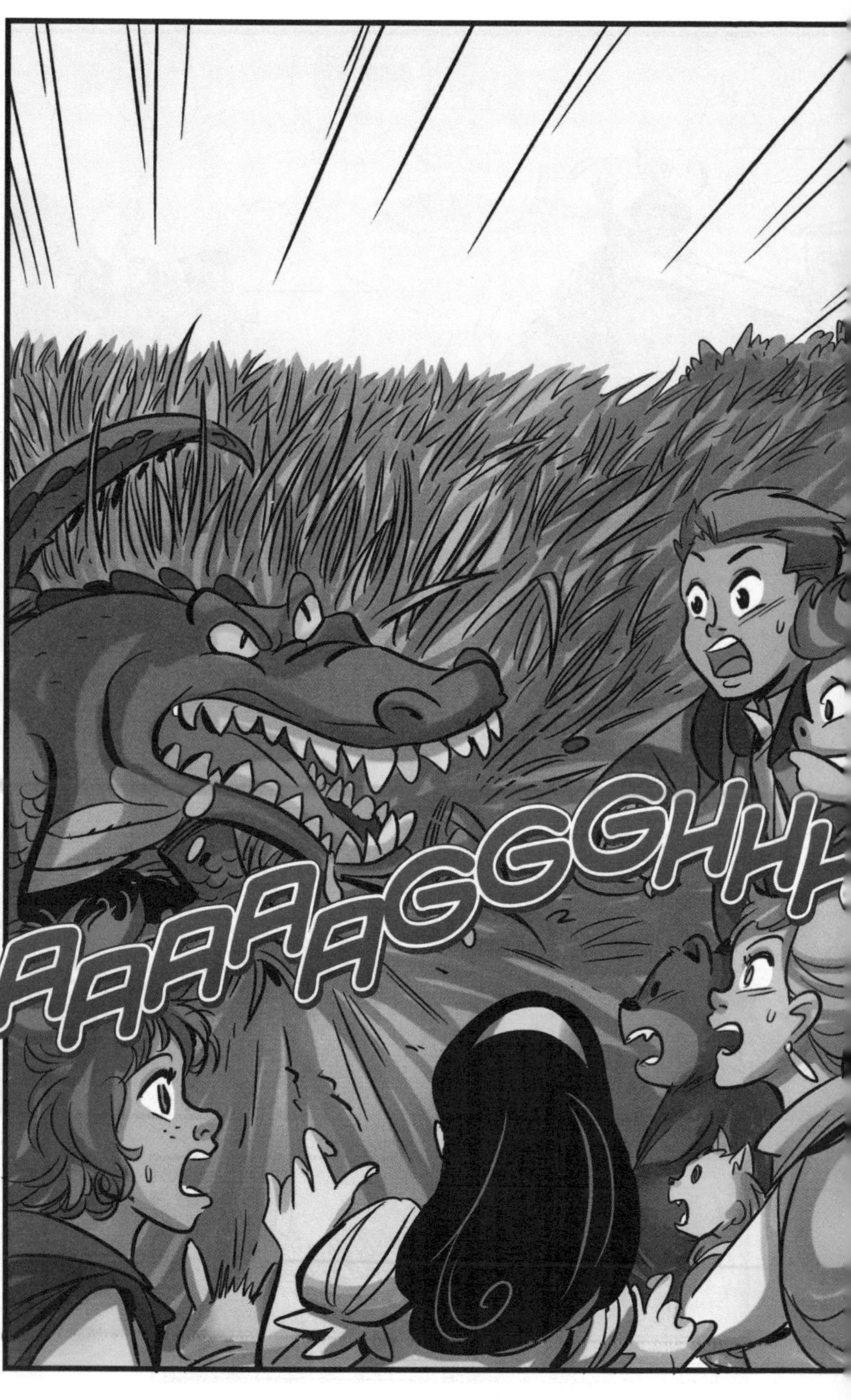
AAAAAAGGGHHH

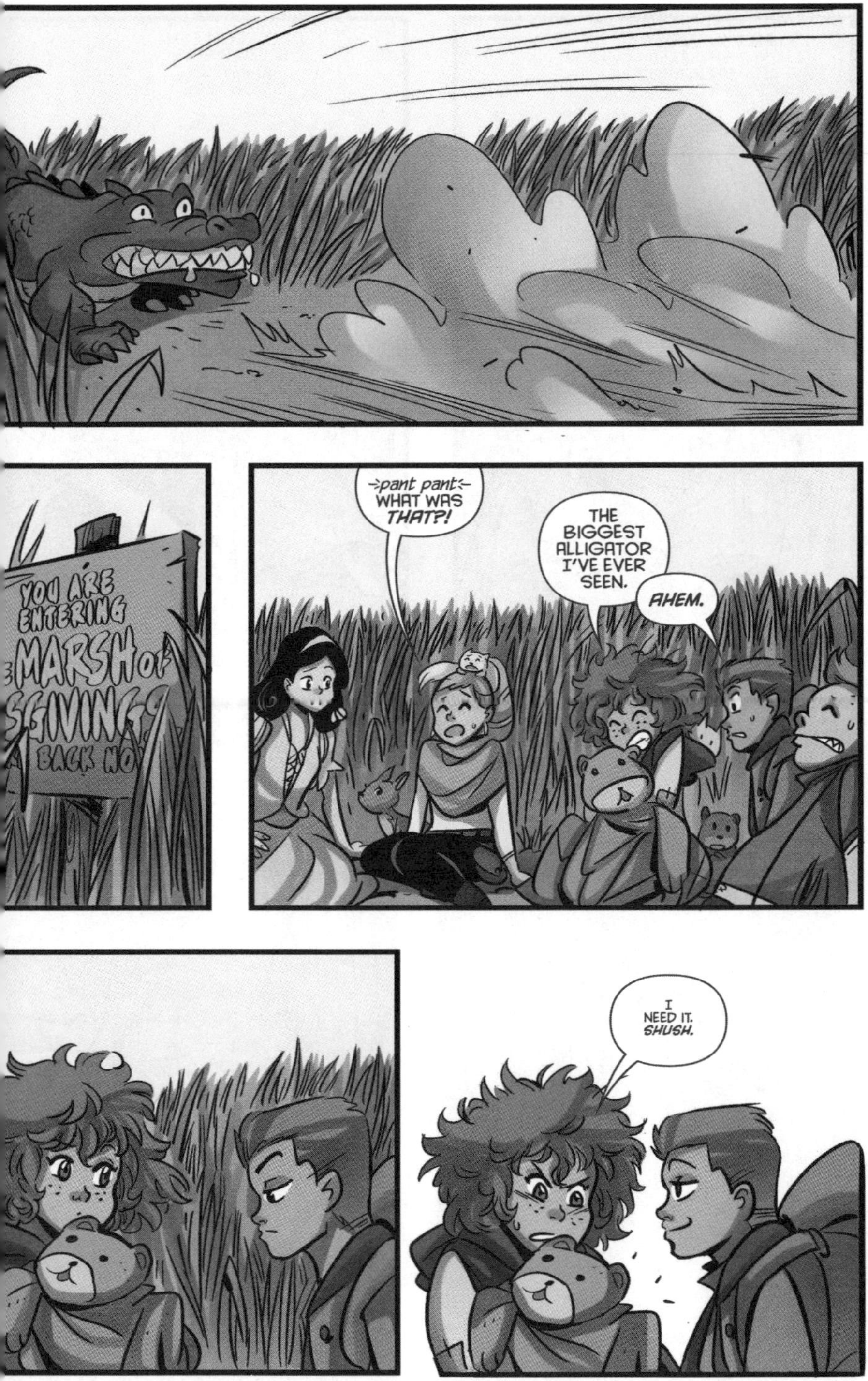
YOU ARE ENTERING MARSH OF SGIVING BACK NO
pant pant WHAT WAS THAT?!
THE BIGGEST ALLIGATOR I'VE EVER SEEN.
AHEM.
I NEED IT. SHUSH.

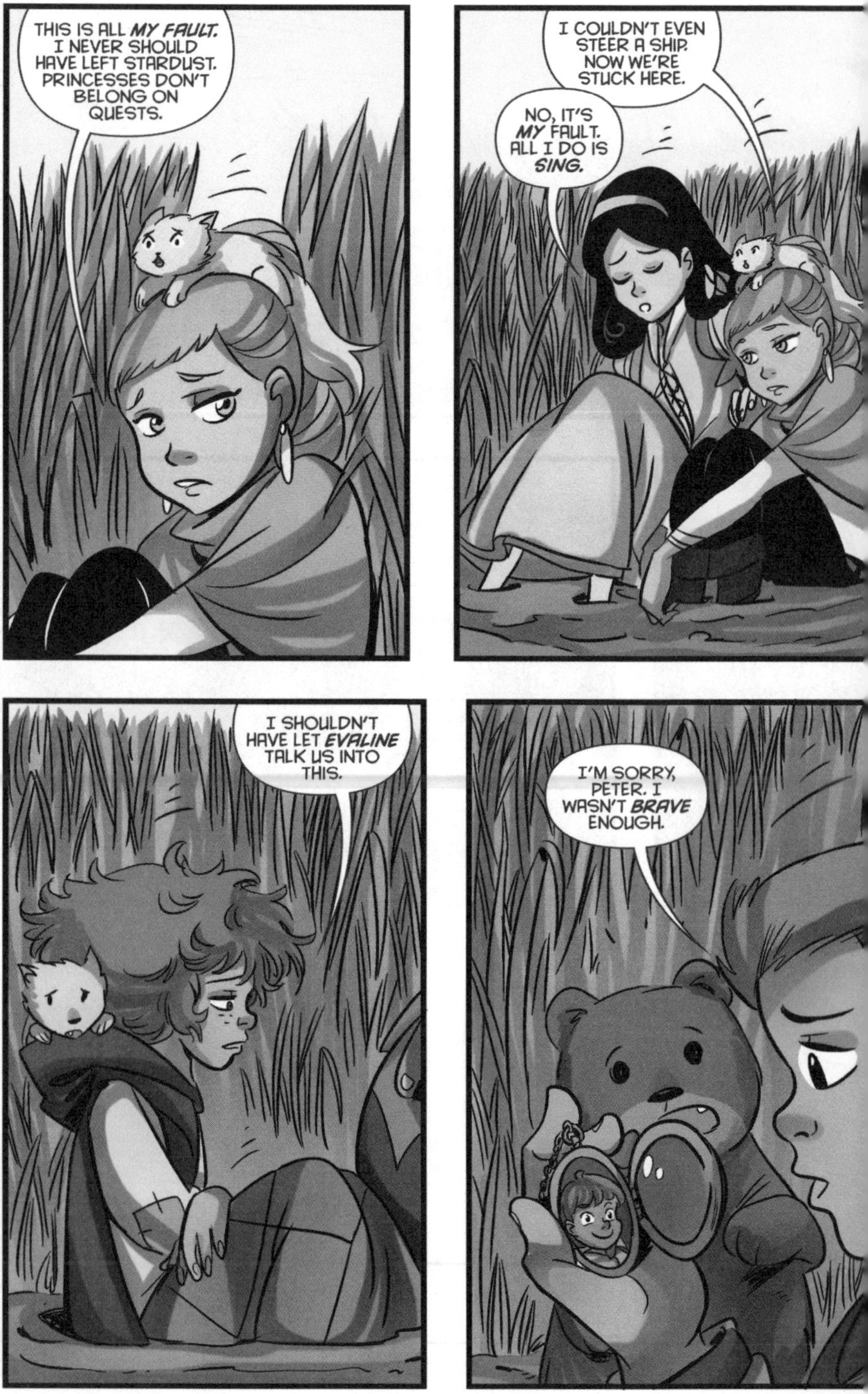
THIS IS ALL MY FAULT. I NEVER SHOULD HAVE LEFT STARDUST. PRINCESSES DON'T BELONG ON QUESTS.
I COULDN'T EVEN STEER A SHIP. NOW WE'RE STUCK HERE.
NO, IT'S MY FAULT. ALL I DO IS SING.
I SHOULDN'T HAVE LET EVALINE TALK US INTO THIS.
I'M SORRY, PETER. I WASN'T BRAVE ENOUGH.

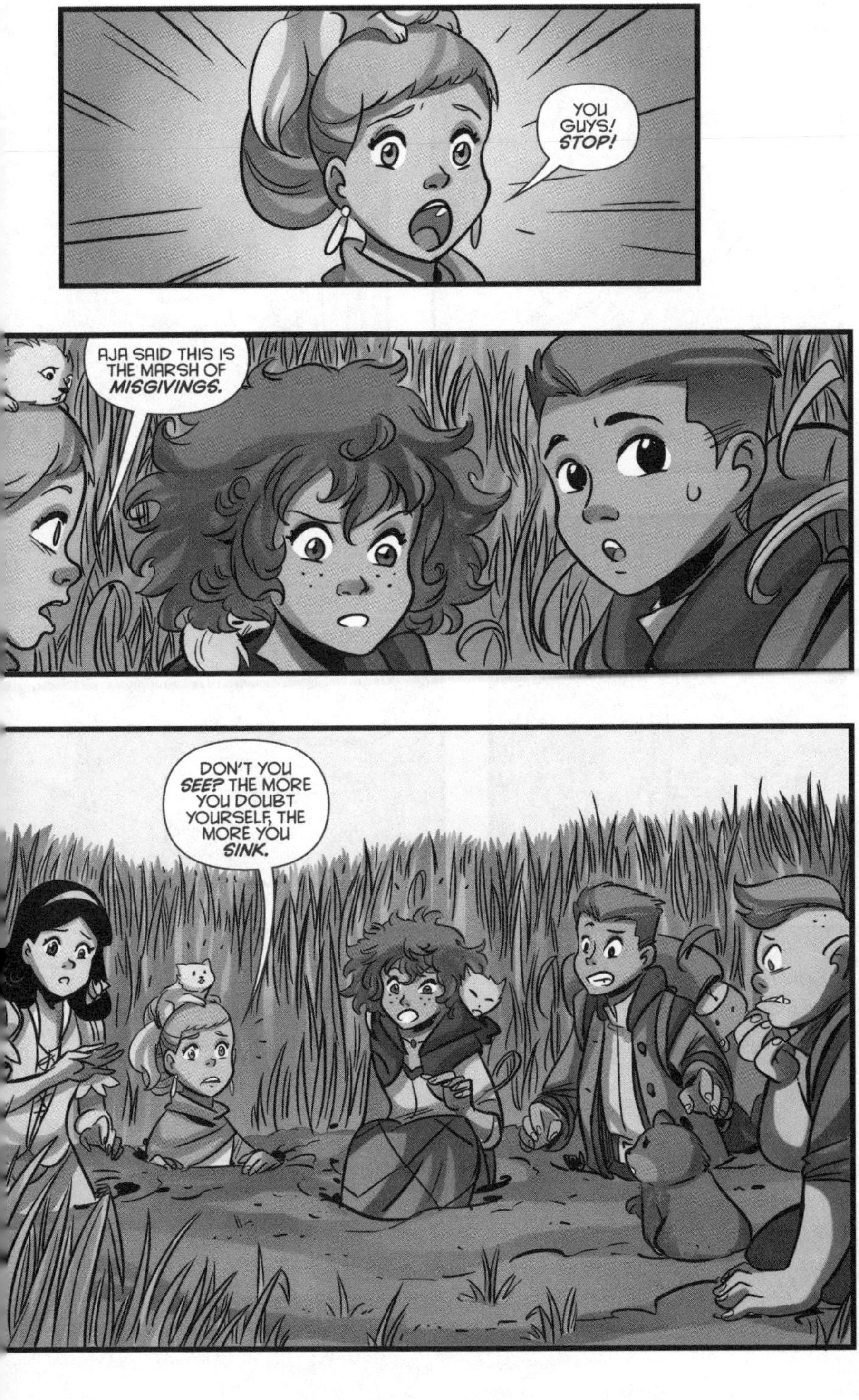
YOU GUYS! STOP!
AJA SAID THIS IS THE MARSH OF MISGIVINGS.
DON'T YOU SEE? THE MORE YOU DOUBT YOURSELF, THE MORE YOU SINK.

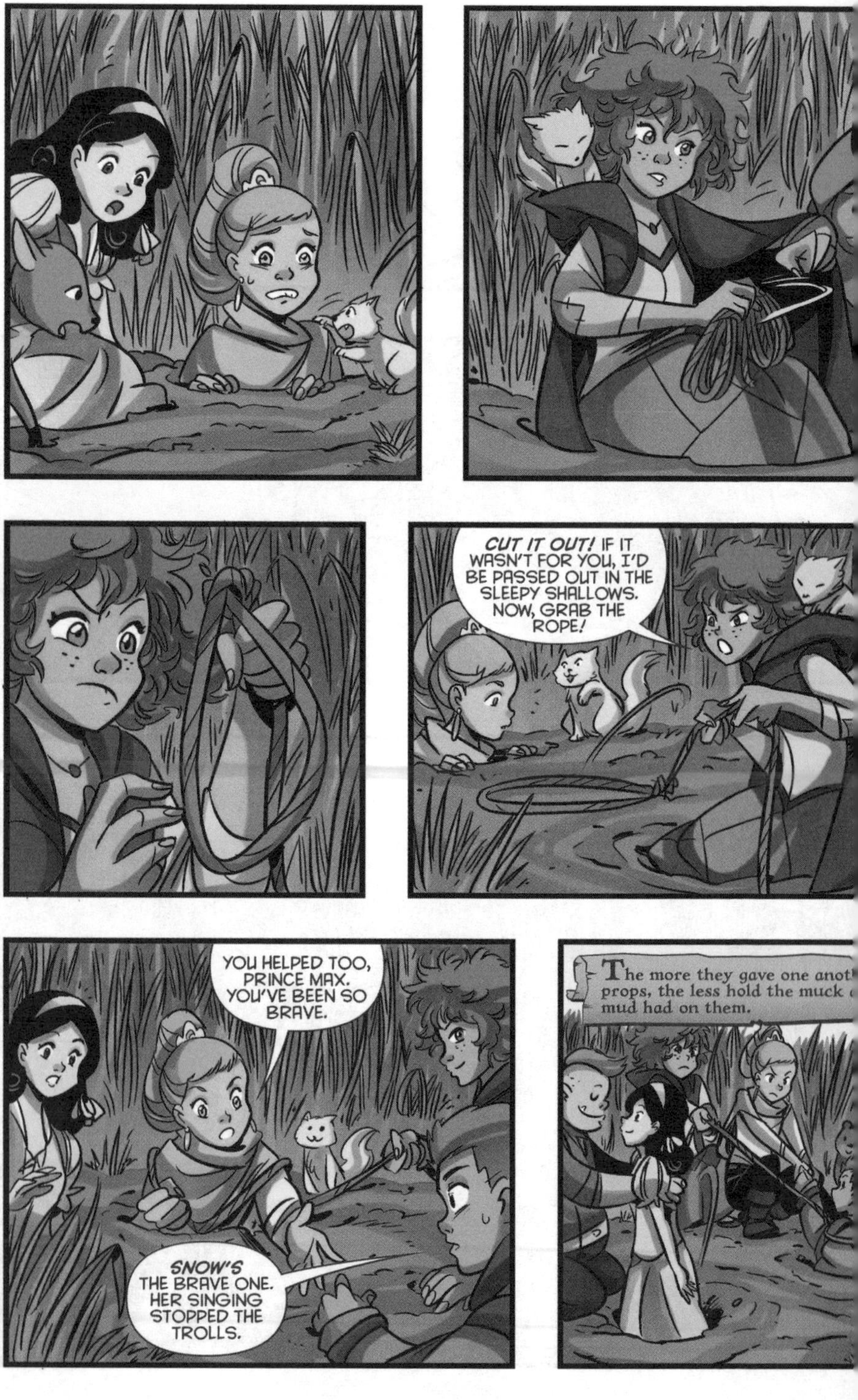

CUT IT OUT! IF IT WASN'T FOR YOU, I'D BE PASSED OUT IN THE SLEEPY SHALLOWS. NOW, GRAB THE ROPE!
YOU HELPED TOO, PRINCE MAX. YOU'VE BEEN SO BRAVE.
SNOW'S THE BRAVE ONE. HER SINGING STOPPED THE TROLLS.
The more they gave one anot
props, the less hold the muck
mud had on them.

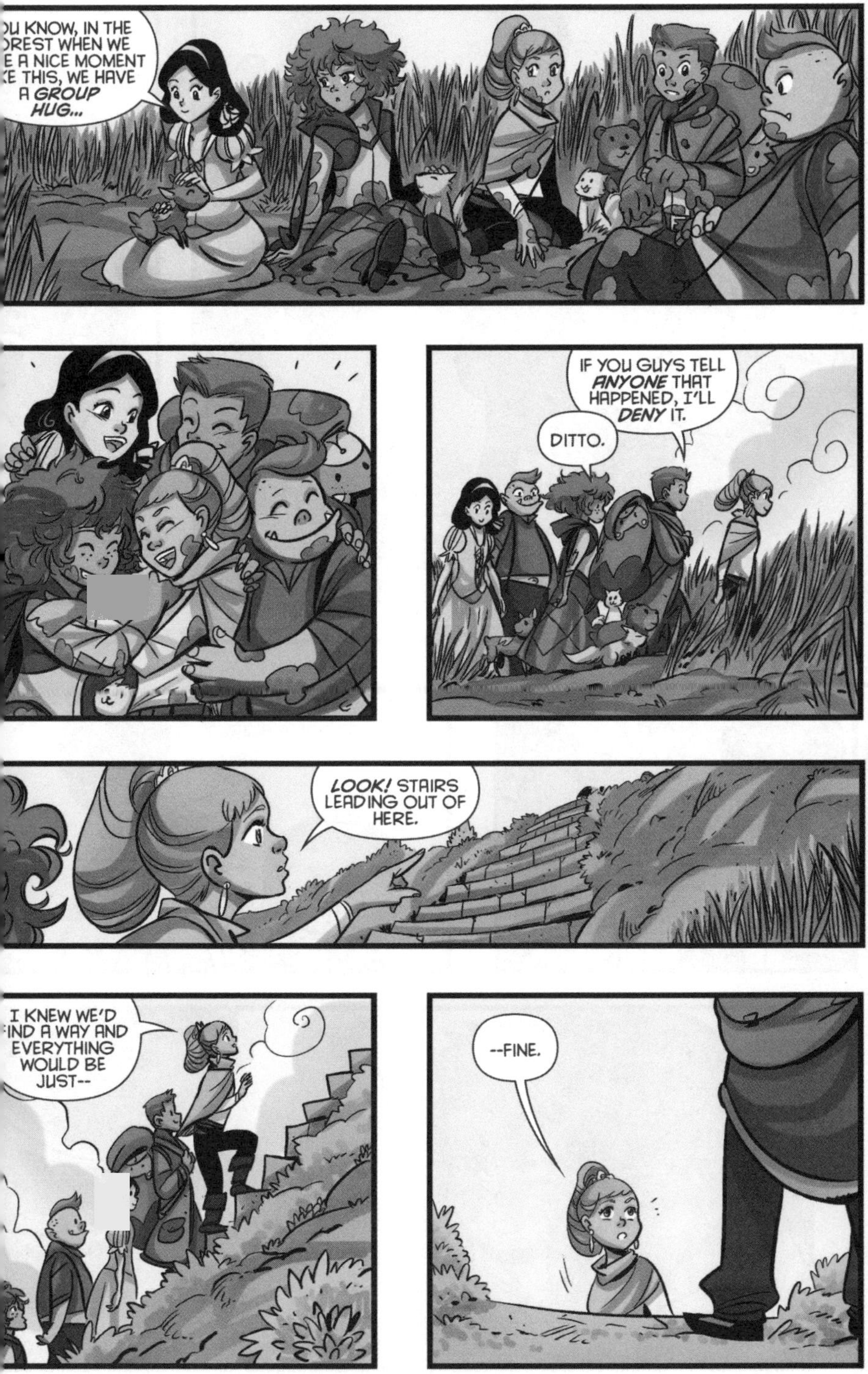
U KNOW, IN THE OREST WHEN WE E A NICE MOMENT KE THIS, WE HAVE A GROUP HUG...
IF YOU GUYS TELL ANYONE THAT HAPPENED, I'LL DENY IT.
DITTO.
LOOK! STAIRS LEADING OUT OF HERE.
I KNEW WE'D IND A WAY AND EVERYTHING WOULD BE JUST--
--FINE.

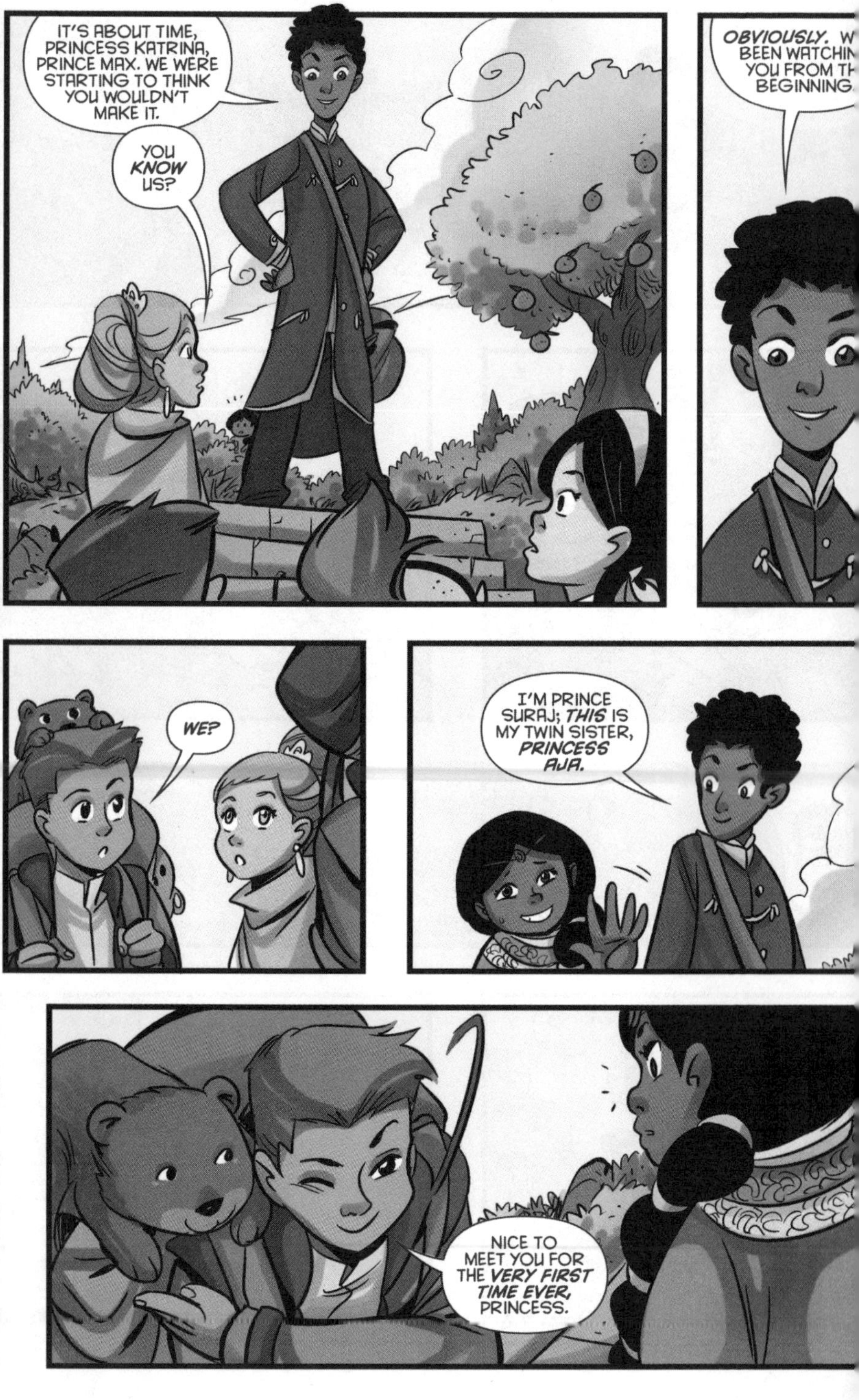
IT'S ABOUT TIME, PRINCESS KATRINA, PRINCE MAX. WE WERE STARTING TO THINK YOU WOULDN'T MAKE IT.
YOU *KNOW* US?
OBVIOUSLY. W
BEEN WATCHIN
YOU FROM T
BEGINNING.
WE?
I'M PRINCE SURAJ; *THIS* IS MY TWIN SISTER, *PRINCESS AJA.*
NICE TO MEET YOU FOR THE *VERY FIRST TIME EVER,* PRINCESS.

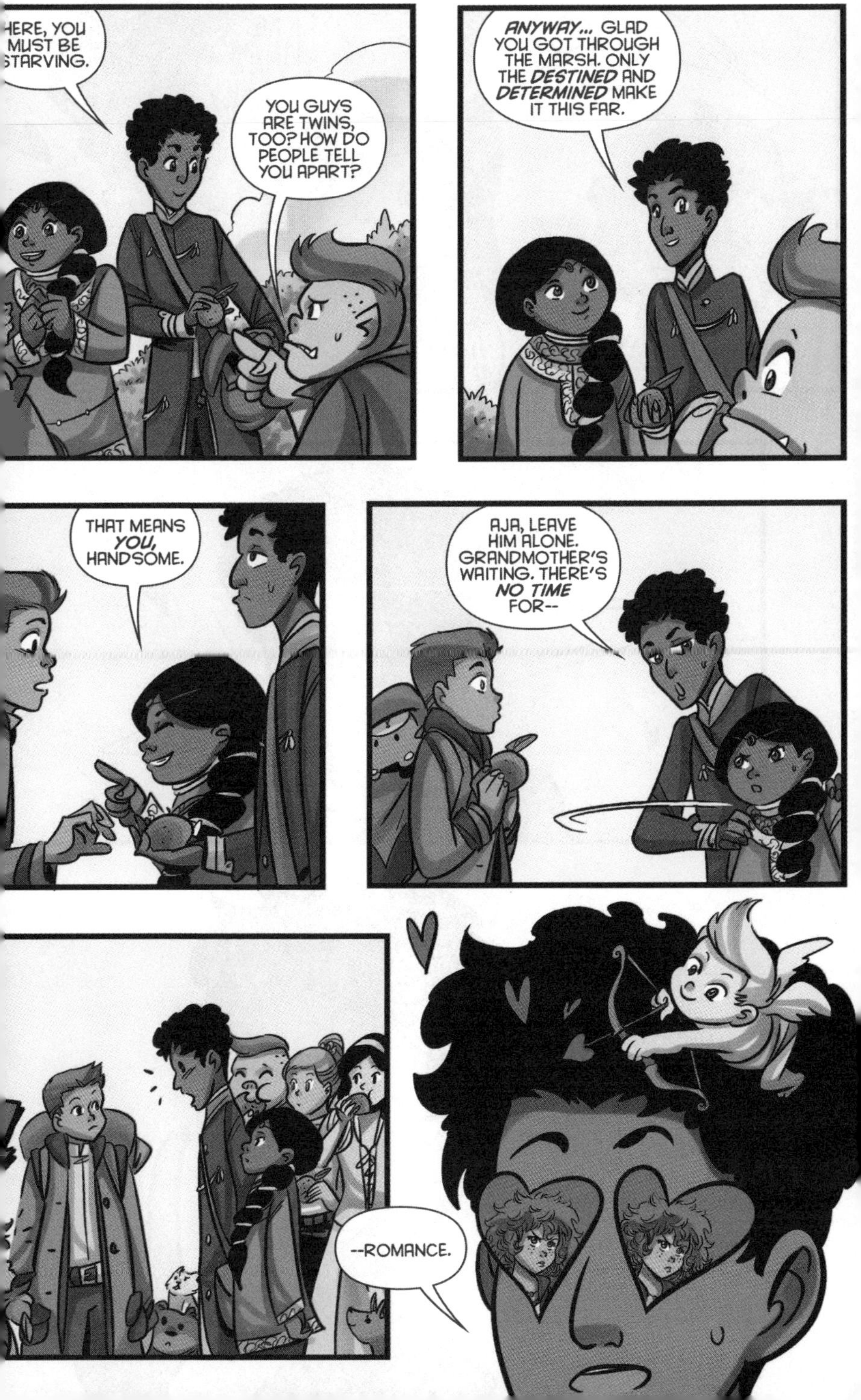
HERE, YOU MUST BE STARVING.
YOU GUYS ARE TWINS, TOO? HOW DO PEOPLE TELL YOU APART?
ANYWAY... GLAD YOU GOT THROUGH THE MARSH. ONLY THE DESTINED AND DETERMINED MAKE IT THIS FAR.
THAT MEANS YOU, HANDSOME.
AJA, LEAVE HIM ALONE. GRANDMOTHER'S WAITING. THERE'S NO TIME FOR--
--ROMANCE.

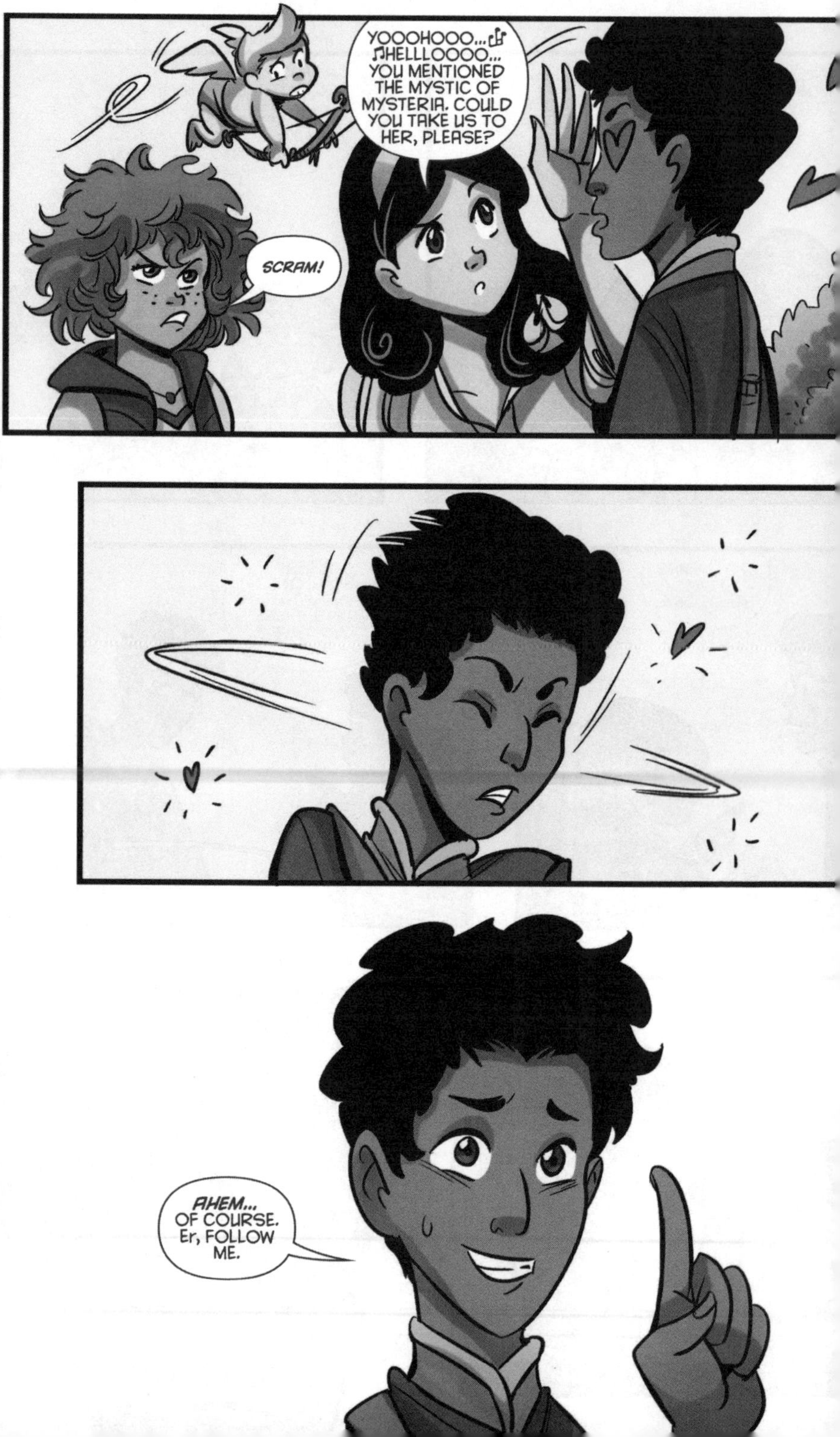
YOOOHOOO... ♫HELLLOOOO... YOU MENTIONED THE MYSTIC OF MYSTERIA. COULD YOU TAKE US TO HER, PLEASE?
SCRAM!
AHEM... OF COURSE. Er, FOLLOW ME.

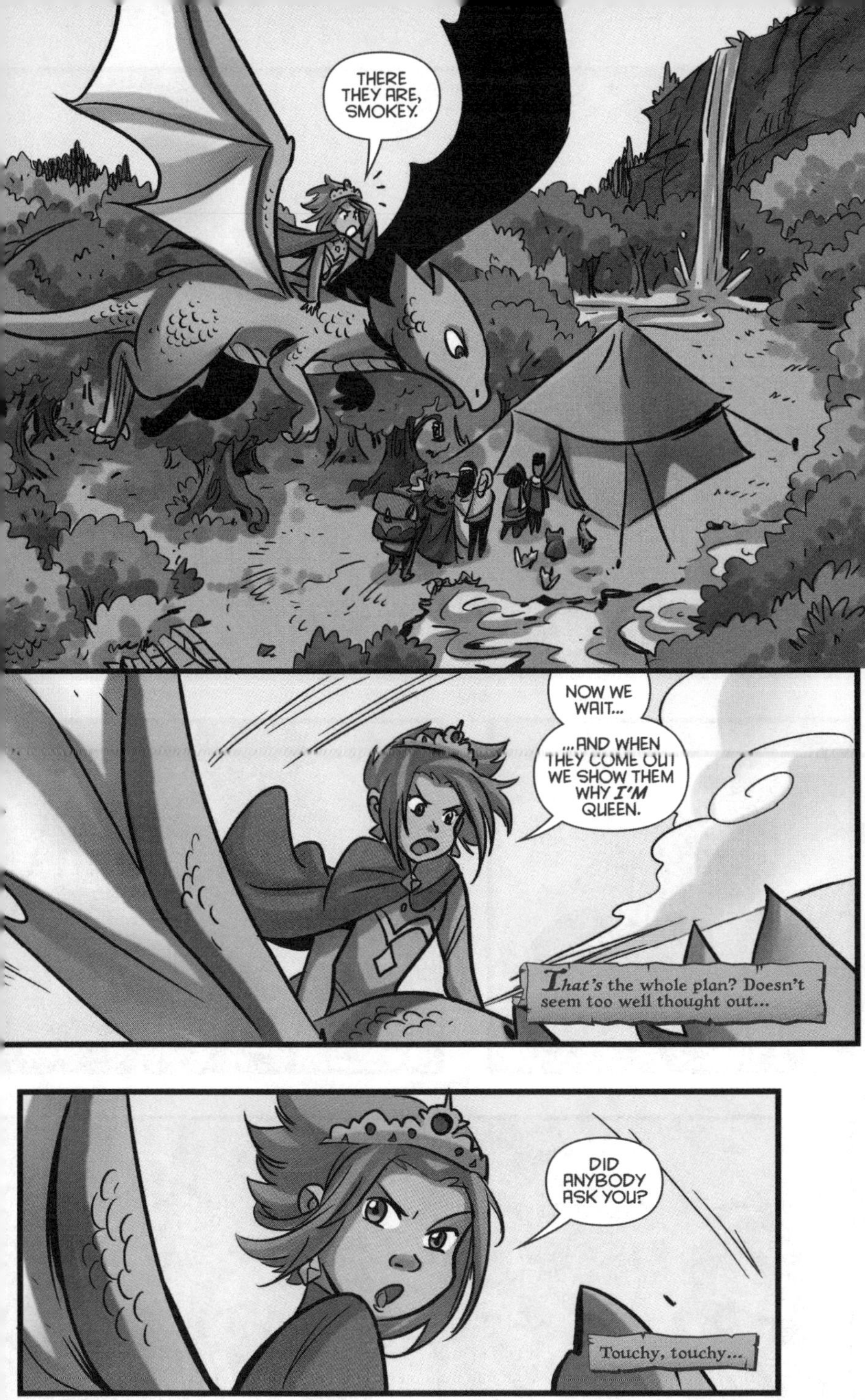
THERE THEY ARE, SMOKEY.
NOW WE WAIT...
...AND WHEN THEY COME OUT WE SHOW THEM WHY *I'M* QUEEN.
That's the whole plan? Doesn't seem too well thought out...
DID ANYBODY ASK YOU?
Touchy, touchy...

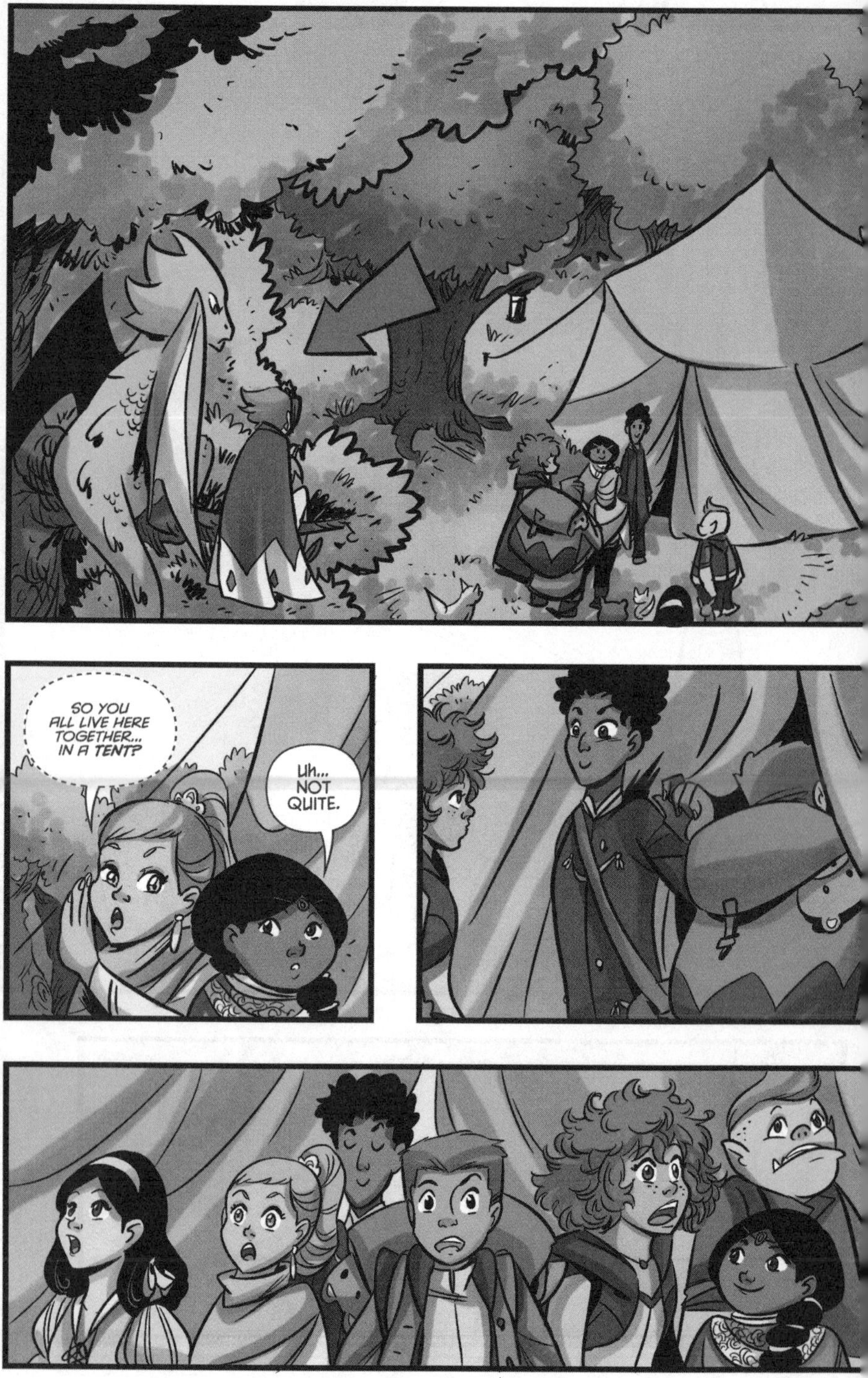
SO YOU ALL LIVE HERE TOGETHER... IN A TENT?
UH... NOT QUITE.

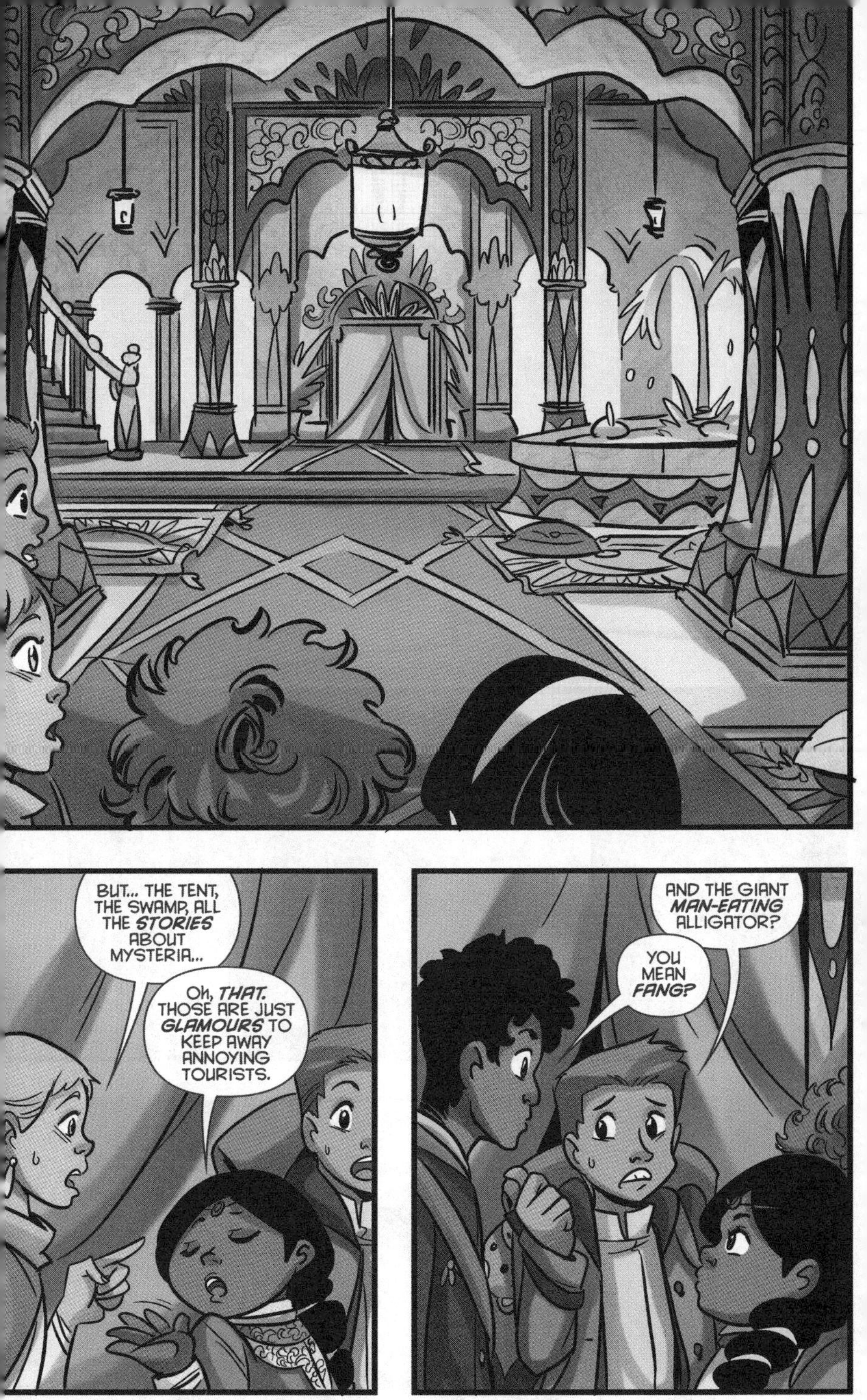
BUT... THE TENT, THE SWAMP, ALL THE STORIES ABOUT MYSTERIA...
Oh, THAT. THOSE ARE JUST GLAMOURS TO KEEP AWAY ANNOYING TOURISTS.
AND THE GIANT MAN-EATING ALLIGATOR?
YOU MEAN FANG?

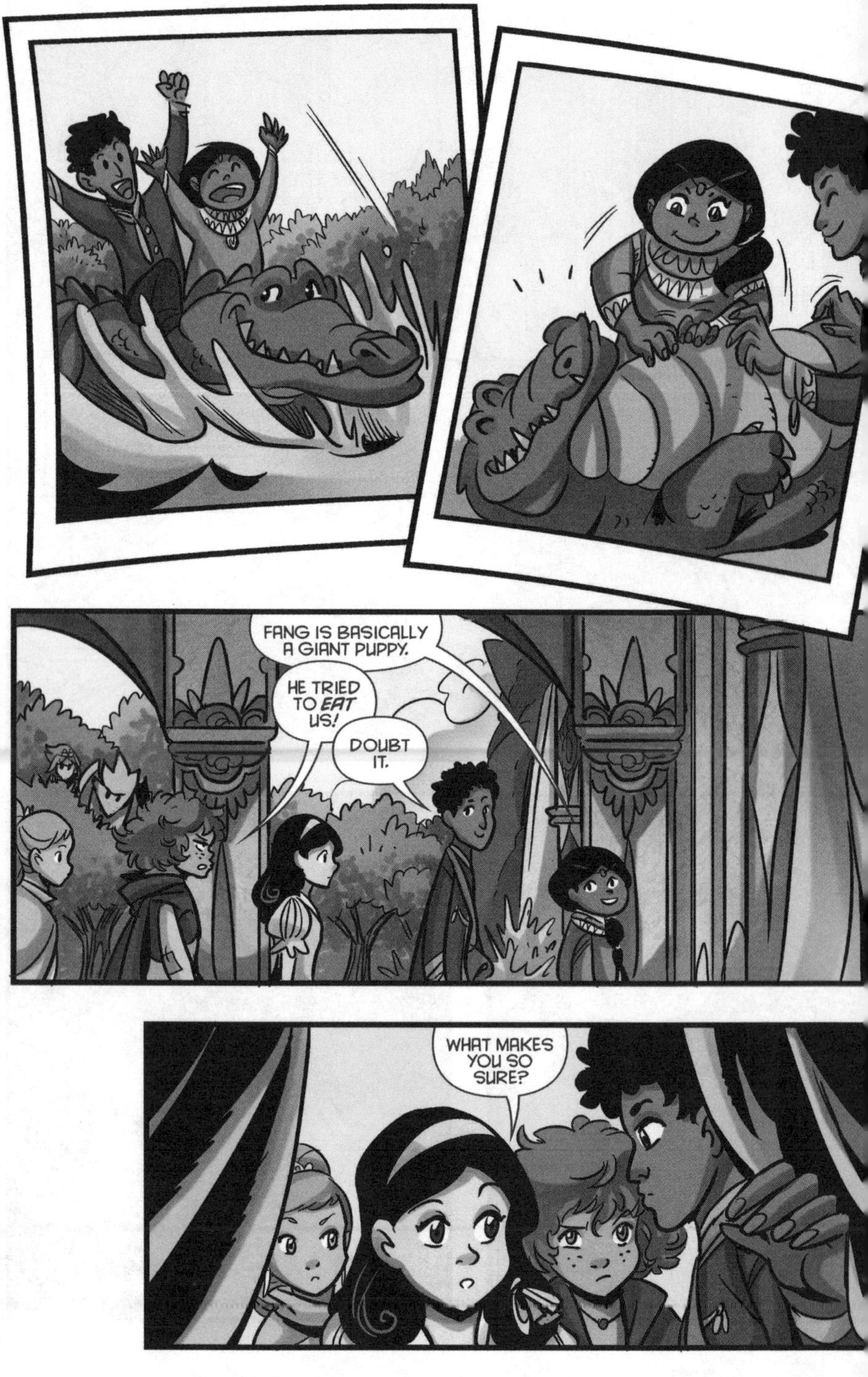
FANG IS BASICALLY A GIANT PUPPY.
HE TRIED TO *EAT* US!
DOUBT IT.
WHAT MAKES YOU SO SURE?

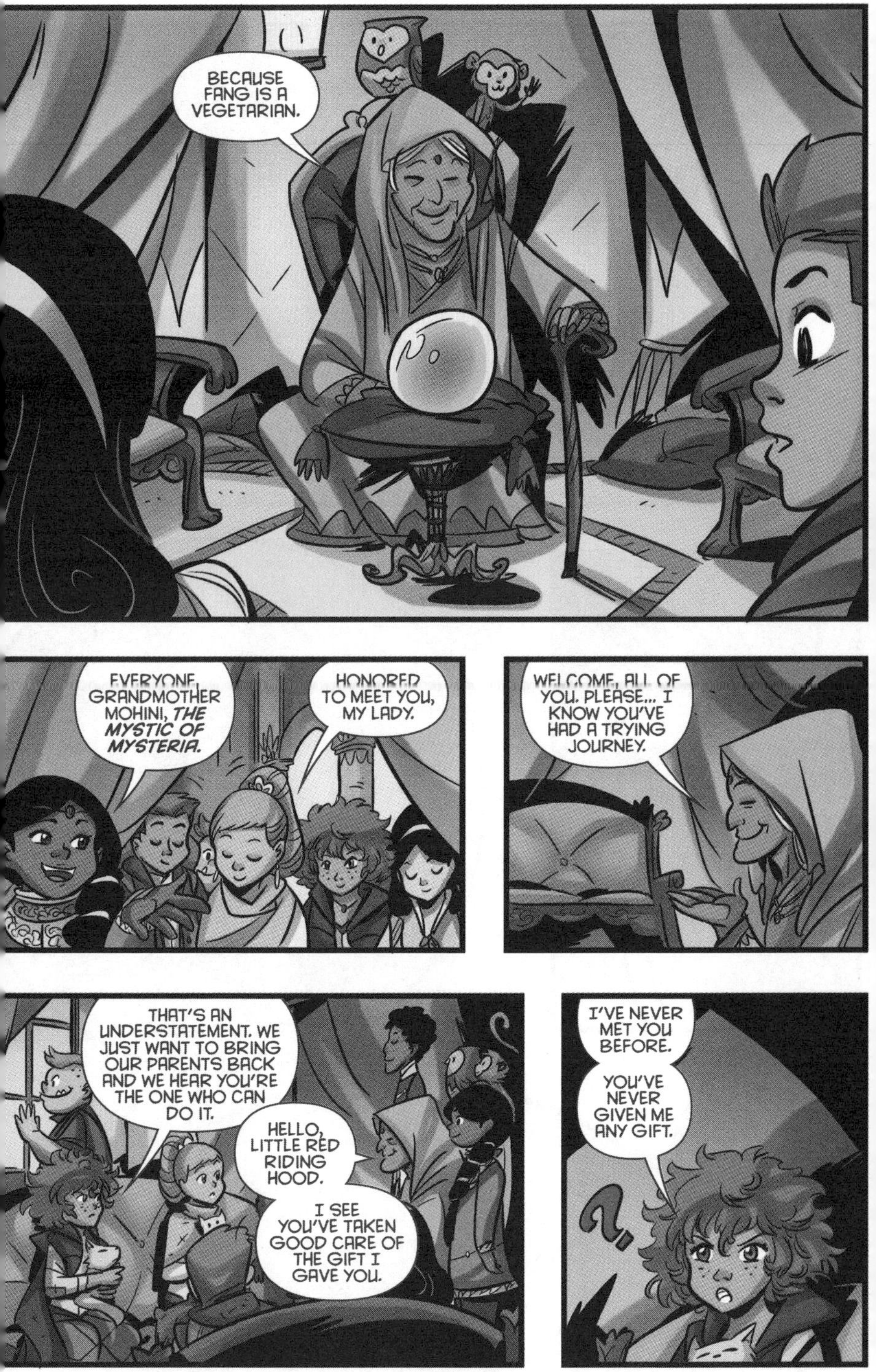
BECAUSE FANG IS A VEGETARIAN.
EVERYONE, GRANDMOTHER MOHINI, *THE MYSTIC OF MYSTERIA.*
HONORED TO MEET YOU, MY LADY.
WELCOME, ALL OF YOU. PLEASE... I KNOW YOU'VE HAD A TRYING JOURNEY.
THAT'S AN UNDERSTATEMENT. WE JUST WANT TO BRING OUR PARENTS BACK AND WE HEAR YOU'RE THE ONE WHO CAN DO IT.
HELLO, LITTLE RED RIDING HOOD.
I SEE YOU'VE TAKEN GOOD CARE OF THE GIFT I GAVE YOU.
I'VE NEVER MET YOU BEFORE.
YOU'VE NEVER GIVEN ME ANY GIFT.

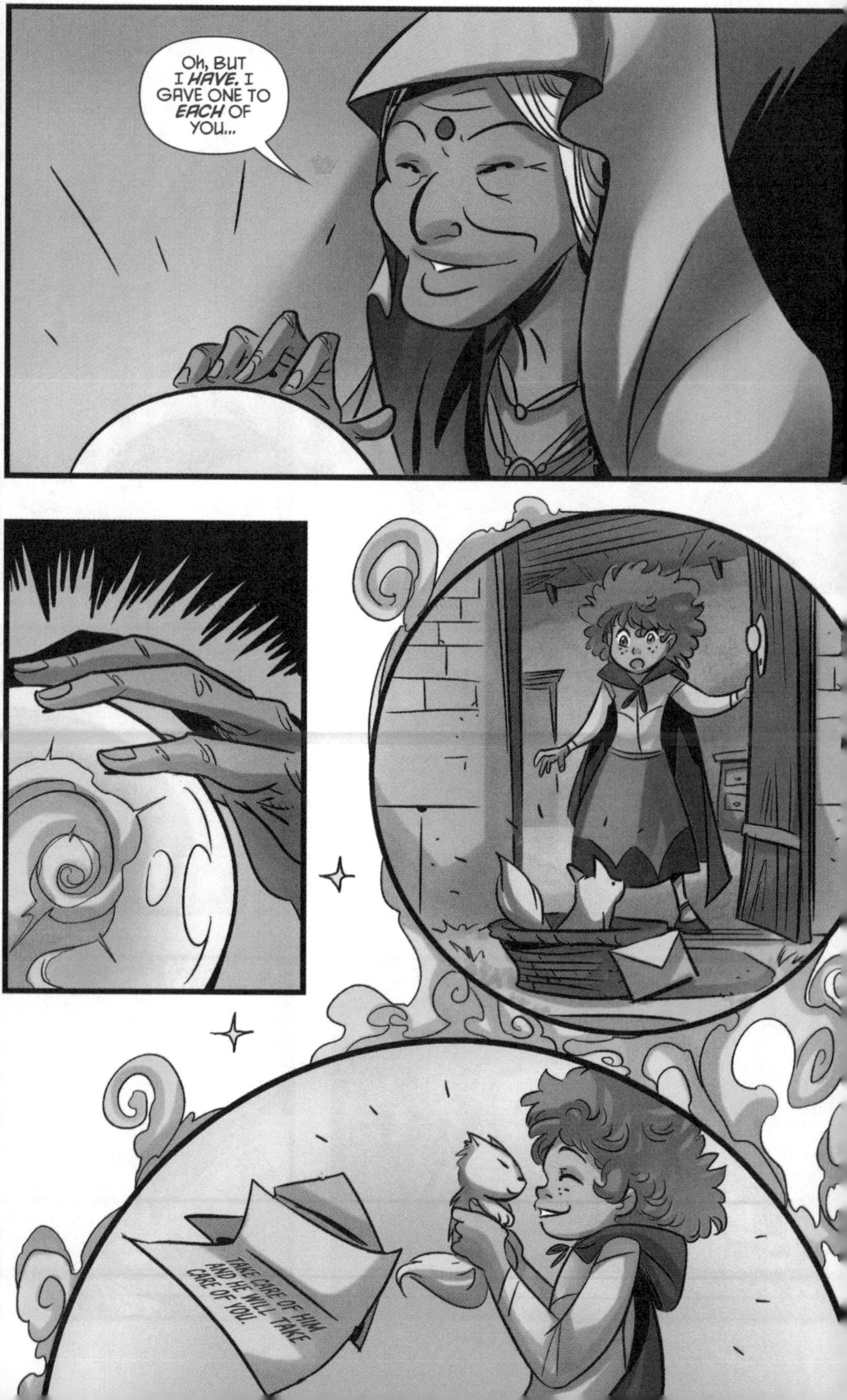
Oh, BUT I HAVE. I GAVE ONE TO EACH OF YOU...
TAKE CARE OF HIM AND HE WILL TAKE CARE OF YOU.

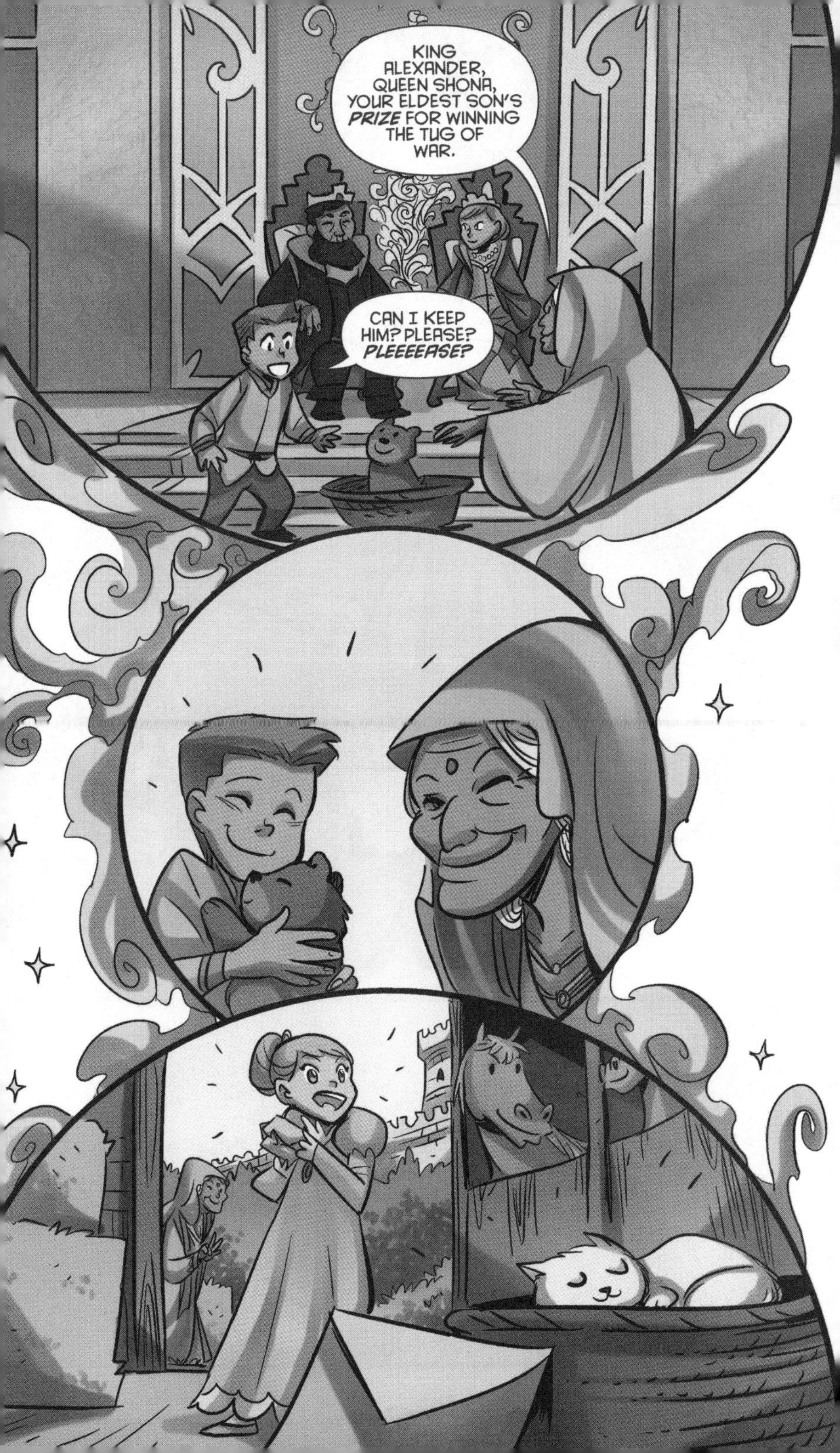
KING ALEXANDER, QUEEN SHONA, YOUR ELDEST SON'S *PRIZE* FOR WINNING THE TUG OF WAR.
CAN I KEEP HIM? PLEASE? *PLEEEEASE?*

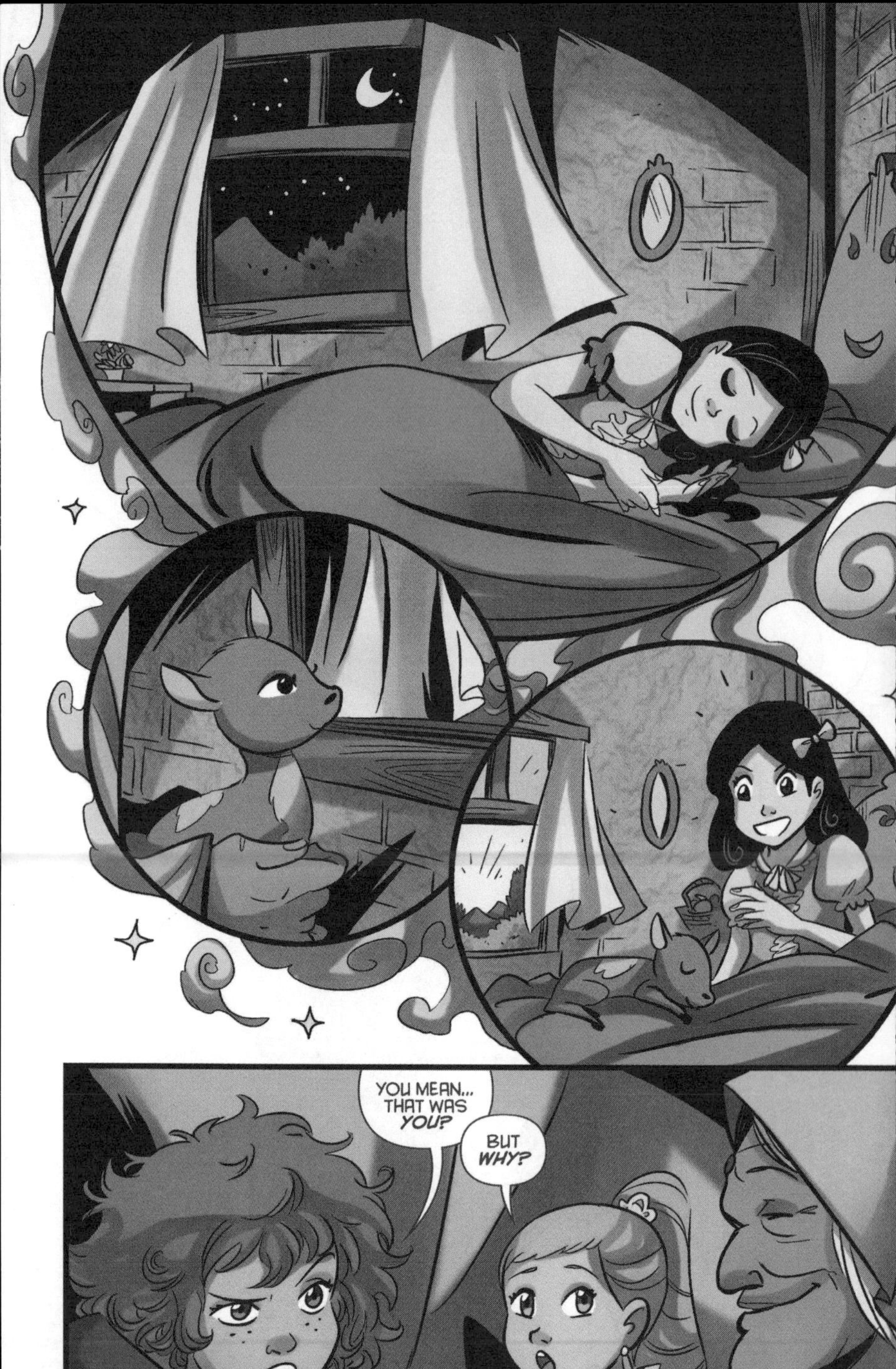
YOU MEAN... THAT WAS *YOU?*
BUT *WHY?*

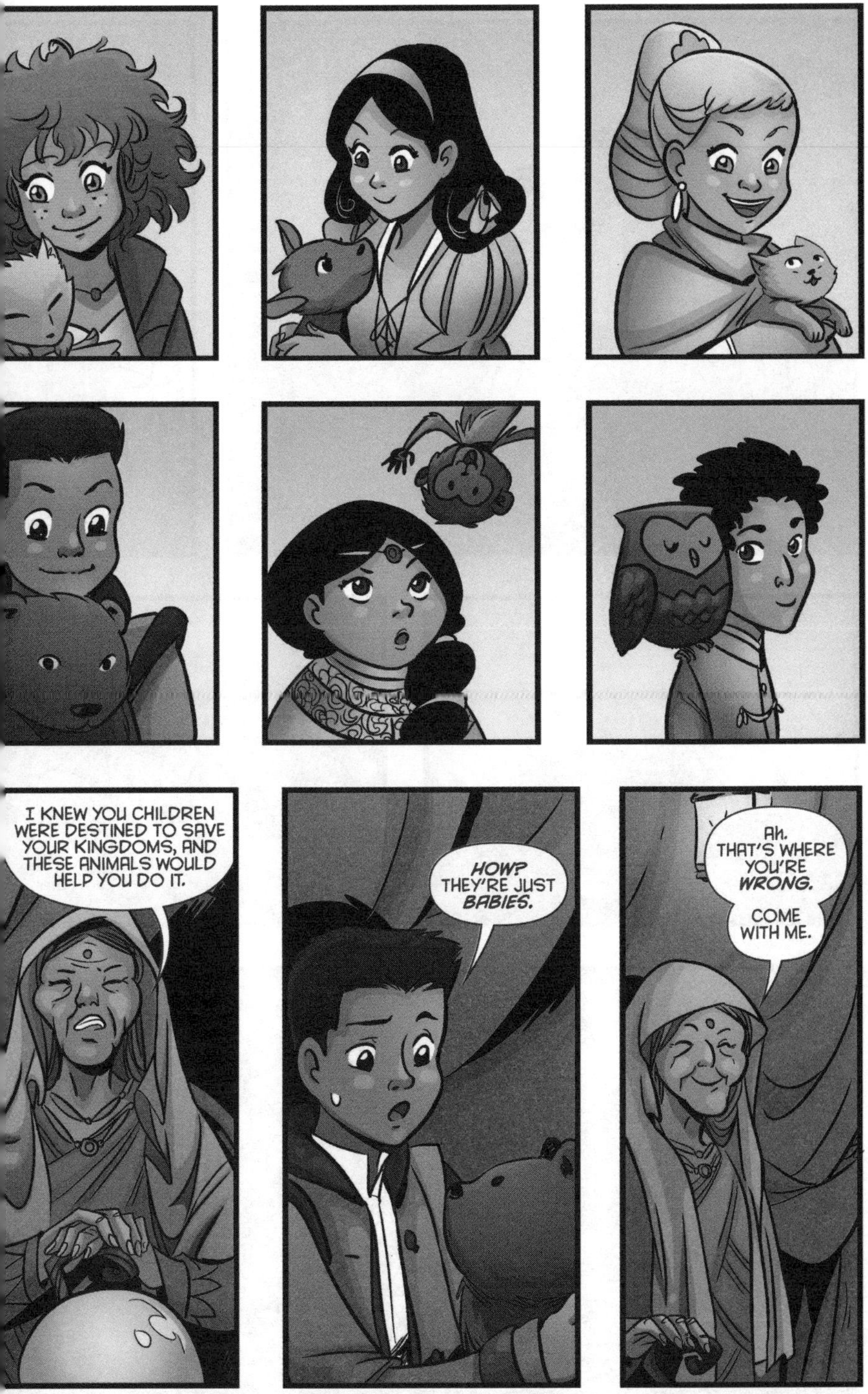
I KNEW YOU CHILDREN WERE DESTINED TO SAVE YOUR KINGDOMS, AND THESE ANIMALS WOULD HELP YOU DO IT.
HOW? THEY'RE JUST BABIES.
AH. THAT'S WHERE YOU'RE WRONG.
COME WITH ME.

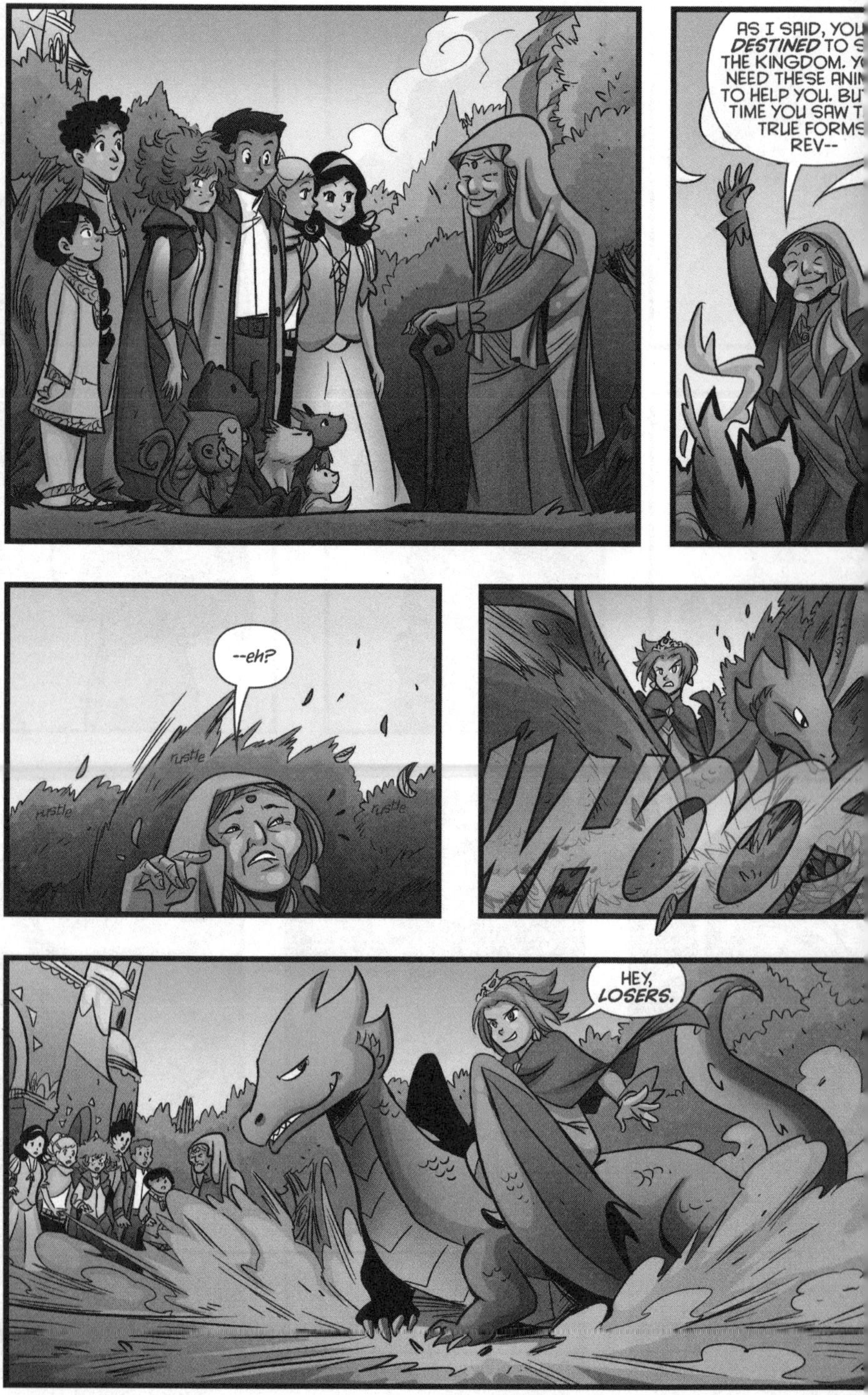
AS I SAID, YO *DESTINED* TO THE KINGDOM. NEED THESE TO HELP YOU. TIME YOU SAW TRUE FORMS REV--
--eh?
rustle
rustle
rustle
HEY, *LOSERS.*

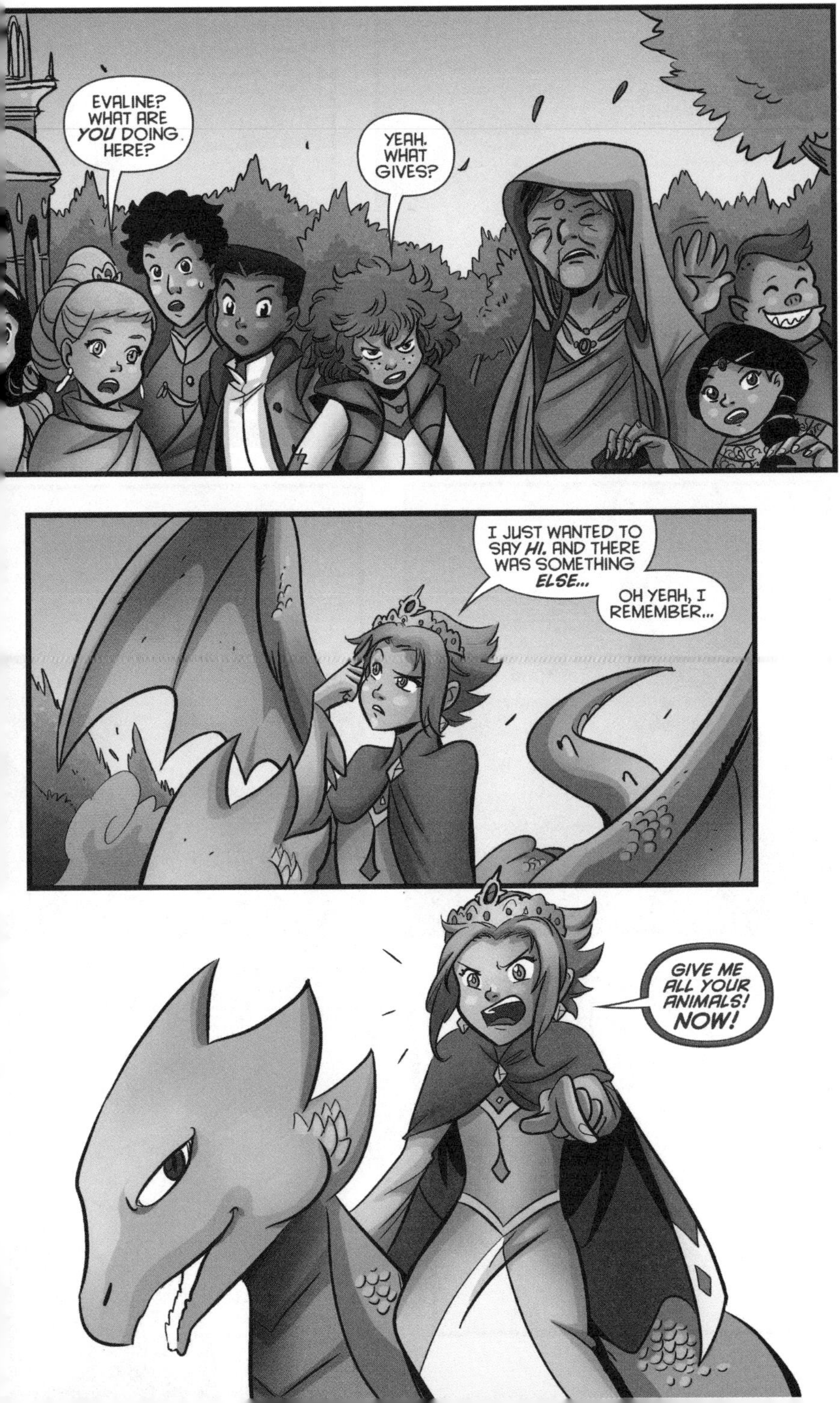
EVALINE? WHAT ARE YOU DOING HERE?
YEAH. WHAT GIVES?
I JUST WANTED TO SAY HI. AND THERE WAS SOMETHING ELSE...
OH YEAH, I REMEMBER...
GIVE ME ALL YOUR ANIMALS! NOW!

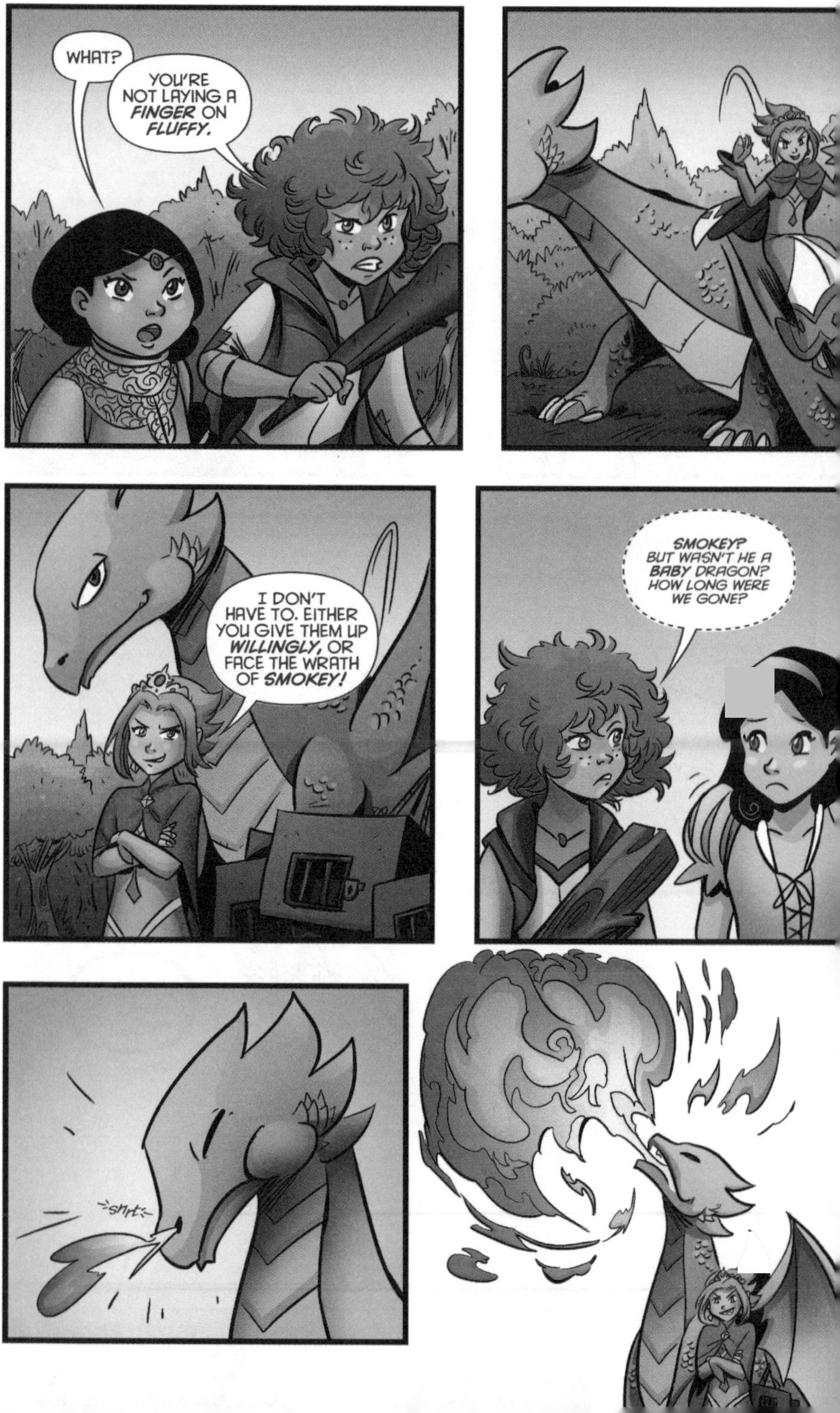
WHAT?
YOU'RE NOT LAYING A *FINGER* ON *FLUFFY.*
I DON'T HAVE TO. EITHER YOU GIVE THEM UP *WILLINGLY,* OR FACE THE WRATH OF *SMOKEY!*
SMOKEY? BUT WASN'T HE A *BABY* DRAGON? HOW LONG WERE WE GONE?
snrt

BUT WHY DID YOU TAKE OUR ANIMAL FRIENDS?

THE MYSTIC BIRD! WE NEED THEM TO COMPLETE OUR QUEST AND--

DUH. I *KNOW.* I'VE BEEN LISTENING IN *THE WHOLE TIME.*

WITH THE GROWN-UPS GONE, *I'M* THE QUEEN OF STARDUST AND I'M NOT ABOUT TO LET YOU *CHUMPS* GET IN THE WAY. SO COME ON, COUGH UP THE FURBALLS.

FINE. HAVE IT YOUR WAY. SMOKEY, *LIGHT 'EM UP...*

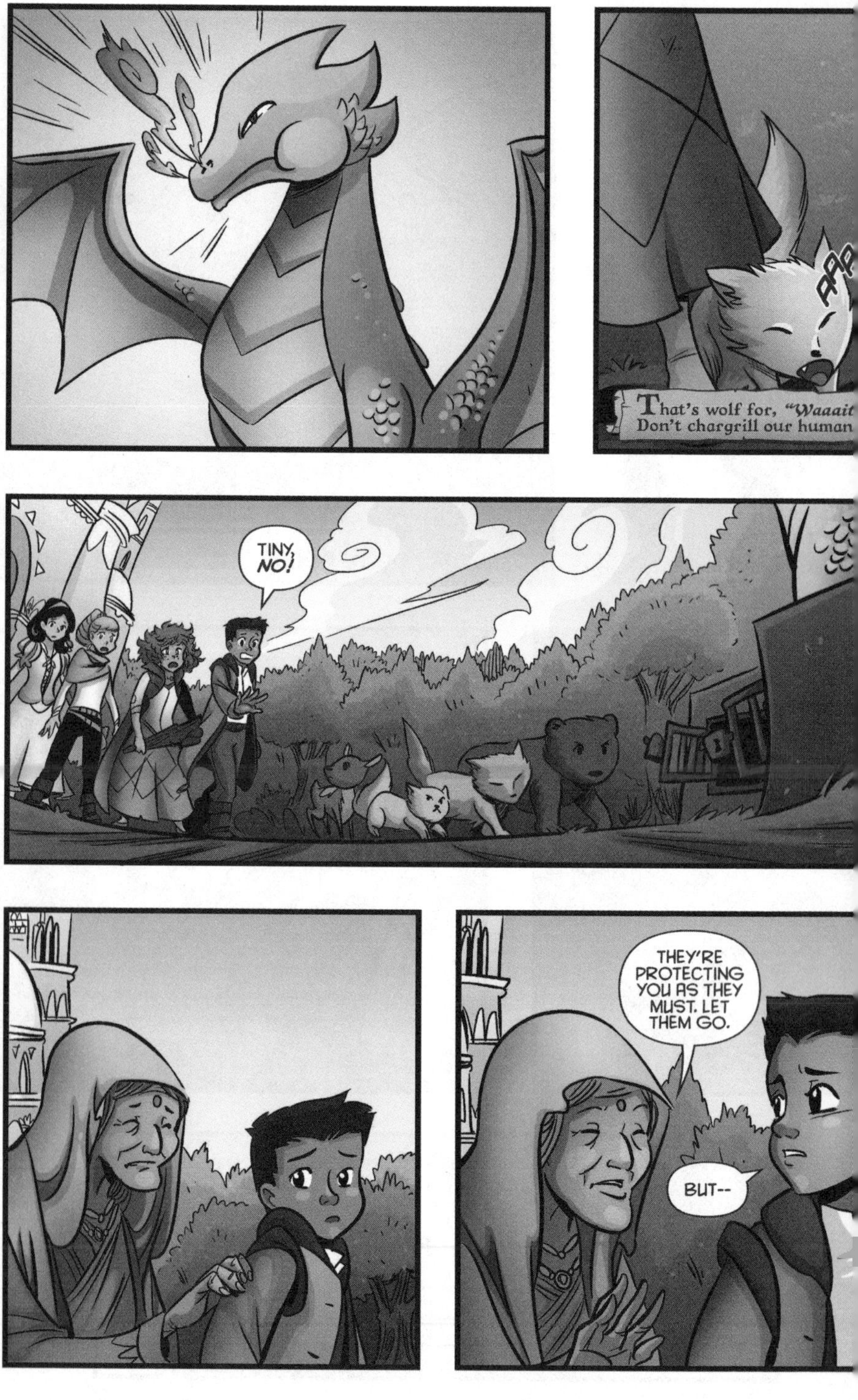
That's wolf for, "Waaait
Don't chargrill our human
TINY, NO!
THEY'RE PROTECTING YOU AS THEY MUST. LET THEM GO.
BUT--

TRUST THEM.

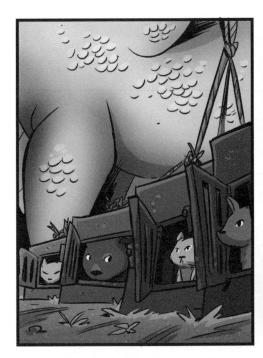

GOOD CHOICE.

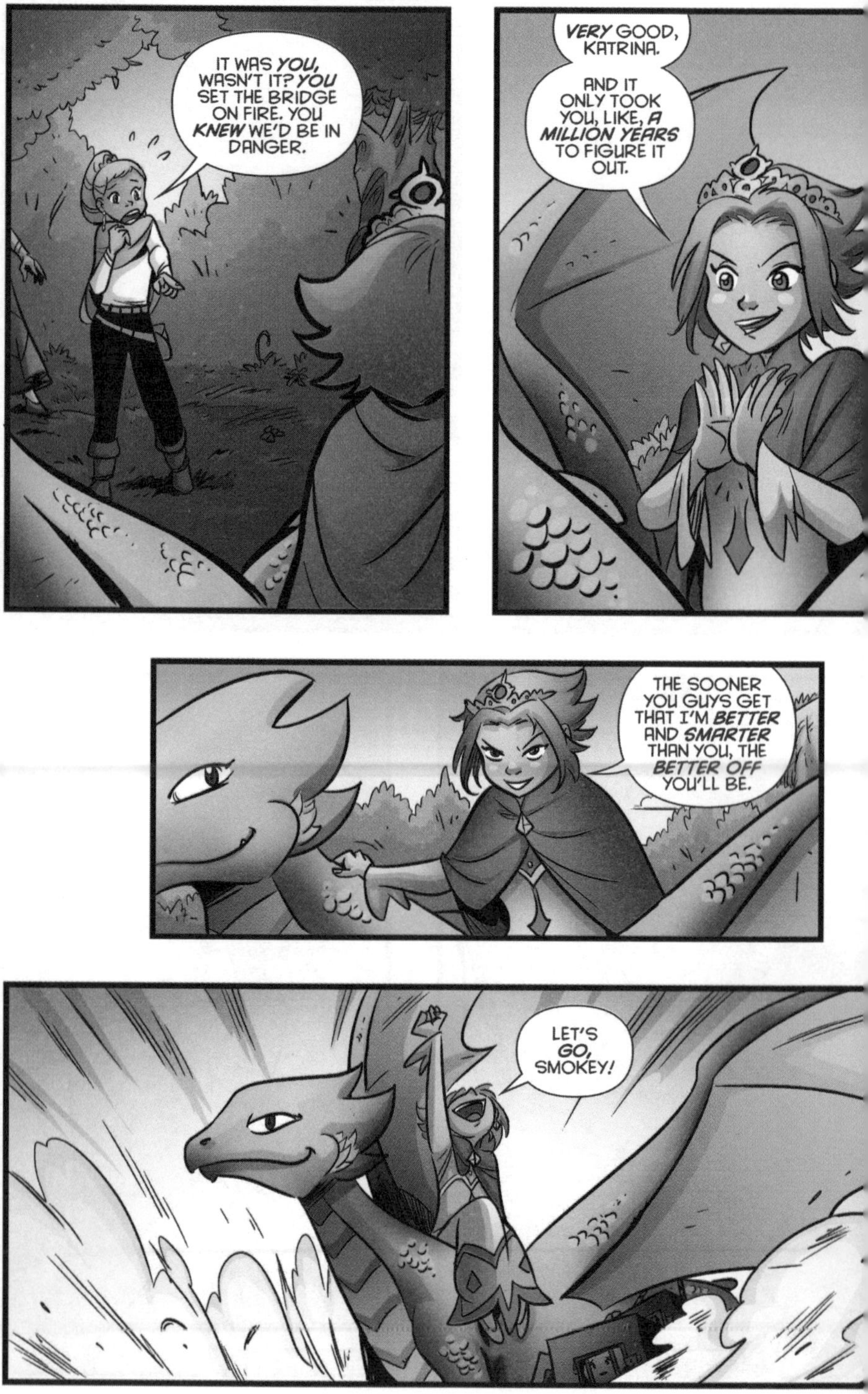
IT WAS YOU, WASN'T IT? YOU SET THE BRIDGE ON FIRE. YOU KNEW WE'D BE IN DANGER.
VERY GOOD, KATRINA.
AND IT ONLY TOOK YOU, LIKE, A MILLION YEARS TO FIGURE IT OUT.
THE SOONER YOU GUYS GET THAT I'M BETTER AND SMARTER THAN YOU, THE BETTER OFF YOU'LL BE.
LET'S GO, SMOKEY!

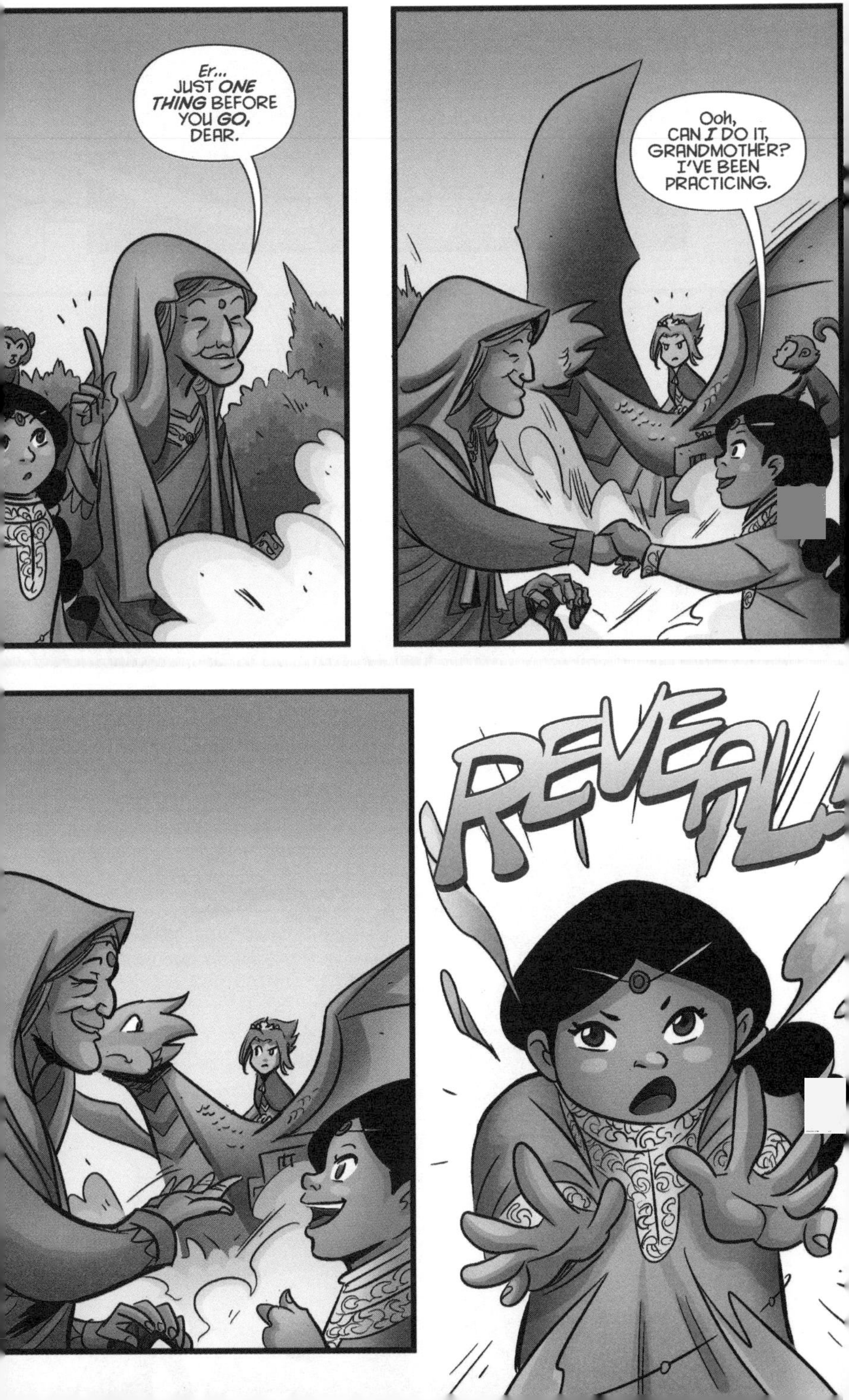
Er... JUST ONE THING BEFORE YOU GO, DEAR.
Ooh, CAN I DO IT, GRANDMOTHER? I'VE BEEN PRACTICING.
REVEAL

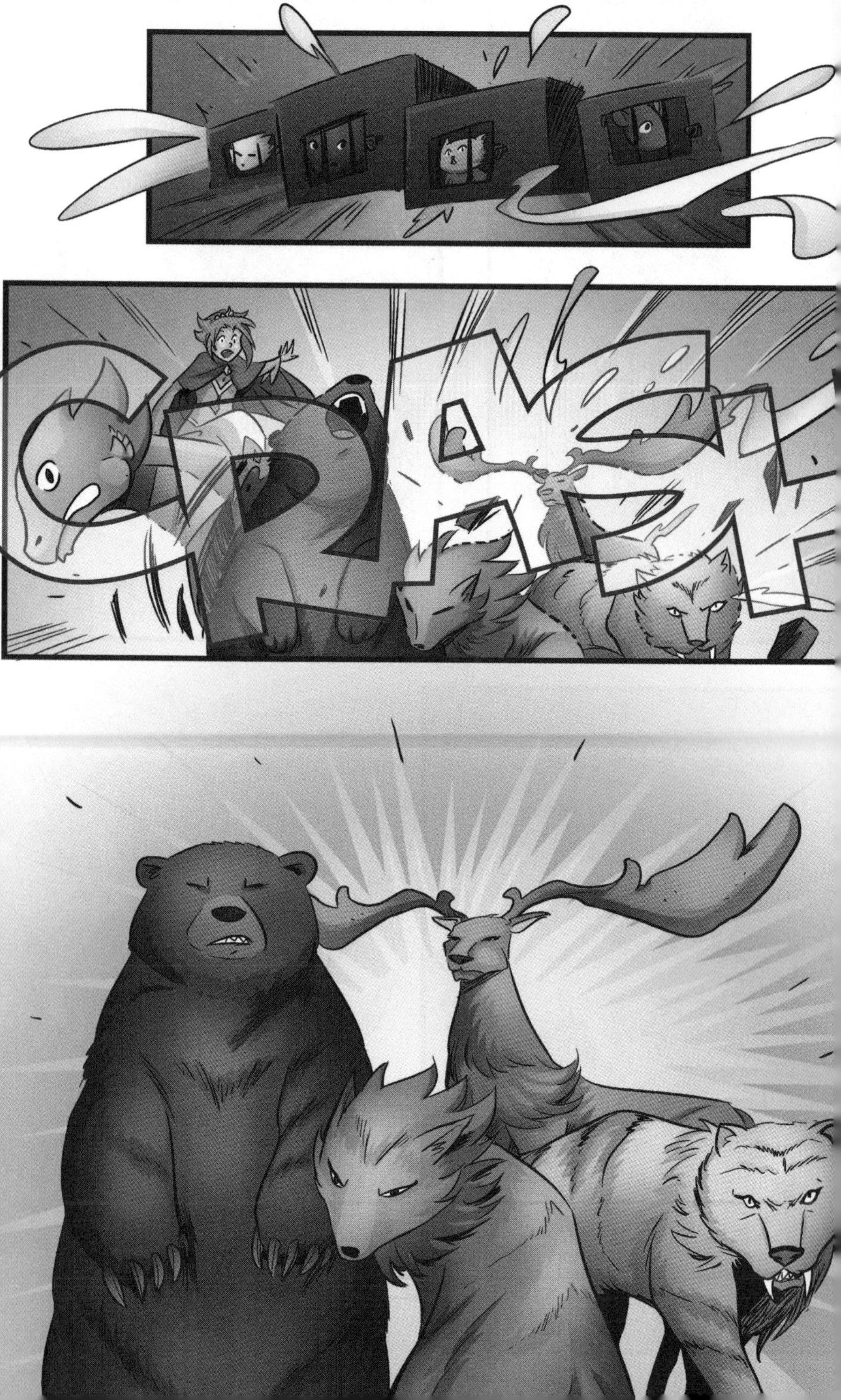
CRASH

PAKKA

NANDI

SMOKEY, YOU'RE *NOT* THE ONLY ONE? *CURSES!* LET'S GET OUT OF HERE.

UH-OH.

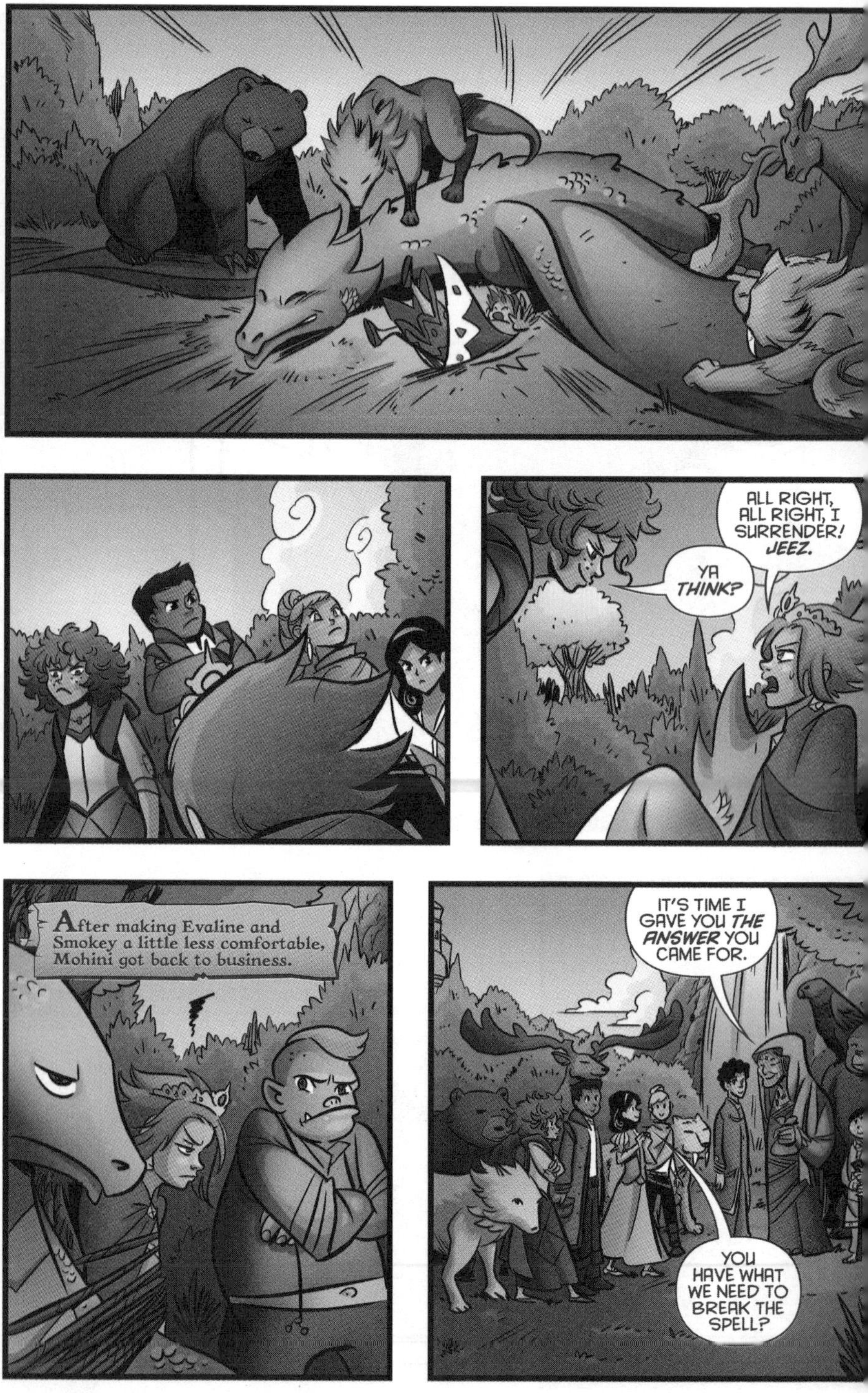

ALL RIGHT, ALL RIGHT, I SURRENDER! JEEZ.
YA THINK?
After making Evaline and Smokey a little less comfortable, Mohini got back to business.
IT'S TIME I GAVE YOU THE ANSWER YOU CAME FOR.
YOU HAVE WHAT WE NEED TO BREAK THE SPELL?

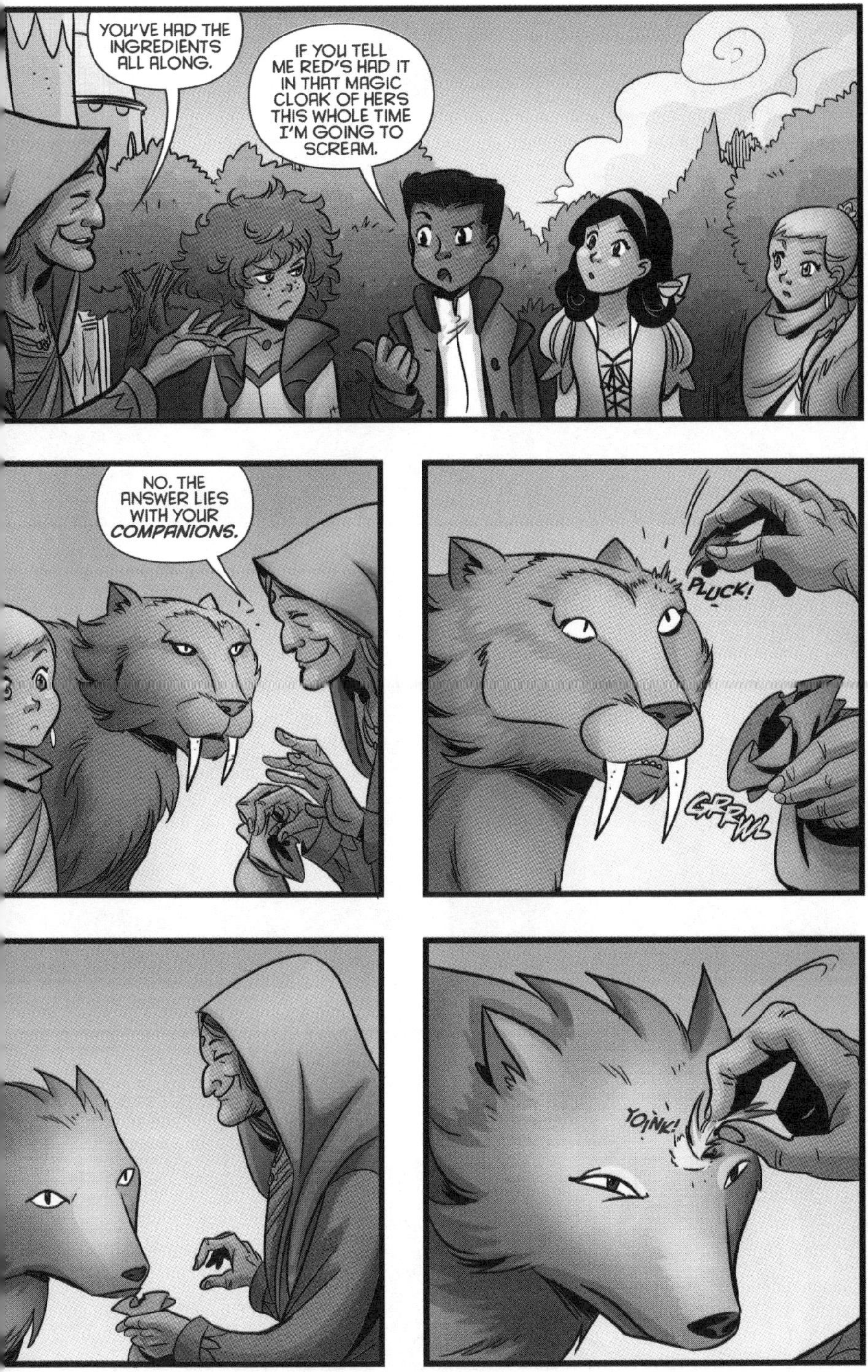
YOU'VE HAD THE INGREDIENTS ALL ALONG.
IF YOU TELL ME RED'S HAD IT IN THAT MAGIC CLOAK OF HERS THIS WHOLE TIME I'M GOING TO SCREAM.
NO. THE ANSWER LIES WITH YOUR *COMPANIONS.*
PLUCK!
GRRWL
YOINK!

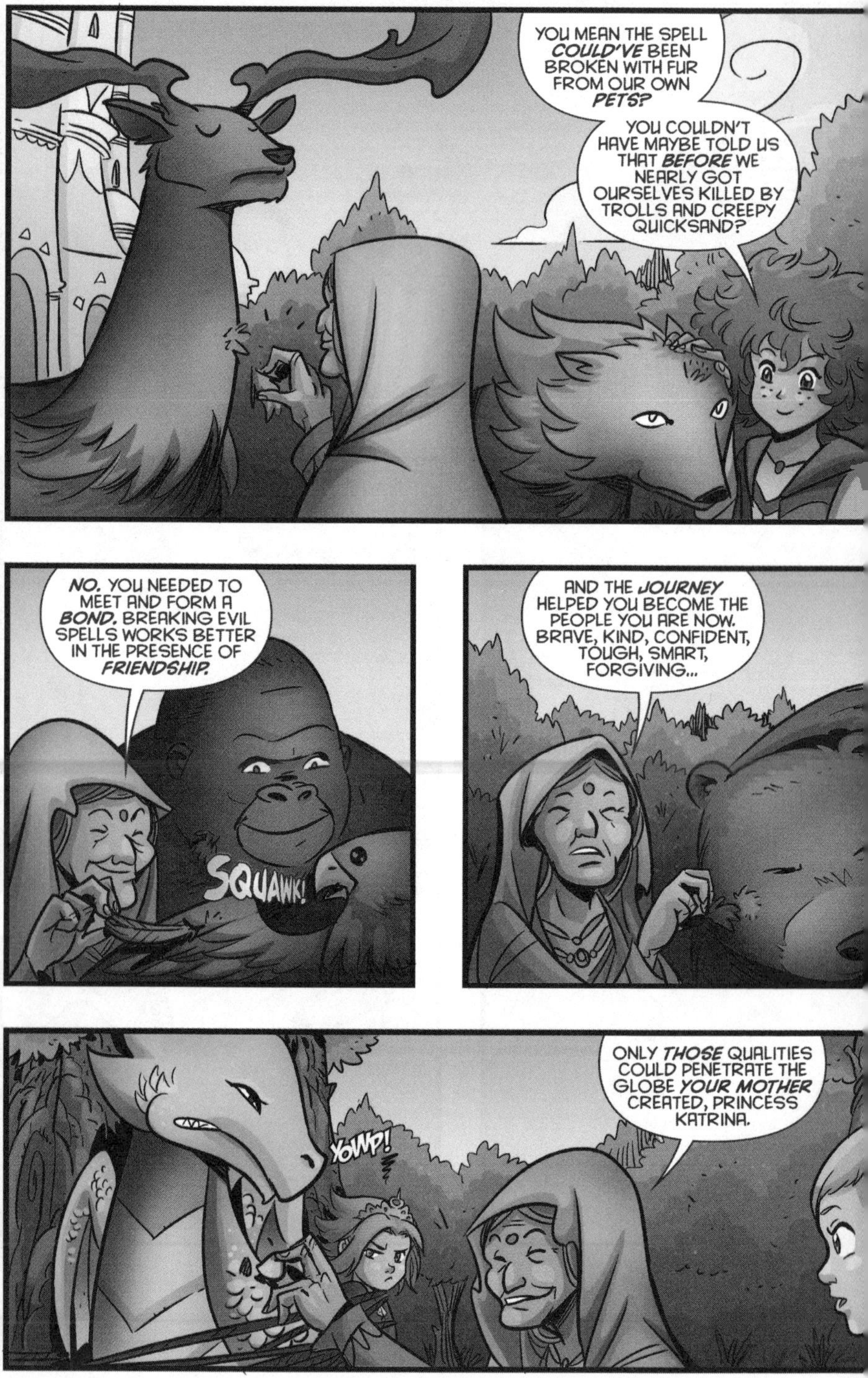
YOU MEAN THE SPELL COULD'VE BEEN BROKEN WITH FUR FROM OUR OWN PETS?
YOU COULDN'T HAVE MAYBE TOLD US THAT BEFORE WE NEARLY GOT OURSELVES KILLED BY TROLLS AND CREEPY QUICKSAND?
NO. YOU NEEDED TO MEET AND FORM A BOND. BREAKING EVIL SPELLS WORKS BETTER IN THE PRESENCE OF FRIENDSHIP.
SQUAWK!
AND THE JOURNEY HELPED YOU BECOME THE PEOPLE YOU ARE NOW. BRAVE, KIND, CONFIDENT, TOUGH, SMART, FORGIVING...
ONLY THOSE QUALITIES COULD PENETRATE THE GLOBE YOUR MOTHER CREATED, PRINCESS KATRINA.
YOWP!

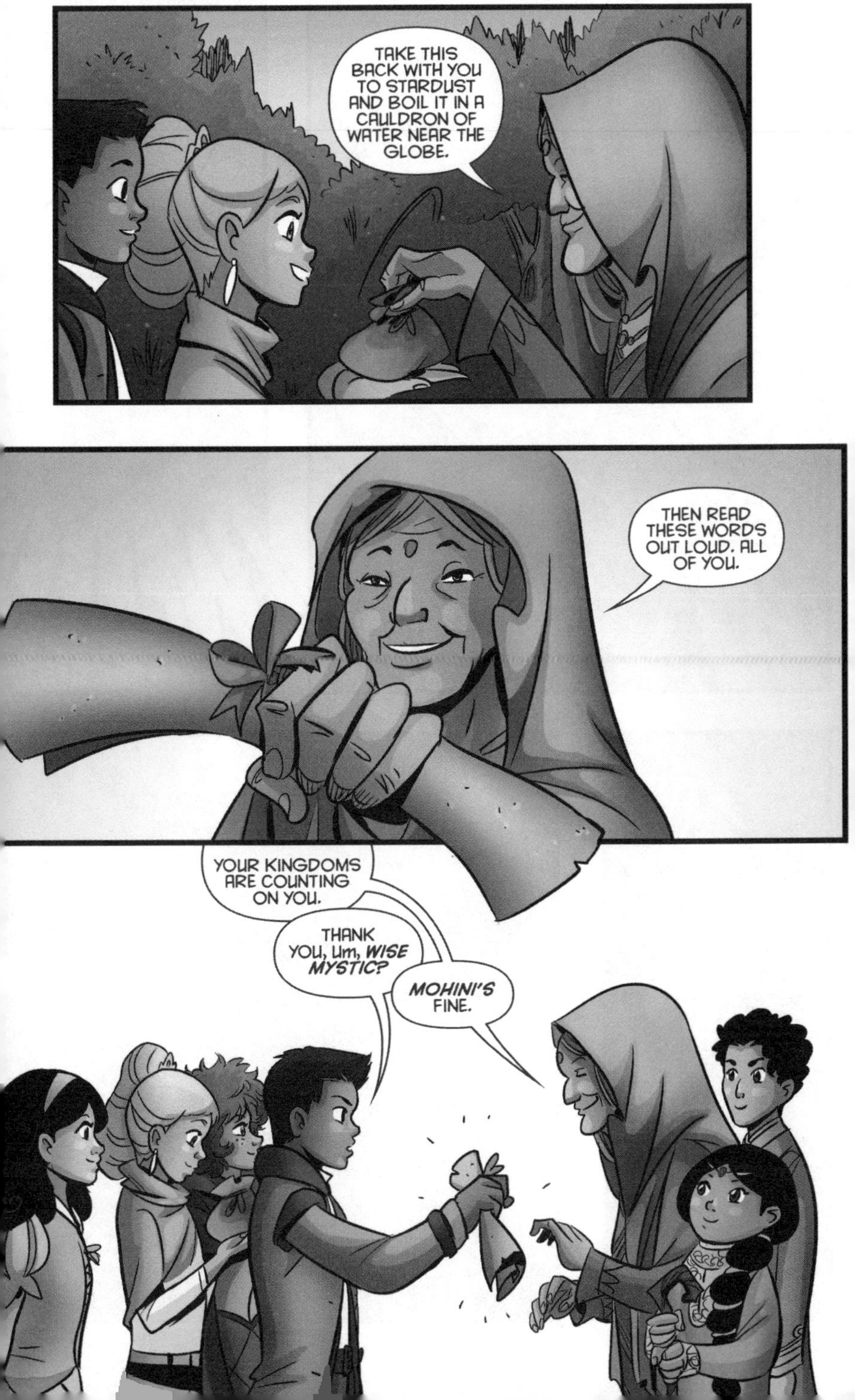
TAKE THIS BACK WITH YOU TO STARDUST AND BOIL IT IN A CAULDRON OF WATER NEAR THE GLOBE.
THEN READ THESE WORDS OUT LOUD. ALL OF YOU.
YOUR KINGDOMS ARE COUNTING ON YOU.
THANK YOU, UM, *WISE MYSTIC?*
MOHINI'S FINE.

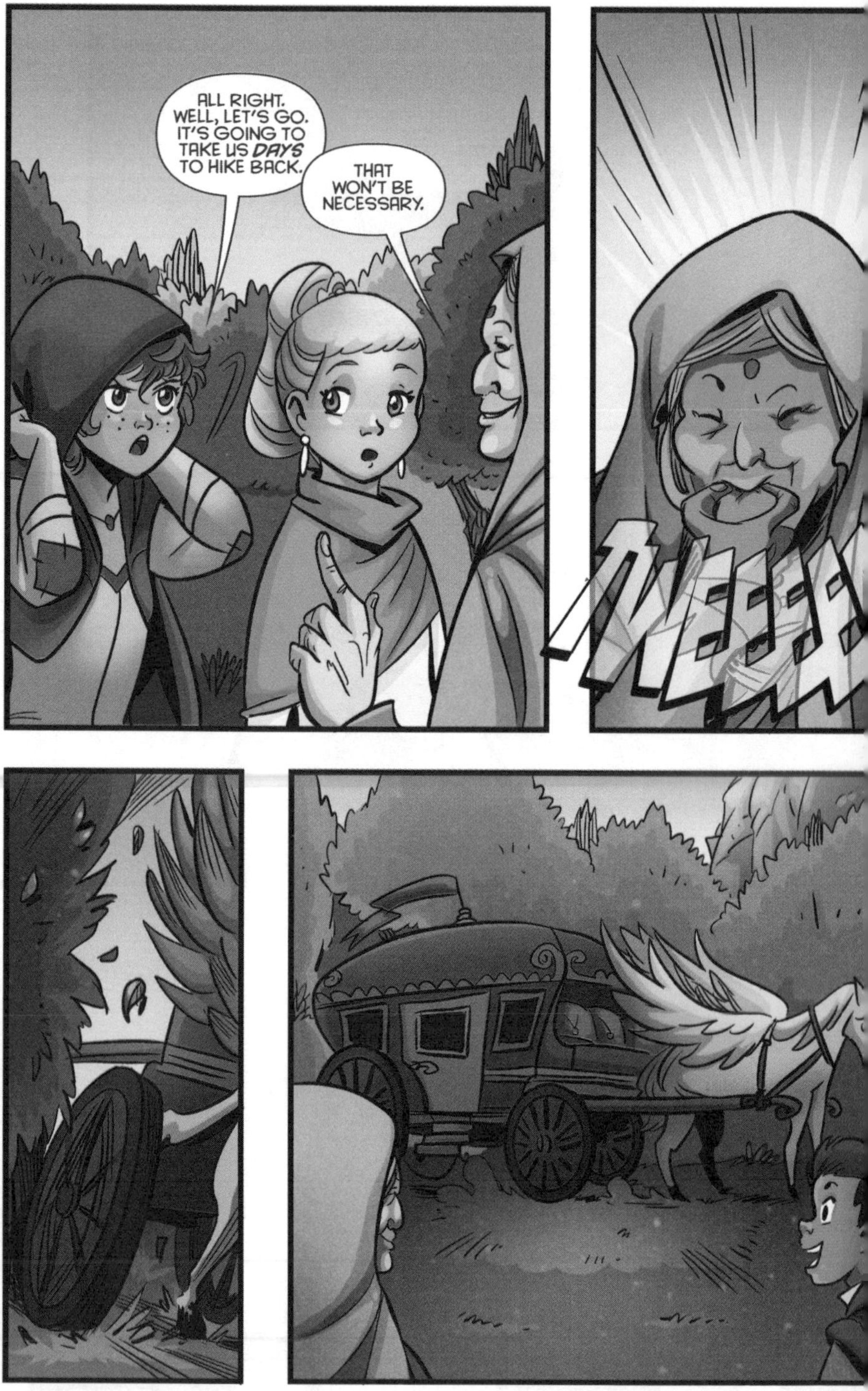
ALL RIGHT. WELL, LET'S GO. IT'S GOING TO TAKE US *DAYS* TO HIKE BACK.
THAT WON'T BE NECESSARY.

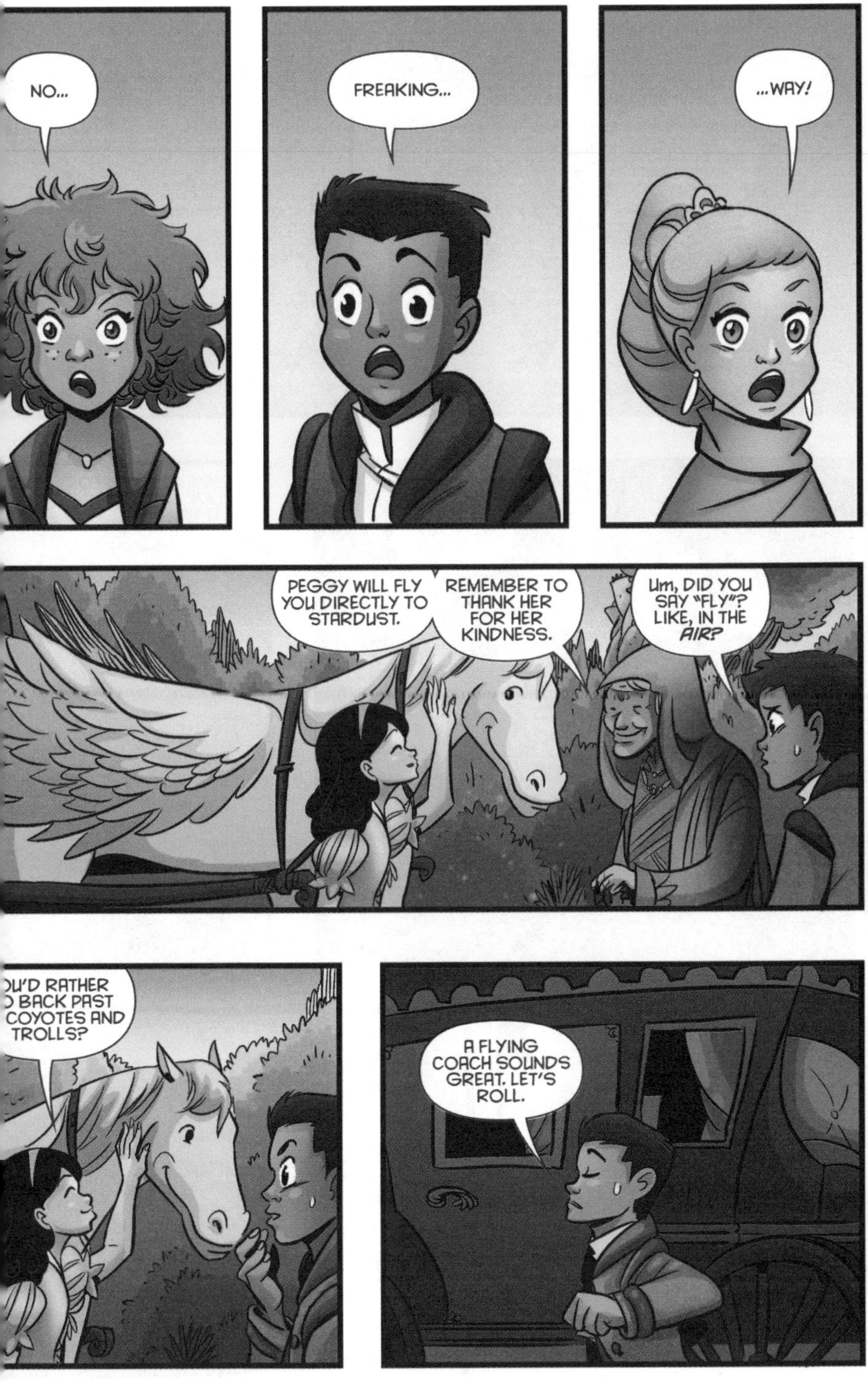
NO...
FREAKING...
...WAY!
PEGGY WILL FLY YOU DIRECTLY TO STARDUST.
REMEMBER TO THANK HER FOR HER KINDNESS.
Um, DID YOU SAY "FLY"? LIKE, IN THE AIR?
OU'D RATHER O BACK PAST COYOTES AND TROLLS?
A FLYING COACH SOUNDS GREAT. LET'S ROLL.

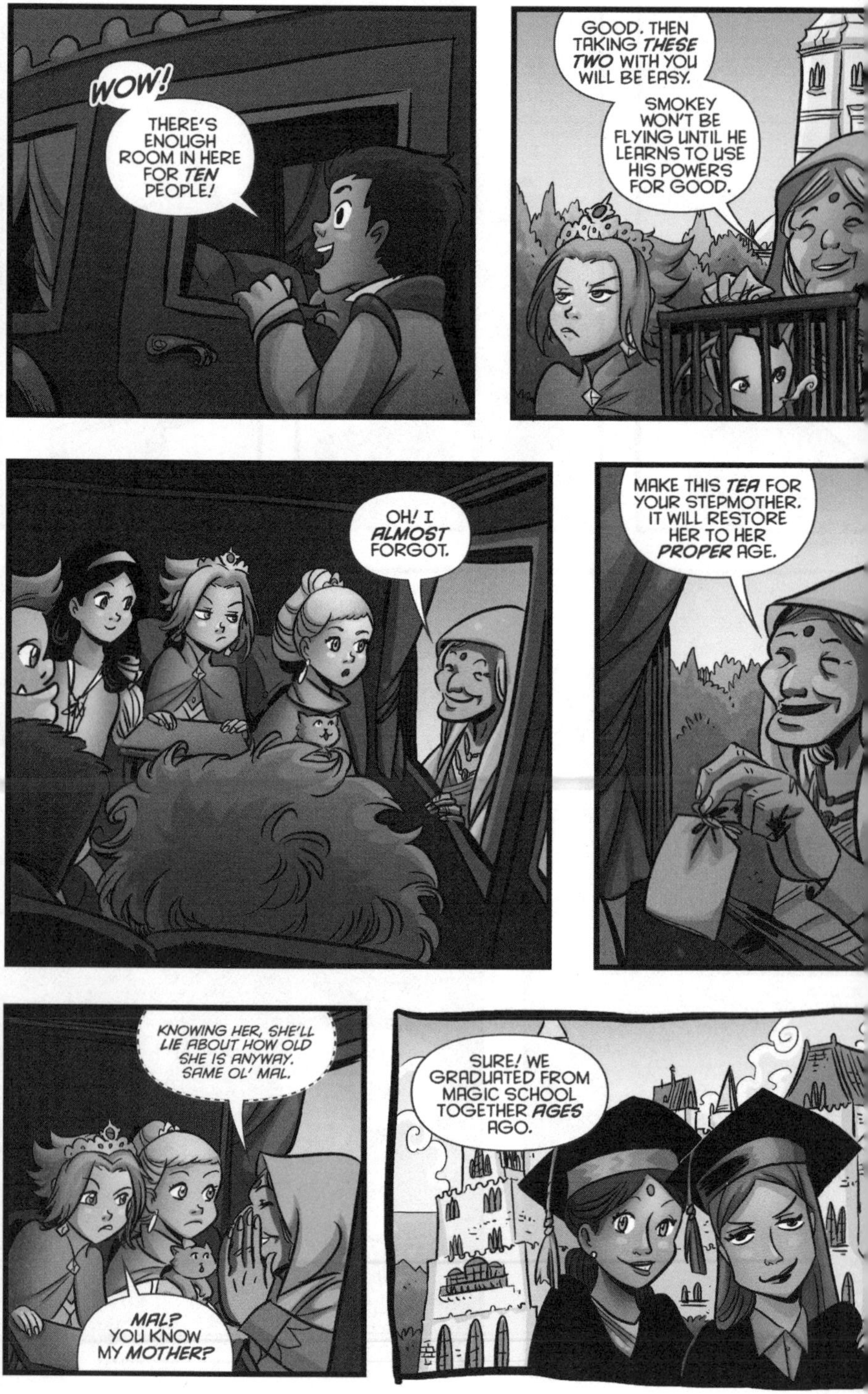
WOW!
THERE'S ENOUGH ROOM IN HERE FOR *TEN* PEOPLE!
GOOD. THEN TAKING *THESE TWO* WITH YOU WILL BE EASY.
SMOKEY WON'T BE FLYING UNTIL HE LEARNS TO USE HIS POWERS FOR GOOD.
OH! I *ALMOST* FORGOT.
MAKE THIS *TEA* FOR YOUR STEPMOTHER. IT WILL RESTORE HER TO HER *PROPER* AGE.
KNOWING HER, SHE'LL LIE ABOUT HOW OLD SHE IS ANYWAY. SAME OL' MAL.
MAL? YOU KNOW MY *MOTHER?*
SURE! WE GRADUATED FROM MAGIC SCHOOL TOGETHER *AGES* AGO.

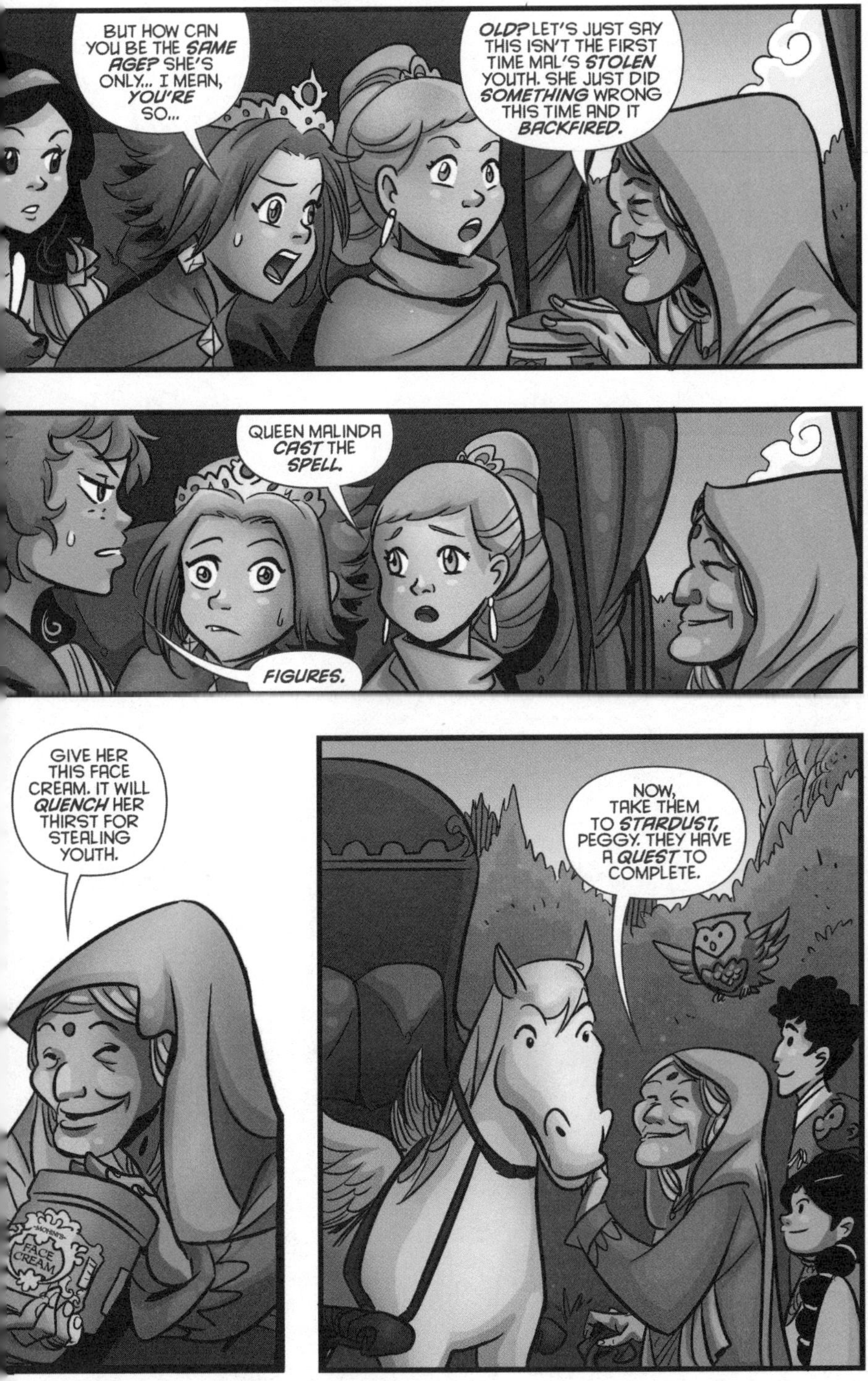
BUT HOW CAN YOU BE THE SAME AGE? SHE'S ONLY... I MEAN, YOU'RE SO...
OLD? LET'S JUST SAY THIS ISN'T THE FIRST TIME MAL'S STOLEN YOUTH. SHE JUST DID SOMETHING WRONG THIS TIME AND IT BACKFIRED.
QUEEN MALINDA CAST THE SPELL.
FIGURES.
GIVE HER THIS FACE CREAM. IT WILL QUENCH HER THIRST FOR STEALING YOUTH.
FACE CREAM
NOW, TAKE THEM TO STARDUST, PEGGY. THEY HAVE A QUEST TO COMPLETE.

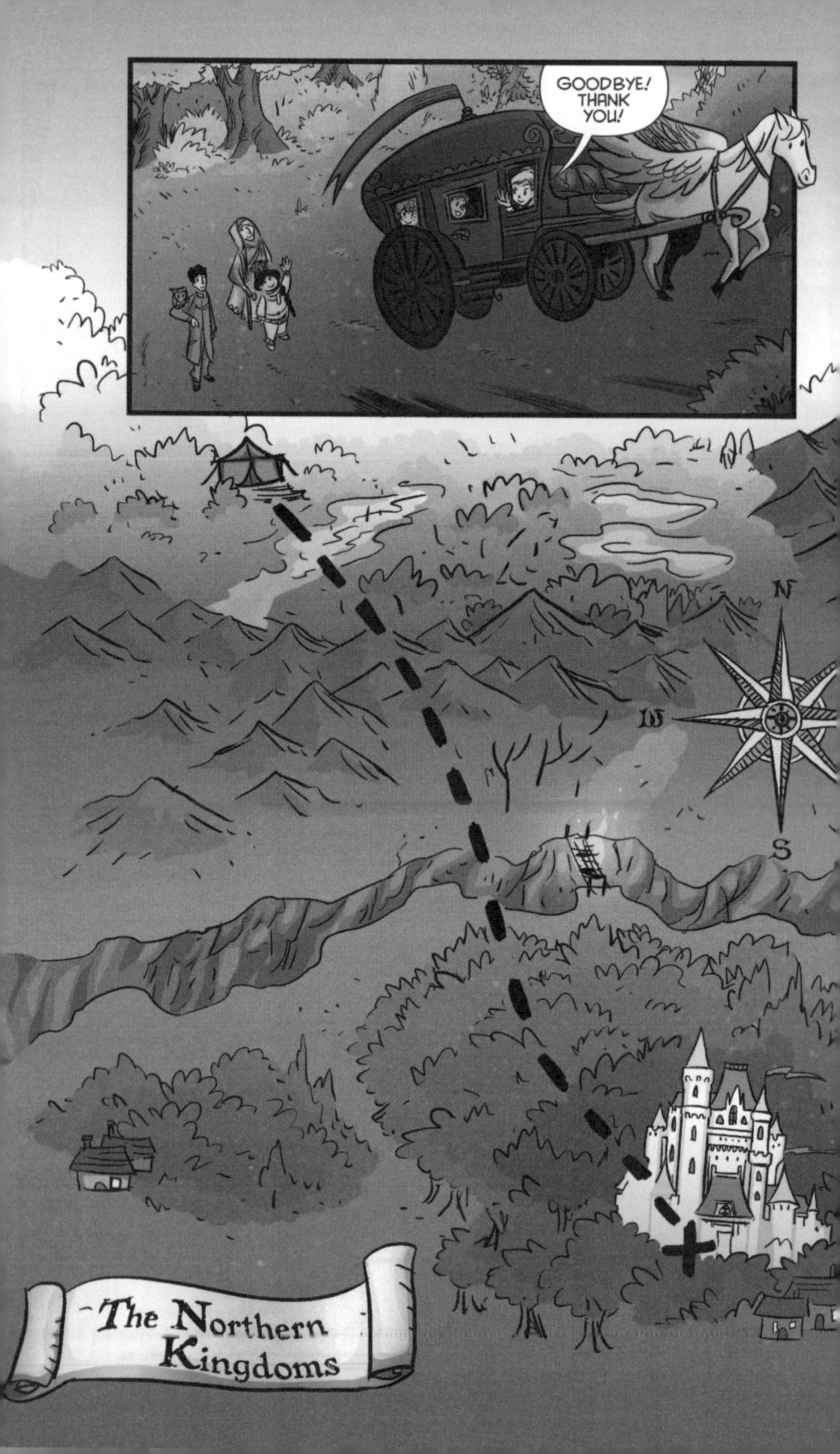
GOODBYE! THANK YOU!
N
W
S
The Northern Kingdoms

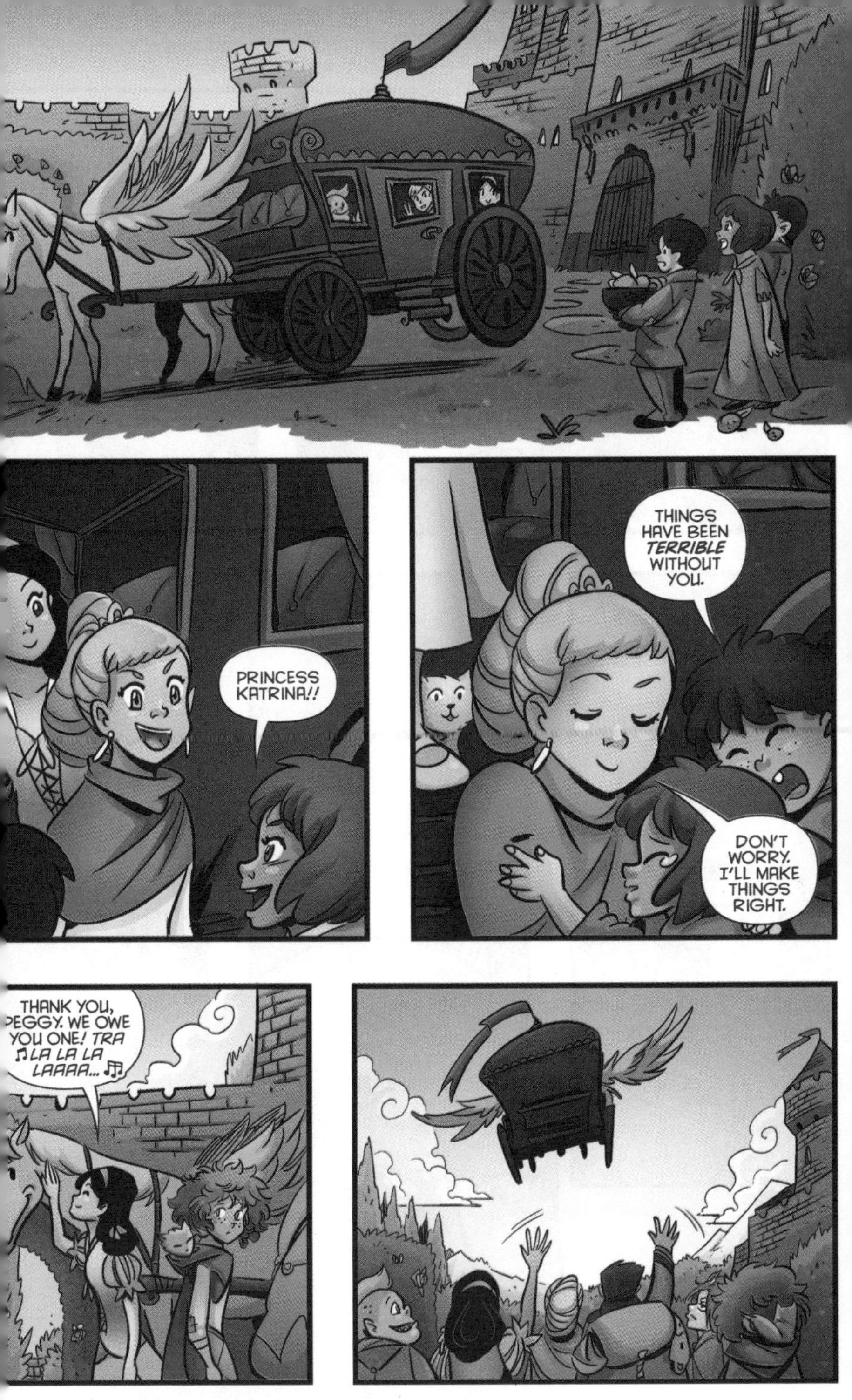
PRINCESS KATRINA!!
THINGS HAVE BEEN *TERRIBLE* WITHOUT YOU.
DON'T WORRY. I'LL MAKE THINGS RIGHT.
THANK YOU, PEGGY. WE OWE YOU ONE! *TRA LA LA LA LAAAA...*

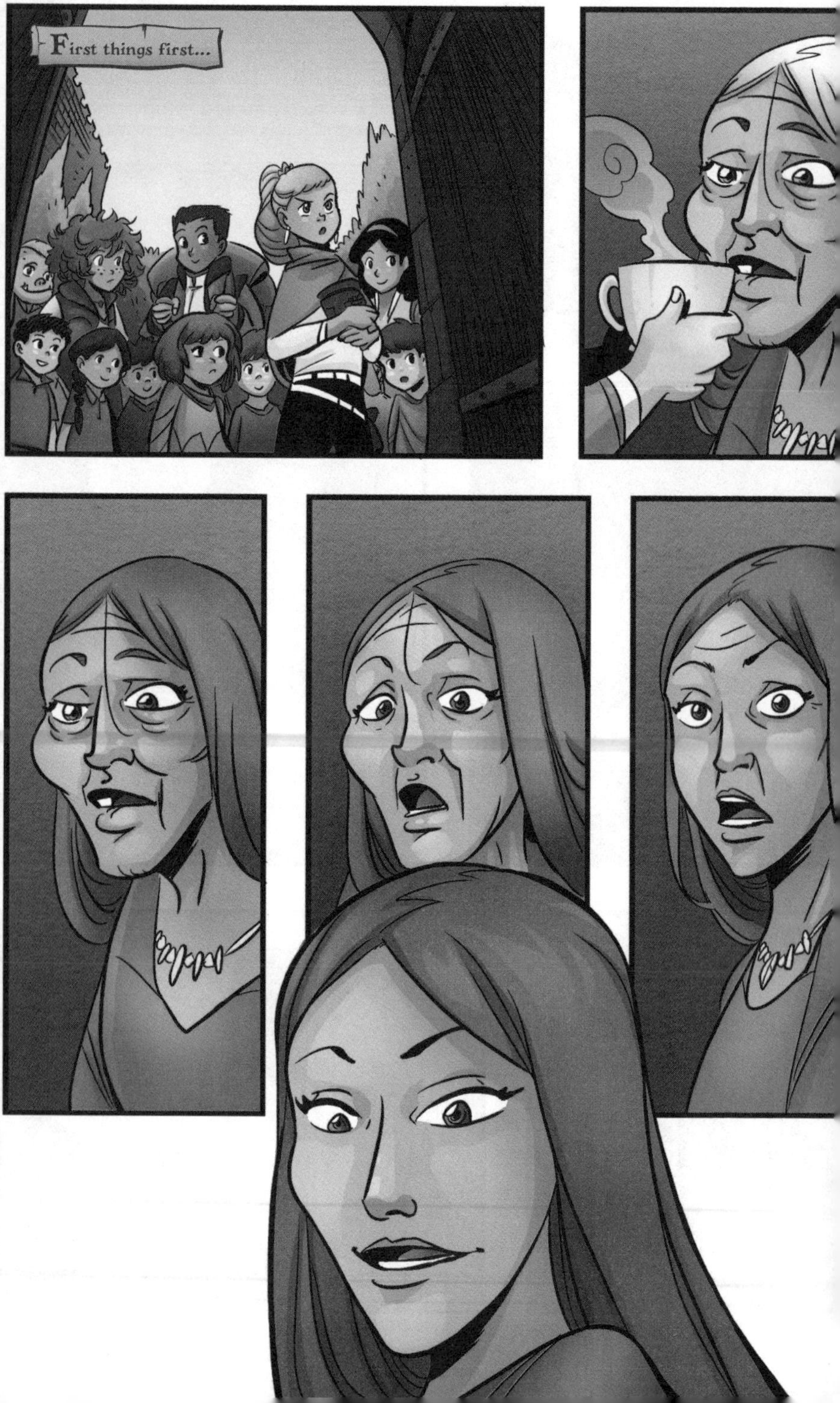
First things first...

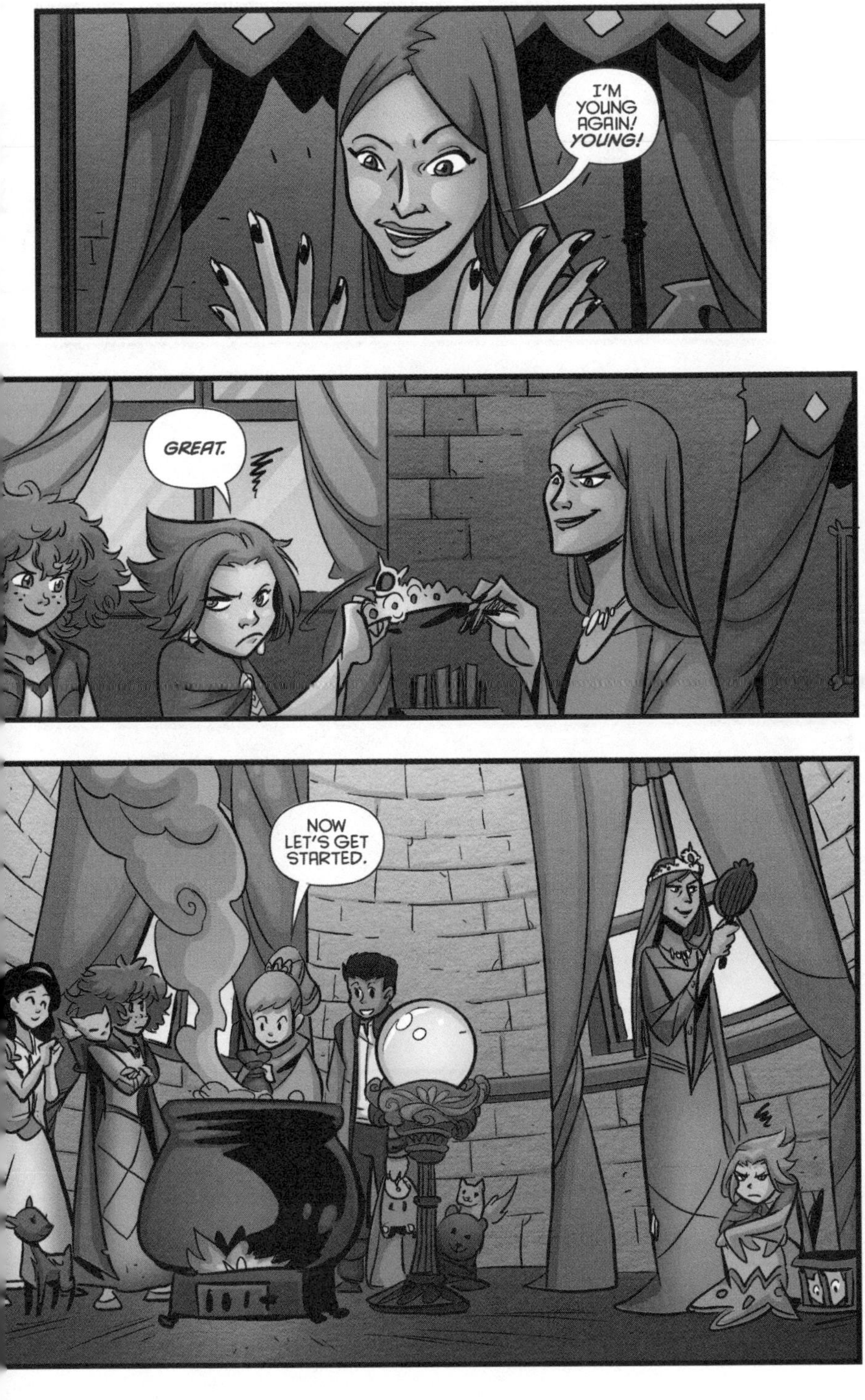
I'M YOUNG AGAIN! YOUNG!
GREAT.
NOW LET'S GET STARTED.

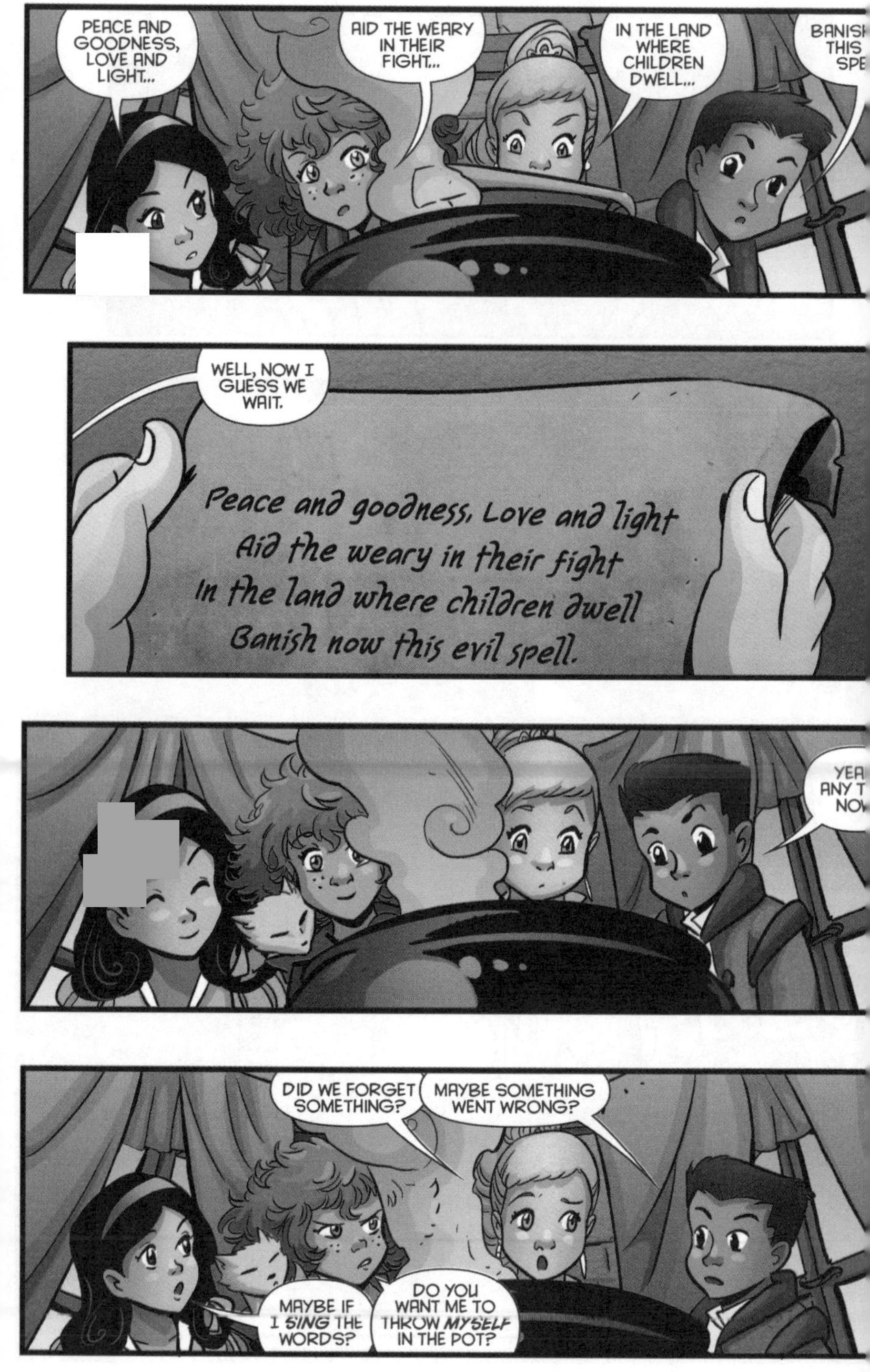
PEACE AND GOODNESS, LOVE AND LIGHT...
AID THE WEARY IN THEIR FIGHT...
IN THE LAND WHERE CHILDREN DWELL...
BANIS THIS SPE
WELL, NOW I GUESS WE WAIT.
Peace and goodness, Love and light
Aid the weary in their fight
In the land where children dwell
Banish now this evil spell.
YEA ANY T NOW
DID WE FORGET SOMETHING?
MAYBE SOMETHING WENT WRONG?
MAYBE IF I SING THE WORDS?
DO YOU WANT ME TO THROW MYSELF IN THE POT?

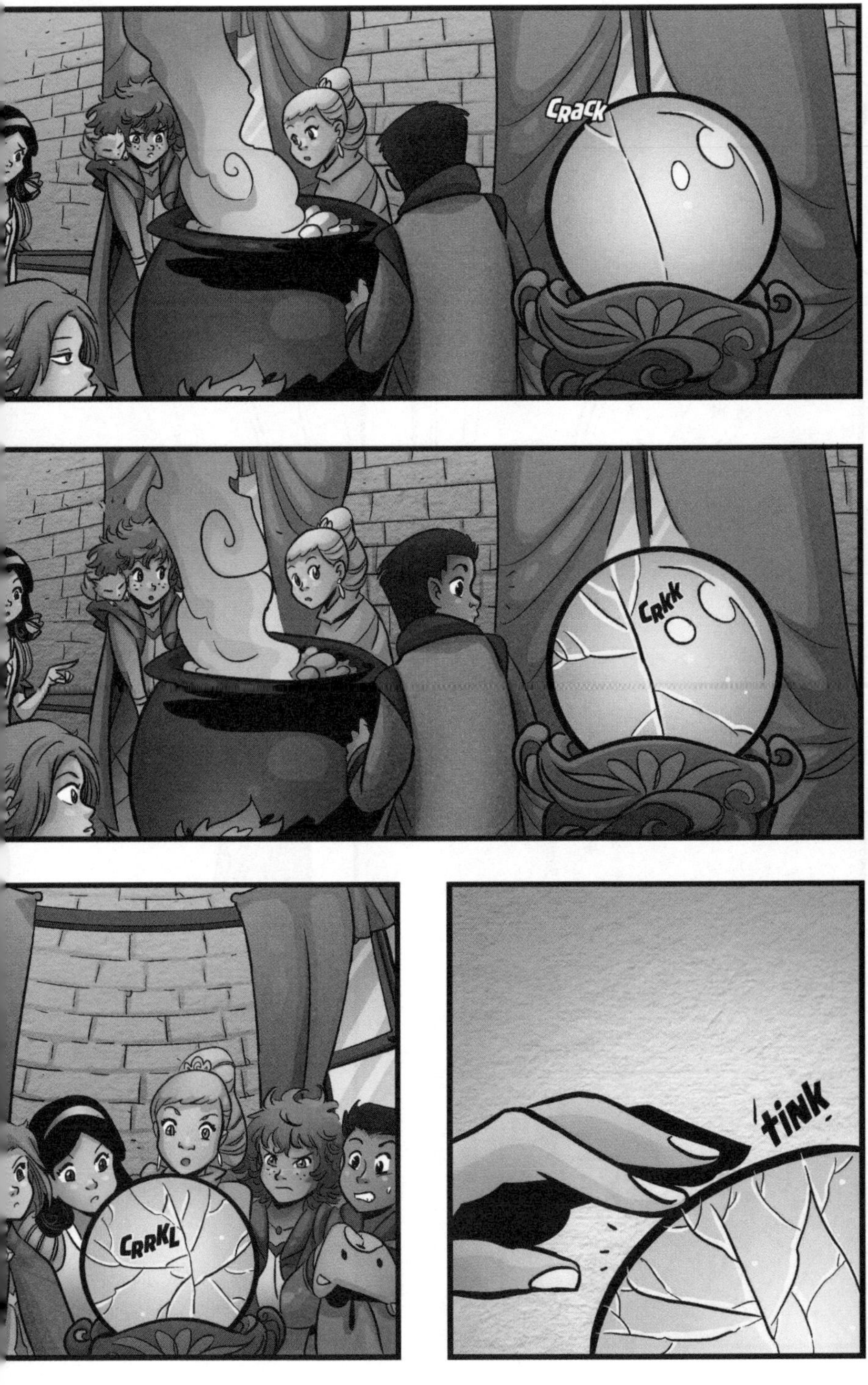
CRACK
CRKK
CRRKL
TINK

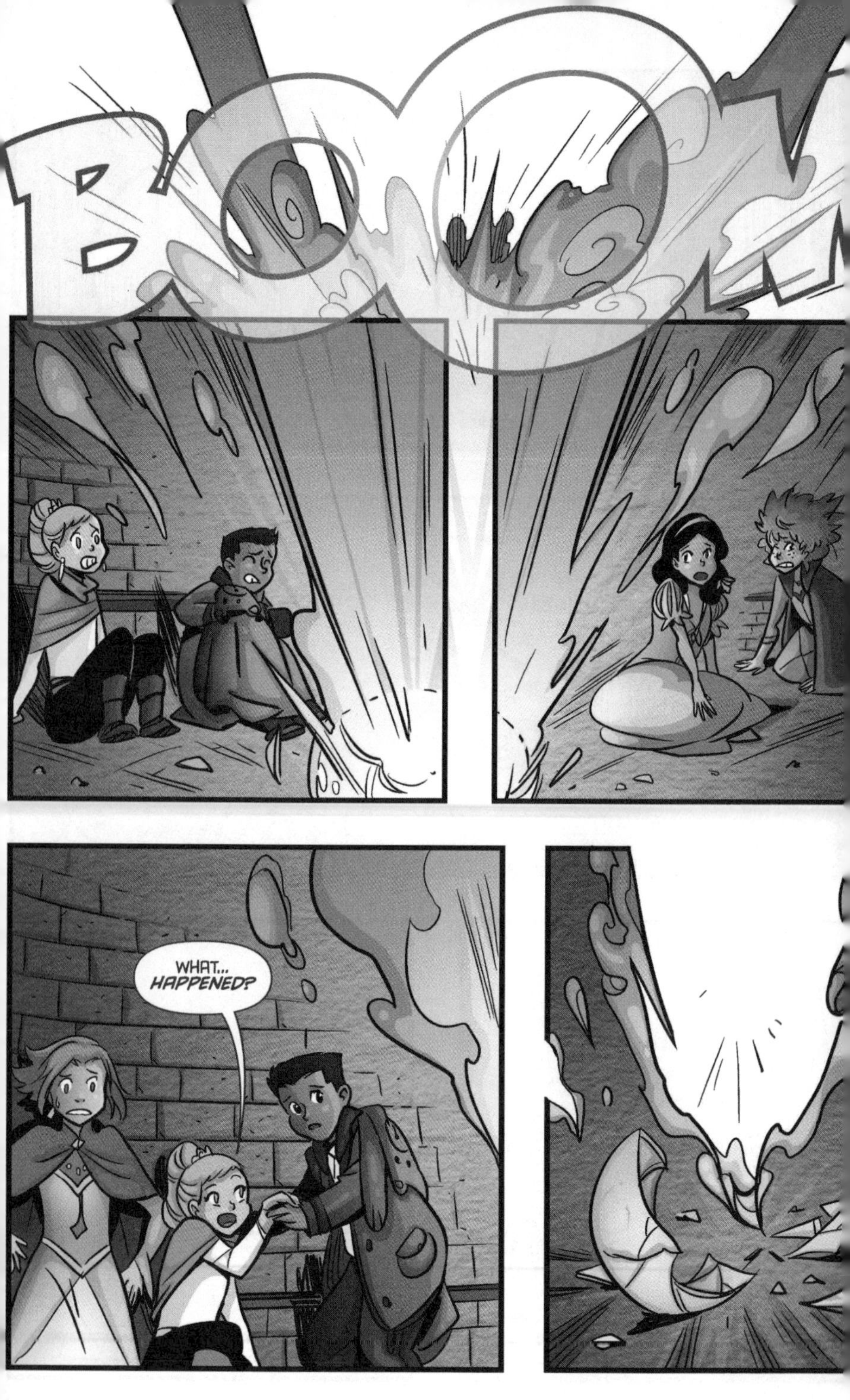
BOOM
WHAT... HAPPENED?

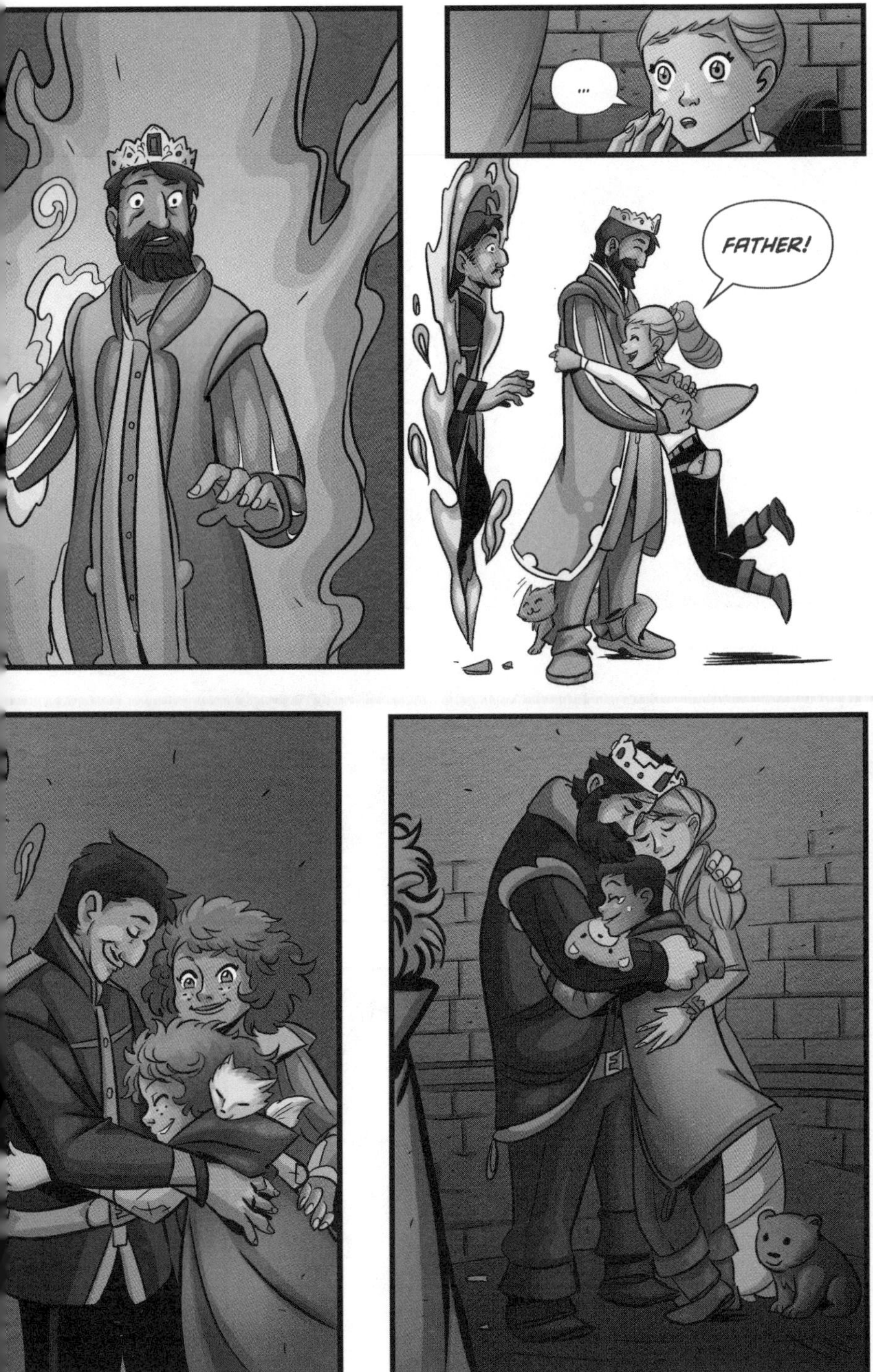
...
FATHER!

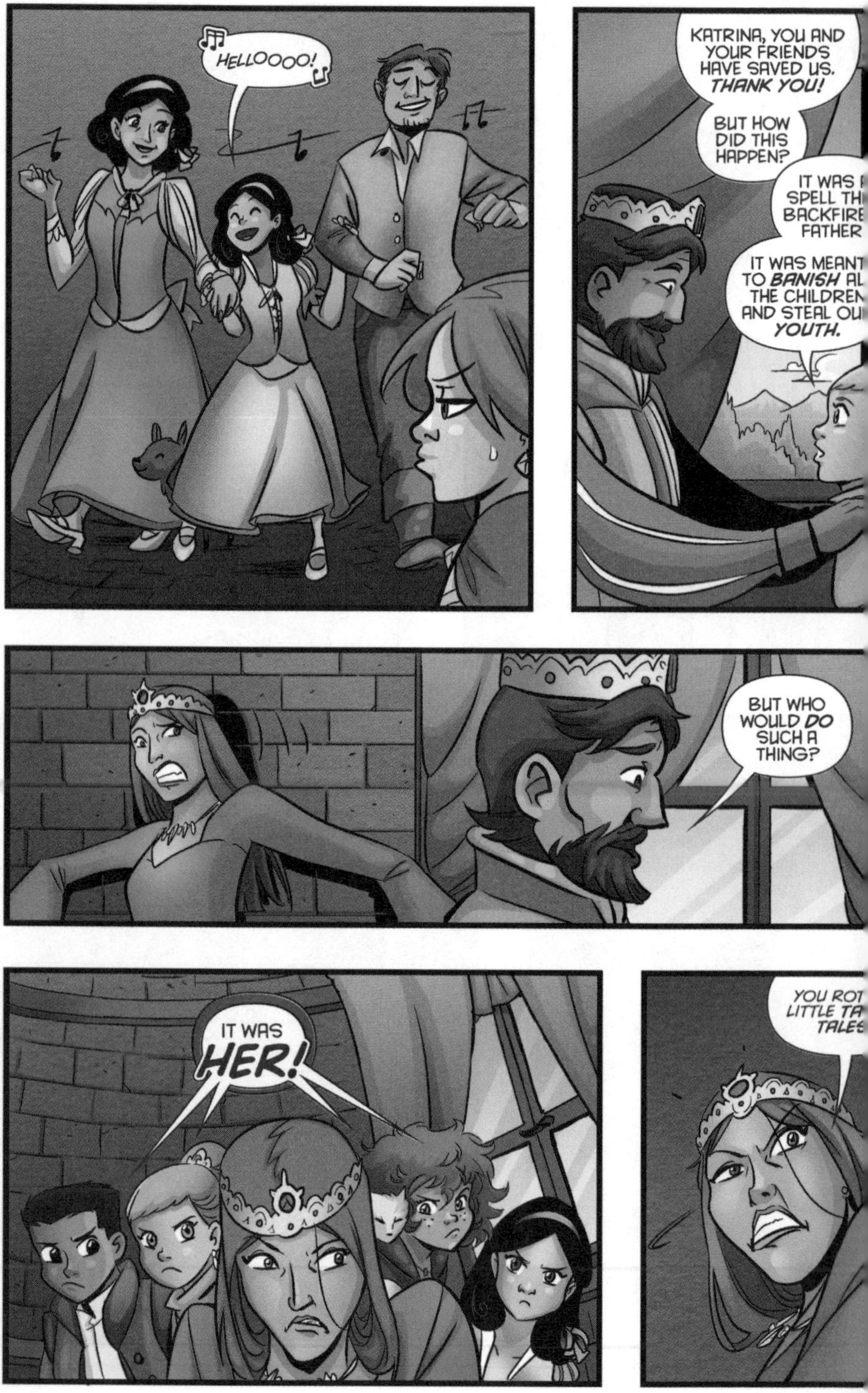
HELLOOOO!
KATRINA, YOU AND YOUR FRIENDS HAVE SAVED US. THANK YOU!
BUT HOW DID THIS HAPPEN?
IT WAS SPELL TH BACKFIRE FATHER
IT WAS MEANT TO BANISH AL THE CHILDREN AND STEAL OU YOUTH.
BUT WHO WOULD DO SUCH A THING?
IT WAS HER!
YOU ROT LITTLE TA TALES

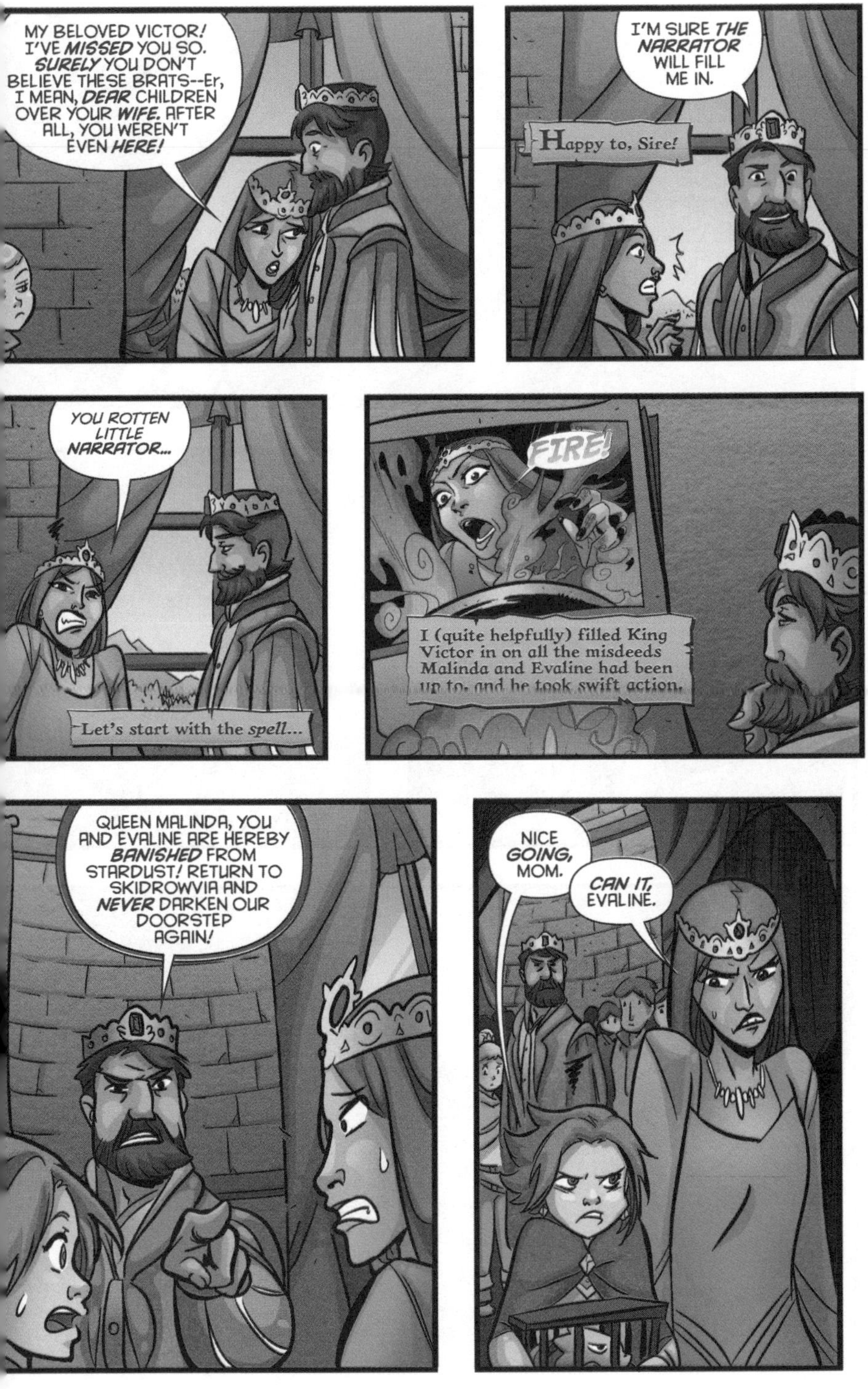

MY BELOVED VICTOR! I'VE MISSED YOU SO. SURELY YOU DON'T BELIEVE THESE BRATS--Er, I MEAN, DEAR CHILDREN OVER YOUR WIFE. AFTER ALL, YOU WEREN'T EVEN HERE!
I'M SURE THE NARRATOR WILL FILL ME IN.
Happy to, Sire!
YOU ROTTEN LITTLE NARRATOR...
Let's start with the spell...
FIRE!
I (quite helpfully) filled King Victor in on all the misdeeds Malinda and Evaline had been up to, and he took swift action.
QUEEN MALINDA, YOU AND EVALINE ARE HEREBY BANISHED FROM STARDUST! RETURN TO SKIDROWVIA AND NEVER DARKEN OUR DOORSTEP AGAIN!
NICE GOING, MOM.
CAN IT, EVALINE.

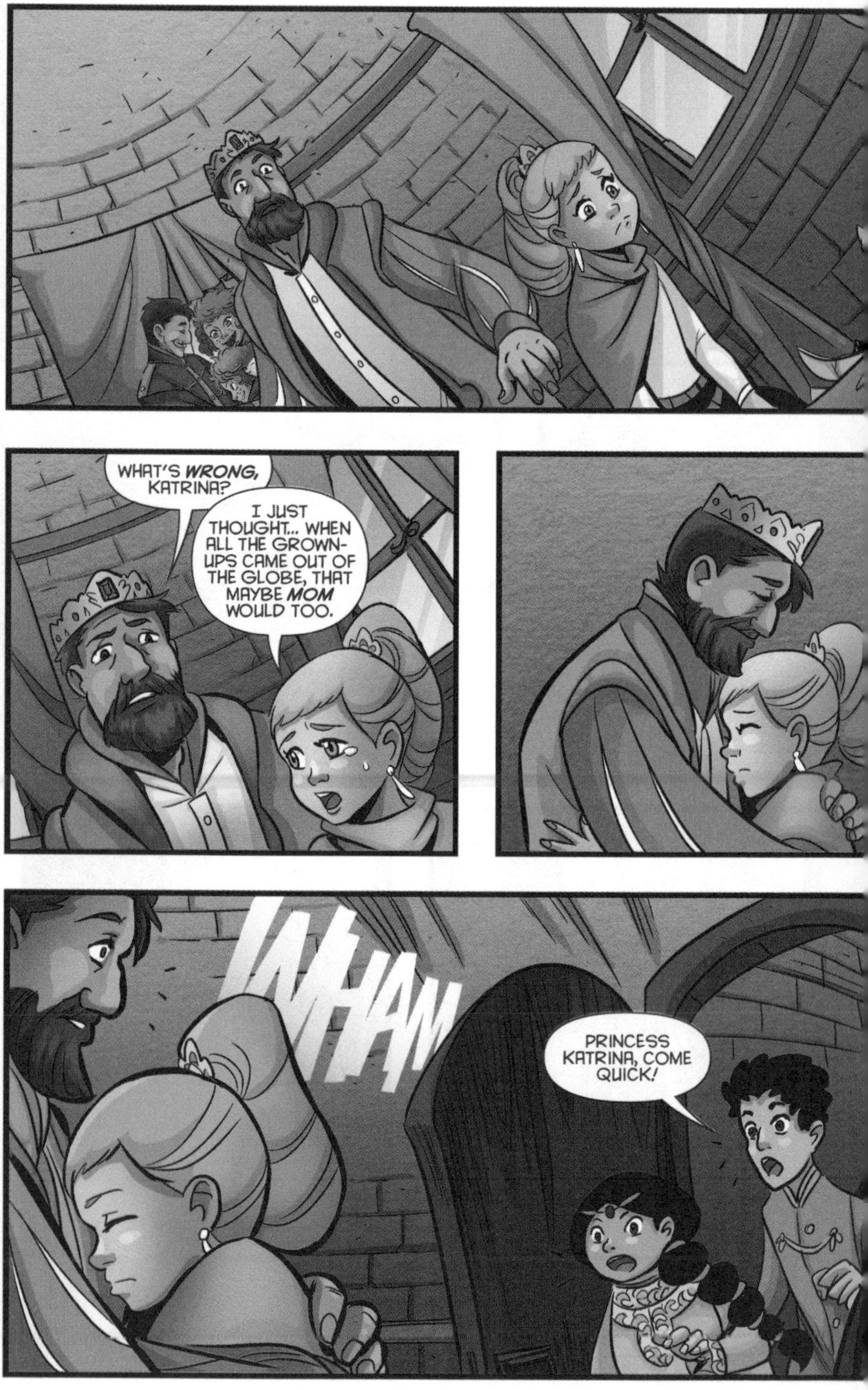
WHAT'S *WRONG*, KATRINA?
I JUST THOUGHT... WHEN ALL THE GROWN-UPS CAME OUT OF THE GLOBE, THAT MAYBE *MOM* WOULD TOO.
WHAM
PRINCESS KATRINA, COME QUICK!

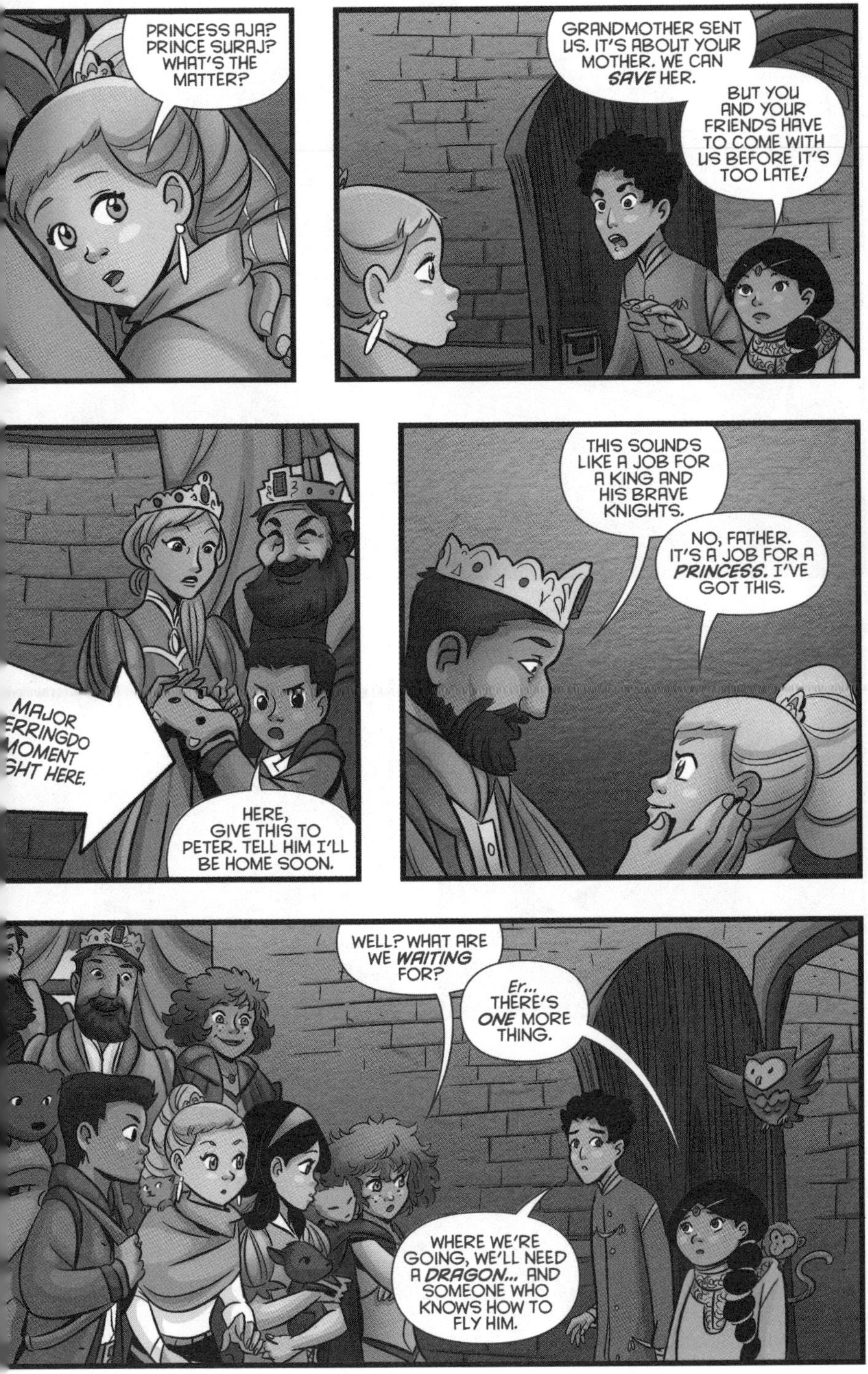
PRINCESS AJA? PRINCE SURAJ? WHAT'S THE MATTER?
GRANDMOTHER SENT US. IT'S ABOUT YOUR MOTHER. WE CAN *SAVE* HER.
BUT YOU AND YOUR FRIENDS HAVE TO COME WITH US BEFORE IT'S TOO LATE!
MAJOR ERRINGDO MOMENT GHT HERE.
HERE, GIVE THIS TO PETER. TELL HIM I'LL BE HOME SOON.
THIS SOUNDS LIKE A JOB FOR A KING AND HIS BRAVE KNIGHTS.
NO, FATHER. IT'S A JOB FOR A *PRINCESS.* I'VE GOT THIS.
WELL? WHAT ARE WE *WAITING* FOR?
Er... THERE'S *ONE* MORE THING.
WHERE WE'RE GOING, WE'LL NEED A *DRAGON...* AND SOMEONE WHO KNOWS HOW TO FLY HIM.

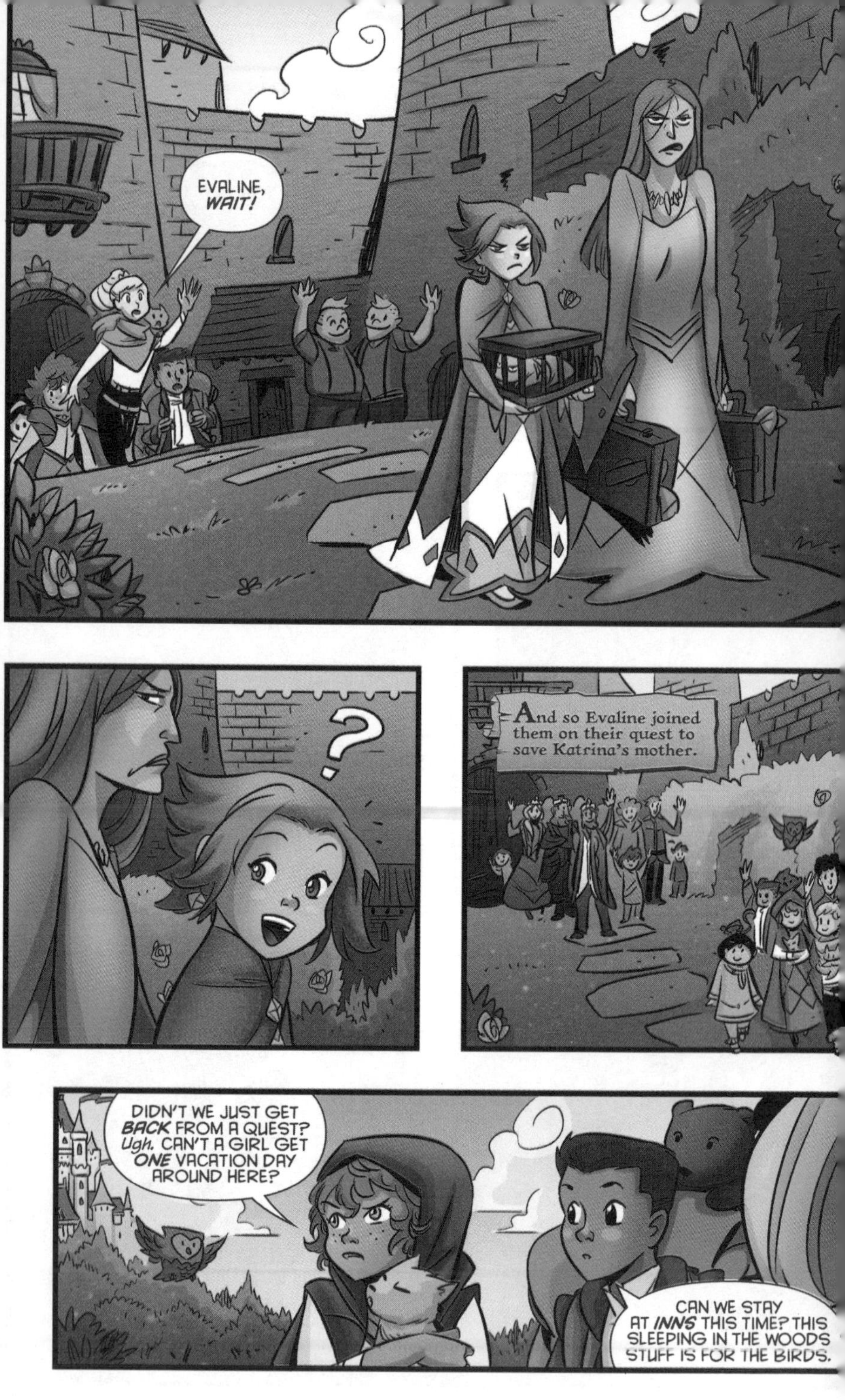

EVALINE, WAIT!
?
And so Evaline joined them on their quest to save Katrina's mother.
DIDN'T WE JUST GET BACK FROM A QUEST? Ugh. CAN'T A GIRL GET ONE VACATION DAY AROUND HERE?
CAN WE STAY AT INNS THIS TIME? THIS SLEEPING IN THE WOODS STUFF IS FOR THE BIRDS.

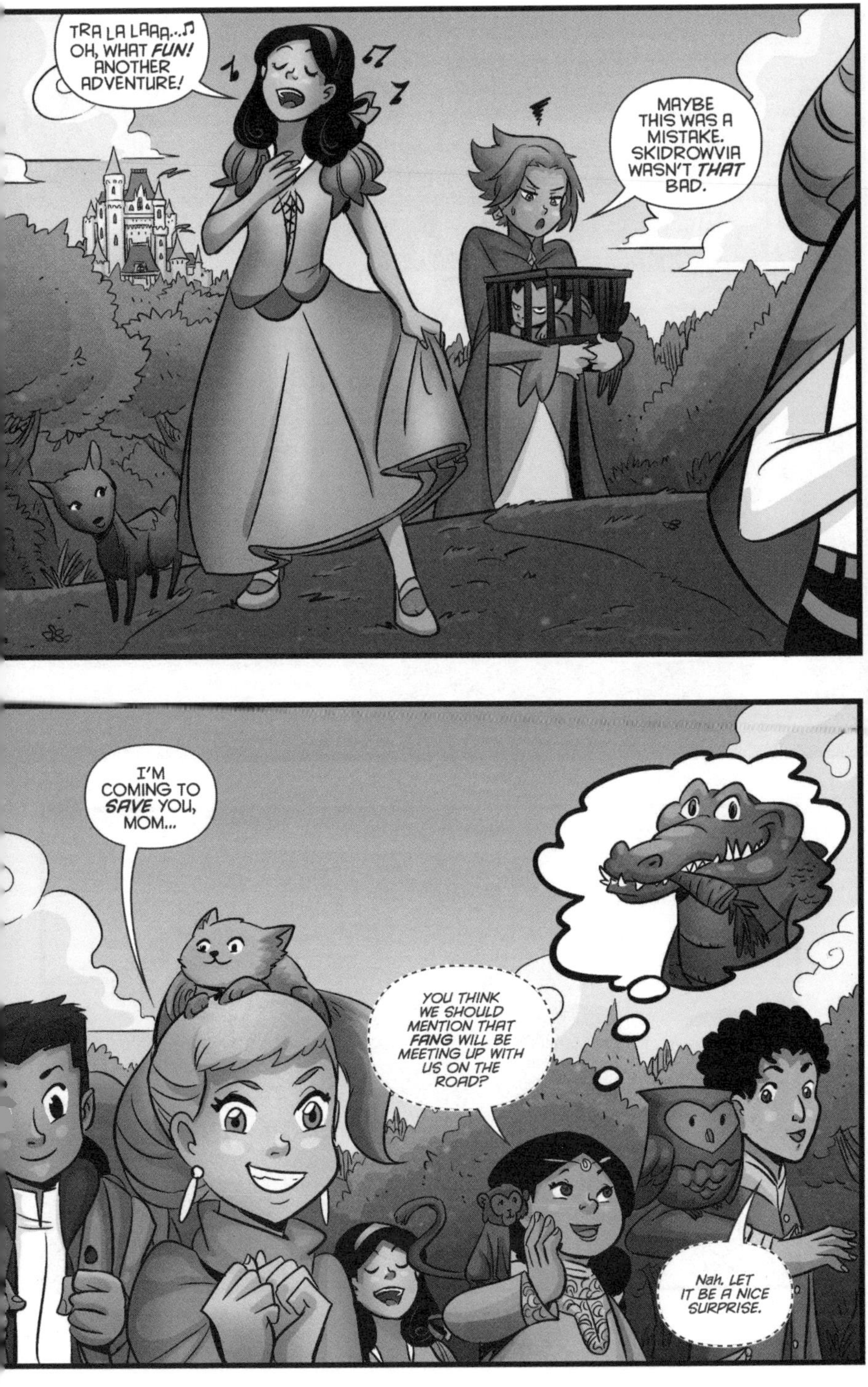
TRA LA LAAA...♫ OH, WHAT FUN! ANOTHER ADVENTURE!
MAYBE THIS WAS A MISTAKE. SKIDROWVIA WASN'T THAT BAD.
I'M COMING TO SAVE YOU, MOM...
YOU THINK WE SHOULD MENTION THAT FANG WILL BE MEETING UP WITH US ON THE ROAD?
Nah. LET IT BE A NICE SURPRISE.

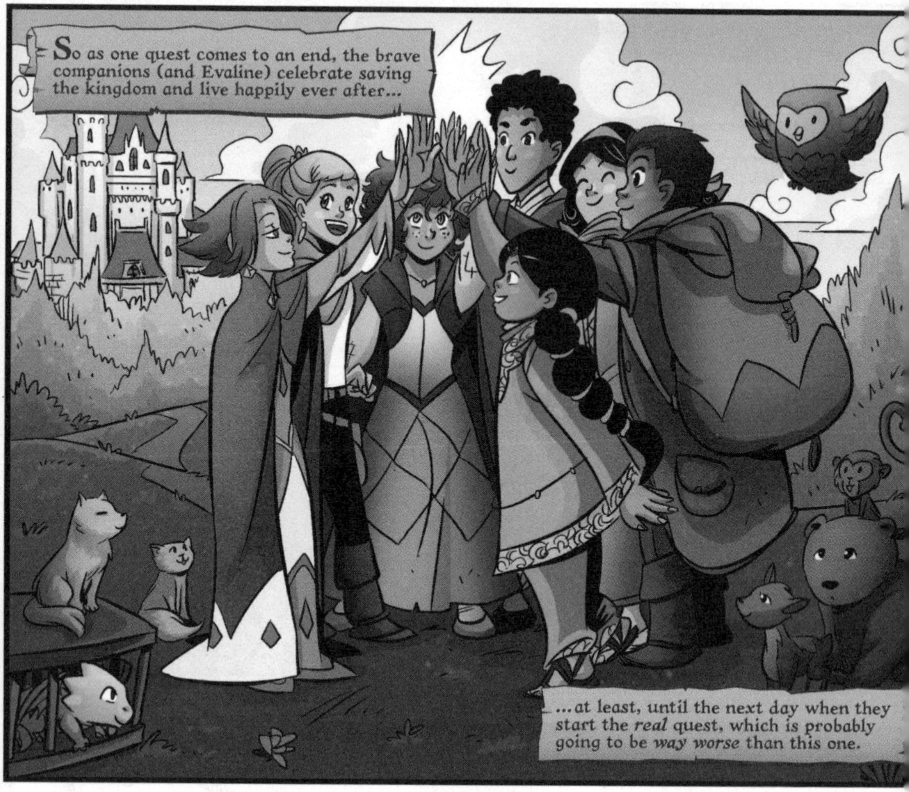
So as one quest comes to an end, the brave companions (and Evaline) celebrate saving the kingdom and live happily ever after...
...at least, until the next day when they start the *real* quest, which is probably going to be *way worse* than this one.

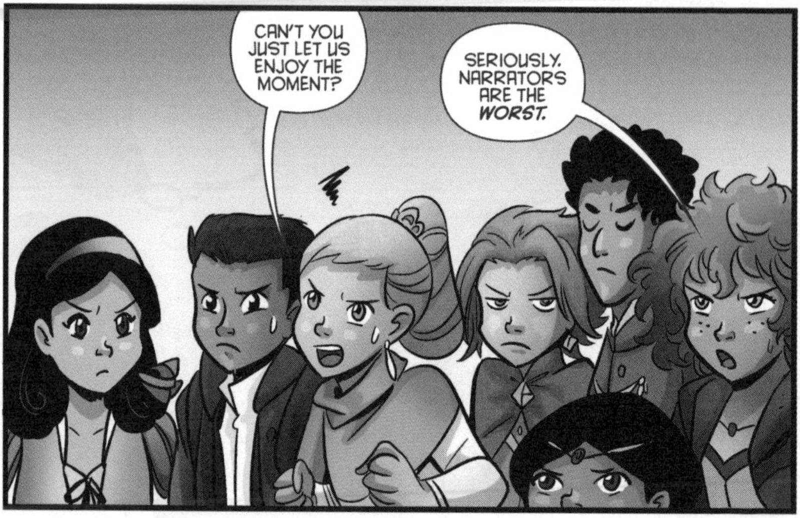
CAN'T YOU JUST LET US ENJOY THE MOMENT?
SERIOUSLY. NARRATORS ARE THE *WORST.*

THE END.